Robert Williams Buchanan

God and the Man

A Romance

Robert Williams Buchanan

God and the Man
A Romance

ISBN/EAN: 9783337007935

Printed in Europe, USA, Canada, Australia, Japan

Cover: Foto ©Andreas Hilbeck / pixelio.de

More available books at **www.hansebooks.com**

GOD AND THE MAN

A ROMANCE

BY

ROBERT BUCHANAN

AUTHOR OF 'A CHILD OF NATURE' 'THE SHADOW OF THE SWORD' ETC.

THE GREAT GOD CASTETH AWAY NO MAN'

A NEW EDITION, with ILLUSTRATIONS by FRED. BARNARD

London
CHATTO & WINDUS, PICCADILLY
1890

Dedication.

I.

TO AN OLD ENEMY.

I would have snatch'd a bay leaf from thy brow,
Wronging the chaplet on an honoured head;
In peace and tenderness I bring thee now
A lily-flower instead.

Pure as thy purpose, blameless as thy song,
Sweet as thy spirit, may this offering be:
Forget the bitter blame that did thee wrong,
And take the gift from me !

R. B.

October 1881.

II.

TO DANTE GABRIEL ROSSETTI.

Calmly, thy royal robe of Death around thee,
Thou sleepest, and weeping Brethren round thee stand—
Gently they placed, ere yet God's angel crown'd thee,
My lily in thy hand !

I never knew thee living, O my brother !
But on thy breast my lily of love now lies;
And by that token, we shall know each other,
When God's voice saith 'Arise !'

R. B.

August 1882.

₊ *This romance is the third work of prose fiction from the writer's pen. In each of these works, a subject has been taken, which, though poetical in itself, involved a treatment transcending the exact limits of verse. 'A Child of Nature,' written in 1870, though not published till nine years after, was the first of the series; the 'Shadow of the Sword' was written and published in 1875; the present work, and the 'Martyrdom of Madeline,' were planned together and written in close sequence. Each of the last three works has a particular 'idea' or purpose, and descends to what some critics call the heresy of instruction. The 'Shadow of the Sword' is a poetical polemic against public War; 'God and the Man' is a study of the vanity and folly of individual Hate; the 'Martyrdom of Madeline' has for its theme the social conspiracy against Womankind.*

R. B.

I HAVE to thank both the press and the public for their generous reception of this romance, or (as it has been styled) tragedy in prose. Despite a title which alarmed the librarians, and a subject which some critics considered transcendental, it was received with the utmost kindness in almost every quarter. Certain sections of the religious world (by which I mean the world which calls itself ‘religious’) may possibly have found it uninteresting; for it neither supports nor attacks the Church of Rome, it has no bearing whatever on the English or any other Establishment, it has nothing to do with theological or ecclesiastical vested interests, and it has never been blest, or curst, by a Bishop. It is of little consequence, therefore, to the higher controversy—if that controversy can be called ‘higher’ which consists of constant wrangling over religious institutions, theories, forms, and fictions. The author holds that true Christianity is an inheritance belonging to all men alike, whatever may be the form of their creed; and that the patience of the world is wasted, and the millennium of love indefinitely delayed, by an eternal dispute over miserable forms.

Since this work was first published, the ' Old Enemy ' to whom it was dedicated has passed away. Although his name did not appear on the front of the book, as it would certainly have done had I possessed more moral courage, it is a melancholy pleasure to me to reflect that he understood the dedication and accepted it in the spirit in which it was offered. That I should ever have underrated his exquisite work, is simply a proof of the incompetency of all criticism, however honest, which is conceived adversely, hastily, and from an unsympathetic point of view; but that I should have ranked myself for the time being with the Philistines, and encouraged them to resist an ennobling and refining literary influence (of which they stood, and stand, so mournfully in need), must remain to me a matter of permanent regret.

ROBERT BUCHANAN.

LONDON: *August* 18, 1882.

CONTENTS.

ILLUSTRATIONS.

'ALL men, each one, beneath the sun,
    I hate, shall hate, till life is done,
But of all men one, till my race is run,
And all the rest for the sake of one!

'If God stood there, revealed full bare,
    I would laugh to scorn His love or care,—
Nay, in despair, I would pray a prayer
Which He needs must grant—if a God He were!

'And the prayer would be, "Yield up to me
    This man alone of all men that see!
Give him to me, and to misery!
Give me this man, if a God Thou be!"'

GOD AND THE MAN.

PROEM.

' ALL men, each one, beneath the sun,
I hate, shall hate, till life is done,
But of all men one, till my race is run,
And ail the rest for the sake of one !

' If God stood there, revealed full bare,
I would laugh to scorn His love or care,—
Nay, in despair, I would pray a prayer
Which He needs must grant—if a God He were !

' And the prayer would be, " Yield up to me
This man alone of all men that see !
Give him to *me*, and to misery !
Give me this man, if a God thou be !"'

    .   .   .   .   .   .

Shape on the headland in the night,
  Gaunt, ghastly, kneeling on his knee,
He prays ; his baffled prayers take flight,
Like screaming sea-birds, thro' the light
  That streams across the sleeping sea.
From the black depths of man's despair
Rose ever so accurst a prayer ?
His hands clench and his eyeballs roll,
Hate's famine sickens in his soul.

Meantime the windless waves intone
Their peaceful answer to his moan,
The soft clouds one another chase,
The moon-rays flash upon his face,
The mighty deep is calm; but see!
This man is as a storm-swept tree.

And, silvern-sandall'd, still as death,
The white moon in her own pure breath
Walks yonder.   Doth he see her pass
Over the glimmering water-glass?
Sees he the stars that softly swing
Like lamps around her wandering,
Sown thick as early snowdrops now
In the dark furrows of the Plough?
Hears he the sad, still, rhythmic throb
   Of the dark ocean where he stands,—
The great strong voice still'd to a sob,
   Near darken'd capes and glimmering sands?
Nay, nay; but, even as a wight
Who on a mirror fixeth sight,
And screams at his own face of dread
Within the dimness pictured,
He useth God's great sleeping sea
To image hate and agony.
He kneels, he prays,—nay, call it not
A prayer, that riseth in his throat;
'Tis but a curse this mortal cries,
Like one who curses God and dies.

.   .   .   .   .   .

' Yield up to me, to hate and me,
One man alone of all men that see!
Give him to me, and to misery!
Give me this man if a God thou be!

' But the cruel heavens all open lie,
No God doth reign o'er the sea or sky,
The earth is dark and the clouds go by
But there is no God, to hear me cry!

'There is no God, none, to abolish one
Of the foul things thought and dreamed and done!
Wherefore I hate, till my race is run,
All living men beneath the sun!'

   .   .   .   .   .   .

To-night he rose when all was still,
   Left like a thief his darkened door,
And down the dale, and o'er the hill,
   He flew till here upon the shore
Shivering he came; and here he trod
Hour after hour the glooms of God,
Nursing his hate in fierce unrest,
Like an elfin babe upon the breast!
And all his hunger and his thirst
Was vengeance on the man he cursed!
'O Lord my God, if a God there be,
Give up the man I hate to me!
On his living heart let my vengeance feed,
And I shall know Thou art God indeed!'

      Again rings out that bitter cry
      Between the dark seas and the sky—
      Then all is hush'd, while quivering,
      With teeth and claws prepared to spring,
      He crouches beast-like . . . Hark, O hark
      What solemn murmur fills the dark?
      What shadows come and go up there,
      Through the azure voids of the starry air?

The night is still; the waters sleep; the skies
Gaze down with bright innumerable eyes:
A voice comes out of heaven and o'er the sea:
'I AM; AND I WILL GIVE THIS MAN TO THEE!'

CHAPTER I.

Granddad, granddad! look up!—it is Marjorie. Have you forgotten your niece, Marjorie Wells? And this is little Edgar, Marjorie's son! Speak to him, Edgar, speak to granddad. Alack, this is one of his dark days, and he knoweth no one.'

In the arm-chair of carven oak, stained black as ebony by the smokes of many years, and placed in the great hall where the yule log is burning, the old man sits as he has sat every day since last winter; speechless, to all seeming sightless; faintly smiling and nodding from time to time when well shaken into consciousness by some kindly hand, and then relapsing into stupor. He is paralysed from the waist downwards. His deeply wrinkled face is ashen gray and perfectly bloodless, set in its frame of snow-white hair; hair that has once been curly and light, and still falls in thin white ringlets on the stooping shoulders; his hands are shrivelled to thinnest bone and parchment; his eyes, sunken deep beneath the brows, give forth little or no glimmer of the fire of life.

Ninety years old. The ruin, or wreck, of what has once been a gigantic man.

The frame is still gigantic, and shows the mighty mould in which the man was made; the great head, with its broad overhanging brows and square powerful jaw, is like the head of an aged lion of Africa, toothless and gray with time.

Kick the great log, and as the sparks fly up the chimney thick as bees from out a hive, his eyes open a little, and he seems faintly conscious of the flame. Flash the lamp into his sunken eyes, and as he mutters curiously to himself, and fumbles with thin hands upon his knees, a faint flash of consciousness comes from the smouldering brand of brain within.

He is not always so inert as now. This, as the grave matron who is bending over him says, is one of his dark days. Sometimes he will look around and talk feebly to his children's children, and seem to listen as some one reads out of the great family Bible which stands ever near his elbow; and the gray old face will smile gently, and the thin worn hand lie lightly as a leaf on some flaxen head. But to-night, though it is Christmas Eve, and all the kinsfolk of the house are gathered together, he knows no one, and sees and hears nothing. He breathes, and that is all.

All round the upland hall the snow is lying, but over it, since last night, have fallen, in black tree-like shadows, the trails of the thaw. The woods are bare. The great horse-chestnut on the hill-top has long since shed its sevenfold fans, intermingled with jagged brown buds bursting open to show the glossy nuts within. Bare even is the ash, which keeps a goodly portion of its leaves so long, and stands scarcely half stript, darkening in the chill autumnal wind. All the landscape round looks dark and ominous; the shadow of winter is seen visibly upon the shivering world.

'Put a drop to his lips—perhaps he'd know us then.'

The speaker, a tall, handsome widow of fifty, with grim, weather-beaten face, holds by the hand a dark-eyed boy of ten, swarthy as a quadroon. Friends and kinsmen of the family—of both sexes and all ages—gather round. It is a festival, and all are more or less gorgeously clad, bright-ribbon'd caps and gorgeous silk gowns being predominant among the women, and blue swallow-tail'd coats and knee-breeches among the men. Next to the centenarian, the chief centre of interest is the handsome widow and her little boy. She has been long absent from England, having married a West Indian planter, and long ago settled down in Barbadoes. A widow with one child, she has at last returned to the village where she was born, and though she has been some months at home, the novelty of her presence has by no means worn away.

'Put a drop to his lips,' she repeats, 'and speak up to grandfather.'

'Grandfather!' cries the boy, taking one of the cold bony hands.

No stir—no sign.

'It's no use, Marjorie,' observes the good matron with a dolorous shake of the head. 'When he goes like this, he is stone deaf and blind. Some of these days, doctor says, he'll never wake up at all, but go out like a spark, as quiet as you see him now.'

'And no wonder,' returns the widow. 'The Book says three score and ten, and he is over a score beyond.'

'Four score and ten, and seven weeks,' pipes a thin voice from the background. 'Ah, it be a powerful age.'

He who speaks is himself an old man, very thin and very feeble, with a senile smile and purblind eyes; yet, gazing upon the figure in the arm-chair, he assumes an appearance of ghastly youth, and feels quite fresh and boylike.

'Four score and ten, and seven weeks,' he repeats, 'and the master was a man growed before I was born. He puts me in mind of the great oak by Dingleby Waste, for it stood many a hundred year before it fell, and now, though it be fallen with its roots out o' the ground, its boughs do put out every summer a little patch of green, just to show there be a spark of life i' the old stump yet.'

The members of the family group gaze open-mouthed at the speaker, and then, with mouths still wider open, at the tenant of the arm-chair; one and all with a curious air of belonging to another and less mortal species, and having nothing in common with a thing so fallen and so perishable. And still the old man does not stir. Lying thus, he does indeed seem like some mighty tree of the forest, gnarled and weather-beaten and bare, uprooted and cast down, with scarcely a sign to show that it has once gloried in the splendour of innumerable leaves, and stood erect in its strength against the crimson shafts of sunset and of dawn.

All the long winter evening there has been mirth-making around him. The hall is hung with holly, green leaf and red berry; and from the quaint old lamp that

'Facing the fire, and the great Yule log, sits the old man,
Christian Christianson, of the Fen.'

swings from the centre beam is pendent a bunch of whitest-berried mistletoe. Fiddles and flutes and pipes have been playing, and nimble feet have beaten merry time on the polished oaken floor. And throughout it all grandfather has kept his silent seat on the ingle, and hardly seemed to hear or see.

It is a grand old hall, fit to be a portion of some grand manorial abode; and such indeed it was once upon a time, before the old manor house fell into decay, and became the home of the Christiansons. Facing the great ingle is a large double entrance door, studded with great nails and brazen bars like a prison gate; and whenever this door—or rather one half of it—is swung open, you see the snow whirling outside, and can hear a roar like the far-off murmur of the sea. The hall is long and broad, and at one end there is a wide staircase of carven oak, leading to a gallery, which in turn communicates with the upper rooms of the house. In the gallery sit the musicians, led by the little old cripple, Myles Middlemass, the parish clerk. Great black beams, like polished ebony, support the ceiling. The fireplace is broad and high, with fixed oaken forms on either side, and projecting thence, two sphynx-like forms of well-burnished brass; while facing the fire and the great yule log, sits, in his arm-chair of polished oak, the old man, Christian Christianson, of the Fen.

The music begins anew, and the folk begin a country dance. Farm maidens and farm labourers lounge in from the kitchen, gathering like sheep at one end of the hall, close to the kitchen door. Then Farmer Thorpe, who is master of the house, which came to him with Mary Christianson, the old man's daughter, leads off the dance with Mistress Marjorie, his grim kinswoman from Barbadoes. The others follow, young and old, and the oldest as merrily as the youngest. Loud cries and laughter rise ringing to the rafters; there is struggling in corners, girlish laughter, patter of light and peal of heavy feet; and the louder the mirth sounds within, the louder roars the winter wind without. But old Christian sits moveless, with his blank eyes, half-closed, fixed on the fire. Like a fallen tree, did we say? Rather like some gray pillar of granite rising grimly out of the sea; with the innumerable laughter of ocean around it, and flight of white wings around it, and brightness above it; dead, dead to all the washing of the waves of life, and blind to all the shining of the sun.

As he sits there, some look at him in awe, and whisper to each other of his past, and shake the head ominously as they think of his strange adventures sailing up and down the world. For he has lived much of his life in foreign lands, a wanderer for many years without a place whereon to rest his feet; he has been a master mariner, and a trader, and an owner of sailing ships; and far away, long ago, he gathered wealth in some mysterious fashion, and brought it back with him to buy the ancestral acres that his father's father lost. A stormy life and a terrible, say the gossips; not without blood's sin and such crimes as, twice told, lift the hair and shake the soul; for if they speak sooth, he has sailed under the black flag on the Indian seas, and taken his share in the traffic of human life. Those who are oldest remember dimly the days of his passion and his pride—days when his hand was against every man, and when his very name was a synonym for hate and wrath. The women-folk speak, moreover, of his strength and beauty, when his white locks were golden as a lion's mane, and his gray eyes bright with the light of the Viking race from whom he drew his fiery blood.

While the mirth is loudest, pass out through the hall door into the night. The great door closes with a clang; the brightness fades into the murmuring darkness of the storm. Stand on the lonely upland, and see the white flakes driving tumultuously from the sea; far across the great marsh with Herndale Mere glistening in its centre like a great shield, and beyond the dark sandhills which stretch yonder like tossing billows for miles and miles beyond, the sea itself is tossing and gleaming, and crashing on the hard and ribbed sand of the lonely shore. The heavens are dark, and neither moon nor star is visible; but the air is full of a faint mysterious light—like moonshine, like starshine, like the light that is in the filmy falling flakes. In this faint phosphorescence the frozen mere flashes by fits and the distant sandhills loom dimly in the distance, and on every side gathers the whiteness of the fallen sheets of snow.

Behind the great farm, with its windows flashing out like bloodshot eyes, and its shadows coming or going on the crimson blinds, stretch the upland fields, deep in drift of mingled snow and sand; and inland, here and there, glance the lights from clustering homesteads and solitary farms. A lamp is burning in every home to-night, for all the folk are awake, and the coming of the Christ is close at hand.

A long lane, deep with many a waggon rut, and closed on either side by blackthorn hedges, leads from the upland, across fields and meadows, to the highway, only a mile along which is the village, and the quaint old village church. Listen closely, and the faint peal of bells comes to your ear in the very teeth of the wind! —and look, even as you listen, lights are creeping up the lane, and soon, shadows of human forms loom behind the lights, and you see the carol singers, with William Ostler from the Rose and Crown at their head, coming along, lanthorns in hand, to sing at the farm door.

William Ostler staggers as he comes, and tumbles sprawling into the snow; whereat there is loud laughter and scuffling of heavy hobnailed feet. Young men in heavy woollen coats, and girls in red cloaks with warm hoods, and little boys and girls following behind, come trooping along the lane. Now they meet the bitter blast upon the upland, and the lanthorns are blown out, but with the light from the farm windows to guide them, they come stamping along, and, facing the hall door, range themselves in a row. Then William with a tipsy hiccough, gives out the word, and the voices ring out loud and clear.

Scarcely has the carol begun, when all sounds cease within the farm; the dance has ceased, and all are standing still to listen. As the last note dies away, the door swings open, and Farmer Thorpe, with face like a ribstone pippin, and white hair blowing in the wind, stands on the threshold, with shining faces peeping out behind him in a blaze of rosy light.

'Come in, come in!' he cries, cheerily. 'Welcome all!'

Stamping the snow from their boots, shaking it from their garments, they troop in and gather together at the kitchen end of the hall, where warm spiced ale is poured for them, and chucks of home-made cake put into their chilly hands. Left outside in the dark, the village children pelt each other with snowballs, and run races in the snow, and shout shrilly in through the key-hole, and beat with tiny mittened hands on the mighty door.

It is close on midnight now. The carol-singers have gone their ways, to make their music elsewhere, and get good entertainment for their pains. The house is full of the pleasant smell of meat and drink.

But the great hall is empty; empty, that is to say, save for the old form sitting before the fire. There he crouches still, conscious of little save the pleasant warmth; breathing faintly, otherwise not stirring hand cr limb.

The musicians, the labourers, the farm maidens, are busy feasting in the kitchen; whence comes, through the half-closed doors, the sound of loud guffaws, of clattering dishes and jingling glasses, of busy, shuffling feet. There is plenty of rough fare, with libations of strong beer and cider and ginger-ale. In the low-roofed dining-room, which opens out up three oaken steps at the other end of the hall, the genteeler portion of the company sit round the supper board,—a snow-white cloth of linen, piled with roast and boiled meats, fat capons, knuckles of ham and veal, Christmas cakes and puddings, great rosy-cheeked apples, foaming jugs of ale, flasks of ruby-coloured rum, and black bottles of foreign vintage. Farmer Thorpe heads the table, in his swallow-tailed coat of bottle-green, his long buff waist-coat with snowy cambric at the breast and throat, his great silver chain with dangling charms and seals; and facing him, at the other end, is Mary his good dame, splendid in silk and flowered brocade, with a cap, to crown all, that is the envy and admiration of every matron in the happy group. On either side are ranged the guests in their degree,—Squire Orchardson of the

Willows, a spare thin-visaged man in deep mourning, having the place of honour at the farmer's right hand, and pretty Mabel Orchardson, the squire's only daughter, blushing not far away, with young Harry Thorpe, a tall yeoman of twenty-one, to ply her with sweet things and sweeter looks, and to whisper tender nothings in her ear. The light of swinging lamps and country-made candles gleams all round upon happy faces, red and bright, with fine shadows behind of oaken furniture and wainscoted walls. The mirth is real, though solemn; for the wine has not yet had time to tell its tale. The old folks pledge each other in old-fashioned style; healths go round; pretty maidens sip out of the glasses of their cousins and lovers, while fond feet meet, and knees touch, under the table. There is a clatter of dishes and knives and forks, a murmur of voices, which only ceases at intervals, when the wind shakes the house and causes the roof and walls to quake again.

But all at once, above the crying of the wind and above all the noise of the feast, rises a sound so shrill and terrible that all mirth ceases, and the company listen in terror. It sounds like a human shriek, coming through the half-closed door that leads to the hall—a human shriek, or something superhuman, so strangely does it ring through the merry house. Hark, again! There can be no doubt now. It is the shriek of a man's voice, sharp, fierce, and terrible.

The more timid among the company—both men and women—keep their seats, shiver, and look at one another; the braver spirits, headed by Farmer Thorpe, push through the open door, and gather on the steps leading down into the hall.

In the middle of the hall stands, ghastly pale now, and terrified, the swarthy boy from Barbadoes, his hands clenched, his eyes staring, every fibre of him trembling with terror. Near to him is another boy, stronger and bigger, of coarser make and breed; young Walter Thorpe, the farmer's nephew, whose father lives down at the Warren. A little way off their little cousin, Mary Farringford, crouches dumb with terror, her large blue eyes dilated and misty with timid tears.

All the three children gaze one way—the dark boy

fascinated, like a murderer caught in the act, with the murderous look of hate and venom found by fear upon his face and frozen there; young Walter a little frightened too, but preserving a certain loutish stolidity; little Mary quivering like a reed. All gaze towards the great fireplace, for there, still fixed in his chair, but with head erect, eyes dilating, and skinny finger pointing, sits the old man, awake at last indeed!

His mouth is still open, panting, and it is clear now that the shriek which startled the company came from his throat. His finger points to the dark boy, who recoils in dread; but his eyes are fixed, not on the boy's face, but on a glittering object which lies upon the floor, close to the boy's feet.

An open clasp-knife, with dagger-like blade and steel spring, the kind of knife that seamen use, too often, upon one another.

Farmer Thorpe steps into the hall, with the wondering company behind him.

'What is the matter?' he exclaims. 'Who was it that screamed out?'

Walter Thorpe, who has recovered his composure, shuffles his feet, grins stupidly, and jerks his thumb at the old man.

'*Him!*' he replies with characteristic indifference to grammar.

'And what—what's this?' cries the farmer, following the old man's eyes and looking at the knife. 'Eh, eh, whose knife is this?'

'*His!*' replies Walter again, nodding his head at the other boy.

'*Edgar's!*' exclaims the voice of the widow Marjorie Wells; and as she speaks she comes forward very pale, and touches her son with an angry hand. 'Edgar, what does it mean?'

He scowls, and makes no answer.

'Have you been quarrelling?' she continues sternly. 'How dare you quarrel, you wicked boy?'

'He struck me,' pants Edgar, still with the murderous look in his face.

'No, I didn't,' cries Walter.

'Yes you did.'

'I didn't—leastways till you pushed me against little Mary and threw her down. Then when I slapt your face, you pulled out that knife, and tried to stick me like a pig!'

A murmur of horror runs through the company.

'You hear, madam?' says Farmer Thorpe, sharply. 'I think your boy's to blame, and if he was my son, I'd give him a sound thrashing. Fancy the young imp carrying a knife like that, and trying to use it too.'

'Edgar is passionate,' says the widow, haughtily; 'but I daresay he was provoked.'

'He said that I was black,' cries Edgar, looking up at his mother with his great eyes, 'and that when I was a man I ought to marry a black woman—and cousin Mary laughed—and so I pushed him; and when he struck me, I pulled out my knife, and I *would* have stabbed him, if grandfather had not screeched out.'

'Fine doings o' Christmastide,' exclaims Farmer Thorpe, shaking his head grimly; 'and look you now at father,' he continues, passing across to the old man, who still keeps the same position, with eyes staring and finger pointing. 'How goes it, father? Come, come, what ails you now?'

At the voice of his son, the old man drops his outstretched arm, and begins to mutter quietly to himself.

'Eh?' says Farmer Thorpe, putting down his ear to listen. 'Speak up, father.'

The words are faint and feeble exceedingly, but they are just intelligible:

'Take—away—the knife!'

At a signal from the farmer, one of the neighbours lifts the knife from the floor, touches the spring, closes it, and hands it over to the farmer, who forthwith consigns it to the lowest depths of his breeches' pocket. All the company look on, breathless, as if upon a veritable miracle—the dead coming back to life.

There is a pause. Then again the feeble voice comes from the worn-out frame,

'My son John.'

'Here, father.'

'Call them!—call the children!'

For a moment the farmer is puzzled, but seeing the old man's eyes again wander towards young Edgar Wells, he begins to comprehend.

'Come here,' he says sharply; 'grandfather wants you.'

The boy at first shrinks back, then, with natural courage, forces a smile of bravado, and comes boldly forward. As he passes into the crimson firelight, the old man's eyes perceive him, and the wrinkled face lightens. But the next instant the feeble eyes look round disappointed.

'Both,' he murmurs—'both my children.'

Again the farmer is puzzled, but his good dame, with woman's wit, hits the mark at once.

'I think he wants our nephew Walter,' she says softly. 'Go to him, Walter.'

With a sheepish grin, Walter Thorpe steps forward, and so the two boys stand face-to-face close to the old man's knee. As his feeble gaze falls upon them, his lips tremble, and he gazes vacantly from one to the other from beneath his rheumy lids. Then suddenly reaching out one hand, he holds Walter by the jacket-sleeve, and with the other, which trembles like a leaf, tries to clutch at Edgar. But Edgar, startled by the sudden movement, has shrunk back afraid.

'What doth he mean?' whispers a neighbour.

'Now, God be praised!' says Dame Thorpe, 'I think he means the lads to make friends. See, Marjorie, how he feels out to touch your boy; and hark, what is he saying?'

They listen closely, and at last they catch the words:

'The children—put their hands into mine.'

At a look from the farmer, Walter puts his coarse brown hand between the old man's trembling fingers, which close over it and clutch it convulsively. But Edgar scowls and hangs aloof, till his mother comes forward and touches him.

'Put out your hand—at once!'

Thus urged, the boy partly stretches out his arm, when the widow takes his hand and places it, like the other's, between the old man's fingers. As the hands of the two boys touch in that sinewy cage, which now holds them firm as iron, their eyes meet with a momentary gleam of defiance, then fall.

'Hush!' murmurs Dame Thorpe, softly; and there is a long silence. The old man's lips move, but no sound comes from them. His eyes no longer seek the faces around him, but are half-closed, as if in prayer.

Presently there is a faint murmur. The farmer bends down his ear, and catches the words, murmured very feebly, . . .

'Love one another.' . . .

Deeper stillness follows, and a solemn awe fills the hearts of all the company. Presently the old man's hands relax, and with a quiet sigh, he leans back smiling in his chair. His dim eyes open and look round, his lips begin to move quietly again.

'When I was a boy . . .'

They catch no more, for the words die away, and he seems to fall into a doze, perhaps into a dream of the days that once have been. While he thus lies, and while the company return with spirits solemnised to table, let us stay by him in the lonely hall, and with eyes fixed upon the fire, recall the troubled memories of his life.

CHAPTER II.

THE YEARS ROLL BACK: A DEATH-BED.

As far back as he could remember,—when, though his body was a useless log, and his eyes dim with dust of age, his memory was still green,—the Christiansons had hated the Orchardsons, and the Orchardsons had returned the hate with interest. The two families were heat and frost, fire and water, peace and war; their spirits could never cross each other without pain. Physically, even, they were as unlike as tall stalwart trees of the forest and creeping shrubs of the common: the male Christiansons, tall, stalwart yeomen of six foot upwards; the Orchardsons narrow-chested, stooping figures, below the middle height.

There was, moreover, this great difference between them : good luck was ever on the one side, while the other seldom throve. A shilling in the pocket of an Orchardson multiplied itself to a pound, and the pound to ten, and the ten to a hundred ; while in the pockets of a Christianson, hundreds melted like withered leaves, like the cheating pieces given to foolish folk by the fairies. The Christiansons never could keep money; the Orchardsons never could let it go. For all this, and for a thousand other reasons, they hated each other the more.

It was such an old hate, such a settled feud, that no one quite knew when or how it began ; indeed, there was a general disposition in the neighbourhood to trace it back to a mythical period, somewhat farther back than the Conquest. But certain it was, that even in the times of the great Civil Wars, the two families were on different sides—cavalier Orchardsons hunted down by roundhead Christiansons, and being hunted down in turn when at last, with the Merry Monarch, came time and opportunity.

Mention a Christianson to an Orchardson, and the latter would look evil, shrug shoulders, and show a certain sort of easy hate tempered with proud contempt. Name an Orchardson to a Christianson, and it was a very different matter ; the blood in his veins would turn to gall, his gorge would rise, and he would feel his strong frame convulsed with wrath, while his hands were clenched for a blow. The Orchardsons were more than shadows on the lives of the Christiansons ; the very thought of them lay like lead upon the breast, choking the wholesome breath.

As years went on, and milder influences supervened, the fierceness of the vendetta between the two families died away, leaving only a great frosty chill, in which the families, without any active hostility, fell farther and farther asunder. The Orchardsons remained at the old manor-house, ever increasing their substance both in money and land. The Christiansons kept tight hold of their farms down towards Herndale Mere and the sea, but it was whispered in more than one wise quarter that they were deeply involved, and that when

Robert Christianson, the reigning head of the house, went the way of all flesh, there would be revelations.

One evening, late in the autumn, as young Tom Rudyard, the doctor's assistant, sat quietly smoking a pipe in the bar parlour of the Rose and Crown, with pretty Nancy Parkinson by his side, and buxom Mrs. Parkinson looking on with a smile, he received an unexpected summons. A tall young lad of about fourteen, clad in a rough yeoman costume, and carrying a riding switch, came bolt into the room.

Tom started up guiltily, for he knew that to enter that bar-parlour was forbidden to Dr. Marshman's assistants (all of whom had in succession 'gone wrong' through a too great love of festivity), and then, recognising the new-comer, grinned, and gave a hoarse laugh. Standing thus erect, the young doctor showed a very long spare body and attenuated legs, clad in a costume rather too loud for that of a regular practitioner, and encroaching indeed on the privileged style of the jaunty veterinary surgeon.

'What, Master Christian, is it you?' cried Nancy, with a smile; then, seeing at once by the boy's pale face that something was wrong, she added, 'Is anything the matter?'

'Yes,' answered the lad with quivering lips. 'The doctor's wanted at once up to the farm. Father's taken bad.'

One cry of commiseration rose from the two women.

'What is it?' asked Tom, reaching up for his beaver hat, which hung on a hook behind the door. 'Not a fit, I hope? At his time of life——'

'Don't waste time talking,' said the boy, 'but come along. Mother sent for the old doctor, but he's out and away at Deepdale; so I came to look after *you*.'

Although he was only a boy, he spoke with a certain authority, and through his great height and powerful frame, looked almost a man; certainly a man in strength, though his form was as yet shapeless and awkward, and his hands and feet too large. That he was greatly troubled and alarmed was shown by his bloodless face and the pale, dry lips, which he moistened every moment with the tip of his tongue.

C

'It's a goodish stretch up to the farm,' said the young doctor, with a rueful glance at the cosy fire. 'I shall want a horse.'

'Take my mare,' returned the lad, 'she's standing at the door, and she'll carry you up at a gallop.'

'I dare say, and break my neck on the road. I don't know a yard of the way.'

'But the mare does; give her her head, and she'll go home straight as a shot.'

Doctor Tom still looked doubtful.

'I shall want my instruments, may be.'

'Then do you ride on, while I go to the surgery, and bring them after you. I'll take the short cut across the marsh, and be there nigh as soon as you.'

Walking out to the front door of the inn, they saw the light from the porch flashing against a great wall of rainy blackness. It was a wild night of wind and rain. The sign was shrieking and tossing like a corpse in chains, and the air was full of a rushing hiss of water.

In front of the door, just discernible in the darkness, stood a dripping horse, or pony, held by a ragged stable-boy.

'Lord, what a night!' cried the doctor, with a shiver, and an inward imprecation on the inconsiderate people who were taken ill in such weather.

'Quick! quick!' said young Master Christianson, impatiently. 'Mount the pony.'

'Is he quiet?'

'As a lamb—only mind to give him his head.'

Quiet as a lamb he indeed seemed, standing drawn together in the rain, perfectly still; but no sooner were the young doctor's long legs thrown over him, than he was off at a bound. The rider had only just time to clutch the bridle, and to utter a startled yell—then darkness swallowed him up.

Good Mistress Parkinson stood at the inn door, with her daughter at her side.

'Master Christianson,' she cried, as the lad moved away; adding as he turned his head, 'let me get you a drop of warm ale, or a posset. You be soaking through.'

The lad shook his head, and buttoning his coat tight round his throat, ran swiftly from the inn door, leaving the good women full of perplexity and simple pity. For Christian, though a wild and headstrong lad, or rather just because he was headstrong and wild, was a prime favourite in all that neighbourhood. 'The true Christianson breed,' all admitted, with wise shakes of the head and secret admiration—quarrelsome, irritable, fierce and fiery, yet withal forgiving and open-handed; proud, like his father and mother before him, of the old name and of the typical family strength; so strong and handsome, that young maids, much his elders, had already been known to cast tender looks at him; yet so simple and boy-like, that he preferred snaring a rabbit or setting a woodcock spring to the brightest pair of eyes in Christendom.

Swift as a deerhound, he ran up through the village, setting his right shoulder against the slanting rain, until he reached the old doctor's cottage, and knocked sharply at the little low door. An old woman opened, and with scarcely a word to her, he ran into the parlour, or 'surgery,' looking for the doctor's case of instruments, and for such simple remedies as might be needed. As he searched, he rapidly explained to the old dame, who knew him well, the state of affairs; and then, having secured what he wanted, and buttoned them tight under his coat, he ran out again into the rain.

Swiftly still he ran along the dark road, not losing breath, though it was rough and steep; presently, with one bound, he leapt a hedge and alighted in a field of rainy stubble. Though he seemed to be in pitch darkness, it was clear that he knew every inch of the way, as, crossing a field, he came out upon an open common or waste, covered with dark rainy pools. Across the common, and up a miry lane; then he saw flashing on a hillside before him the lights of a farm.

When he reached the farm door, he found it standing open, and Doctor Tom, splashed from top to toe, on the point of entering, while the little mare, which he had ridden in fear and desperation, was standing with head down, quiet as a lamb.

c 2

' How's father? ' asked the lad in a whisper, as he followed the doctor into the hall.

A shock-headed farm-maiden answered something in a whisper, and Christian led the way upstairs. Passing up a broad oaken staircase, he reached an open corridor, out of which opened several doors; approaching one of which, he knocked softly.

The door was immediately opened by a young girl, about a year older than himself. She put her finger on her lips, as he was about to speak, and beckoned the doctor, who quietly approached.

In a large old-fashioned bedroom, with a polished floor of slippery black oak, and a low ceiling close to the black rafters of the roof, was a large wooden bedstead, on which lay the figure of a man, a great gaunt yeoman, with iron-grey hair and clean shaven face. Some of his clothes had been hastily thrown off, and by the bedside were his high riding boots; but he still wore his shirt and waistcoat, the former torn open to free the powerful workings of the throat. His eyes were closed, his face ghastly pale, his whole attitude that of exhaustion and semi-stupor, and his breathing was very heavy and hard.

By the bedside stood a tall, pale matron, some few years his senior, and close to her, on a chair, was an open Bible.

Doctor Tom came in on tiptoe, and standing by the bedside, sucked the knob of his stick, and gazed with rather vacant eyes at the man; then, reaching down his coarse red hand, felt the pulse, and found it very jerky and feeble.

' Brandy—have you given him brandy, mistress? ' he asked, in a hoarse whisper.

The matron nodded her head.

'Well, give him some more, at once, please; 'tis the only thing to keep life in him. How did it begin? What doth he complain of most? '

In a low voice, the matron explained that her husband had been seized, while sitting at supper, with a violent pain in the region of the heart. He had come in very wet and weary from a long ride to the neighbouring market town, and he had been fasting all day. He had been a good deal troubled, too, she said, and that made him neglect his food. When he was first seized with pain, she thought he would die at once, but when he had drank some spirits boiling hot, he got a little relief. Presently another attack of pain came on, and then they got him to bed, and put warm bottles to his feet ; since then he had been easier, and had seemed as if he were asleep.

As the two stood whispering together, the sick man suddenly opened his eyes.

' Who's that ? ' he said, feebly. ' Be it the doctor ? '

' Yes,' said his wife, ' young Mr. Tom.'

' Tell him I don't want no doctor's stuff; I shall be all right i' the morning.'

' How's the pain, master ? ' asked the doctor.

' Middling—middling bad,' answered the patient; then with a groan he put his hand upon his chest. ' There be a weight here like a millstone, right down upon my heart.'

' Doth it pain you when you breathe, master ? '

' Ay, surely ! like a knife a-cutting me in twain. But I don't want no physic—no, no ! '

He closed his eyes, moaning, and seemed to sink into a doze.

Doctor Tom led the matron aside.

' Your good man's powerful bad, mistress. He'll have to be bled straight away.'

' Is he in danger, think you ? '

Maybe yes, maybe no. If the blood flows free, it may ease his heart a bit; his viscera be gorged with black blood, mistress, and his heart doth not get room to beat.'

So without more conversation or delay the young leech opened a vein in the farmer's arm. The dark blood came freely but feebly, and as it flowed, he really seemed to breathe with greater ease. When about an ounce of blood had been taken away, and the artery carefully bound up, he seemed to lie in comfortable sleep.

' He'll do now,' said Dr. Tom. ' We'll look round in the morning, and see how he thrives.'

The matron, who had exhibited rare nerve during the blood-letting, and had herself assisted without a word, now looked wildly up in the doctor's face.

'Will my man live?'

'Why not, mistress? See how easy he do breathe, now! Ay, he'll live, I hope, for many a long year!'

Down the great stairs slipped Doctor Tom, followed by young Christian. He was well satisfied with himself, and quite unaware that, in the true spirit of the science (or nescience) of those days, he had finished his man, and drawn from an exhausted arterial system its last chance of recovering its shattered strength.

'Will you ride back?' asked the boy.

'On the back of that brimstone mare?—not I. I'd rather walk barefoot, young master. Good-night.'

The lad did not offer to escort him beyond the door; but leaving him to wander home as he might along the dark roads, returned to the room up-stairs, and rejoined his mother and sister.

That night none of the three retired to rest. The mother sat watching by the bedside, while the girl and lad sat upon the hearth, waiting and listening. Not a sound broke the silence but the monotonous breathing of the sick man, and a faint murmur from the lips of the mother, as, with horn-rimmed spectacles upon her nose, and the old Bible upon her knee, she read softly to herself.

The room was dimly illumined by the faint rays of a wood fire, and by the light of a small oil-lamp, which was fastened against the wall over the chimney-piece. Seen even thus, the boy and girl seemed made in very different moulds: he, strong, herculean, rough, with blue eyes, and curly flaxen hair; she, tall, thin, and delicate, with swarthy skin, dark eyes, and chestnut hair. The boy, in his build and complexion, resembled the figure on the bed. The girl resembled the wan woman who sat reading by the bedside.

Christian Christianson was scarce fourteen years old; his sister Kate was rather more than a year older. Their parents had married somewhat late in life, and the two children were the only living issue of the match.

Both in name and frame did the rough lad show his Scandinavian origin, his connection with those far-off ancestors of his who swept down from the north in the old times, harried the seas and the sea-coasts, and scattered their seed far and wide on those tracts of territory which pleased them best. Nothing foreign seemed to have entered the light current of his blood. While he lay there, rough and awkward as a lion's cub, he might have been taken for the heir of some old viking, bespattered from his cradle with the salt sea foam.

But young Christian was heir to little save the surname of his father and the monopoly of certain fruitless feuds. His father and his father's father had farmed the lands verging on the great sandhills, and within hearing of the sea; and it was to be supposed that he would farm them also, when his turn came. His father's father had died in debt, and his father had been more or less in debt when he was born, and the shadow of mysterious obligations had been over the house ever since he could remember. He had been brought up to no profession, and with no particular occupation; but by looking on and using his wits, as boys can, he had learned a little of farming, and the value of farm stock. His education had been rough-and-ready enough. While his sister could play a little on the harpsichord, and sew a fine sampler, besides being able to read and write fairly, he possessed no accomplishments, save, of course, those which he had acquired by sheer force of physical courage and perseverance. He could sit any horse barebacked, he knew every beast of the field and fowl of the air, he could wrestle and swim, and he was an excellent shot at birds on the wing—this last being a much rarer accomplishment in those days than we, with our modern notions, might imagine. But he had little or no taste for books, and beyond a good ear for a tune, and a good deep voice, which might have made him a fair singer, little capacity for any of the arts.

As he sat before the fire, his eyes were lifted ever and again to the pallid face of his mother, who read on monotonously to herself. Kate Christianson sat with her hands in her lap, gazing at the fire. So hour after hour passed, until it was past midnight; and then, all at once, the invalid's sleep began to grow disturbed. He tossed upon his pillow, and clutched the counterpane with his strong hand, muttering half-articulate sounds. Suddenly his wife started as if stung, for she heard the sound of a hated name.

'Five thousand five hundred pounds . . . five per cent. per annum . . . Richard Orchardson, his heirs and assigns . . . witness . . .' Here his words became in-articulate, until he added, gasping, his own name, 'Robert Christianson, of the Fen.'

Young Christian heard, and looked up with a strange darkness on his fair face.

'Mother,' he whispered, 'did you hear?'

'Hush!' cried the matron with uplifted finger; for her husband's eyes had opened again, fixing themselves strangely upon hers. They watched for a few moments, then, with a low cry, the man started up and tried to spring out of bed.

'Father! father!' cried Mistress Christianson, rising and pushing him back. 'What ails you, father? Christian, come—help to hold him down.'

The lad sprang up, and putting his strong arms gently round his father, tried to soothe him; for it was clear that his wits were wandering.

'Who's that? My son Christian?'

'Yes, father.'

'Get me my hat and staff, lad. I be going out.'

'Not to-night, father.'

'Ay, to-night. Tell thy mother not to sit up, for I shall be late.'

'Speak to him, mother!'

'Father, don't you know me?' cried his wife.

'Ay, ay, dame, I know thee well enough, but I can-not stay talking. I be going out.'

'Where are you going?'

'Down to the Willows. I must see Dick Orchard-son, and tell him my mind.'

The listeners looked at one another aghast. The very mention of the name of an Orchardson sounded strange on those lips, but to hear one of the hated brood named so glibly, as a being with whom it was possible under any circumstances to have human intercourse, was positively startling.

'God help him!' cried his wife with a cold shiver.

Exhausted by his efforts to rise, the farmer sank back upon his pillow. His breathing was now very difficult, and his face was convulsed as if with acute pain. They moistened his lips with brandy, and chafed his trembling hands.

'Father!' cried Christian, trembling; and Kate, standing close to him, echoed his tender cry.

The farmer opened his eyes again, and looked round.

'Who's there? Is that my boy Christian?'

'Yes, father.'

'Come closer, lad, and take my hand. Where's thy mother?'

'Here, father,' said Mistress Christianson. 'Oh, Christian, thy father's dying!'

'No, no, mother,' cried the boy.

'Tell Dick Orchardson——'

So far the farmer spoke, then paused again. Again that hated name.

There was a long pause. The farmer lay with eyes wide open, looking upward, and muttering to himself. They could make nothing now of his words, and a dreadful awe was upon them, for the shadow of the coming angel was already upon his face. Kate Christianson cast herself down by the bedside, hiding her face and sobbing wildly. The mother stood gaunt and pale, her dim eyes on the man who had been her loving companion so many long years. The lad, clutching his father's chilly hand, was trembling like a leaf.

So they waited, and it seemed, in that solemn moment, that the chamber grew dark. Oh that dreadful silence of the chamber of death! The poet speaks of 'darkness visible;' *this* is silence heard—a silence ominous and strange, in which the very beating of the heart is audible, and we feel the stirring motion of the unconscious life within.

They listened and waited on. At last a few faint words were audible.

'Down by the four-acre mere. Is that Dick Orchardson? Tell him . . . Get me a light, lad, I cannot see tho letters, I cannot read . . . Ask thy mother, forgive, forgive . . .'

One last faint cry, and the voice was for ever still. Of what was a living face but a few minutes before, only a marble mask remained. All knelt and prayed, for the shadow which follows all men was in the room.

CHAPTER III.

SHADOWS AT THE FEN FARM.

WHEN Robert Christianson was dead and buried, there came at last the revelations that had long been predicted. First of all, it was discovered in a general way that he was far more heavily in debt than any one had guessed; that, indeed, his affairs were a ravelled skein which it would take all the ingenuity of the law or all its cruelty to disentangle. Then, when the various threads of obligation were separated from each other, and the widow and her children thought that the coast was clear, came a letter, like a thunderbolt, announcing that the freehold of the greater part of the farm lands was under a mortgage, that the interest was long in arrear, and that, to crown all, the holder of the fatal mortgage was their hereditary enemy, Richard Orchardson of the Willows.

At first it was too horrible for belief. The very thought was an outrage on the beloved dead. The widow sat with stern sceptical face, while the boy Christian was loud in his expression of indignation. But confirmation quickly came. It was made only too clear that the deceased farmer, in the extremity of his distress, had accepted assistance from the enemy of his father and his father's father, and had given as substantial security the mortgage upon the choicest of the farm lands.

Bitterer even than death itself came the humiliating discovery; bitterer, because for the moment it killed all reverence and respect for the poor dead, and showed

him as a man yielding, forgetful, and barren of pride.
Better to have starved, thought the widow, than have
sought or taken succour from that quarter. Alas! she
little knew how long and terrible had been the farmer's
struggle before he did yield, how cruel the pang had
been, and how the pain of the secret had preyed upon
the poor man's heart, until it broke in shame.

When all was thought that could be thought, the
mother and son spoke out by the fireside, while Kate
looked sadly on.

'"Twas a trap for thy poor father,' said the widow,
'be sure of that. Dick Orchardson set it many a long
year, and at last thy father, poor man, was caught.
Ah, if he had only come home to me and told me of his
trouble! This comes of having secrets out-o'-doors.'

'What shall we do, mother?' asked Christian.
'Can we pay the money?'

'Nay, my boy.'

'And Lawyer Jeffries hath given notice that we
must pay up or yield the land.'

'One or other, Christian.'

The lad clenched his hands and uttered a fierce cry.

'They shan't take the land away from thee, mother.
Let them try it! I'll go down to the Willows, and
make old Dick Orchardson own it was all a cheat, and
if he denieth it——'

The boy paused, livid with hate and rage. As he
did so, his sister Kate, who had been looking on in
terror, interposed tearfully.

'Nay, who knows,' she said, 'but the squire is more
kindly than folk say? Why did he lend our father the
money, and help him out of his trouble, if he hated him
so much?'

'Hear her, mother!' cried Christian, 'hear the foolish
wench! And yet she hath heard the preacher say that
figs grow not on thistles, and roses spring not from
thorns. An Orchardson kindly! Mother, do you
hear?'

'Kate is a girl,' returned the widow, grimly, 'she
cannot understand. It began long since.'

'What began, mother?' asked Kate.

'The trouble between our houses. If there had

ne'er been any Orchardsons, we should be rich folk now. They robbed thy father's father, a hundred years ago.'

'But, mother——'

''Tis something in the blood,' cried the widow. 'A fox is a fox, and a kestrel a kestrel, and an Orchardson is an Orchardson, till the world doth end. The wicked breed! If God would blot it out.'

'Amen, mother,' cried Christian; and Kate, knowing their temper, did not dare to say another word.

So it remained in their minds as a settled thing that Robert Christianson had, by some kind of devilish malignity, been beguiled into taking help of the Orchardsons, whose sole desire had been to crush the hapless family, and perchance close the mortgage. They waited a little time in great dread and anger; but no more word came from the lawyers, and their whole lives were poisoned by the suspense.

That portion of the freehold embraced in the mortgage included the best and richest part of the farm lands, leaving untouched only some ninety acres and the old farm-house, which latter had fallen into great dilapidation, and stood, quite solitary, over against the sandhills, with its face from the sea, which formed a broad estuary two miles away. Inland before it stretched the farm fields, in a great hollow which had once been a fen, and still bore that name, but sloping gradually to rich pastures and clumps of cheerful wood. Over these pastures and woods peeped the village spire —the glistening of which, in all kinds of weather, was a cheerful and comfortable sight to the inmates of the farm.

The very solitude of the situation gave to the owners of the Fen Farm a feeling of possession and mastery. Standing at his own door, a Christianson was monarch of all he surveyed—of the broad and comparatively barren acres of the old fen; of the narrow osier-fringed stream which wound through these acres and then, curving suddenly, ran in among the sand-hills towards the sea; of the rich slopes beyond, where crops waved green and yellow, or frosty stubble glittered, through the various seasons of the year.

There was only the spire to remind him of the world of men beyond, of the red-tiled village hidden from his sight, and of the heaven above. Then the sandhills behind the house were his; and these, though comparatively worthless and only affording combes of arid pasture for cattle here and there, were large in extent, and gave a lordly sense of territorial sway. And among the sandhills was the rabbit warren, let to a cousin of the family on profitable terms.

With the ancient freehold of the Fen Farm went, by right immemorial, the privilege of coursing and shooting. Every boy Christianson might run a hound or handle a gun on his own acres. Not only did rabbits swarm in the sandhills, but the sands were the resort, at certain seasons, of the hare, which would seek deserted rabbit-burrows and lie there till discovered *perdu*, and hunted out, by man or dog.

Small wonder, then, if the Christiansons loved the place, and clung to every inch of the soil. Even the house, though a rambling tenement and scarcely weather-proof, with cheerless rooms and rat-haunted wainscots, was very dear to them for the sake of the generations which had lived and died within. In summer time, with its red front covered with creepers and wild roses, its dove-cot on the red-tiled roof, and the white doves wheeling and settling in the sunlight, it looked quite pretty and bright. There was an ancient orchard, too, with broken-down walls, and trees so old and gnarled they yielded little fruit, and grass as thick and deep as the grass that grows on graves.

But if the cruel debt of the mortgage was not paid, what remained? Only the old house, and the sand pasturages, and the arid acres of the old fen; only, in other words, a barren stretch of soil, not to be farmed with profit by any but a man of means. The pasturages and combes of the upland slope, which ever filled the eye with a certain sense of prosperity—the woods where the nightingale sang in summer and the woodcock was flushed in the frost—the rich fields which grew the best grain—all these would surely go. It was an ugly thought. To stand at the farm door, and know that possession ceased at the stream, and that the cattle

grazing on the slopes beyond belonged to another, would
be almost too much to bear.

A few days after mother and son had discussed that
cruel business of the mortgage, and come to the conclu-
sion that devilry had been at work, young Christian
was rambling among the sandhills with his greyhound
Luke—an English dog, with a cross of the coarser Irish
breed. Not far from the farm, he came upon the track
of a hare, printed with filigree delicacy in the sand.
The marks were confused and mingled, crossing and re-
crossing one another, for poor Puss had been obviously
'running races in the mirth' through the morning dew,
but at last the lad hit upon the true trail. It led him a
good mile between the sandhills. On the top of each
sandhill or mound grew thick coarse cotton grass and
grassy weeds, and whenever the track led thither he
set the dog's nose to work. Presently, reaching the
summit of one of the highest of these sandhills, he came
in sight of the long flat stretch of black sand and mud
fringed by the waters of the sea.

He stood for a time and gazed. The sea was quite
calm, in the grey silver light of a still November day,
with quiet clouds piled upon the horizon like a range of
hills. A lobster-boat, with flapping brown sails, was
crawling along by means of sweeps towards the distant
fishing beds. On one spot of the sands, close to the
sea, was a white swarm of gulls, sitting perfectly moveless, save when now and then a solitary bird would rise
with sleepy waft of wing, fly a few yards, and settle
again. All was very still, but from a sea-creek not far
distant he could hear from time to time the cry of the
curlew.

While he stood, he saw sailing towards him, slowly,
methodically, hovering always at the same distance from
the earth, a large raven, followed at a distance of about
fifty yards by another bird, the female. They came
slowly, for each in turn, hovering over each sandhill, on
the grassy summit of which something edible might
hide, searched the grass for prey. From time to time
the foremost bird uttered a thoughtful croak or chuckle,
which the hindmost bird echoed after an interval.
Christian knew the two birds well. Once, indeed, he

had shot at the male bird at very short range, eliciting no other result than a defiant croak and a few falling feathers. Since then he had let the birds alone. They too had a freehold of the place, and had used it for a hunting-ground years before he was born.

He watched the birds carelessly, till they passed in succession over his head, greeting him with a croak of sublime indifference, and then, poised slanted in the air, glided more rapidly away. Turning his eyes to the sea, he saw that the swarm of gulls had risen and were hovering in the air, their cries, made faint by distance, reaching him where he stood.

Riding along the sands, at a trot, was a horseman, whom, in the distance, he did not recognise.

Idle, and tired of hunting the hare, he sat down and watched the rider till he disappeared behind the sand-hills, and the flock of gulls settled again on the fringe of the sea. Then, after a little time, Christian rose and walked down the side of the sandhill. In the smooth hollows between the mounds, it was impossible to see or be seen for many yards away; and presently, as he turned round a sandy corner, he came full in view of a gentleman on horseback—doubtless the same he had seen approaching by the side of the sea.

A man of about forty years of age, dressed in velvet riding-coat, breeches, high boots, and low-crowned beaver hat. He was portly, but somewhat unhealthy-looking, his skin being deeply marked with the small-pox, his eyes being somewhat shrunken and inflamed, and his hair and short-cropt whiskers of deep black.   .

He was not alone. By his side, upon a small Welsh pony, rode a boy of about twelve years of age, evidently his son, for he had his father's eyes and complexion without their disfigurements. At a first glance, he struck one as a disagreeable boy, with a supercilious expression, and a peculiar look of lying-in-wait. As he was riding, he did not exhibit his chief physical deformity. Though scarcely a cripple, he was lame. One limb had never grown rightly, and though he could walk tolerably and comfortably, he could do so with neither ease nor grace.

At sight of these two figures, Christian turned red

as crimson, for he knew them well. The gentleman was his father's enemy, Squire Orchardson of the Willows; the boy was Richard Orchardson, the squire's only son.

To his surprise, the squire rode right up to him along the sands, and then drew rein.

'You are young Christianson of the Fen?' he asked in a sharp authoritative voice.

Christian stood scowling, but made no answer.

'Have you no tongue, sirrah? I was just coming to see your mother.'

Christian started as if stung, and went from red to pale. Meanwhile his greyhound, seized by a fit of excitement, began to bark furiously at the heels of the boy's pony, which pranced and plunged, causing its rider to utter a timid cry.

'Call up your dog!' cried the squire. 'See you not 'tis frightening my son's pony?'

Christian turned towards the dog and called it to him, with such a scowling sneer upon his face as was irritating beyond measure.

'Come, Luke,' he said, and turned away.

'Stay!' cried Mr. Orchardson, involuntarily raising his riding-whip. 'Is your mother at home, boy?'

No reply.

'A Christianson all over,' muttered the squire. 'A cub of the old breed. Come, Dick.'

So saying, he trotted off, with his son following; the latter, as he urged his pony away, greeting Christian with a mocking grimace. Christian clenched his fists, while, with a shrill contemptuous laugh, the boy disappeared.

His blood boiling with rage, Christian stood for some minutes; then, remembering the squire's question, he began to hasten homeward. Was it possible that the squire meant to insult his mother by darkening her door during her affliction. If so, let him take care. He would at least warn his mother.

Excited beyond measure, he ran among the sandhills, till, emerging from them, he came in full view of the farm.

He was too late.

The squire and his son were sitting on horseback before the farm door; the squire was talking and gesticulating loudly, and on the threshold, as if pointing them from it, was Mistress Christianson, stern, and pale as death.

Christian strode up to the door and joined the group, just in time to hear the last few words of their conversation.

'I am sorry you are so bitter, dame,' the squire was saying; 'God knoweth, I have no wish to be hard upon you, and I will gladly grant you grace.'

'We want no grace from an Orchardson,' answered the dame; 'I pray you, sir, quit my door.'

'Yes, quit our door!' echoed Christian, coming up at this moment.

'Like cub, like vixen,' muttered the man to himself; then, turning to his son, who sat smiling upon his pony, he added, 'Come, Dick, we are not wanted here.'

The boy laughed, and said something in a whisper, which brought a dark smile to his father's cheek. At the whisper and the look, Christian felt sick with mingled hate and rage; and he made a movement with clenched hands as if to advance upon the pair, when his mother put her hand upon his arm to command him back.

So the two Orchardsons, father and son, rode slowly from the door, the boy pausing a moment at the gate to give a wicked laugh and sneer, before he cantered away by his father's side.

'Mother, what did they want?' asked Christian, trembling.

The dame did not reply; she was too busy with her own gloomy thoughts. Turning back into the house, and entering the dark wainscoted parlour, she took down the old Bible from its niche, put on her horn spectacles, and began to read, as was invariably her custom when her dark hour was upon her. Rocked upon the dreary billows of her favourite 'Psalms,' she felt with David the terror and the tumult of a wild unrest. In imagination, at least, her enemies were now scattered and smitten hip and thigh, and her soul went up in gloomy thankfulness to God.

CHAPTER IV.

SOWING THE BLACK SEED.

EMERGING from her trance of wrathful prayer, Mistress Christiansou gradually led her children to understand the real facts of the interview between herself and Richard Orchardson. The hereditary enemy of her husband and her family had, it appeared, made overtures of a seemingly friendly nature, and had offered, if the dame wished it, to withdraw all pressure for the payment of the mortgage money. He had no wish, he said, to be too hard on a helpless woman, or to visit the husband's folly and improvidence on the head of his widow. At this first allusion to the dead, she had been unable to restrain her indignation, and in a few fierce words she had launched her life-long hate at her enemy's head, demanding that he should cease to darken her door.

'Why did he come to the house he hath made desolate?' she now cried angrily. 'To lay some other trap, sure, for the folk he hath destroyed. I knew when he rode up, with that fox-smile upon his face, and the boy grinning by his side, that he meant some hidden mischief; so that, when he spoke of kindness, my soul went sick.'

'And mine too,' said Christian, 'when I met them i' the sands.'

Days passed, and the Christiansons heard no more of the Orchardsons. They waited and waited, in hourly dread and expectation of the fatal missive which should announce to them that the mortgage would be closed, and the money due realised on the land. But the missive did not come; instead of it, there was an ominous silence. At last, however, some weeks after the interview at the farm-door, came another letter from Lawyer Jeffries, on behalf of Richard Orchardson, requesting in formal terms, but polite, the payment of the moneys due. To this the dame replied curtly,

saying that payment was impossible, and that, to make
an end, the mortgagee was at liberty to take what
course he pleased. This brought over Lawyer Jeffries
in person—a little, hard, dry, but good-natured man of
business, who drove down in his gig from the neighbouring town, ten miles away.

He was closeted with the dame for hours, and
Christian, listening at the door, could hear high words
from his mother, and soft persuasive periods from the
visitor. Lawyer Jeffries strongly advised a policy of
conciliation. His client, he avowed, had no wish to
press hard upon the widow, though she was entirely in
his power, and he himself was sure that, if she only
asked respectfully for time and consideration, both
would be given. It was throwing words away, however. The good dame was obstinately resolved never
to ask any favour from the man who, she devoutly
believed, had planned her husband's ruin.

The little lawyer rode away in despair; but being,
as we have said, a good-natured man, and kind-hearted
withal, he carried to the squire such a message as
seemed conciliatory enough, and Orchardson, who had
just then no mind for harsh measures, instructed him
to let the matter stand. So weeks passed away, and
though the Christiansons were still in constant anticipation of a notice of ejectment from the rich Fen lands,
nothing more was said or done.

The doubtful peace thus attained between the two
houses might have lasted long but for one of those
events, trifling in themselves but often fatal in their
issues, which so often complicate the relations of human
beings.

One day in December, Christian took his gun, and,
followed by his sister, strolled out over the Fen lands.
Their larder was empty, and he was looking for a hare.
Though it was winter, the weather was almost spring-
like. The mist had lifted like a night-cap from the
fens, and from the clear patches in the sky the sun sent
down revivifying rays, as if to inspire new joy and
bring fresh hope to the heart of every man, now
Christmas-tide was nigh. It brought cheer at least to
young Christian Christianson, who, strolling along over

the fen, with his gun flung across his shoulder, had probably never felt more magnanimous in his life.

The mingled feelings of stern pride and bitter
hatred, which had been handed down to him as the
woeful inheritance of his house, and had taken their
place only too firmly in his heart, seemed to fade temporarily before the beneficent light of the sky. The
words which his dying father had uttered came back to
him, and resounded again and again in his ears like a
wail of admonishment and pain. ' Forgive—forgive! '
— Yes, those had been the last words on the lips of the
poor worn-out man, and no one had heard them but the
family whose souls, warped with hatred, sick with
pain, were only too ready to forget that dying prayer.
Christian, at any rate, had not quite forgiven even his
father; and as for the Orchardsons, he had met hate
with hate, scorn with scorn; and while standing up, as
he thought, in manly defence of his house, he had
plunged into the blackest gloom of a mad Inferno.
But to-day, boy though he was, he asked himself why
should these things be? why not bury the past, as
generations of men are buried, and with the help of
God look forward to bright and happy days to come ?

Forgive ? nay, he did not feel even yet he could
forgive—that he possessed sufficient strength to reach
forth his hand in friendship to human beings who had
so often and so cruelly stung him and his. Forgiveness such as that would be unnatural, would demand
superhuman strength and kindliness.

The utmost he could do was what he then resolved
to do : bury the Orchardsons deep down amid the ruins
of the sad and bitter past ; and with all memory of
their existence blotted from his soul, try to live a new
life.

He paused, and turned to his sister Kate, who
was walking quietly beside him.

' Kate,' he cried, ' think you, when our father lay
a-dying, and said, " Forgive—forgive," he meant that
devil's brood up at the Hall ? '

' Nay, I know not,' answered Kate, timidly, for she
feared the theme.

' I think rather he meant mother to forgive *him* for

ever having taken aid from the enemies of our house. His conscience pricked him sore for that misdeed.'

' Poor father ! '

' But he was to blame. Small wonder his conscience stung him.'

' Alas ! '

' How now, Kate ? '

' Perchance Squire Orchardson meant kindly—perchance he will be kindly still—nay, did he not say as much ? It is mad to cross him ; will you not forget old troubles, and give the Orchardsons your hand, and speak to mother, and then—and then——'

She paused trembling, for Christian's face was dark with passion.

Poor Kate was a gentle girl, with more of her father's softness than her mother's determination.

She was utterly incapable of feeling a life-long hatred for the Orchardsons, not perhaps because she was usually more tender-hearted than her brother, but because her memory was imperfect and her feelings evanescent. She would forget a benefit as easily as an injury, while her brother was capable of keenly remembering both. And he did remember them as he listened to his sister's words—he remembered also the feelings of gladness and hope which had filled his soul only a few minutes before. He remembered also his father's dying words, and he struggled to say, ' I will forgive,' but his lips would not utter the words.

' Kate,' he said, ' I can never forgive, but I'll try, if I can, to forget ! '

' Nay, Christian, say not so,' pleaded Kate, quietly. ' What doth the Bible say ?—why, that we should forgive our enemies, ay, seventy times seven ! '

She paused, but her brother did not reply. His eyes were fixed with gloomy distrust upon an object close at hand. She turned, and beheld standing only a few paces off young Richard Orchardson of the Willows.

He had evidently heard every word of the conversation, for on his pale, pinched face there was a quiet sneer. If looks of bitterness and hatred could kill, young Christian had at that moment lain dead at his feet. Kate, seeing with terribly sinking heart the dangerous looks ou the faces of the two lads, endeavoured to become peacemaker. She laid her trembling hand on her brother's arm.

'Come, Christian,' she said, eagerly, 'we'll get home.'

The youth, almost frightened at himself, was yielding to her influence, and would have walked silently away but young Orchardson stopped them.

'Give me that gun,' he said, 'or you shall answer for carrying it on my father's land!'

Christian flushed up angrily. A hot reply came to his lips, but with an effort he suppressed it.

'Nay, not so fast, young sir,' he said. 'The Fen Farm belongs to the Christiansons to-day, if it goeth to the Orchardsons to-morrow. 'Tis you that are a-trespassing, not I; I be on our own land!'

'You lie,' returned the other; 'the land is ours— my father paid for it to keep you folks from starving. 'Tis like a Christianson to hate the hand that fed him!'

Christian again controlled himself with a mighty effort.

'Nay, I'll not talk with thee,' he muttered. 'Come, Kate.'

But the boy interposed.

'You shall not go,' he cried. 'Give me that gun, or I will take it from you.'

Christian smiled grimly, amused to see the puny thing stand before him, pale and tremulous with passion, to hear him talk of using force to one who could have bent him like a reed at one touch of a strong hand.

Kate turned to young Richard with outstretched hands.

'Do not provoke my brother. He is strong, and you are so weak; I know he would not wish to hurt you, but you say such wicked things.'

'My father is too soft,' cried the boy with a sneer. 'Had I my will, I would rid the fields of such vermin.' Then he cried more angrily, 'Why did you set your cur at my pony's heels yesterday? It is a foul brute,

forehead bloody where it had struck upon a stone. With the blood trickling down his face, he staggered to his feet; then, seeing the blood on his hands, he began to cry piteously.

'Stop!' cried Christian, as he turned to go. 'Tell me you did not harm the poor hound, and I will ask your pardon.'

Young Orchardson made no reply, but, sobbing still, cast one look at the dead dog, and made a movement as if to spurn it with his foot; then, with a blood-stained face, rushed rapidly up the hill.

Kate, still sobbing, wrung her hands. 'We are undone, we are undone!' she moaned. 'What will Squire Orchardson say when he hears that you struck his son?'

But this time her brother did not heed her, or scarcely seemed to hear. No furious flame of anger now burnt in his heart, but on his face there was a fixed look of horrible pity and pain. In weary sorrow he raised his eyes to the still smiling sky.

'Forgive!' he murmured; 'nay, father, I can never forgive *now*. Since there is a God above us, why doth He let such things be?'

He raised the poor stiffening body of his dog, and carried it tenderly homewards in his arms, choking down his tears as he went.

As he passed the house door his mother came out to question him, and he told her what had passed. She went very pale, but said little; she did not even chide her son for his violence.

Christian laid the poor hound tenderly in the porch, and then all went into the house together.

An hour later, there came a great rapping at the door. Anticipating evil, they went and threw the door open, and there stood Squire Orchardson, mounted on his black horse, and shaking his heavy whip at them all. He was livid with passion, and the moment he saw Christian, shrieked aloud,

'Where is he that struck my boy? Where is the coward that smote a poor lame lad? Come out, you dog! come out! that I may punish you as you deserve!'

Christian was about to leap out and face the speaker, when his mother, grim as death, ordered him to keep back. Accustomed to obey her, he paused.

'My son did not strike your son,' answered the dame coldly; 'he fell, and so was hurt.'

''Tis a lie!' cried the squire. 'He struck him' My boy never lies, and he hath told me all.'

'Your son is the liar, sir,' said Christian, 'if he saith I struck him. I gave him a push in anger, and he fell upon a stone. But he poisoned my dog!'

'And if he did, what is the life of your wretched cur to a scratch upon my son? Your dog poached upon our preserves, and had I seen it, I would have shot it with my own hand. My boy did well. Had he poisoned the whole of your wicked brood he would have done better still.'

'You are a brave man,' returned the widow, with a cold smile, 'to talk thus to a lonely woman. Had my man been living, he would have reckoned with the father as his son did reckon with the son.'

'Enough, woman!' cried the squire, madly. 'If there is law or justice in the land, you shall all moan for this. Beggars that you are! I will be even with you *now*. No more mercy—no, no! I'll grind you down to dust!'

'Begone, sir! you darken our door.'

And without another word, she closed the heavy door in his face. Listening within, they heard him muttering and cursing aloud, and striking on the door with his whip; then, with a loud threatening oath, he galloped away.

They had not to wait long for the issue of that sad dispute. The very next day came the legal intimation that the mortgage money was to be realised to the last penny, and that if they could not pay up both principal and interest, they must yield the well-loved land.

Thus the thunderbolt fell not quite unexpectedly, and they looked at one another with stupefied faces.

Kate was the first to speak, and her words were characteristic.

'Mother, mother! do not let us be undone. Let me go to Mr. Richard. Let me tell him that we beg his pardon, let me sue for pity. I know he will listen to me, if I plead humbly enough.'

'Silence!' cried Christian. 'How dare you think of it? Your father's blood flows between you and——'

He paused, for Kate was kneeling on the floor and sobbing, and the dame was standing over her like a ghost, pointing at her with a lean forefinger, and trembling as a leaf.

'Christian!' cried the girl. 'Speak for me! Mother!'

Christian pnt his hand upon his mother's arm. For a moment the dame did not speak; her lips moved, but she was too troubled to find words. It was terrible to see her white stony face, with its wrathful eyes. At last she gasped, pointing to the great Bible which stood open upon the sideboard,

'Give me the Book!'

Christian placed it upon the table near her.

Stooping, she seized Kate's cold hand and placed it among the leaves. Poor Kate shivered and moaned, and tried to draw her hand away, as if she feared the touch might do her harm.

'Now, swear!' said the mother.

Kate only sobbed aloud.

'Swear on the Book, that you will never again willingly exchange words with any of that name or that blood; swear that in sickness and in health, as long as life lasts, you will never take the hand of an Orchardson or knowingly worship under the same roof with any of that blood or name; swear that your prayers shall rise nightly against them, wherever you may be.'

Kate seemed overcome with terror.

'I promise, mother—do not ask me to swear!'

'Swear on the Book!'

Thus urged, Kate Christianson took the oath.

The dame turned suddenly to her son.

'You shall swear too!' she said sharply.

The boy swore right eagerly. Then he stooped and caught his sister in his arms, just as she was swooning away.

CHAPTER V.

ENTER PRISCILLA.

So it came to pass, through the issue of ill-blood between mere children, and between men and women who were as children in their foolish passions, that the breach between the two houses widened into a gulf as deep as hell. On the one side of this gulf of hate and darkness, sat the Orchardsons, rich, prosperous, in the full sunshine of fat meadow and plenteous vineyard. On the other side crouched the Christiansons, a beggared family, bitter at heart, ever waiting for the evil hour which might bring vengeance. The mortgage was closed. The fat Fen lands passed into the hands of their hereditary foes ; and all remaining to them now were the old house, fast falling into decay, and the barren hills and burrows of sea-lying sand.

Well, there are compensations even in the deepest shadows of trouble. It was something at least to have the old house, and not to be turned out by the bailiffs, like conies by the ferret, into the open cold ; something more, to possess the ancestral sandhills, barren and desolate as they were. At a pinch, they could at least exist, though no human soul but themselves knew how sore at times the pinch became.

Fortunately, they had never been free livers, and even in their days of prosperity had known little but homely fare. With keen thrift, now, they contrived to preserve a decent appearance before the world.

Widow and daughter kept their needles busy, and their spinning-wheels as well ; so that Christian, who had a rough boy's knack of destroying apparel, never went otherwise than neatly clad. And the boy, who was the idol of both, had his luxuries too. Many a time the two lonely women went without common necessaries themselves in order that the head and hope of the house might have gentlefolk's fare.

In this sad season of poverty and social disgrace, it

is hard to say what would have become of young
Christian Christianson if he had not relieved his angry
moods by that free physical exercise of which he had ever
been so fond. The women had their Bible, their constant means of communication with some strange far-off
Divine sympathy; his, on the contrary, was not a
religious nature, and in more respects than one he
belied his name.

For weeks and months the shame and outrage of
that cruel legal revenge dwelt within him, poisoning
every thought and feeling, distorting every hope and
dream. At first, but for the piteous pleading of his
sister and the sad command of his mother, he would
certainly have gone off and committed murder. For
weeks afterwards he was in the mood, had either father
or son crossed his path, to have shot him dead, or to
have sprung upon him and tried to tear him limb from
limb.

Fortunately, his mad rage was suffered to consume
itself, and to die away, without receiving any fresh fuel
from without.

So the boy went and came, somewhat more dark
and sullen than before, but to all outward seeming,
little changed.

Years passed on, and the bitterness of seeing others
in possession of the ancestral land, which stretched
rich and plenteous before the very door, had begun to
wear away. Poverty was so familiar that it no longer
seemed very unfriendly or quite unkind. The widow
had accepted her cross patiently, and by dint of strict
parsimony, had saved a trifle. At all events, affairs
could grow no worse,—unless the very roof fell in upon
their heads, a not altogether unlikely contingency, taking
into consideration the state of the farm-repairs.

It is to be feared that, in one particular respect,
Christian had suffered severely. His education had
been unduly neglected. It is doubtful, however, if
much more attention would have been given to his
training, even had the family not fallen on evil days.
In those times, many a wealthy farmer was too illiterate
even to write his own name, and book-learning was
generally regarded as so much vanity, not to be in-

dulged in by scusible folk whose lives were occupied in tilling the land and accumulating gold.

What he lacked in knowledge, Christian Christianson gained in manly strength and beauty. At twenty years of age, he might have sat to a painter for a youthful Thor.

His short clustering ringlets, his firmly-chiselled face with its grave blue eyes and splendid chin, his strong yet shapely neck, his perfectly-moulded arms and limbs, were all in keeping. Though of great height, he had none of the unwieldiness of giants. His only defect was a peculiar stoop in the shoulders, a not unusual characteristic, I have noticed, of brooding and determined men.

For the rest, his disposition, it is to be feared, was sullen and stern. He had strong and stirring passions, as we have seen, but they had been subdued to a gloomy sense of wrong. Brave, honest, incapable of meanness or treachery, he yet conveyed in his manner a certain feeling of dangerous repression. His bitterness against the world had been fostered by constant loneliness; for the family had now few friends.

It was his twentieth birthday, and the day, a clear June day of unusual brightness, broke with warmth and splendour over the sandhills and the sea. He had risen early, and gone down to the sea for a swim. Emerging from the water, light and glistening as a naked god, and happy for the time in the glowing consciousness of life, he cast on his clothes, and turning inland, he threw himself on one of the hot sandhills, to bask in the sun.

All was perfectly still—the clear heaven, the calm throbbing ocean, the long flat sands still wet from the receding tide: not a sound broke the summer silence. All at once, however, the stillness was broken by the sound of a voice, singing.

So suddenly did it rise, and so near at hand, that he was quite startled. Half-rising he listened. Yes, there could be no doubt whatever; some one was singing close by.

A clear silvery voice, like that of a woman. Stranger still, the words seemed merry and foreign, belonging to some language he did not understand. It seemed like witchcraft, and Christian, who was not without his superstitions, felt a trembling thrill run through his frame. This lasted only for a minute; then, rising to his feet, he moved over the sandhills in the direction of the voice.

A few quick strides brought him within sight of the singer.

Down beneath him, in a green space between the sandhills, sprinkled with canna-grass and yellow flowers, a young girl was walking, singing clearly to herself as she moved and sang in the summer sunshine.

She was dressed in black, without one trace of any ornament. Even her bonnet was black, which she had taken off and was swinging by the strings. The contrast between her gloomy dress and her bright face set in golden hair was sufficiently startling; but equally as great was the contrast between that dress and the clear gay trill of her girlish voice.

Christian stood looking on in wonder. He was used to country maidens, but this apparition seemed something quite different. She wore dainty boots and gauntlet gloves, and her attire, though so sombre in colour, was of fine material and elegant in form.

As he gazed she ceased to sing, and stooping down gathered one or two of the yellow flowers; these she fastened to her bosom, and as she did so, gave a silvery laugh.

Christian was fascinated. He had never seen a human being so completely at ease with herself and with the world. In her complete contentedness with her own company and thoughts, she realised Wordsworth's lines:—

> Solitude to her
> Is sweet society, who fills the air
> With gladness and involuntary song.

He looked on in wonder.

Presently the girl resumed her walk, and her voice rose again. This time the tune was even gayer, though the words were still foreign and strange. Then, finishing a verse, she laughed again, out of sheer delight of heart.

It seemed hardly fair and honest to play the spy in that fashion, without letting the young lady know that she was not unobserved; so Christian, though he felt bashful for the first time in his life, gave a cough to attract her attention.

She looked up at once, and, to his astonishment, smiled and beckoned.

Scarcely knowing what he did, he walked down towards her, and soon encountered the full fire of a pair of blue eyes, directed right into his own.

Then came a point-blank question.

' How long have you been listening, if you please ? '

Christian stammered, blushed, and looked confused. Before he could find an answer, came another question.

' Do you belong to this place ? '

' Yes,' he said.

' Then perhaps you can help me. I have lost my way.'

' Lost your way,' said the young man, looking puzzled. ' Why——'

He was about to ask the question which she at once, without hearing him, answered offhand.

' I was wandering along the sea-shore, and I turned off among the sandhills ; and each is so like the other that I got lost among them.'

' You did not seem to mind.'

' Nay, but I was singing to keep my courage up. You heard me ? '

' Yes.'

' Did you think I was singing a hymn ? '

Christian stared, and involuntarily shook his head.

' Since it was in French, perchance you could not tell,' she added, smiling, seeing the shadow of a smile on Christian's face. ' Well, perchance it was not a hymn at all, but a *chanson* I learned over in France.'

There was something so frank and artless in the girl's manner, something so utterly different from the self-conscious timidity and blushing stupidity of country maidens, that Christian was perfectly bewildered. To be addressed so fearlessly and carelessly by a complete stranger was in itself a novelty. He felt for the time like an awkward lout, tackled for the first time by a fairy of the wood or sea.

'Do you—live here ?   Nay, in the neighbourhood, I mean ? '

'I am staying with my father, over in Brightling-head.'

Brightlinghead was a small fishing village, situated some miles away, upon the sea-shore.

'And you ? ' she asked.

'I live at the Fen Farm, in yonder.'

'What is your name ? '

'Christian Christianson.'

She looked at him from top to toe, with the frank yet modest look that was peculiar to her.

'You must be a good Christian, in sooth, if you are like your name.'

Christian coloured up, and said awkwardly,

'What is your father ?   Not of these parts ? '

'Nay,' she replied, 'he is a stranger.   He hath come down hither to preach God's Word.'

Christian wondered again; to his simple sense, there seemed something most inconsistent between gospel-preaching and a vision so bright and sweet.

'Your father is a parson, then ? '

The girl shook her head.

'Nay, he is not in holy orders, though he hath had a call.   Since he heard good Mr. Wesley preach, the Spirit hath moved him to discourse for poor folks' conversion.'

Another change. She spoke now with a quite different intonation, recalling the prim phrases of the dissenting chapel.   Her eyelids drooped demurely, and the edges of her pretty mouth were just turned down—like a roseleaf folding.

While speaking, they had moved on quietly towards an opening in the sandhills, and they were now within view of the open sea sauds.

'I shall know my way now,' she said, quietly. 'Good day, friend.'

But Christian, with the fascination of her presence strong upon him, was not to be parted with so easily. He kept by her side saying :

' If you will suffer me, I can show you a short cut back to your village. 'Tis but going round yonder by the skirts of the water-meadow, instead of winding along the curves of the sea.'

' Point me the path, prithee, and I will take it.'

' Nay, I will go with you a piece of the way.'

The girl smiled, and looked at him again with her bright eyes.

' A good Christian, as I said! Come, then, good Christian ! '

And she tript along with happy unconcern, he following.

As they went, he had a better opportunity of observing her, and the more he looked, the more his wonder grew. She could not have been more than seventeen or eighteen, and yet her manner had the perfect repose of a mature woman. Her complexion was very pale, yet clear, her eyes matchlessly bright, her eyebrows dark, yet her hair the lightest of gold. He noted, too, that she had tiny hands and feet. Her figure was slight yet very graceful, and she walked with a light elastic tread.

By this time she had put on her bent bonnet, a structure of the then fashionable coal-scuttle shape, yet wondrously becoming to a plump and pretty face.

Christian had seen few women save his own mother and sister, and such rustic beauties as he knew were of the red-cheeked, not to say red-elbowed, order. Of ladies proper he knew little or nothing. There was the vicar's wife, who might have once been comely, but was now sedately grim ; and her daughters—young ladies with shrill voices and high waists. Lawyer Jeffries' daughter was a bold-looking, handsome girl, and so were many of the farmers' daughters round about. But the one invariable characteristic of all these persons, plain or fair, was that they had two distinct manners— the ' stand off ' manner and the ' come on ' manner— whenever they were in company with a person of the other sex. In one word, they were either flirts or prudes; in either case ridiculously conscious of the sexual distinction.

Now, the curious charm about this pretty stranger

was her complete unconsciousness of anything of the sort.

She spoke to Christian as frankly as one young man might talk to another, with perfect modesty, perfect unconsciousness, and perfect ease. She took him at once, as it were, into her confidence, as a human being, and yet, all the time, she preserved a certain pretty virginal dignity, which warned him that it would be a dangerous thing to encroach.

So he followed her as a dog might follow its mistress, happy, yet conscious of the command of a superior spirit.

They passed along the sea-shore, along the border of the water-meadow, and then, crossing a field, found themselves in a dusty country road deeply furrowed with old cart-ruts, yet thickly sprinkled with growing grass. The hedges were high, and the grass all under them was thickly sprinkled with speedwells and dog-violets. The thick hedge shut out the distant sea, and it seemed like walking in a wood.

Presently the maiden paused.

'You must not come any further—I am quite right now.'

''Tis but a short step further,' returned Christian, 'and I will not leave you yet. Perchance before I go,' he said, 'you will tell me your name.'

'Did I not tell you, friend? It is Priscilla.'

'Mistress Priscilla——'

'Priscilla Sefton, at your service,' she cried, smiling and dropping a little curtsey; 'and now, since you have proved yourself good Samaritan as well as good Christian, I prithee come no further.'

The young man tingled and blushed each time she played upon his name.

'I have naught to occupy me, and I am going your way.' he replied.

'Naught to occupy you?' she cried, with a smile. 'Know you not the rhyme, "Satan doth find some mischief still, for idle hands to do"? But there, since you are so willing, come along.'

So they went side by side. Presently they came to a little bridge, arched like a maiden's foot, spanning a bright brook, that went leaping down to the sea.

Priscilla paused, and leant over, looking at the sparkling water. Just below the bridge, it made a pool, fringed deep with sedge and reeds, and in among the reeds white water-lilies were just unfolding, each with a pinch of gold in its heart, and on the banks hung wild rose-bushes, with pink flowers fluttering open to see their images in the water beneath. Just then, a bright little bird, in gorgeous summer clothing of red, blue, and gold, darted through the arch of the bridge, paused as if to alight on an outreaching twig of the rose-bushes, and then, seeing Priscilla, flew on rapidly with a sharp cry, keeping very close to the water, and following with rapid precision every winding of the brook.

'What a beautiful bird!' cried the girl. 'Do you know its name?'

''Tis a kingfisher.'

'And look—there is another!'

On a stone in the middle of the pool was a little bird with a snow-white breast, dip-dipping in rapid motion as it stood, with its head cocked on one side, and its sharp eye so intent on the water that it did not see the human forms above it.

As Priscilla spoke, it quietly slipt into the water and disappeared from sight.

'That is a water-ouzel,' exclaimed Christian.

The little bird re-emerged, stood on the stone again dip-dipping, and then, startled, flew off after the kingfisher, down the stream.

'How nice to be a country lad,' said Priscilla, 'and to know all the pretty birds and flowers. 'Tis almost my first visit to the green fields. I have lived all my life in smoky towns.'

'London born, perchance?' queried Christian.

'Yes; but since I was twelve years old, I have dwelt with my good Aunt Dorcas in Liège. It was pleasant there, but I love our England best.'

CHAPTER VI.

FATHER AND DAUGHTER.

As they lingered there, leaning over the keystone of
the little bridge, they formed a fine contrast; he, so
mightily and grandly made, with his sunburnt cheeks
and air of Arcadian simplicity; she, so delicate and
fairy-like, in her tight-fitting dress of black, with her
little gloved hands and fairy feet. Down below them
in the shadows the gnats swarmed, and the minnows
sparkled, and the trout leapt; birds were singing on
every side; in heaven, there was full sunshine; on
earth, perfect fruition of the summer tide. Delicious
was the birds' song, delicious the cool trickling sound
of the running brook. Like a child delighted, Priscilla
listened, and her pure face reflected the joy of all the
happy things around her.

Young Christian looked and gladdened. He did not
know it yet, for he was a boy, but the divine hour had
come: the hour which does not come to all (for to some
men capable of infinite affection it never comes at
all), but which, when it does come, means transfigura-
tion. This delicate being, bringing with her the per-
fume and the beauty of some unknown world, this
dainty stranger, who talked with him already as frankly
as if he were an old friend, held him spell-bound. Yet,
strange to say, he was not tongue-tied; to his own
astonishment, he found himself catching the contagion
of her frankness, and talking with a freedom unusual to
him.

'This is Thornley Beck,' he said; 'down yonder, a
mile away, it runneth into the sea. I have seen the
white trout trying to climb it in autumn floods, but
they cannot pass the bridge, and there are no pools, so
they cannot stay. Down close to the sands, there be
silver mullet in hundreds, and the fishermen take them
in the net.'

Christian spoke as a country lad, loving sport better
than sentiment. To him, the fishing possibilities of

the beach were of infinitely more consequence than its
natural beauties, for the artistic sense had never been
born within him.

'Had I my will,' said Priscilla, thoughtfully, 'none
should snare the pretty fish. 'Tis a sin to slay what the
good God made.'

The lad stared, for such talk was to him incomprehensible.

'God made the fish for food,' he answered, 'and th.
beasts, and the birds of the air. Our Lord Himself did
go a-fishing once.'

'Nay, 'twas a miracle,' answered the maiden, 'and
these things are hard to understand. God meant it for
a merry world, but our sin hath transformed it. Had
you seen what I have seen, in the wicked city, you
would be sad.'

'What have you seen?'

'Human folk dwelling in places dark and foul; men
and women pining away for lack of the sweet air; little
babes starving at the breast; and I have heard cursing
and gnashing of teeth, such as the good pilgrim your
namesake heard when he lay him down in a den.'

'What took you into such evil places?' asked
Christian in surprise.

'I went with my father, to save souls.'

'How?'

'By reading to them out of the Blessed Book, and
by telling them of Him that loved them and laid down
His life for their sakes. I have stood by and sung sweet
hymns to them, while they smiled and died.'

The lad's wonder deepened. The girl's words were
so sad and terrible, and yet her face remained so bright
and simple. Here and there in her intonation he seemed
to catch the twang of the preacher, but the manner was
so different, so calm and innocently assured.

A sudden question occurred to him, and he uttered
it at once.

'You wear black,—you are in mourning perchance?'

She shook her head.

'My mother died long ago, when I was a babe; but
my father doth not think light colours seemly, nor do
any of our folk.'

'Your folk?'

'We are of good Master Wesley's flock, and he him
self hath sent my father hither.'

Now Christian had heard of the great preacher, as of
one malignant in all respects, disaffected to Church and
State and King; and he had heard of his people, as of
people to be avoided and distrusted by all good subjects.
Nay, in his own district there were sprinkled a few
infected individuals, who were at war with the parson
and exiled from society in general. Notably, there was
one Elijah Marvel, a shoemaker of grim and forbidding
aspect, who would bandy words with the vicar himself,
and had in consequence lost all custom, fallen on evil
days, and alas! taken to strong ale—fortified by which,
he became even more malignant than before. His mother,
he knew, often spoke of Mr. Wesley with a certain respect, but she had never openly fallen away from the
Church, and had sent her children to church and Sunday-
school, and had a stately welcome for the pastor of the
parish whenever he paid her an official visit. Altogether,
Christian shared to the full the popular prejudice against
dissenters of all kinds; for he had not learned to think
for himself on religious subjects, and took his religion as
it came to him, with the other traditions of his race and
blood.

Priscilla noticed his astonishment, and looked at him
with grave thoughtfulness.

'You are not of my father's persuasion?'

'Nay,' cried Christian, quickly, 'I am for the
King.'

Priscilla's face blossomed into an amused smile.

'And so are we all!'

'Nay, I thought——'

'Well, good Christian?'

'—That Master Wesley was a Pretender's man, and
an enemy to all good subjects.'

'Master Wesley is for the Lord Jesus, the King of
kings,' she replied simply, 'and I fear you have heard
him belied like his Master before him. I would you could
hear him preach: he is so terrible, yet he can be so gentle
when he lists. His voice is as the sounding of trumpets,
yet his smile is kindly as the sunshine upon the sea.

Though he cometh to call sinners to repentance, he is sorest of all upon himself.'

So speaking, in her natural tones, as if she were uttering mere matter-of-fact, she walked on. The language of the conventicle had grown so familiar to her, that it came to her lips as naturally as girlish laughter. She seemed a strange contradiction; so bright and fearless, and yet so full of grave discourse; so sweet in her manner, yet in her matter so solemn and even sad; so pious-minded, yet so happy. Now, Christian knew, even in his little experience, that the Methodist people inclined more to the dark than to the sunny view of human affairs. Cobbler Marvel had once roundly rated the vicar himself for cooking hot dinners on the Sabbath, and for over-finery of personal attire. His talk was much of Armageddon, and of brimstone, and of the pit. Moreover, once or twice Christian had got a peep at certain forbidden gatherings in the open air, where common men gathered together and spake as the Spirit moved them; and he had thought their discourse the very reverse of cheerful, nay, gloomy and dull exceedingly. Such, in his simple eyes, were Methodists—fate-haunted and distracted men. Yet here was something so different, under the same name: a sunbeam of a maiden, happy in a sinful world. Her piety was like her black dress; it only showed her brightness to more advantage. He had read few books, but one of them was the 'Pilgrim's Progress;' and already he felt that Priscilla was like one of those shiningly-vestured beings, who talked to that other Christian and encouraged him upon his way.

And now, leaving the brook behind them, they passed along the hot lane, and coming to the brow of a hill, saw again the sea glittering before them; and between them and the sea was the fishing-village of Brightlinghead, clustering with red-tiled houses, and brown sails, and drying nets upon the sea-beach.

Priscilla led the way, followed by her new acquaintance, and paused near a tiny cottage, with a narrow patch of front garden, upon the roadside. Inside the garden gate stood two men, seemingly in angry conversation.

One was a short, squat, bullet-headed man in black,

who wore a clerical hat and carried a cane, and who
was obviously in holy orders. The other was a tall,
thin man, with a countenance of ghastly pallor, and
large blue eyes full of a somewhat wandering light.
He did not seem more than fifty years of age, but his
hair was as white as snow.

'Now mark me,' said the clergyman, shaking his cane,
'I will have no malignant and disaffected wanderers—
whom no man knows, and have no authority from God or
man—meddling with my people. 'Tis my care to look
after the souls of this parish, and I want no meddlers. I
warn you, therefore, to quit the place, or to let my
people be.'

The person whom he addressed answered him, with
a curious far-off look in his eyes.

'Nevertheless, I must do my Master's bidding.'

'At your peril! I have but to give the word, and
they would duck you in the horsepond, or stone you from
the town.'

'For what?' gently said the white-haired man. 'For
telling simple folk the way to God's mercy? For warning them to save their souls alive, ere yet they fall to the
place where the worm never dieth?'

The clergyman, a very hot-tempered little man, gave
a grunt of complete disgust.

'I know the canting jargon, Master Methodist, but it
won't do down here. My people have been taught that
the best way to save their souls is to do as I bid them, to
work hard for daily bread, not to meddle with themes
they cannot understand, and to honour the King and the
clergy. There, go to! You have come to the wrong
place, that is all, and the sooner you depart as you came
the better we shall all be pleased.'

With these words the indignant clergyman bustled
through the garden gate, cast one sharp look at Priscilla,
who was entering in, and walked rapidly away.

Approaching the white-haired man with an anxious
look, the maiden touched him on the arm. Strange to
say, he did not turn his eyes upon her, but still preserved
in them the curious far-off look we have already described.

'Priscilla!'

'Yes, father, it is I. What hath been the matter?'

'The good pastor of the parish is angry that I have been preaching to his flock. I am grieved in sooth to have offended him, but I cannot serve two masters, and the good seed must be sown.'

'Verily, father; but come, some one wants to speak with you. To-day I have lost my way, and found a friend.'

So saying, she took the old man's hand and drew him towards the gate, where Christian still stood wondering. When they were quite close, she beckoned to him with a smile.

'Will you speak to my father?' she said. 'Father, this is a young man who showed me the way home. His name is Christian Christianson.'

'A good name, at all events,' said the man, with the glint of a smile upon his wan cheeks, 'and I trust a fitting one. Young man, you are very welcome.'

As he spoke he reached out a thin white hand, and Christian now perceived for the first time that he was blind—stricken by the species of disease of which Milton so pathetically yet patiently complained. The *gutta serena*, or 'thick drop serene,' had invaded both orbs, and left him in perpetual night.

Christian shrank back, but both father and daughter invited him to enter the cottage, and though bashfulness had now fallen upon him like an uncomfortable garment, curiosity made him assent. He followed the strange pair into a low-roofed parlour, with black rafters and white-washed walls. The only furniture was a plain deal table and some chairs. The floor was of deal, with no carpet. All would have seemed squalid indeed, but upon the table there was a plate of water, with fresh-called pansies from the garden, close to an open Bible, very stained and old.

The man sat down, and Priscilla motioned their guest to do likewise.

'Nay, I cannot linger,' he murmured, flushing; 'I will depart now, and——'

'Stay a short space,' said the blind man. 'Priscilla, get Mr. Christian some refreshment. Perchance, when he hath broken bread with us he will remain and offer up thanks with us to the Giver of all mercies.'

A sweet look from the maiden's eyes did more to persuade the lad to remain than any prospect of praise or thanksgiving. So he kept his seat, and tripping forth to the kitchen, she brought him plain brown bread and new milk, which he made pretence, for courtesy's sake, to taste.

Meantime, his eyes sought the face and figure of the blind man; and he was surprised to find in one so afflicted so complete a calm. Looking closer, he noticed that, though the man's dress was plain, it was of excellent material, that he wore wondrously fine linen, that his hands were white and delicate, and had never been used in any manual labour. This puzzled him more; for all the Wesleyans whom he had seen, or of whom he had heard, were common handicraftsmen or labourers in the fields. There was, moreover, in the man's manner a curious stateliness and grandeur. He spoke with an accent of extreme refinement, which even Christian, though country-born, could not fail to perceive.

As they sat, there was a tap at the door, and a grim-looking man, clad in fisherman's style, quietly slouched in. He was followed almost immediately by another younger man, then by an elderly woman leading a child, and lastly by a good-humoured-looking blacksmith, fresh from the forge, in his leather apron. Some of these people were evidently expected; for at the sound of their entrance the blind man rose to his feet and gave them welcome.

'Good even, master,' said the blacksmith, cheerily. 'I hear thou'st had a visit from t' parson. Well, never heed *him*, for he be an old wife.'

'What is your name, friend?' asked the blind man.

'Seth Smith, master,' was the reply.

'Have you come of your own will to join our circle in prayer?'

'Ay, if you please, and I will tell you why. Because parson he did dare me to come and pray wi' Wesleyans. "Mind thy own soul," said I, "and I'll mind mine," and off I came—for I'll pray in what company I please.'

'Be seated, friend,' said the blind man, quietly.

'And I'll tell thee more, master,' cried the smith, who was both garrulous and aggressive. 'They say thou'rt one o' the right sort—a rich man who has divided all his riches among poor folk. Now, t' parson he gives nought, but is a swaggerer in gentry's company, and cares only for 's tithes. So I be come to listen, and if I like thy ways I'll come again; and if I like not thy ways, I'll stay at home.'

This at least was frank, and the stout smith took his seat like a man who did not mean to be imposed upon, but was determined to criticise, boldly yet honestly, the proceedings which were to follow.

Christian rose to depart, but at an eager sign from Priscilla, he remained. Then he beheld, and indeed took a part in, the simple ceremonies of his new acquaintances.

The proceedings were opened with a short prayer by the blind man, whose face as he prayed shone with a soft beatified light. Then Priscilla, who was seated by his side, gave out the words of a simple hymn; and afterwards, in a clear beautiful voice, led the singing. How sweet yet solemn seemed the tones! Could this be the same voice that he had heard, but a little time before, trilling out the gay cadence of that incomprehensible French song? Yes, it was the same, but the effect was so different, so holy and so grave. He raised his eyes and peeped at her face. A deep shadow lay upon it, and though the eyes were still clear, they seemed full of the sadness of recent tears.

Then the blind man began a short discourse, taking for his text the terrible words, 'I am he that liveth, and was dead; and, behold, I am alive for evermore, Amen; and have the keys of hell and of death.' Commencing in a low and somewhat feeble voice, the blind man spoke of Christ's life on earth, its pains and tribulations, its temptations—which come likewise to every man; then of His terrible death, rendered necessary by the iniquities of the world He came to save. A deep awe fell upon those who listened; with dark imagination, the speaker reproduced for them the picture of that night of Calvary, which was only a colossal likeness, he said, of the crisis which must occur in miniature to every soul before it can be saved. Raising his voice, he passed on to speak of the ever-living God, to whom the keys of hell and of death belong. His hearers trembled, for it seemed as if the very spirit of earthquake shook beneath them The countrywoman moaned and clutched her child; and on the smith's hard-hammered face the perspiration stood in great beads, while his breath came and went like the sound of the forge bellows.

Christian, not unmoved himself, looked again at Priscilla. She seemed listening, but none of the trouble seemed to touch her. To what can we compare her? To a sunbeam on a graveyard; to a white dove floating over stormy waters. Her eye was fixed on vacancy, and her face was quite bright. Perhaps, after all, her thoughts were far away.

Suddenly the smith gave a great groan and threw up his hands, crying, ' Lord, what a miserable sinner I be ! Lord, Lord, have mercy upon me ! ' And the others fervently cried 'Amen ! ' At this moment Christian became conscious of an ugly face, surmounted with a head of shock hair, gazing in through the latticed window.

'Yaw ! Methody ! Methody ! ' shrieked a voice; and immediately came a loud howling and hooting from many voices around. But the blind man made no sign, and continued his discourse as if he heard nothing. Then some one outside mimicked the howling of a dog, and there was loud applause.

Ceasing solemnly, the blind man made a sign to Priscilla, and again she gave forth the words of a simple hymn, and herself led the singing as before. At the sound of the music, the noise without increased tenfold—howls and catcalls and savage laughter arose—and finally, a heavy stone, hurled by some cowardly hand, struck the window and broke several of the diamond-shaped panes.

Notwithstanding this interruption, no one stirred; it seemed as if all were prepared for such interference. Priscilla finished the hymn with perfect calm and gravity, and after another short prayer, the service concluded.

The smith strode over to the blind man, and reached out his hand.

'Give me thy hand, master! Thee hast made me see what a poor lost wretch I be! I like thee, and I'll come again; and if any man molests thee, I'll take thy part.'

Then he shook hands with Priscilla and patted her kindly on the head, for he had a daughter of his own, he said.

Christian followed suit, and said good-bye to father and daughter. The latter seemed almost to have forgotten his presence, for now the service was done, she was talking anxiously to her father; but she gave him her hand civilly, and he thrilled at the touch.

Passing out to the road, he found a gathering of some twelve or fifteen men and boys, blocking up the way, some scowling, some grinning. The smith went first, with little ceremony, and they cleared the way for him quickly enough; but at sight of Christian, they murmured loudly.

'Yaw! Methody!' cried the same voice he had heard before.

Christian smiled, rather amused than otherwise. This they took as a sign that they might encroach, and gathered round him; but a closer look at his square jaw and powerful frame kept them from laying hands upon him.

He walked through them, and away from them. There was a wild yell, but he did not turn.

Suddenly a stone whizzed past his ear, and another fell at his feet. He turned quickly, and saw, in advance of the rest, the thrower—a great hulking fellow of four- or five-and-twenty, ostler at one of the inns.

Christian strode back, and before the other could stir they were face to face.

'Did you throw that stone?'

The fellow grinned savagely, and made no reply; but the others hooted.

'Answer me,' cried Christian, 'or I'll wring your ugly neck!'

'Best try!' snarled the other; then he uttered a terrified yell, for Christian had him by the throat. There was a quick struggle, a cry of voices, and in another minute the ostler lay like a log on the road,

with bruised body and bleeding nose. Christian stood
panting, and faced the shrieking group.

At this moment, the group parted, and there appeared
the same clergyman whom Christian had seen before in
conversation with the blind man.

'What's this? what's this? How dare you strike
one of my people?'

'He stoned me first,' answered Christian, 'and he
hath only got what he deserves.'

'Who are you, boy? What's your name?' demanded
the clergyman, sharply.

'My name is Christian Christianson, and I dwell
away yonder at the Fen Farm.'

'I have heard of you; and to no good, I promise
you. Squire Orchardson of the Willows knoweth you
and yours only too well.'

'As the thief knoweth those he hath robbed!'
retorted Christian, turning fiercely on his heel.

As he did so, he saw, standing at the cottage door,
the figure of Priscilla Sefton. She was looking at him,
with a face full of admiring sympathy and terror. He
smiled and waved his hand to her; then he walked
away along the road, with all his young spirit troubled,
his body flushed with victory, and his heart trembling
(though he scarcely knew it) with the new-born flame
of love.

CHAPTER VII.

A DISAFFECTED SPIRIT.

A few days after the first meeting of Christian
Christianson and Priscilla Sefton, Cobbler Marvel stood
leaning over his garden gate, and looking moodily at
vacancy. His hymn-book was in his hand, his red
cotton nightcap was on his head, and he was in his
shirt-sleeves. Nevertheless, the church bells were ringing, and it was Sunday. Cobbler Marvel's only recognition of the day was significant, though peculiarly
simple : he had washed his face.

'*He lifted his eyes, and encountered the vision of a fresh young face.*

He was a gaunt, grim-looking man of about sixty, with grey hair and beard, a copper-coloured nose, and a weather-beaten complexion. His long legs were cased in rusty brown small-clothes and torn stockings; his shirt was of red wool; his waistcoat, which he wore unbuttoned, for coolness, of brown cloth. His night-cap was cocked somewhat fiercely over the only eye he had—the right one—and he had altogether the appearance of a person who would stand no nonsense.

It was a golden summer morning, and the sound of the bells fell sweetly on the Sabbath air, but Cobbler Marvel was the very reverse of amiable.

'You may ring, and you may ring,' he muttered to himself, as he listened; but I've heerd as fine music as that played on Satan's fiddle; and parson may pray and preach sarmon, but I'd as lief hear the howling of the Beast. And he'll gang home to 's roast and boiled and fine company, and drink his port wine wi' Old Nick at his elbow, and a wail of weeping and gnashing of teeth all round. Well, the Lord's above, and hell's below, and

Adam's fall
Doth doom us all
Until the Judgment Day.'

It was a gloomy view of the world to take for one who, despite his appearance, was a not entirely un-prosperous person. For Cobbler Marvel stood in his own garden, or orchard, a full acre in size; in one corner of it there were bee-hives, with gold-thighed swarms hovering near them; and amid the trees stood the little red-brick cottage—small, but weather-worthy, with a bench of stone in front for the cobbler to cobble upon in fine weather, when he was tired of gardening and keeping his bees in order. But Cobbler Marvel was misanthropical by nature, and what was worse, a woman-hater to boot, although a married man. As the country people passed, dressed gaily in their Sabbath best, he paused, frowning and sniffing, more especially at the women. He had not forgiven the fair sex its original participation in the collapse of human nature.

The church bells ceased, the country people dis-appeared, and Cobbler Marvel was still scowling at the country, when a voice startled him. He lifted his eyes, and encountered the vision of a fresh young face, gazing at him with frank and peaceful eyes.

' Good-morrow, friend,' said the voice, with a ring as sweet and clear as that of the bells.

The cobbler screwed up his eye, looked the speaker from head to foot, and then, failing to recognise in her any of his acquaintances or foes in the village, grunted defiantly,

' And why good-morrow, young mistress ? why good-morrow, eh ? ' he demanded.

' Because it is fair weather, and the sun shines, and it is the Lord's Day,' was the quiet reply. ' So it is good-morrow indeed.'

This time Cobbler Marvel did not deign to respond, but hunching np his shoulders scowled again at vacancy, waiting to be left alone.

But Priscilla—for it was no other than she—persisted.

' What may be your name, good man ? '

' What be that to thee ? ' answered the misogynist, still averting his one eye, muttering to himself, in the words of an obscure but pious poet,

> ' And Eve she came a-questioning,
> And caused our father's fall.'

Priscilla smiled, and shrugged her pretty shoulders, a trick she had learned across Channel.

' Be not afraid, good man,' she cried ; ' I am only a simple maiden, and a stranger—and you need not fear me.'

' I fear no man,' growled the cobbler ; ' nor no woman.'

' Then you mislike them, which is next to fear, and that, good man, is wicked, and unseemly for a true Christian—which I hope you are.'

Something in the calm, cool, matter-of-fact tone startled Marvel, and he turned his head round to glare at Priscilla. Then he looked the pretty figure from head to foot again. He was not in the habit of being tackled so quietly. Most of the neighbours avoided him and feared his tongue, and even with his inveterate adversary the parson, he was able to hold his own.

' And who may *you* be that talks so pert ? No good.

mayhap! Get thee out o' the way, I be thinking on
solemn things!'

'I have heard Master Wesley say——'

'Eh?' interposed the cobbler, with a start at the
name.

'——That none was so solemn as Tom Fool, and that
Tom Fool, with himself for company, was as good as
two fools in a show.'

Elijah Marvel started and gasped. The words were
not spoken rudely, but with the quiet precision of one
making a true but apposite quotation.

Before he could speak again, the girl proceeded,
'I think I can tell your name now, good man. It is
Elijah Marvel.'

'How learned you that?' said the other sharply.

'I was bidden to seek the surliest man in the village,
and, by that token, you are he.'

The cobbler uttered an exclamation which, on less
profane lips, would have sounded like an oath. The
sweat stood on his forehead, and the light in his eye
grew positively baleful. But something in the sweet
superiority of the maiden awed even him. As he stood
panting and hesitating, Priscilla came nearer.

'What a pretty garden you have!' (A grunt from
Marvel.) 'And what fine trees, full of fair fruit.'
(Another grunt.) 'And you keep bees to make you
honey—I see the yellow hives, and I can hear the busy
insects humming all about.' (Another grunt.) 'I must
bring my father to hear your bees, good man, for he
loves the sound; and, like good Master Wesley, holds
the simple bees a pattern set by God for human folk.'

Cobbler Marvel had started again at the mention of
the preacher's name. He took off his nightcap, and
mopped his brow. His manner momently grew more
and more respectful.

'And who may your father be, young mistress?' he
inquired, in a subdued voice.

'He is Master Sefton.'

'From London?'

'Yes.'

In a moment the man's manner changed. His grim
features broke into the semblance of a smile.

'Lord, lord, what a goose I be! I might ha' known you were from none o' these parts, you do speak so bold. And you be Master Sefton's daughter from London? I heerd he were coming to these parts, for to spread the good tidings, and save folks' souls alive from flaming fire.'

'Yes; and he has come.'

'Praised be the Lord! There be plenty of brands here for to pluck from hell's burning, for the parson, he be a Pope's man, and his flock be like the flock o' swine that were drowndead through entering of devils. Where be thy father staying?'

'Over at Brightlinghead,' answered Priscilla, 'but we have walked over to-day, and he is resting at the foot of the hill.'

'Nay, then, I'll come to him at once,' cried the cobbler.

Priscilla looked at him quietly, and smiled.

'First get thy coat, good man; my father does not commend vanity of attire, but he loves neatness and seemliness, most of all on the Lord's Day.'

Cobbler Marvel went very red, and, for the first time in his life, felt ashamed of his defiant *déshabillé*.

'I've heerd tell as Master Sefton is blind,' he muttered irritably, 'and if so be——'

'Nay, good man,' cried Priscilla, 'what the sun can see, God can see, and a good Christian should be seemly clad.'

The cobbler grunted disapproval, and muttered something about the vanity of personal adornment, and the necessity of every man despising vanity for the sake of his precious soul. But the grace and ease of Priscilla had quite mastered him, and after a moment's hesitation he stalked into his cottage, and in a few minutes re-emerged, looking, for him, exceedingly spick-and-span. Then Priscilla tript down the road, and the cobbler stalked after her; and on a stile leading into a green field just on the skirts of the village they found the blind gentleman sitting, murmuring quietly to himself, with the sunshine on his snow-white hair.

The cobbler looked upon him with no little respect, and when introduced to him by name, saluted him with great reverence. For even over the aggressive mind of

Cobbler Marvel the serene self-possession and refine‑
ment of Sefton exercised an immediately subduing in‑
fluence. After a little conversation on general subjects,
Sefton said,

'And where do our people meet to-day?'

'In my poor cottage, master,' was the reply; 'and
'tis nigh upon the hour. Will you join us, master? or
if so be ycu be too weary, I'll fetch them along, and
we'll worship out in the open air.'

The blind man rose, and smiled as he answered,

'I am never weary when about my Master's work.
Lead the way, and we will come to your house. Priscilla,
let me lean upon your arm.'

'Nay, master, lean on mine,' cried the cobbler, 'I be
the stronger.'

Sefton thanked him, and took his arm, and they
walked slowly up the hill. Priscilla followed quietly.
As they went it seemed as if all the shadow went with
them—with the grim old tatterdemalion and the afflicted
gentleman, while all the sunshine remained behind with
the girl. She moved on lightly, with a full enjoyment
of the fair prospect, the golden weather, the azure sky.
Of these wonderful revelations of an Almighty Love
the men saw nothing—the one because he was physi‑
cally, the other because he was mentally, blind; but the
maiden, in her sweet unconsciousness and content, was
at one with Nature. Her somewhat gloomy creed, like
her demure dress, could not touch the brilliancy and
purity of her young life. Indeed, she scarcely realised
its gloom, though, from early habit, she was so familiar
with its vocabulary.

In a few minutes they were again close to the
cobbler's garden gate, which they entered, and passing
through the rows of heavily-laden fruit-trees, approached
the cottage door. Here they encountered an inter‑
ruption, which made the moody cobbler look exceedingly
uncomfortable for the time being. On the threshold
stood a middle-aged and rather good-looking woman,
dressed in a Sunday bonnet and bright-coloured gown,
and gazing at the cobbler, and from the cobbler to his
companions, with impatience and irritation depicted in
every lineament of her face.

This, if the sad truth must be admitted, was Marvel's wife, the only person in the village who was in any sense of the word a match for him. Much of his hatred for the female sex might be traced, possibly, to the discomforts and incompatibilities of his wedded lot. The woman was many years his junior, and a sturdy opponent of all innovations in Church, State, or domestic institutions. She attended the parish church regularly, and in matters of doctrine was in close league with the parson against her husband.

On seeing the strangers, she drew back with a bound and disappeared into some mysterious part of the cottage. With a low groan, expressive of commiseration for her or his own forlorn condition, the cobbler led the way across the threshold.

Entering the parlour, which was quite empty, the cobbler assisted Sefton to a chair, while Priscilla walked up to the window, where sweet-smelling musk plants were flowering in great profusion, and fixed her large eyes longingly on the sunny garden. All was so dark and quiet one could hear distinctly the buzzing of the flies amidst the musk plants—the monotonous drone of the bees in the tea-tree outside. But presently a rap on the front door announced visitors; and Cobbler Marvel, trotting off, soon ushered the new-comers into the room.

They consisted of three or four very weather-beaten figures in wide-awake hats and rough suits, half rustic, half nautical. They entered in single file, hat in hand, and looked around them with the vacant look peculiar to persons entering church or chapel.

In a few minutes all the men were on their knees, and Cobbler Marvel delivered an extempore prayer of no little length and with one chief fault, that it touched rather on the gloom than the cheerfulness of the life of man, and dealt somewhat unmercifully with sin and sinners. Then the men stood up, and one of them began a hymn, in which all the others gruffly joined.

After this Mr. Sefton rose, and in a few touching words, contrasting favourably in matter and manner with those of the local leader, touched on some points in his own simple spiritual experience. After a few words of a similar kind from a country character with a very rubicund face and a very faint far-away voice, and another hymn, the proceedings terminated.

No sooner had the company departed than the kitchen door opened violently, and Mrs. Marvel, still in her Sunday finery, sailed into the parlour.

'It don't become *thee*, Elijah Marvel,' she cried, 'to turn my house into a meeting-house, and set all the neighbours scorning us, and ha' parson preaching agin' us out o' pulpit, driving away thy custom and breaking thy dame's heart! If thou must pray, pray like a decent man among decent folk, and live cleanly. They do say you be plotting wicked things agin' Church and King, and soon or late thou wilt come to be hung on gallows tree.'

'Nay, dame,' interposed the blind man gently, 'you speak of things you do not understand. Thy good man is no plotter, nor are we who are to-day his guests. We are only grievous sinners like yourself, seeking to save our souls.'

'And who may you be, kind sir?' asked the house-wife, with some asperity; adding as she turned to Priscilla, 'and you, young madam?'

'The gentleman is my father,' replied Priscilla; 'and we are strangers. But come, father, it is time to go.'

Appeased and subdued by the appearance and manner of the speaker, Dame Marvel gave a courtesy, and became apologetical.

'Your pardon if I ha' spoken sharp, young madam, but Cobbler Marvel he would fret a saint. Since you be gentlefolk, as indeed we may plainly see, you are kindly welcome. Maybe you'll rest a bit, and taste a glass of my cowslip wine?'

'Nay, dame, we must depart,' said Mr. Sefton, 'though I thank you all the same.'

Leaning on his daughter's arm, he moved to the door, while the dame, with another great courtesy, made way for him to pass. Cobbler Marvel hobbled after them, with a fierce scowl at his wife, who answered him with a defiant toss of the head. So they crossed the garden, and after bidding the moody cobbler fare-

well, and bidding him join them at their gatherings
in the neighbouring village, passed quietly across the
green fields towards Brightlinghead.

CHAPTER VIII.

CLOUDS IN THE SKY.

SEVERAL weeks had passed away since Christian
Christianson and Priscilla Sefton had met accidentally on
the sands, and since that day the two had scarcely been
alone in each other's company. True, they had met;
for was not Christian now a constant attendant at the
religious services held in the cottage at Brightlinghead ?
Indeed, so absorbed had he become in religious fervour
that he completely forgot to watch how affairs were
going on at home. It seemed to him now that he was
continually sitting in the little cottage listening to the
beautiful voice of the girl as she sang the quaint new
hymns, or watching her beautiful bowed head as she
joined her father in prayer.

Then when the service was over, he, longing yet
dreading to stay, walked out with his brother wor-
shippers and strode moody and dissatisfied towards his
home.

But one night, when he rose as usual to take
his departure, Priscilla motioned to him to stay, and
having bowed a sweet good-night to her father's
fellow-worshippers, passed with Christian out into the
garden.

It was one of those calm, still summer nights,
which are rendered even more beautiful by their promise of a golden morrow. On emerging from the
house, Priscilla looked round her with a sigh of
pleasure; then she turned to Christian. He had been
looking full at her; as soon as their eyes met his
dropped, and he turned his head away.

'Nay, friend, you have no need to turn away,' said
the girl, laying her slender hand upon his sleeve. 'Do

you know, good Christian, of what I was thinking when I looked at you to-night?'

At these words Christian felt his whole frame tremble, and an unaccountable feeling of joy fill his heart, but he answered quietly enough,

'Nay, Mistress Priscilla.'

'This—you will become the best Christian in Brightlinghead!'

The young man started, looked into the eyes that were gazing so fearlessly up at him, and answered confusedly enough,

'Nay, Mistress Priscilla.'

'But I say yea, good Christian Christianson; for you are good, I aver, because, although you have youth and manly strength, and plenty of carnal temptations, you withstand them all, and while improving yourself set a good example to others.'

'Verily, Mistress Priscilla,' returned Christian aghast, 'how do you guess all this?'

'I do not guess it, I know it,' returned the girl, quietly; 'why else should you come so often to the cottage to the old blind man and his daughter? Ah! do not think, because I have not spoken, I have not watched you well. I have, and approved you; therefore I have come out to-night to shake hands with you in a brave new light of hope.'

So speaking, with more than her usual quaintness of phraseology, she held out her small white hand; Christian took it, but he did not speak a word. Somehow the girl's laudatory words did not bring with them that degree of pleasure which he felt they should have done. He knew that most of what she had said was true; he knew that he had braved the elements and renounced many daily pleasures merely for the sake of attending the religious meetings at Brightlinghead; but he was not so sure that the fervent preaching of the aged missionary had been such a lodestone as the face of his beautiful daughter. What would those meetings have been to him without Priscilla? Alas! the world without the sun.

For a time they stood at the gate in silence; again Priscilla was the first to speak.

'Good-night, Christian,' she said, quietly. 'You have a mother, you say?'

'Yes, and a sister.'

'Happy mother, and happy sister!' returned the girl quietly. 'Well, I have a father for my share. I must not linger longer here, so again good-night!'

This time she returned to the house, and Christian strode homewards.

For full seven days from that night Christian Christianson did not attend the religious meetings at Brightlinghead. Not that he was over busy at home, but an uncomfortable sense of shame made him shrink again from meeting Priscilla. Yet he longed to meet her, daily and hourly he thought of her; the whole air seemed to be ringing with the echo of her name. His disposition was undergoing a transformation which he himself could hardly understand. Priscilla had come; and as a flower unfolds its petals before the sunshine, his whole nature was expanding under the mysterious light of a woman's eyes.

His temper grew fretful and strange, but every morning the world, in his eyes, grew brighter; it seemed to him that he had never lived before that day when he met the sweet figure on the sands; the past with all its sorrow seemed to fade from his mind, like the blackest night before the brightening of dawn.

And Priscilla? Was *her* day dawning—*her* night fading away? He thought of her face when they had first met on the sands; thought of it as he had seen it night after night during the hours of prayer; thought of it as he had seen it that night at the garden gate, smilingly upraised to his. And as he did so he dared to hope that this little pale, prim girl had come to be to him what the sun is to the earth, the moon to the sea.

'Yes,' he thought, ' her rare sweet love would make amends for half a century of sorrow. Sure 'tis such good fortune as that which makes this life worth living. I will try to deserve all that she thinks of me : with the help of God I will live a brave life and become a Christian man!'

During all this time, as we have said, he kept away from the cottage, because he felt that in going thither he was playing a double part.   He longed to meet Priscilla again alone.

At the end of the weary week he did so.

He came upon her again walking on the sands by the sea; she was singing very cheerfully to herself, but as soon as she saw Christian she ceased, and hurried forward with outstretched hand.

'I am fortunate to-day,' she said, looking steadily into the young man's face. 'I came to seek you and I have found you!'

'You came to seek me!' was all that Christian could reply, for there was something in Priscilla's blunt speech which completely puzzled and confounded him.

'Yes,' returned the girl, quietly smiling, 'I came to seek *thee*, friend Christian! You know the heathen story of Mahomet and the mountain?' she added, with a still brighter smile; 'well, my good Christian has of late become the mountain, and to-day I am Mahomet!'

This time Christian did not reply; indeed he hardly seemed to hear. He was conscious of standing upon a sheet of golden sand; he knew that the glorious golden sun-rays were falling all around him, that the sea was murmuring musically in his ears, that a slender figure clad in black was standing before him, with a face like that of an angel turned smilingly to his!'

How long he stood thus he did not know; his slumbering senses were aroused by the sound of the voice which ever thrilled him to the soul.

'What hath come to you, good friend? you are changing; tell me, then, what is the matter?'

Here was a chance for Christian Christianson to speak. In a moment a burning desire possessed him to take the girl's hand in his and say, 'Yes, Priscilla, I am changed, for you have changed me. I love you—say that you love me too!'

He turned towards her, he half stretched forth his hand, he looked down into her eyes, but before he could open his lips to speak, Priscilla had turned away.

'I did not come with the intention of idling away the day,' said Priscilla, quietly. 'My father is in ill cheer to-day, and would gladly see you. Will you come, good Christian?'

To all outward perception Priscilla's manner was the same as it had ever been; nevertheless, there was something in the tone of her sweet voice which completely dispelled the young man's dream, and brought him back to himself again.

Once more, for the second time in his life, he was walking along the road towards Brightlinghead, Priscilla Sefton by his side—with the sunlight falling all around them and the sky smiling its brightest above. They walked along in silence, and Christian was again falling into that delicious trance which had mesmerised his senses on the sands, when he was again aroused by the sound of his companion's voice.

'You have lived here all your life, have you not?' it said.

'Yes, I and my folk for generations back. I was born at the Fen Farm yonder, and 'tis there I hope to die!'

'In truth,' cried the girl, with a smile, and regaining something of her former ease of manner; 'I trust there is yet time for you to find a place to die in! But since you have dwelt here so long you know all the country-folk around, perchance?'

'Most all.'

'And among them young Squire Orchardson of the Willows? A fair young man, of a goodly disposition!'

The girl had spoken innocently enough, with no thought or wish to wound or anger her companion: yet the young man's face turned from white to red in very rapid transitions, a dangerous light kindled in his eyes, his powerful hand clenched firmly as if for a blow. For a time he stood speechless; when he did speak it was to answer her question by another.

'What know *you* of young Squire Orchardson of the Willows?'

Priscilla looked up quickly, the change in his voice was so marked that it startled her. And how his face had changed! The frank, open, manly look had gone; there was an ugly light in his eyes which she had never seen before.

'What know you of young Squire Orchardson?' he asked again, this time almost roughly.

Priscilla grew reserved.

' In sooth, good friend,' said she, ' I know as little of Squire Orchardson as I know of you. Up till a few weeks ago yon were both strangers to me, but he, like you, has been good Christian enough to come to Brightlinghead of an evening and join our circle in prayer!'

' *He* has come; and *you*—you have welcomed him ——'

' In verity,' said Priscilla, coldly; ' when we open our doors to do the work of the Lord we make *all* welcome!'

Precisely in the same way Priscilla had spoken to him before, and had made his heart leap up for joy. ' Come, good Christian,' she had said, ' when we open the doors in the name of the Lord we make *all* welcome!' How blissful those words had sounded to him then; they seemed to say, You are welcome to come as often as you please and gladden in the sunshine of my presence; but how different it all seemed now! With those self-same words she had given a welcome to his bitterest foe.

The two walked on in silence till they came to the bridge which spanned the narrow part of Thornley Beck. Here Christian paused, and held out his hand.

' Good-bye, Priscilla,' he said.

The girl looked surprised.

' Good-bye ? and wherefore good-bye ? ' she said; ' did I not ask you to come to Brightlinghead ? and you said yes ! '

' I am in no mood to meet Master Sefton to-night ! '

' Then your mood has changed since we started from the sands ! '

' It hath ! '

The young man turned away, leaned over the parapet of the bridge, and looked gloomily down into the water. The girl watched him for a moment; then she approached him quietly and laid her gentle hand upon his arm.

' Christian ! '

' Well ? '

' What ails you ? Have I done aught that angers you ? if so, speak freely, friend ! '

Christian turned, took both her hands and looked into her eyes. Again here was his chance to utter everything! but the tongue clove to the roof of his mouth, and ere he could recover himself, the girl spoke again.

'Hath anything occurred between you and young Mr. Orchardson ?' she said.

A groan from Christian. The hands were dropped, and again he turned away.

By this time the girl had grown quite interested: again she approached the young man and laid her hand gently upon his arm.

'What is it ?' she said.

'Why do you ask ?' he said.

'Because it may be in my power to help you—nay, do not shake your head; tell me your grievance, and the burden may be lighter for you to bear!'

Thus urged, Christian told her all : of the many bitter wrongs endured by him and his, of his undying hatred, and long-cherished hope of revenge; and to all his passionate outburst the girl listened quietly with that calm serene look in her eyes.

'Now tell me,' he said, as she turned away, 'have I not good cause to hate this man, and every one of his name ?'

She shook her head firmly.

'If you are a good Christian, you have no cause to hate him, or any man alive. Our Lord tells us to forgive our enemies, even seventy times seven !'

'Priscilla, it is not possible for a mere man to walk in the footsteps of our Lord !'

'If he doth not *try* to do so, he should not profess to be one of our Lord's followers !'

'I *have* tried—God knows I have.'

'And because you have found difficulties, you have never hoped to surmount them.'

He looked at her with a certain savage passion and laughed.

'What would you wish me to do ? Go to young Orchardson, perchance, and stretch forth my hand ?'

He spoke bitterly, but Priscilla answered quietly and composedly enough :

'Ay, my good friend, that is just what I would have thee do!'

'Then I tell you I would sooner my hand should rot from my arm, than be clasped with his in loving kindness!'

Priscilla turned quietly away.

'In good sooth, I had thought better of you,' she said. 'Good-night.'

And she walked away, leaving him on the bridge alone. He did not attempt to follow her, his heart was too bitter, and he stood leaning moodily on the bridge, watching the slim black figure as it faded slowly away.

His hatred towards the Orchardsons was stronger at that moment than it had ever been before. Priscilla had praised them; she had hinted that they might be right while *he* was wrong; and the thought of this turned the one drop of human kindness in his heart to gall. Were these people, who for generations had been like black shadows upon the lives of him and his, destined now to cast from his lips the only cup of happiness which he had dared to raise?

'O God!' he cried, 'it cannot be. What have I got in all the world but Priscilla? What happiness did I ever know until *she* came? Sooner than he should come between us, I would kill him with my own hand!'

He remained for a time on the bridge, wrapped in his own gloomy thoughts; then he turned towards his home.

It was growing late; daylight was fading fast.

After a while Christian left the high-road and took a shorter route across the fields. It was very quiet here, no one seemed abroad, and Christian walked silently along, still thinking of his interview with Priscilla. Presently he paused, gave one quick glance around; then stood as if listening; a man passed by on the other side of the hedge, and disappeared; then a woman came hurriedly from the same spot, paused within a few yards of where Christian stood, and on looking into his face, uttered a half-terrified cry.

'Kate!'

'Christian!'

Then the two paused in embarrassed amazement. Christian's face darkened terribly. He recalled the man whom he had seen moving stealthily from the spot whence his sister had issued. He turned upon her with a murderous look in his eyes.

'You have been talking with young Richard Orchardson!' he said.

Kate did not reply, but she turned away her head and burst into tears, while her brother, still smarting under the wounds inflicted by Priscilla, still mad with his own bitter wrongs, poured upon her head a torrent of passionate upbraidings.

''Tis the women, the cursed women, who bring bitterness to every house! What will thy mother say, I wonder, when she knows you have spoken with an Orchardson, and met him secretly in the Fen Fields at sunset?'

'Christian, for the love of God, do not tell my mother!'

'Not tell her?'

'She would hate me. She would never forgive me,—she would turn me from her door!'

'You knew all this before.'

'Oh forgive me, brother, forgive me! I meant no harm. I cannot hate as you,—all this bitter feud doth almost break my heart!'

And Kate cried so sorely and pleaded so hard, that out of pity her brother at last granted her prayer.

When they reached home Kate went immediately to her room. Having got there she fell on her knees in passionate tears.

'If he knew! if he knew!' she cried. 'O Jesus, help me, I am a woeful woman!'

For several days Christian scarcely stirred abroad, but at length, solitude becoming too much for him, he resolved to go to Brightlinghead and make his peace with Priscilla. This resolution put him in a better frame of mind; when he entered the cottage garden it was with the full determination to confess his love for her and ask for hers in return.

The cottage door stood open, he tapped gently, and receiving no answer walked in. Two people sat alone in the parlour, Priscilla Sefton and young Richard Orchardson of the Willows.

CHAPTER IX.

THE ENEMY IN THE PATH.

CHRISTIAN started back as if stung, and in a moment his face turned from crimson to deadly white.

'Come in, Christian,' cried Priscilla, quite unconcerned at his appearance, and not rising from her seat; while Richard Orchardson, now a pale, thoughtfullooking young man, plainly but richly drest, looked quietly up, with the supercilious smile that Christian knew so well, and hated so much.

They were seated close to each other in the recess of the old-fashioned cottage window, which, although wide open, was completely smothered in creepers and red and white roses. The room was shadowy and cool, but the humming of bees came with a pleasant sense of sultriness from without.

Christian's head swam, and he turned away. Staggering out of the door he reached the garden, and was moving away, when he felt a touch upon his arm.

'What is the matter?' asked Priscilla, who had risen and followed him. 'Why are you going away?'

He looked at her as if stupefied, but made no reply. It seemed like witchcraft, and for the moment he resisted, with all the force of his soul, her tender spell upon him. Just then, to complete his confusion, the figure of Richard Orchardson appeared on the threshold. Standing up, young Richard appeared to much less advantage than when sitting down; for one leg was much shrunken from the old lameness, and by reason of the contraction in the limb, the body was somewhat bent. But no one, looking at the young man, could doubt his gentle breed. It appeared in the small white hands and neatly-turned foot, no less than in the pallid, handsome face.

Sick and shaking, Christian walked on to the gate. Priscilla followed.

'Why are you angry, friend?' she demanded.

'I am not angry.'

'That is not true,' she returned simply.

'And if I am angry?'

'Then you are to blame,' she said. 'Wherein have I given you offence?'

Trembling from head to foot, and scarcely able to articulate from excitement, Christian pointed at young Richard, who still stood just out of hearing. The girl's gentle forehead contracted, and she looked distressed.

'I remember now what you said,' she said; 'and indeed Mr. Richard himself has told me something of the feud between your families. Yet he freely forgives you the wrong you once did him.'

'The wrong *I* did him!' gasped Christian.

'Yes. You struck him a cruel blow when you were boys. He was weak and you were strong, and you were to blame.'

Christian grew livid. On this subject, of all others in the world, he could not speak with ordinary gentleness even to *her;* nay, he could not discuss it or entertain it at all, so terribly did it disturb his soul. The dark passion covered his face like a cloud, and shocked her.

'Then alas! what he said was true,' she cried, looking at him with angry grief. 'I am sorry for it.'

She turned with a sigh, but he touched her and detained her.

'What did he say? What did he dare to say?'

'That you were cruel and unbending,—more like a wild beast than a Christian man.'

Christian uttered a harsh laugh. In his present temper he was not displeased with his enemy's estimate and description of him; for he felt like a wild beast, and he wished his enemy to believe that his hate was as unreasoning and complete.

'For his own part,' continued the maiden, 'Master Richard is content to let bygones be bygones. He forgives the wrong you did him long ago, and is ready to take your hand. Come to him,—let *me* be peace-maker!'

As she spoke she placed her little hand lightly on his shoulder, and looked up into his face with a smile so sad, so winning, that it would have melted any heart save one where jealousy and hate were contending.

Yes, jealousy; though he scarcely knew it. His cup of hate had been full before, but it lacked until that day the poisonous wormwood of the most miserable of all the passions. Half-unconsciously he glanced towards the cottage door. There his enemy still remained, with an expression upon his face which seemed more like insolent contempt than Christian forgiveness.

'Come and take his hand,' cried Priscilla imploringly.

His only answer was a look of frightful agony. Without uttering another syllable, he flung himself through the gate, and walked wildly and rapidly away.

Priscilla stood gazing after him, lost in sorrowful thought. When his figure had quite disappeared in the direction of the sea, she heard a voice at her elbow.

'Did I not tell you so?' said young Richard in his blandest tones. 'The young cub is like the old she-wolf; he would like to have his fangs in my throat.'

She did not reply immediately; and he stood gazing at her in unmistakable admiration. Standing thus, his slight form would have offered a strange contrast to the yeoman-like proportions of his enemy. His face was very handsome and clear-cut, though its expression was irritating and at times mystifying; his form and limbs, but for the deformity of the one foot and the stoop occasioned by it, were elegant and shapely; while his whole manner bespoke the gentleman of luxury and education. He was clad in a rich dress of velvet, with front and cuffs of the finest cambric, and on his white fingers he wore rings.

'I asked him to shake hands with you,' said Priscilla after a pause. 'I wished to make peace between you.'

'And he refused?' asked Richard, with an airy shrug of the shoulders. 'Did I not say that you would waste your time?'

'It is terrible to see such wicked hate between Christian folk. Ah! had you seen his face!'

'I know the Christianson expression,' returned Richard contemptuously; 'something between the look of a trapt weasel and the glare of an otter at bay.'

'He hates you so much! And you?'

'And I despise him infinitely.'

'To despise is almost as wicked as to hate,' replied Priscilla, looking steadfastly at Richard.

'How then shall I express it ?' exclaimed the young man, with the ease peculiar to him. 'I am, I hope, a fair Christian—at least, with your good counsel, I am in a fair way of becoming one—and I have almost succeeded in forgetting that yonder clumsy fellow once struck me; that is to say, I have not *forgotten*, since my looking-glass reminds me every morning that he has marked me for life.'

Here he pointed to his fair forehead, where indeed the trace of his early injury was still to be seen, in one faint but ineffaceable mark. 'But what is done is done, and, after all, we were boys. I therefore bear no malice, and would take the fellow's hand ; only Heaven keep me from being long in his company, for he is a clown. I shall never go out of my way to do him any harm ; should he attempt to injure me, I shall crush him, if possible, just as I would crush an adder that tried to sting me, or a venomous insect that settled on my hand. You look shocked, Miss Priscilla. Well, instruct me where I am wrong, and I will promise to obey your counsel.'

'You are wrong to despise one of your fellow-creatures.'

'How can I help it ?' said Richard, with a smile. 'Frankly, though, such a fellow would be amusing if he were not so monotonously dull.'

'Why did he strike you ?' demanded Priscilla, quickly. 'You must have provoked him sorely.'

Richard coloured violently, and for the moment, under her clear gaze, lost his usual self-possession.

'A boy's quarrel, as I told you,' he answered; 'I forget how it began, but how it ended I know full well, for I was the weaker, and down I went. For the rest, the feud between our houses is traditional; there never was a time when our folk were on speaking terms with these yeomen of the Fen. 'Tis all very tiresome and very stupid, I grant you, and for my own part I can't afford to have an enemy, since 'tis only a source of irritation. Only in one event should I think it my duty to assert myself and become the aggressor.'

' What event ? ' said Priscilla, startled by the peculiar emphasis in the speaker's last words, no less than by the peculiar look of warmth that accompanied them.

' In the event of his crossing my purpose in one of those affairs which determine a man's happiness on earth, and perchance his qualification for Heaven.'

His look was unmistakable, and she at once understood him; but without a blush, without the slightest sign of self-consciousness, she frankly met his eyes. This frankness and fearlessness embarrassed him not a little. Had she coquetted or blushed, or drooped her eyes in bashful fear, then and there would his bold lips have made a confession of love; but Richard Orchardson, despite his slight physical deformity, had no little knowledge of the fair sex, and he knew that the time was not ripe.

' But come,' he cried, ' let us change the theme. When yonder fellow entered, you were speaking to me of your father's plans for the future. Can you not persuade him to forsake this vagrant life—so unsuited to one of his gentle breeding ? '

' Nay, sir ; nor would I attempt it.'

' Why not ? '

' Is it not a blessed thing to go about on the Lord's work ? '

' Doubtless ; and your father, I grant you, is as noble as one of the apostles of old. But alas ! he has fallen on adverse times. Everyone who disregards the supreme authority of the Church is baited by the parsons as either an infidel, or, what is worse, a political malignant ; and for proselytes you have, in most villages, only the same. Where you strive to do most good, you succeed often in only setting folk by the ears. Look not angry—have I not proved myself your friend ? But I cannot help bethinking me of a homely proverb of my father's—" Would you lead a life of peace and heart's content, keep friends with the parson of the parish ! " '

' Alas ! the parsons chide us sorely, wherever we go.'

' Because you meddle with the work they are paid to do. They would fain drive their sheep to Heaven through the Church door, and when they find you urging them in another direction, they are naturally angry. In sooth, most folk are so foolish and old-fashioned that they can be saved on no other conditions, and in no newer way, than were their fathers before them; and such are the folk in these villages. For my own part, I should deem most of the louts scarce worth saving at all, were I not instructed to the contrary by the creed you teach so well.'

'There is no human being,' answered Priscilla quietly, 'but is worthy to be plucked from the burning. So my father saith.'

'Even at the risk of burning one's own members! Ah, but your father is superhumanly good, as I always tell you. Well, to return to what I was saying. You cannot live this wandering life for ever?'

'For ever?'

'I mean that your martyrdom will end some day, and perchance you will—marry?'

He watched her closely, but her face did not change. She moved over to a rose-bush, plucked a rose, and divided it thoughfully, petal by petal. Then she spoke, as if discussing a subject of the simplest interest.

'I do not think I shall marry. I shall remain with my father all my life.'

'But he is old, and—nay, do not think I speak ont of little feeling—in the nature of things will pass away long before yourself. Then you will be alone.'

She shook her head, and looked quietly upward.

'I shall never be alone,' she said.

The young man looked at her in deepening wonder and admiration. Though there was something in her perfect purity and simplicity of character far beyond his comprehension, he could at least feel the spell of her beauty and the charm of her heavenly disposition. At that moment he did not dare to speak of love; he was too certain that her feelings towards him, and possibly towards all other men, were perfectly passionless; but his eye burned and his face flushed, with a baser and less spiritual emotion. A physiognomist, observing him, would have traced in his fine face the taint of an underlying sensuality, which indeed was inseparable from his nature.

'It is an ill world,' he persisted, 'and you may one day feel its cruelty. Even in your father's company, you are frequently exposed to danger. Yester night, had I not been of your company, the folk here would have used you both roughly—and wherever you go, you meet with enemies who are very pitiless. It pains me sorely to see one so fair amidst such sorry scenes. You should be a lady, leading a lady's life—not a homeless wanderer from place to place.'

'You would have me idle,' answered Priscilla, 'or playing pretty tunes on the harpsichord, or doing foolish embroidery, or dancing in fine raiment. Such vanities are not for me, good friend ; I am happier as I am.'

So saying, she walked back to the cottage door, where, after a few minutes, Richard Orchardson bade her farewell.

How the young man became so familiar a guest in the cottage, is easily told. He had the keenest of senses for a pretty face, and one day, as he rode by, he had seen Priscilla standing at the gate, in all her youthful prettiness and seemliness. A few inquiries at the nearest house of entertainment informed him who she was ; and soon, with characteristic assurance, he joined the little gatherings over which her father presided. All formalities being dispensed with by these simple people, he soon found himself on terms of easy intimacy ; and under the pretence of being moved by a spirit of pious repentance, he had endless opportunities of communing with the object of his admiration.

Quitting the cottage, he walked down to the village inn, where his horse (for owing to his infirmity he seldom walked far) awaited him, and he was soon upon the road towards the Willows. He did not ride straight homeward, however. Leaving the country road on which Christian and Priscilla had lingered that bright morning when they first met, he rode down to the sea-sands ; and seeking the very edge of the water, where the sands are ever hardest and firmest, put spur to his horse and galloped. After a good mile's gallop, he drew rein, and walked his steed in deep thought. His pale cheek was flushed with exercise, and his eye burned brightly.

At last, he turned his horse's head up towards the sandhills, taking much the same way that his father and he had taken, many years ago, when they encountered young Christian among the knolls. He had left the sea-sands, and was proceeding slowly along the arid fields which stretched just above them, when he saw, almost blocking his path, the figure of Christian Christianson.

Christian had been seated in dark thought on a great stone when the approach of Richard disturbed him. He sprang up, and for the instant the other thought he contemplated personal mischief. So Richard went very pale, and with a sharp pull at the rein drew his horse on one side, and passed. Christian glared at him, and their eyes met. The horseman nervously clutched his riding whip, in expectation of an attack; for indeed the face of Christian looked ominous, in its mad expression of frenzied dislike. But he was suffered to pass untouched, and had no sooner done so than he quickened his horse's pace into a trot. Not until he was several hundred yards away did he draw rein, and look round. Christian stood on the same spot, almost in the same attitude, like a shape of stone.

That day, perhaps for the first time, Christian Christianson knew his heart. He was realising in its full intensity the horror of that terrible line of the religious poet, Young :—

The jealous are the damned.

And by the measure of his black jealousy he was able to mete his love. The shock of seeing Priscilla in the company of his hereditary enemy, of the being whose merest breath had the power to poison the sweet air and make life hideous and unbearable, had revealed to him the full intensity of his personal passion. He felt now that to see her talking confidentially with any other youthful man would cause a sickening sense of envy and dislike; but to have seen her so close with what he most abhorred, was stupefying and over-whelming.

He had rushed down to the sea-sands, and had his

dark hour alone. He had spoken out his mad thought to the sea, as so many a poor soul has done, in default of a better listener. He had raged and stormed, with no living thing to heed him, and still his spirit was overburdened.

Grown a little calmer, he had taken his staff, and in a kind of dream, had written with it on the sands, in large round characters, her name,—

' PRISCILLA.'

Then, taken by a sudden fancy, he had added another to it—

' PRISCILLA CHRISTIANSON.'

Again and again he wrote it, hurriedly blotting it out afterwards with his foot, for fear it might be read by eyes profane.

But the last time he wrote it thus, defiance held him, and he let the bold words stand. Yes, he cared not who read them—if they were read by *her*, by all the world! He loved her, he would possess her, he would make her his wife! She should be Priscilla Christianson in good deed.

And yet, how hopeless it all seemed! He felt *that*, even as he toyed with the sweet thought of possession. She was so far above him. He was so common, she so pure and fair. He hated his rude strength, his strong hands, his coarse breeding. Oh, why had he not been born gentle, like—like Richard Orchardson, his foe!

Well, happen what might, no Orchardson should possess her—that he swore to himself over and over again; and as he did so the murderous devil which filled the heart of Cain crept into his. His thought travelled back to the sad morning, long before, when the boy Richard lay bleeding on the ground before him; and oh! he thought to himself, if his enemy had never risen again to cross his path!

He walked wildly away, leaving the name, ' Priscilla Christianson,' written large on the sands. A little later Richard Orchardson rode over that very spot, and had he looked down might have read the words.

As he passed they were obliterated by his horse's hoofs.

That night, and the day which followed it, were hours of fierce torture for Christian; the fiercer because he dared not, or rather would not, show it to either mother or sister. His mother was now very infirm, and seldom left her chair, an ancient piece of furniture of black oak, with high straight back, like that of a *prie-Dieu.* Much sorrow and deep suppressed passion had told terribly upon her senses, which were fast beginning to fail; but her Bible was ever at her right hand as of old. As for gentle Kate, she also had greatly changed, constantly avoiding her brother's presence, and when within his gaze, seeming highly nervous and distraught.

On the morning of the second day, as Christian stood at the door preparing to go forth, a vision came before his eyes. Priscilla herself was tripping up to the gloomy house, with her brightest look upon her.

Directly she saw him she waved her hand, and cried,

'May I enter, good Christian?'

He ran forward, and took her little hand in both of his.

'And welcome!' he said, trembling. 'Why did you come?'

'To see your good mother.'

'My mother!'

'Yes. I have heard that she is sick and ailing, and perhaps I may bring her a little cheer. Your pretty sister, too—I wish to see her.'

'Come in,' said Christian, scarcely knowing what he said.

He led her gently into the dark parlour, where the old dame sat erect, with the film of years upon her eyes. She did not see them till they came quite near and spoke her name. Then Christian told her who the stranger was, and why she had come.

'She is welcome,' said the dame, gloomily.

With the sweetness peculiar to her, Priscilla took her place by the dame's side, and soon beguiled her into conversation; so that presently she brightened a little, and relaxed her look of gloom. Then the maiden opened the Bible, and read a chapter in her musical voice, to which the dame listened well content, though the chapter chosen contained little of the thunder in which she delighted. Finally, at Christian's request, she sang a simple hymn, so sweetly and so simply that Christian, though he knew her gift of song so well, was spell-bound.

As she ended, Kate Christianson came in, and fixed her great sad eyes upon her with timid wonder. The contrast was strange between Kate's soft, wistful, scared-looking face, and the perfectly peaceful lineaments of Priscilla.

'Your sister,' said Priscilla, and kissed her. Then she fixed upon her one of her steadfast, truthful, questioning looks; for something in Kate's expression touched her to the heart.

A little later, when she rose to go, having left sunshine in every part of the house she had entered, Christian followed her. They walked out of the old house together.

'Your sister seems sorrowful,' said Priscilla. 'Hath she had any trouble?'

'All our folk have had trouble,' answered Christian.

'But any great trouble? She looks like one whose heart failed her, and who sought a friend.'

'A friend?'

'Yes,—to speak her sorrows to, and be relieved.'

'She has my mother.'

'Ah, that is different,' returned Priscilla, thoughtfully; and she walked along in silence.

She had a message up to the village, she said, and she was going there straightway. Might he walk with her a portion of the way? She assented with a smile, and he remained by her side.

For the time being he had almost forgotten the existence of Richard Orchardson, or of any possible rival or opponent. He was too happy in her mere presence, in the light of her face, in the sound of her voice. He felt, as before, like the men who walked with angels towards some shining Land.

At last she paused and held out her hand.

'You must come no farther,' she said, smiling.

' Wherefore not ? '

' I do not wish it, that is all.'

Christian bent his head in immediate assent, for he loved, in his strength, to feel her mastery over him.

' That is enough. What *you* wish, *I* shall do.'

' Everything ? '

' Yes, everything ; except——'

.   He paused reddening, for he remembered how she had besought him to take Richard Orchardson by the hand.

' Except forgive your enemy,' she said sadly, finishing the sentence for him. ' Ah well, the day may come when you will not refuse me even *that !* '

He turned back, leaving her to proceed upon her way. Scarcely had he done so, than the evil spirit which is ever at the ear of the jealous began to ask, ' Why hath she dismissed me ? To whom is she telling her message ? ' Sick with the fear which these questions awakened, he followed her at a distance, keeping well from view.

She passed through the village, nodding to Cobbler Marvel, who stood in his usual *déshabillé* at his garden gate ; she passed the church, the village school ; then reaching the further side of the village, she came to a green lane.

All was very quiet and lonely here, though human habitations were so close. Entering the lane she walked more slowly, loitered and waited, and once or twice looked round.

Then Christian slunk back behind a friendly hedge and waited.

Presently she hastened her steps ; and looking out, Christian saw a figure approaching along the lane. She stood and waved her handkerchief ; the figure waved in return. It was the figure of a man.

Christian's head swam—he could scarcely see.

The two figures met, and as they did so, Christian recognised in Priscilla's companion the man he most hated to behold.

Christian stood rooted to the ground, watching the meeting of the two figures. Anyone seeing his livid, distorted face just then would have been startled by its terrible expression. If, as Swedenborg and other supreme mystics have laboriously proved, the face is the index of the soul, and by the face alone an ' angel ' or a ' devil ' (according to the Swedenborgian terminology, with its occult meanings) may be recognised, then surely, at that moment, Christian stood in the category of evil spirits. All the forward-looking lightness, all the dreamy hope and fear, of early and noble manhood, had faded from his countenance, leaving only in their place the black shadow of ignoble passion. Such a look, indeed, might Cain have worn, when he saw his beautiful altar overthrown, and the lightning of heaven playing scornfully upon his sacrifice.

After a minute of rapid conversation, the two figures moved slowly on side by side, along the green lane. Slipping from his shelter, and keeping as well as possible from view, he followed, with his eyes fixed upon them, watching their slightest movement. When they paused, as they did from time to time, he paused too, slipping into the shadow of the green hedge. But they did not once look back. That their talk was animated every gesture proved ; and that it was pleasant talk he also knew, for once or twice she laughed merrily, and turned a bright face upon the face of her companion. Never before in his life had he felt such a sickening sense of moral meanness. To play the spy as he was doing was foreign to his nature ; he hated them, he hated and despised himself ; yet the dark spirit of jealousy had him by the hair, and he felt powerless to resist its cruel hold. So he watched and followed, look by look, and step by step.

The lane passed under a canopy of boughs, made by tall ash-trees intermingling their branches overhead ; at its further end stood the gate of a little old-fashioned lodge, untenanted and fallen into decay. This Christian knew well ; it was one of the lodge entrances to the many-gabled ancestral dwelling where his enemies dwelt—the Willows.

He saw Richard Orchardson swing the gate open, while she passed in. Something merry passed between them, and he saw their faces turn again to each other in the sunshine ; then they passed into the shadow of trees beyond and disappeared.

He felt that he could follow no further. Duped
and baffled, like the evil spirit in the play when he saw
the sign of the pentagram on Faust's threshold, he
shrank back, and turned his weary footsteps home.

CHAPTER X.

UP AT 'THE WILLOWS.'

RICHARD ORCHARDSON and Priscilla walked on side by
side beneath the trees, a straggling colonnade of ash,
planted many a long year before; and emerging thence,
came out upon an open space of green, in the centre of
which was a large tarn or pond, surrounded on every
side by water-willows, with silver tresses dangling and
dipping upon the water's brim. Fronting the tarn was
the house, a quaint Elizabethan structure of red brick,
with a terrace, where once upon a time (if traditions
were true) Queen Bess herself had walked and mused,
one night when she had rested, a stately guest, beneath
that roof. It was a quaint and lonely habitation, only
partly tenable, for the Orchardsons were ever a small
family, and used few of its many rooms.

Approaching the terrace, they ascended to it by a
broad flight of crumbling steps, and came upon a semi-
circular space, in the centre of which was a sun-dial
surrounded by flowers, and not far from the dial a
rustic seat.

'How beautiful!' exclaimed the maiden; and she
added, looking at the dial, 'And what is this?'

' 'Tis our sun-dial,' answered Richard smilingly.

'To tell the hour by?'

'Certainly, when there is sufficient sunshine.'

'I have heard of such pretty devices; and see, here
are the hours graven letter by letter. Teach me to read
it now.'

'Look where the shadow falls, slanting from the
index. It is past twelve o' the clock, or rather o' the
dial, as you may see.'

' 'Tis so indeed,' cried Priscilla, watching the

moveless shadow with earnest eyes. 'But when there is no sun, how do you reckon then ? '

' Then we go within, and look at the clock ! '

' See the flowers, how they climb around, as if they would cover the dial's shining face. 'Tis a sweet thought, to measure our days by the sunlight, among leaves and flowers. I have heard my father say that in old times they reckoned time with dripping water, as they do still with slipping sand in the hour-glass.'

' Yes ; they had the water-clock, invented by one of their wise men. But sit here, I prithee, and look at the prospect; is it not fair ? And look on what side you will, far as you please, the land is ours.'

Priscilla sat upon the garden-seat, and looked around as he desired. On all sides stretched flowery walks, green plantations, meadows, and fields of grain. Even as she gazed, a thought came to her, troubling her bright expression ; she lifted her eyes to his, and said quietly and slowly,

' Since you had so much, why did you seek more ? '

' I do not understand,' he exclaimed, smiling down upon her.

' Christian has told me,' she said simply. ' Your father coveted his land, and took it from his father.'

Richard's face blackened ; the very name of his foe came like a sting. But he conquered his annoyance in a moment, and replied with well-assumed quiet and indifference :

' If Master Christian has told you that old tale, I hope he hath told it truly. My father loaned to his father large sums of money, and even when these sums were not returned, nor the fair interest paid, my father in pity forbore his lawful claim. 'Twas not till the Christiansons were wickedly ungrateful, till they did us grievous injury passing patience, that we seized our own.'

As he spoke, Richard saw his father approaching—a tall, stooping figure, with something of his own delicacy of feature, but a harsher and less refined expression. The squire expressed no surprise either in word or look on seeing his son's companion, but coming up, took off his hat with an old-fashioned bow.

'This is young Mistress Sefton,' said Richard, 'of whom I have spoken to you.'

Priscilla rose and curtsied; the squire bowed again.

'The young lady is right welcome . . . I have heard of your father from others, and my son, as he saith, has spoken to me much of you.'

The squire did not add that he had heard of Mr. Sefton as a half-crazy fanatic, with most preposterous notions concerning religion. Under ordinary circumstances, Mr. Orchardson, who was a staunch Churchman, more from political than spiritual motives, would certainly not have received a person of 'malignant' connections with so much urbanity; but in this case he had particular reasons (which he had not explained even to his son, but which will presently be apparent) for being civil to his pretty visitor. Urged by the same reasons, he had interposed no objection, uttered no admonition, when he had first heard of his son's acquaintance with the Seftons, but had, on the contrary, quietly encouraged a friendship which, common experience told him, might readily ripen into love.

After some minutes' desultory conversation, throughout which he continued to treat Priscilla with a courtliness unusual to him, he led the way into the house, passing through an open glass folding-door into a great chilly drawing-room, the old-fashioned furniture of which was carefully mummied up in holland cloth. Here he summoned his housekeeper, and ordered tea, which was served very strong, in tiny cups of the rarest china.

'And how fares your father?' he demanded kindly, as Priscilla sat and sipt the pleasant beverage. 'He is a frail man to wander from place to place alone.'

'Not alone,' answered Priscilla, 'since we go everywhere together.'

'Nay, but pardon me, you yourself are but a child. It concerns me to think that you and he, who might be dwelling in comfort like the gentlefolk you are, should be as houseless wanderers upon the earth. 'Tis a strange life, for both.'

'So we are often told,' said Priscilla quietly, 'and so were the apostles told, long ago.'

'" You shall not go," cried the girl wildly, holding him with trembling hands.'

Richard glanced at his father, deprecating any controversy, and the squire, with a smile and a nod, turned the talk into other channels; showed the maiden his pictures, and his few books; told her carelessly some of the old legends of the house, which were many; and altogether proved himself so agreeable and charming a host that even his son was astonished.

An hour later, Richard accompanied Priscilla back to the village, where her father was staying that night under the roof of Cobbler Marvel. Returning thence, after a pleasant parting and a warm hand-shake, he entered the lodge gate and walked slowly up the shadowy avenue,—his eyes still full of Priscilla's loveliness, his heart beating high with the dream of possible possession.

Suddenly he started and stood still, as a figure emerged from the shadow of the trees and stood before him: the figure of a woman cloaked and hooded.

'Richard!'

'Kate!'

The hood fell back, and showed, in the dim light, the pallid face of Kate Christianson.

'I have been waiting for you,' cried Kate quickly; 'thank God you're come at last!'

'What do you seek with me?' returned the other irritably. 'You came upon me like a ghost, and—well, well, what is it?'

She gazed at him with great tearful eyes, and without replying, began to sob bitterly, and wring her hands.

He uttered an angry exclamation, and turned on his heel.

'Go home; we shall be seen.'

'Nay, if we are, I heed not. Things have gone too far between us to let us part so, and I care not now if the whole world know how cruel you have been to me. Richard! for the love of God, be not so hard; speak kindly, Richard, and I will try to forgive you still.'

'You are talking folly,' answered the young man. 'What have you to forgive? Good Kate, I prithee let us talk some other time; to-night I am in haste.'

'You shall not go,' cried the girl wildly, holding him with trembling hands. 'No, not yet!'

'Are you mad ?   Kate, as you love me——'

'God help me, methinks 'tis more like hate than love that fills my poor heart. Who is she you have been walking with so long ? '

He looked at her, and smiled without replying.

'Will you not answer me ? Nay, you need not, for I know her. She is the blind preacher's daughter from Brightlinghead, and you have gone a-courting her as you did come a-courting me; and I have watched you, Richard, and seen you smile upon her as you used to smile on me; but take heed, for more than one has been a-watching, and if I spoke the word——'

'What do you mean ? ' he cried sharply, shaking off her hold upon him, and seizing her arm in his turn.

'Never mind,' she answered, meeting his eyes with a curious look.

'Hark you, Kate Christianson, I am getting tired of your weary words and peevish ways. You used to be pleasant company, but now——'

'But now, since you are tired of my company, you seek another's.'

'And if I do, who can prevent me ? '

She uttered a low cry, and raised her hand threateningly.

'I can ! Nay, Richard, you need not laugh. I can; and I will ! '

'*You !* '

'I have but to speak one word——'

'Speak !—to whom, prithee ? '

'To Christian, my brother.'

He flung her arm from him with a gesture of com-plete contempt, but for all that he trembled, for he knew well that the threat was not altogether a vain one, and the memory of that never-forgotten day, when he lay bleeding upon the ground, and Christian stood frowning over him, passed darkly across his soul.

'I care neither for him nor you. If he dares to cross my path, I will crush him as I would crush a toad. So threaten no more, but let me go.'

'Richard, for God's sake listen ! ' cried the girl, suddenly changing her angry tone to one of despairing entreaty. 'I did not mean to threaten—in good deed

I did not; but you are so cold, so cruel—you do make me mad. 'Twas for your sake I came hither to-night—to warn you against my brother.'

'What!'

'He hath been watching too.'

'Watching?'

'He followed the preacher maiden until she met you, and then he followed again till you entered the lodge gate in her company.'

'And what then?'

'He loves her, Richard, and if you come between him and her——'

'Well?'

'He will *kill* you, Richard!'

Richard grew very pale, but instantly recovering his self-possession covered his real trepidation with an educated sneer.

''Tis like your brother's impudence to raise his eyes to yonder maiden, who is a lady born. Do you know, good Kate, your brother is a boor, and is better placed at the ploughtail than at a gentlewoman's elbow? I do not think you can be serious when you speak of his loving Mistress Sefton.'

Now, poor Kate loved her brother, and though she was naturally of a weak and timid nature, she loved him too well to hear him slighted of; moreover, in this tender question she had double interest at stake, for if Christian was Richard's rival, Priscilla was, by the same token, hers. So she replied bravely, without the least hesitation,

'My brother is as good a man as you, and fit for any lady in the land.'

'Bah! your brother is a clown.'

'If he were nigh, you would not dare to say so, responded Kate, while Richard's face grew paler still, and his lip quivered. 'If I were to go to him this night, and tell him what hath past between us, do you think he would spare you?—And he suspects, remember that!'

'What do you mean?' cried Richard eagerly.

'He witnessed our parting one night near the four-acre mere, and he taxed me fiercely with meeting an

Orchardson. Alack! had he guessed how often we had met, how I had given my heart to the enemy of our house, what would he have said? I dread his wrath and my mother's; she would curse me, for I have broken my oath upon the Book. And they *must* know full soon! Listen, Richard—there is something more I came to tell you—it is terrible, but 'tis time that you should know.

She put her lips to his ear, and whispered; he started as if he had been stung by some venomous snake, and uttered an oath.

'No!'

'God help me, it is true.'

'I tell you it is impossible,—you are a fool, and you are deceiving yourself. No, I'll not believe it.'

'Alas! the day is nigh when you *must* believe it, and all the world too. But I shall not live to see that day—no, for my heart will be broken, and I shall die.'

She hid her face in her hands, crying bitterly, while he stood gazing at her in gloomy dislike and irritation. Night had now fallen, but the skies above were full of a faint palpitating starlight, like the ghost of day.

At last Kate looked up and dried her tearful eyes.

'Richard,' she said, 'I have thought it all over, and there is only one way. When we are married——'

As she spoke the word, he started, and frowned darkly.

'When we are married, we will go to my brother and ask his forgiveness. He will be angry at first per-chance, but seeing 'tis too late, he will work round in time. Dear Richard, let us speak to the parson, and when we are wedded man and woman before God, per-chance we may be forgiven.'

The young man looked at her in growing dislike and dread, and after a brief silence replied:

'Listen, Kate!—Let there be an end to this folly between us twain. I am in no mood to marry, and if I were, I could never marry one of your house. Nay!' he continued, as she wrung her hands with a low wail, ''tis no use to cry and plead. Be a wise woman, Kate. Keep our secret, and when you marry some honest yeoman, as you may, I will take care you shall not lack for dower.'

'Oh, Richard, speak not so! You will keep your promise!

'What promise?'

'To make me your wedded wife.'

'I never promised, and if I did I repent me. Our two houses can never be united; but what we know, no other living soul need know, if you are wise.'

'No, no! I will speak to my brother! I will tell him.'

'You will tell him nothing, good Kate; you love your honest name too well. And if you did, what then? Do you think I fear him? Now, kiss me, and be sure that I remain your friend.'

'Do not touch me! Oh, Richard, you have broken my heart!'

'Not I!—Give me your hand, and swear.'

'I will drown myself this night!'

'You will do no such foolish thing.'

'What have I left to live for? My brother's hate, my mother's curse. 'Twas an evil day when I was born; most evil day of all, when I trusted an Orchard-son. Let me go! 'Tis all over now for ever and ever!'

He tried to hold her in his arms, but she tore herself free with a wild cry, and ran from him into the darkness. For a moment he seemed about to follow her, but refrained, and stood listening to her retreating footsteps. In good truth, he placed little value upon her threats and passionate words, for he was used to such scenes. Again and again, of late, her manner and language had been violent to desperation; again and again she had threatened to let the world know of the relations between them; but nothing had come of it hitherto, and he did not seriously believe that anything would come of it now. At the same time, he could not help reflecting, with a nervous shudder, on the dangerous character of his hereditary foe, who, if seriously provoked, would certainly not hesitate before taking some desperate revenge.

'The fellow is a wild beast in my path,' he reflected, as he walked slowly towards the Willows; 'as long as he breathes the same air, I shall never be quite safe.

Can it be possible that the wench was right, and that he presumes to raise his eyes to Priscilla?—And Priscilla? She is so tender of heart, and she would smile upon the meanest thing in her path; but her smiles mean nothing—she would never cast her thoughts so low. Well, be that as it may, I wish the clown were buried in the churchyard, or lying twenty fathoms deep in the salt sea.'

So musing, and muttering to himself, Richard Orchardson returned to the house, and found his father awaiting him in the large apartment, half parlour, half lumber-room, which was known as the gun chamber. The walls were hung with sporting pictures, fowling-pieces and pistols, and trophies of the chase.

The squire was reading an old book on hunting, but looked up with a smile.

Well?'

'Well, father?'

'Did you see her to her home? A pretty maiden, and gently reared. I am glad you brought her to me, and I hope she will come again. Did you see the afflicted man, her father?'

'Not to-night. We parted at Cobbler Marvel's door.'

'What a place to shelter one so fair!'

'All roofs are alike to them—the richest or the meanest.'

The squire rose and stood facing his son, with a curious expression upon his face.

'And yet, Richard, this blind preacher, who goes about almost as a beggar, and who has scarcely a roof to cover his head, is a richer man than I, your father, and might if he chose be holding up his head among the grandest folk in London.'

'Is it possible?' cried Richard, in no little surprise.

'It is certain,' said Mr. Orchardson; 'and if he were to die suddenly to-morrow, yonder pretty maiden would be an heiress.'

'I thought he had given away his substance in charity, and lived only upon a pittance reserved to him.'

'' Tis not quite so bad as that,' answered the squire, still smiling. 'The poor fool hath squandered much in so-called alms-giving and missionary work, but the bulk remains, and much of that he cannot even touch—which is a mercy, for the sake of the young dame, whom he might beggar.'

'How learned you this, father?'

'From one in London, who knows him well, and whose knowledge has never yet played me false. The pretty maiden herself knows not of her good fortune, or only dimly guesses it; for her father enacts every day and hour the comedy of being apostolically poor. So now, son Richard, that you see which way the hare is running, and know where her cover lies, will you gallop still?'

'What do you mean, father?'

The squire laughed, and placed his hand on his son's shoulder.

'Do you think I know not, lad, when young folk favour one another? Well, win her; I tell you she is worth the winning. Think you I would have suffered you to go a-psalm-singing so long, in such company, had I not been warned that all was well?'

There was a long silence. Richard sat in a chair, gazing thoughtfully down, while his father kept his keen eyes fixed upon his flushed face, well pleased.

At last the young man looked up.

'Father, I shall do my best, for indeed I love the girl; but one stands in my way.'

'Who, lad, who?'

Richard pointed to his forehead, with a venomous smile.

'He who marked me for life. Christian Christianson.'

CHAPTER XI.

ANOTHER LOVE SCENE.

MEANTIME Christian was once more having his dark hour alone; wandering seaward with mad jealousy in his heart, and the shadow of mortal hate upon his face; raging, fretting, planning; darkly, desolately, driven by the wind of his own passion, like a cloud in the wind of its own speed. Had he known the full truth that day, had Kate found him then and told him of the evil wrought by her own feebleness, and the baseness of his rival, he would have flown like a wild beast to avenge his house's in-jury, and expend his own dark desire; and the hours of his enemy would surely have been numbered. But he felt as yet in his own heart, despite his jealous fury, that he had no righteous cause for violence. The woman he loved had her right, as well as he, and if she chose to seek Richard Orchardson's company, he had no claim to control her liberty of choosing. Nothing had passed between them that would justify his interference; and although he felt mad with her for her pertinacity and her indifference to his personal dislikes and hates, he was in no sense master of her life.

It seemed to him, indeed, at that time, that all was ended between them. She had come like a beautiful spirit on his life, stirring its deepest fountains with a new revivifying light; but now it was over. As calmly and as freely as she came to him—nay, as it seemed, with a kinder touch, and a tenderer smile—she had gone, would daily go, to the man he hated most. He had no power to control her. Bitter as it was to bear, he knew it was hopeless to protest, unless she herself should change of her own free will. With one so pure, so passionless, violent entreaty was of no avail. She was the stronger spirit still, his mistress and his superior —that he felt most keenly; and his baffled anger kept him in despair.

Was it true, then, that she loved Richard Orchard-son? Was it fated that, even in love itself, his enemy should wreck his life and darken his dreams? Yes, it was possible. Even amidst the storm of his unreasoning hate, he felt the superiority of Richard Orchardson in all those gifts which are dear to women-folk: in delicacy of nurture, in gentleness of breeding and education, in fairness of feature and courtliness of mien. Priscilla, herself, was a town lady, while he was country bred. In his own sight he was coarse, clumsy, ungainly, while she was delicacy itself. Could so rough a hand as his be suffered to pluck so pretty a blossom? No, he felt that he was fated to lose her, and his anguish was, that what he lost, the enemy of his house might gain.

Had Christian been able to see deeper into the heart of Priscilla Sefton, he might have been a happier and a calmer man. In her eyes, his very wildness and strength had a fascination. Though she rebuked his violent passions, observing them and rising above them with her characteristic serenity, she did not dislike him for them,—any more than she disliked the sea for being turbulent, or the clouds for breaking into sullen thunder. Rather, it was a charm to her to encounter such a nature for the first time, as it was a charm to stand under the clouds and to look upon the sea. Nor could one with eyes so susceptible to natural impressions be blind to Christian's striking physical beauty. He was pre-eminently a handsome man, though his handsomeness was that of a Heracles, perfect in strength and manhood; and his face had the splendour of perfect sincerity and truthfulness, even when shadowed by unreasoning passion. That her Heracles was submissive to her slightest wish or whim, and would at her bidding have cheerfully sat down to the distaff, like Heracles of old, was still no disparagement in her eyes; for his obedience was that of a strong will voluntarily bending to a charm, rather than that of a weak will to be conquered by the nobler and the stronger.

Fortunately for Christian's peace of mind, they met again by accident that very afternoon. As he walked in his favourite haunt among the sandhills, he saw her passing below him towards the sea. She looked up and saw him, and beckoned, smiling. He walked down to her rapidly, scarcely knowing what he did.

'I am going down to the shore,' she said, ' to gather green sea-moss for my father's eyes. Will you come with me ? '

He gazed at her as if in a dream, and made no reply ; but as she moved on he followed close behind her.

She talked on, with her happy unconsciousness of manner.

'Dame Marvel tells me that the sea-moss, boiled

till it makes a jelly, is good for healing soreness of sight, and my father's eyes are very tender.　Will you tell me where to find it?'

'Yes,' said Christian, in a low voice; 'but the moss you seek grows on the shiny pebbles below high tide mark, and you cannot gather it now.　You will see it in great patches like stains upon the sand; the gray plover feed upon it in winter, and the black brent geese swim in to seek it, from the open sea.'

He hardly knew what he was saying, but he spoke out of the fulness of his country knowledge, and the words came.　She looked at him curiously, with a certain admiration.

'You know everything, good Christian,' she cried, smiling; 'all the flowers that grow, and all the fowl of the air, and even the virtues of the herbs of the sea. Will you gather some for me to-morrow, and bring it to me, or shall I come again?'

'I will bring it to you, if you please.'

'We sleep to-night at Cobbler Marvel's.　Bring it there.'

She turned as if about to leave him, but he reached out his hands to detain her.　Surprised at the touch, and even more by his sudden change of manner, she flushed a little, and her smile faded.

'Do not go yet,' he exclaimed.

She raised her eyes to his face, and saw it burning. For the first time during their acquaintance she trembled, and partly lost her self-possession.

'Well, good Christian?' she said, forcing another smile.

'When we parted to-day, I followed you; yes, I suspected something, and I followed to watch—and I saw you meet with *him.*　You met him, and you walked with him upon his father's lands, perchance into his father's house.　Nay, do not deny it, for I saw it with mine own eyes!　I watched you, till I could watch no more, and came away.'

The words came rapidly without premeditation, and before he knew it he found himself arrogating a power over her which he knew she must resent.　But he was desperate.　He scarcely cared what he said, or what

might be the consequences of his words. He felt a
wild desire to come to open quarrel with her, and so
ease his choking thoughts—even if he should afterwards
have to fall upon his knees and crave her pardon.

She looked at him in surprise and pain; when he
ceased, she looked at him still, but kept silence. Then
he went on:

'When I first knew you, I thought you were kind
and good, too good and kind to give me pain; those
first days were the happiest of my life; I worshipped
you—nay, the very ground you trod on, for I thought
you something so far above me. But since he hath
come between us, you have been different. You have not
seemed to care, and when I have warned you, you have
seemed to think better of him than me. Let there
be an end to it all this day. Tell me with your own
lips that you love him, and I will never trouble you
again.'

The words were strange, coming from one who had
never, save in the most far-off hints and looks, revealed
his heart before. She seemed greatly surprised, nor
was her surprise without a certain tinge of indignation.

'What do you mean?' she said. '*Love* him?—
love whom?'

'*Him*—the very name chokes me: the man you
kept tryst with to-day.'

'Mr. Orchardson?'

'Yes. Is it true? Speak!'

'You are asking a foolish question. If I loved any
man—even if it were true, I mean—do you think I
should reply?'

'Then you do not deny it?'

'You have no right to ask me.'

He leaned his face close to hers, and she felt his
breath upon her cheek.

'I have this right, Priscilla—that I am mad with
love for you myself; that my love is torturing me,
killing me; that I would die if I knew for certain that
you loved that man.'

'You know not what you say,' she cried quickly.
'You are a boy, and you talk without thinking. If I
did not think that, I should be angry.'

Before she could say another word, or move away, he was on his knees before her, holding her by both hands.

'For God's sake, pity me.   I love you, Priscilla!'

A warm flush suffused her cheek, but she retained her self-possession. She tried to release herself, but finding herself helpless in his strong hold, struggled no more.   Gazing intently into his upturned face, and meeting his ardent and reckless gaze, she said firmly,

'You must not speak to me like that.   No man has ever done so before, and I will not suffer it.'

'Then you hate me, and you love him?'

'I do neither.'

'Tell me the truth—I can bear it!'

'I will tell you nothing.   Release me, sir!'

But he had gone too far now to retreat.   Having once broken the ice, he persisted in passionate confession.   In a torrent of burning speech, he spoke of his wild adoration.   Despair made him eloquent, and, though usually reticent, he found no lack of words.

'I am so sorry,' she cried, when he paused in agitation.   'I thought you a true friend, and now, it is all different.   Why do you speak of such things?   We are both too young.'

He sprang to his feet, with trembling outstretched arms.

'I am a better man than he,' he said.   'Put us face to face, and let the bravest win: unless—unless you are like all the rest, and choose him who has the most of land and gold.'

'I choose no one.   I shall never marry, and if I did——'

'You cannot always abide alone.   I will work for you, slave and toil for you.   Tell me that I may perchance win you if I prove myself worthy, and I shall be content.   Promise me.'

'I will promise nothing.   It is wicked to vex me so. Let us be friends.   Be my good Christian still, and I will try to forget that you have spoken what it is unmaidenly to hear.'

'You can listen cheerfully enough when *he* speaks.'

'He has never spoken as you speak,' she replied

sorrowfully; 'he is gentle, and would not so distress me.'

'But you know he loves you.'

'Nay, I do not know it.'

'He loves you, Priscilla, and who would not? But bethink yourself—he will never feel for you as I feel, never! You are more to me than the light of the sun, than the breath of my nostrils, than my immortal soul. Without you I cannot live; with you, I should be a happy man—the happiest in all God's world!'

It was not in Priscilla's gentle nature to be unmoved by such an appeal, spoken with so intense and spirit-stirring a sincerity. As she listened on, she sighed deeply, and finally, reaching out her little hand, she said in a voice broken by quiet tears :

'Good Master Christian, how can I answer you ? I am sure you speak out of your heart, and would not willingly give me offence; but what can I say now, further than I have said ? Only this, that I would you cared for some better and worthier woman—one who would make you a fitting wife and helpmate, and love you as you deserve. For myself, what am I but a simple maiden, neither thinking nor dreaming yet of wedlock ? My place is with my father; where he goes, I follow; and soon, perchance, we shall be far from here.'

'You are not going away!' cried Christian, with a sickening sense of dread.

'I cannot tell,' was the reply. 'My father hath done all he can do in these parts, and he hath many calls to other places.'

'And if you go, what will become of me ? Priscilla, I cannot live without you.'

She shook her head sadly.

'We are like two ships in the sea; we have spoken with each other, that is all, and the world is wide. When I am gone, you will be as you were before I came. Bethink you, it is only a few short weeks since first we met. You were well content before I came, and when I go ——'

'No, no!' exclaimed Christian. 'All is changed for me; I myself am changed. I am another man, in another world. I cannot live without you.'

'Nay, we have both work to do,' answered Priscilla ' you in your place, I in mine. I shall always remember you, and this fair country place; and I think, good Christian, you will remember me. Shake hands upon it!'

He took her hand, and, pressing it to his lips, kissed it passionately.

'I will follow you to the world's end!' he cried.

'You will do better,' said the maiden, withdrawing her hand gently. ' You will try to become a better man, for my poor sake.'

'A better man!'

'Yes, Christian. Since you have said so much, may I be frank with you in turn? Even if it could be, even if I willed to marry, I should fear your violent disposition.'

'Priscilla!'

'Nay, hear me out. Your love and your hate are both so mad, so wild. You cherish such strange animosities.'

'Only against one man in all the world.'

'And to hate one man is hate enough,' said Priscilla, firmly. 'Sometimes, when I have listened to you, when I have heard your stormy words, I have been in terror lest some day you should do some dreadful deed.'

'God help me, and so I might if my love were cast away. You can save me from that, you can make me worthy in God's sight.'

'Nay, Christian, only your heart can do so much. You must learn to chasten it; you must learn that all hate is evil; and when you have learned that, you will be able to bear your cross, as our Lord did, as any soul on earth may do.'

She turned away and walked a few paces from him; then pausing, reached out her hand again, with her old smile.

'Let us part now for to-day,' she said. ' To-morrow—— -'

'To-morrow I will bring you the moss for your father's eyes!'

'And so you shall,' she cried; and still smiling, she walked away.

She left him happy. Something peaceful came upon him, out of her gentle looks and words. He watched her with adoring eyes till she passed from sight; then with a low cry, he hid his face in his hands, and sobbed.

Not in sorrow now. The tears came welling up from his overburthened heart; for he felt she pitied him, and knowing her heavenly pity, he did not feel wholly cast away. There was a comfort, too, in the fact that he had spoken; that thenceforth, whatever might happen, she could not fail to understand him. So he looked round on the earth, and on the sea, and up to the peaceful heaven; and he blessed, in the name of all these, the maiden who had come to make them clearer, to put new light and colour into their ever-changeful hues, as well as into the tangled thread of life.

When the sun had set, he wandered home, and entering the house found his mother sitting alone in the dark room.

'Where is Kate?' she asked. 'I have called for her, but she does not come.'

Christian called his sister's name aloud, and then, as she did not answer, he went to seek her. He passed from room to room, but could not find her. This seemed strange, for Kate was a home-loving girl, and seldom absent from the house. He returned to his mother, bearing a light with him for the room.

'I cannot find her,' he said. 'Belike she has gone on some errand up to the village, and will soon return.'

The dame looked pale and astonished; after a pause she said:

'When did you see her last, my son?'

'Not since before noontide. I left her then in the house.'

'She went forth soon after thyself, promising to be back within an hour. Have you searched in her room?'

'Yes, mother.'

'Then go forth and look for her. 'Tis time she was come home.'

Accustomed by habit to obey his mother's slightest wish, Christian did not hesitate a moment, but ran forth; searched all the outbuildings, looked up and down the farm-fields; shouted his sister's name aloud without eliciting any reply. It was now quite dark, and he began to be seriously alarmed; for Kate, as we have said, was home-loving, and little likely to gad about after nightfall. Returning into the house, he told his mother the state of affairs, and was at once bidden to go up to the village and make inquiries. This he did, but to little avail. Kate was nowhere in the village.

Things now looked ominous. No one had seen the girl since early in the afternoon; and the person who had met her last, an old labourer, had seen her hastening homeward, by the path which wound along the side of the four-acre mere. Could any accident have happened to the girl? When the moon rose, Christian stood by the mere side, and looked at the black palpitating water with a fearful heart. Could his poor sister be lying *there?*

As he gazed and gazed, a vision rose before him of the girl's pale face, as he had often seen it lately. He had been too much absorbed in his own new dreams to take much heed of it at the time; but he remembered now, with a twinge of pain, how changed she had been Then came across his brain the memory of her encounter that night with Richard Orchardson. Was it possible that they had encountered at other times, or that Orchardson was in any way, however remotely, connected with the fact of her disappearance? No, he could scarcely believe it. He would not wrong his sister so much as even to entertain the suspicion for a moment. She had sworn her oath upon the Book, and she could never have broken it so desperately.

That night, Kate Christianson did not return home; nor the next, nor the next again. Though Christian searched high and low, he could gain no clue to the cause of her disappearance. On the third day they dragged the four-acre mere, but found nothing there.

Pale and terrible in grief, the mother kept her eyes on her Bible, as if the end of the search was to be found within it.

But Kate did not come, and a shadow worse than death remained in the lonely house.

CHAPTER XII.

KATE CHRISTIANSON'S TROUBLE.

THE stream of our narrative now turns aside, to follow Kate Christianson. On parting from Richard Orchardson, she moved rapidly away through the surrounding shrubberies, following a footpath that she knew well, and which led her to the loneliest part of Squire Orchardson's demesne. As she went she kept up a low moaning, like one in pain, and looked neither to right nor left; indeed, she seemed, for the time being, deaf and blind to the objects around her. At last she paused, in the shadow of a small plantation, not far from the highway, and sitting down upon a bank, hid her face in her hands and rocked herself to and fro.

She waited thus for hours, as if half stupefied. The place was solitary, and no one beheld her, or heard the low moaning which still came from her mouth. The setting sun touched her with a finger of crimson fire, but she did not see or feel it. Not till it was nearly dark did she rise to her feet and move away.

Her mind seemed now made up. She returned to the highway; concealing her face with her cloak, and shrinking from every form she met, she hastened homeward; passed rapidly through the village, and took the lane leading down to the waste mere. That some desperate purpose animated her was evident from her gestures; for ever and anon she threw her arms in the air, and uttered a cry to God.

Quitting the lane, she ran across a water-meadow, and came upon the side of the mere. The sun had just disappeared, but a faint reflected light still hung over the scene, and in that light the dark water looked more than ever sombre and forbidding. She looked at the black shallows, she looked at the sad chill sky. Shuddering, she shrank back, and began to sob. The hot tears came, and saved her from self-murder. No, she could not die—not at least that way.

'O God!' she cried. 'What shall I do? what shall I do?'

Then, in her despair and fear, she thought she would return home. She was not yet missed, and it was not too late to return and take her place in the house. And even if the worst came to the worst, she would fall upon her knees, tell the truth—part of it, not all—no, no, not all—and perhaps they might forgive her. Even if they killed her, what then? She wished to die, though she lacked the courage to go flying up and falling at God's feet, a suicide.

Even as she turned her face towards the farm, something stirred within her, like the quickening of another life within her own. A new horror passed through her. Then, as if she had been pursued, and flying in mortal terror, she fled away—not homeward, but across the darkened fields.

A thick white vapour was rising from the cold earth; she passed through it like a ghost, from meadow to meadow, from field to field, instinctively familiar with every step of the way, though sight was useless to guide her. Before long, she was out upon the open road, and walking rapidly away from her native village.

Her mind was now made up. She would leave her home, and seek shelter as far away from pursuit as possible; for she knew now that if she lingered even a single day, her shame would in all probability be discovered. With a sickening horror in her heart, and her brain stupefied with a nameless dread, she fled on and on.

Poor Kate was country-bred, and in youth had learned the free use of her limbs in all manner of rustic exercise; so although her mind was crushed down and darkened, her body still retained a certain strength. She walked on with little or no consciousness of fatigue until two hours before midnight; by that time she had left her home ten long miles behind her. She found herself on a solitary highway, crossing level flats, with a clear view of the open moonlit sea.

By this time she had partially recovered her self-possession, and with the instinct of a hunted thing, when the first flash of fear has passed, began to plan her movements with a certain cunning. Not many miles away, she knew, was a small seaport town, from which ships sometimes sailed to distant parts—even as far as London, she had heard. She would reach the town and go on shipboard, first sending a message to those at home and entreating their forgiveness. After that, she cared not what became of her. She would creep to some lonely corner of the world, and bury herself past all search, all remembrance.

On the road before her she saw lights burning, and pressing on, she found that they came from a little roadside inn. The door was closed, and there seemed no company indoors; but she went up and knocked timidly.

Some chains were loosened and a bolt drawn; a shock-haired head looked out upon her, that of a man holding a rushlight. He glared at her with true country suspicion.

'Who be there?' he growled. 'A woman! What d'ye want at this hour o' night?'

'How far away, good man, to Norton-by-the-Sea?'

The man looked at her suspiciously for a few moments before he replied.

'To Norton? Why, five mile and more. Be you going there to-night?'

'Yes.'

Reassured by her obvious timidity of manner, the man threw open the door, and came out upon the threshold.

'Let me have a look at thee,' he cried, holding the light to her face. 'Where do you come from, that call so late? You be a stranger, mistress?'

'Yes, that I be! Good-night, and thank you kindly.'

'Stop!' cried the man. 'If you be a stranger, and come o' decent folk, you can ha' a bed here for payment, a clean bed and supper too, if you will. 'Tis time all honest folk should be a-bed, and there bo bad chaps about these roads.'

But Kate would not rest yet. She thanked the man, and turned away.

'Good-night,' she said again.

I

'Good-night,' growled the man, and closed the door upon her.

She walked on for another hour; then she saw, far away before her, the lights of the town she sought. The sight gave her new strength, and she hastened towards it.

By midnight, she was on the skirts of the town. All was very still; no one stirring. She went on, looking for some place where she might knock for shelter. As she did so, she felt the same sickening and terrifying sensation that she had felt by the mere side. In a moment she became dizzy, tottered to a doorstep, and without a sound, fainted away.

When Kate Christianson opened her eyes she found herself in a strange room lying upon a truckle bed. She started up with a cry, and gazed with a terrified look around her.

The next moment she sank back moaning upon the bed. She was alone; the room, a wretched garret, was strange to her; it was evidently night, for a guttering rushlight burnt dimly on the table, and all the house was hushed.

What had happened? She could not tell, but something terrible must have taken place, for her brain was throbbing, her lips and eyes burning feverishly, and her hand, which looked so white and thin, was clammy and cold, as if with the chilly touch of death.

For a time she lay with her burning eyelids closed, and her poor weary over-wrought brain trying to recall the past; then some movement attracted her attention, she opened her eyes and looked around again. This time she saw that she was not alone. On a wicker arm-chair beside a smouldering fire, a woman was seated.

She had evidently been sleeping, but her face was now turned somewhat anxiously towards the bed. Their eyes met; she came over and took the girl's wasted hand kindly in her own.

'Where am I?' said Kate, faintly; then overcome by her own weakness, she burst into tears.

It was some time before she could calm herself

again; but while she sobbed the woman patted her hand, and did her best to soothe her again to sleep.

But Kate was too excited to rest; question after question came eagerly from her feverish lips, until at length she knew all. Yes, thus she learned that two days before the master of the garret had lifted her senseless form from the ground, had borne her to his room, and committed her to the care of his wife; that a few hours after a child had been born prematurely, and that since that hour the mother, stricken with fever, had lain almost at the point of death.

'The child, the child?' gasped the agonised girl. The woman, mistaking her agonised cry, said softly,

'Don't grieve, poor wench: the poor little ba'rn is dead.'

For one moment the girl's parched, feverish lips opened to breathe a word of thankfulness to God; then, overcome by her own misery, she uttered a heart-breaking cry, and burst again into weary sobs and tears.

Kate learned little more that night, for the woman, alarmed at her excessive grief, refused to speak again; she returned to her seat by the fire, and left Kate to lie and think over all that had taken place. What a night she passed! As every weary hour dragged by, the fever which had seized her seemed to increase.

In the morning, the woman, going to the bedside, found that the fever had reached its height, and the poor patient was raving in wild delirium.

And for several days more Kate Christianson was as one gone mad, she raved in the height of fever; then her feverishness abated, and her senses returned to her. Her child had been buried, and the people, grown weary of the mystery, were anxiously inquiring who the unfortunate mother might be.

'What is your name, wench? tell me, and I'll write to your friends,' asked the woman for the twentieth time one day.

'I have no friends,' said Kate wearily. 'I want to die!'

Then she thought of her mother, of her brother, of the man who had brought all this sorrow upon her, and prayed again to die. But her prayers were vain,—God had deserted her; she still lived, and her **troubles** grew.

What could she do ? To stay there was impossible, to return to her mother was impossible: she resolved to seek the father of her child, and cast herself on his protection. To do this, she must escape alone; to reveal her plans would be to reveal her identity, to bring all her terrible secret to light, and call down shame and sorrow upon those she loved.

She would tell no one of her wild desire; she would creep from the house at dead of night, and fade like an evil shadow from the place. Daylight died, and night came on: the invalid seemed better and inclined for sleep, and the poor woman who had attended her so kindly retired to get that rest of which she was herself in need.

'You shall write to my friends in the morning,' Kate had said. 'Prithee let me pass this night in peace!'

'In peace ; nay, in this world there is no peace for me!' she murmured a few hours later, as she rose from her sick-bed and tremblingly drew on her clothes.

It was several hours past midnight; every sound was hushed, all within the house were sleeping peacefully, as the sick girl, dragging her trembling limbs along the floor, descended the stairs and passed quietly from the house.

There was a bolt to the door; with trembling hands she slid it back, and then, at the sound, stood shivering and listened. No one stirred. She opened the door stealthily, slipt out, and drew it to behind her. She stood in the empty street of the sleeping town, hesitating, bewildered, not knowing what to do.

It was the dark hour that precedes the dawn, but the silvern moonlight was lingering in placid places of the heavens. The air was very cold, for during the night there had been rain, and some was still falling in a thin imperceptible mist.

Kate looked wildly round her. The cool air came sweetly upon her fevered brow, the damp dew fell upon her loosened hair. All seemed so still, so peaceful.

As she paused in hesitation, all her past life came upon her as in a dream. Her eyes filled with tears. With trembling feet, she turned her face towards home.

Yes, she would go back. In the place where she had been hidden no one knew her, no one could follow. If she hastened, she might reach her native village before the world was well astir. And even if the news of her shame should follow her, what then? She would lie down and die in the old place, and they would place her in the little green churchyard, by her poor father's side.

In the light of a golden summer morning, pleasant and peaceful after a night of rain, Priscilla Sefton rose, and looked out of the little attic window of the cottage at Brightlinghead. The garden lay beneath, newly baptised in morning dew; and across green slopes beyond, sparkled the innumerable laughter of the sea. She opened the casement; the scent of flowers crept sweetly in. She listened; and heard birds singing, as if it were the world's first day.

Coming down into the little parlour, she found her father already up, and awaiting her. They knelt down in loving prayer together, as their custom was, and then began their simple morning meal. After breakfast, Priscilla walked out into the garden, leaving the blind man seated in his chair, in those holy meditations which were necessary to him as the very breath of life.

As she moved in the sunshine, plucking a flower here and there, the garden gate opened, and Richard Orchardson appeared. He was booted and spurred, and carried in his hand a nosegay and a basket of choice fruit from the manor garden.

'I am an early visitor,' he said smiling. 'My father hath sent me over with these nectarines for Mr. Sefton, and some rare flowers for yourself. I was bidden also to ask you to become our guests for a few days up at the Willows.'

'My father is within,' returned Priscilla with a certain coldness. 'Will you come and speak to him?'

'Presently,' said Richard, lingering by her side. 'What a fair morning!'

' Yes.'

Her manner seemed unusually thoughtful and reserved, and the young man at once noticed the change.
Instead of looking him in the face as was her wont, she
kept her gaze averted, and moved slowly towards the
cottage.

' Do not go in yet,' said Richard quickly. ' I wish
to speak to you.'

Without speaking, she turned, and for the first time
looked him in the face. She saw something there
which caused a shadow to fall upon her own.

' My father is waiting for me,' she said, embarrassed,
but not agitated, as she had been when she saw the
same expression in the face of Christian Christianson.

' Pray listen a moment,' persisted Richard. ' I have
ridden over on purpose to see you. I must speak to
you ; alone.'

Seeing now that it was inevitable, she paused, but
the shadow remained upon her.

' Dear Priscilla—nay, suffer me to call you so—when
you know what hath brought me, perchance you will
pity me ; without your pity, surely I am a lost man.
Since you came hither to Brightlinghead, there hath
been but one thought in my soul—how I might make
myself worthy in your eyes. I have spoken with my
father, and he approves what I am about to say to you.
Priscilla, will you become my wife ? '

Even now, her colour did not change, though she
looked nervously upon the ground. Encouraged by her
silence, which he misconstrued, he took her hand, and
proceeded in a strain of greater confidence and gallantry.

' Sweetheart, I am sure you could not have miscon-
ceived me. The face is a tell-tale, and sure mine hath
betrayed me from the first. Nay, did I not hint the
truth before, though my sweet was too roguish to understand ! Let me speak to your father straight, and tell
him that I have won your heart.'

' Nay,' returned Priscilla, ' for it is not true.'

Richard still kept her hand.

' You will not refuse me, Priscilla. I am the squire's
son, and though I say it, shall be a rich man. I know
you are poor in the world's goods' (here he watched

her keenly, to see the effect of his words), 'but in you I shall have a treasure far surpassing gold. And you shall be a great lady! There shall ever be maids at your elbow, horses for you to ride, a grand house for great company, and troops of gentle friends.'

'Such things are not for me,' said Priscilla simply. 'Prithee speak of it no more.'

'Perchance you will chide me because I am so bold—but it is your heavenly beauty that leads me on. Sweetheart, I love you!—ay, more than all the world!'

As he spoke, Priscilla started and uttered a half-terrified cry. Surprised, he turned and followed the direction of her eyes. At the same moment he heard a low voice, the sound of which chilled the blood in his veins.

'Richard!'

On the garden-path before them stood a woman, wild-eyed, ghastly pale, woe-begone, her raiment soaked with the night's rain, her hair falling loose upon her shoulders. As she uttered his name, wild tears ran down her cheeks, and she fell moaning upon her knees, and stretching out her arms to him in wild entreaty.

CHAPTER XIIL

KATE COMES HOME.

THE young couple stood petrified, but the woman, after uttering that terrible cry, fell prostrate upon the ground.

Priscilla rushed forward, raised her gently, gave one look into the pale, sorrow-stricken face, and then turned to Richard Orchardson.

'Who is she?' she asked; 'she named your name, and seemed to know you. And I—I seem to have seen her face before. You know her, friend?'

He was standing upon the spot where Priscilla had stood two minutes before, but he had almost turned his back upon the two girls; he stood so, as he answered Priscilla's question.

'Yes, I know her well,' he said; 'we have known each other since we were children. Her name is Kate Christianson; she is a daughter of Dame Christianson of the Fen Farm.'

'Kate Christianson!—his sister Kate—ah, I remember.'

Richard Orchardson turned now—turned and looked at Priscilla with quite a new light in his eyes, and the terror which a few moments before had filled his heart was replaced by a feeling of bitter irritation. The tone in which Priscilla had uttered those few words had told him something. She had been deaf to his proposal because, foorsooth, her heart had been turned towards another man, and that man was his bitterest foe!

Priscilla, meanwhile, for the time unconscious of the presence of her would-be lover, was still bending over the form of the unconscious girl, chafing her hands, smoothing back her hair, and allowing the sun to shine upon her face.

Then, as there were still no signs of returning consciousness, she turned to Richard again.

'Will you help me to bear her into the house?' she said. 'I thank the Lord who did direct her footsteps to our door.'

For a time the man remained silent, utterly at a loss what to say or do. He was like one tossed hither and thither on conflicting tides, each one of which seemed likely to engulf him. Of the strange turn of events which had brought Kate Christianson to her present pitiable state he knew almost nothing, neither could he guess the motive which had led the girl to Priscilla Sefton's door. But of this he felt certain, that should she be carried into the house, and there recover her consciousness, his cause with Priscilla would be lost. What to do? how to avoid the catastrophe? His heart sickened within him, and he inwardly prayed that every breath which the unconscious woman drew might be her last.

But Priscilla awaiting his answer, presently he spoke.

'Sweetheart,' he said, 'your kind disposition doth you wrong. Such women as that are best outside your door. Take my advice, send her to the Fen Farm, and when she passeth beyond the sunshine of this spot think of her no more.'

'Why do you speak so ?' asked Priscilla.

'Because I know 'tis sacrilege for one roof to cover you two.'

'Sacrilege! nay, then, I tell you 'tis my duty to attend to such sore trouble as this—a Christian's help is given where it is needed; the prosperous and the happy do not call us, but we listen for the voices of those in distress. What saith the Lord ?—"Come unto me, all ye that are weary and heavy-laden, and I will give you rest." Therefore, good Master Richard, I prithee call my father, who will give me what help I need!'

But Orchardson did not seem inclined to do that.

'Forgive me, Priscilla,' he said; 'I was wrong and you have put me right. You will always keep me right, sweetheart, and I would do anything to please you!'

So saying, he lifted the unconscious Kate in his arms and carried her into the house; when he had placed her upon the bed he turned again to Priscilla.

'Sweetheart,' he said, softly, 'can I do more for thee ? In sooth, though I have no cause to love the name of Christianson, I feel grieved for the poor wench, and would gladly serve her. 'Tis a sad story, now I remember. The maiden disappeared from her home several days ago, and all at the Fen Farm believe her dead.'

Priscilla did not reply; she was bending over the sick girl, trying to find some glimmer of returning consciousness; but none came. She lay like one stone dead.

Priscilla raised her head.

'You have your horse at the gate, good friend ?'

'Yes.'

'Then you will gallop away with two letters from me—one for the doctor, one for Christian Christianson?'

The young squire's face reddened; he was about to give a hasty refusal, when he suddenly checked himself, and said,

' Whatsoever *you* wish, I will do.'

Priscilla immediately proceeded to scribble off two notes.   The one to Christian ran as follows :—

' MY DEAR FRIEND,—Your sister lieth under this roof, grievously sick.   An hour ago, as I stood at the gate giving good morning to young Squire Orchardson, a weary woman staggered up and fell at my feet.   The young squire, recognising her sooner than I, told me her name; he carried her into the house for me, and is now waiting to be the bearer of two letters, one to the doctor, and this one to yourself.   You will come, good friend, as soon as you receive this; and in the meantime I shall do all in my power for the poor sick maid.

' Your faithful friend,
' PRISCILLA SEFTON.'

Priscilla, while sealing this letter, felt that she had phrased it well.   The wish had of late become strong within her to be the peacemaker between these two men, for to her gentle nature the hatred which they bore to one another was terrible beyond endurance. So in despatching this missive Priscilla thought that by judiciously mentioning the service of young Orchardson, she would at least gain for him his enemy's thanks.

As Orchardson took the lines, he was gratified at receiving a sweet word of thanks from Priscilla, and an earnestly expressed hope that she would soon see him again.

' For of course,' she added, quickly, suddenly remembering their conversation of a few hours before, ' you will be curious to hear how the poor maid goeth on.'

' I shall be very curious,' returned Orchardson, as bending over her hands he pressed them affectionately, then took his leave.

He delivered the doctor's note himself—the other he gave to a boy; for much as he wished to serve Priscilla, he could not bring himself to ride up as a messenger to the Fen Farm.

Having done his work he rode leisurely homewards.

He was in anything but a comfortable frame of mind, though he had decided what must be his own course of action. So far, he had been fortunate, the girl had remained senseless; but sooner or later she must recover, and then, perhaps, Priscilla might learn all. At first he had thought of communicating with Kate, and trying to ensure her silence; but now he had decided upon a better plan. She had no witnesses; if she accused he could deny; nay, more, he could put this forth as another evidence of the wish of the Christiansons to disgrace him and drag him down.

On reaching home he found his father about to sally forth; at sight of his son's face the old man turned and re-entered the house.

'Well, lad?' he questioned, laying his hand affectionately on Richard's shoulder, 'how sped thy wooing?'

'I am baulked again by a Christianson.'

'Curse them,—curse the whole breed!'

'So say I, father; Priscilla was gentle as a lamb until his runaway sister staggered up and fell at her feet. Then her heart melted, and she forgot me; bade me help the girl into her house, and then despatched a message for her brother. My suit will never thrive with Priscilla till the Christiansons are away.'

For three days young Orchardson nursed his wrath against the Christiansons, but mostly against Kate; and during the whole of that time he was in a state of terror as to how matters would end between Priscilla and himself. On his own course of action he had, as we have said, fully decided, but for a time he shrank from the idea of meeting the girl, and commencing the false tales which he knew he should have to tell.

But gradually he grew accustomed to the thought of them, and on the evening of the fourth day he had conquered himself sufficiently to walk down to the cottage at Brightlinghead, ostensibly with the intention of inquiring how the poor outcast fared, but really to discover how much of her sad story had been told to Priscilla.

It was long past sunset, the evening prayer-meeting at the cottage was over, the small congregation had dispersed, and Priscilla herself, a light shawl thrown over her head, was walking up and down the road in the fast-gathering twilight.

She was much paler and more pensive-looking than usual, but when her eyes fell upon the young man her face brightened with a strange smile.

He saw at once that he was safe. ' Good Mr. Richard, you are welcome,' she said, ' I was thinking of thee !'

The young man's heart grew light. He kissed the hand which she gave him, then held forth a posy of his father's choicest flowers.

' I have come to inquire for your patient,' he said quietly, ' and my father hath sent these flowers to cheer thee in the sick-room.'

' Your father is too good. When you return, thank him for me.'

And she took the flowers, and held them to her sweet face.

For the moment he felt impelled to give an affection-ate reply, but remembering that to be too precipitate might mean the loss of all, he contented himself with watching Priscilla's beautiful pale face as it bent above the nosegay to inhale the posy's fragrant breath.

' They are very sweet,' said Priscilla, softly, ' but in-deed I have no sick-room to put them into now. Our poor little maid hath gone away.'

' Gone away ? ' echoed Orchardson, and for a moment there arose within him a wild hope that Kate Christian-son might be dead.

But Priscilla quietly replied,

' Yes, so soon as she was strong enough to move her brother took her home.'

After that they both remained silent. Orchardson longed yet dreaded to hear more, and Priscilla knew not what to say. Her scheme of becoming peacemaker between these two strange men had completely fallen through. But since she could not make peace, she would try not to create a stronger hatred. She would never mention to Orchardson how Christian, on hearing that the man had dared to touch his sister even in kindness, had shown ungovernable wrath, and had in his frenzy even accused Priscilla of wishing to humiliate him before his foe.

He had succeeded in arousing the gentle maiden's wrath at last. But the anguish which had followed her wrath told her only too plainly the state of her heart

'I will go away,' she had said to herself. 'We have no longer any mission here. It requires a stronger will than mine to lead these men from the errors into which they are falling. God is far-seeing, and He may choose some other means of bringing them right at last.'

'Will you come in?' asked the girl, quietly; but Orchardson shook his head.

'Not to-night, Priscilla. If I may, I will come again. Good-night, and may God bless you!'

He uttered the benediction with strange earnestness, then he bent again and kissed her hands. For that night at least he spoke no word of love, but walked away with a strange look of relief, like one reprieved from death.

CHAPTER XIV.

THE WIDOW'S CUP IS FULL.

RICHARD ORCHARDSON might breathe in peace. Kate Christianson, in recovering from her swoon, said nothing to incriminate him or herself, but answered all questions with vague words and moans. Then Christian Christianson had indeed taken his poor sister home, and the shock of the removal had again overpowered her, and for many hours she lay like one stricken unto death.

The mother and brother watched her; each looking, wondering, but saying nothing. Not even to each other in the silence of the night had they spoken of the terrible fear which was heavy upon the hearts of both.

For a time they thought that the girl would die, and the mother in her anguish and suspicion guessed at times that it might be better so; but God willed it otherwise; Kate gradually recovered—arose from bed, the mere ghost of what she once had been, and again resumed her place in the house. This was a hard time for Kate, for now that her delirium had passed away, Dame Christianson, unable longer to restrain her anxiety, began to question her daughter as to the past.

But Kate had the tenacity and reticence of some otherwise feeble natures. She would say nothing. She gazed into her mother's stern, cold face with pitiful pleading, and when pressed closely, fell into violent paroxysms, and in her anguish wildly prayed that she might die.

So it came to pass one evening that Dame Christianson, sitting by the fire with the old Bible upon her knee, looked at the trembling, cowering figure before her, and resolutely steeled her heart.

'Thou wilt not speak, thou wilt tell me naught,' she said, 'but for all that I fear that thou art not fit to share this roof with righteous folk. If it cometh to pass that thou hast brought shame upon our name, I will turn thee like a dog from our door!'

'Mother, mother!' cried the trembling girl.

But the stern old woman held up her hands.

'Call me not mother till I hear thy tale. Perchance thy sin is not so great as I deem it, but since thou triest to break my heart, do not name my name. Here in thy father's house is food and shelter, but while thou hidest aught from me, thou art no child of mine!'

So Kate sobbed and cried, and rocked herself in her agony of grief; the mother read the Bible, looking up now and again to watch the tear-stained face of her daughter—but neither spoke.

When Christian came in from his work in the fields, she quietly did what work was required of her, then, like a stricken hound, she crept up to her room. As she was leaving the chamber for the night, Christian called her back.

'Good-night. Katie,' he said.

The sound of the old childish name, spoken so fondly by her stern brother, was too much for poor Kate to bear. Pausing, she held up her sunken cheek for her brother's kiss, then, with one last look into her mother's stern face, she crept upstairs, and having gained her room sank on the floor in passionate tears.

When she was gone and the door was closed, the mother and son spake no word. Christian, whose heart had melted for a moment at sight of his sister's silent pain, had far different thoughts to occupy his brain. Only two hours before he had met Priscilla on the sands, and received her last farewell.

Yes, Priscilla was gone from Brightlinghead; she had come like a spirit of light and love, to bring gladness to the hearts of many, but now the Divine Hand which ruled her life pointed onwards, and again she followed her blind father forth into the wilderness of the world.

Well, it was some comfort to Christian that she had wished to say ' good-bye '—that she had given him a few words of counsel, and expressed a hope that they might some day meet again.

' We have both our work to do,' she said, sweetly, ' you as well as I.   God give you strength to do it manfully and well, dear Christian.'

' Priscilla ! ' he cried, wildly, ' before you go, hearken again ! '

But Priscilla put up her hand.

' Nay, we have both said o'ermuch already.   Good-bye, and may God bless you, dear friend.'

' God's blessing comes to me through you only; when you are gone it will be to me as if I had been plunged into the darkest depths of hell ! '

' Alas ! say not so.'

' But I say so, in good sooth.   Give me some hope, Priscilla !   Leave me not to waste and die.   With your help, I might become a better man.'

The girl shook her head, sadly.

' I have tried,' she murmured, faintly; ' and I have failed.   My place is with my father, and even if I were free, I should fear your disposition.   Good-bye, dear Christian !   Perchance we may meet again some day, soon, and till then, remember me ! '

With such words upon her lips, and a calm, placid smile upon her face, she had faded from his sight.

The memory of that interview was ever in his mind, the light of that sweet smile ever before his eyes, making the world seem brighter to him, and softening his heart to all mankind.

To-night, particularly, Priscilla's influence was strong

upon him, as he sat looking at his mother's, stern, cold face, and thinking of his heart-broken sister.

'Perchance she is too hard, he thought; 'perchance we are both too hard. Poor Kate! if she hath sinned, she suffers sorely.'

A little later, when he went upstairs, he looked into his sister's room. Kate's passionate pain had passed away; pale and exhausted she sat now upon the bedside.

'Kate, my lass,' said Christian, going up to her, and lifting one of her wasted hands, 'the mother's heart is sore because she loveth you—remember that; maybe, the soreness will pass away, and she'll come right again. She hath had overmuch trouble, Kate, and it makes her hard sometimes; but she loves you; nay, we all love you.'

The girl said nothing; with the docility and timidity of a poor dumb animal, she pressed her cold, trembling lips to her brother's hand, and sank back again upon the bed.

But when he was gone, and she was alone again, alone with her load of sorrow, which was surely breaking her heart, she moaned aloud in anguish :—

'If he knew, if he only knew! would he not curse me as my mother would curse me? would he not drive me forth as she would drive me forth? Yea, even although it sent me to my death. What shall I do? Dear God, what shall I do? I cannot live like this, I cannot go out into the world. If only I could die!'

She wiped away her tears, tried to calm her ever beating heart, and sat down to think. What *could* she do? Nothing, nothing! Confess to her mother that she had grievously sinned, and that Richard Orchardson, the mortal enemy of their house, had won her love, and afterwards brought her to shame? Nay, for then with a mother's curse she would be driven forth to become a hopeless outcast on the pitiless street.

Suddenly, in the midst of her blackest despair, came a ray of hope, a ray so bright that for the moment the dead light in the girl's eye kindled into something of its old brightness. She thought of Priscilla Sefton, the blind missionary's daughter; she was known to be good and kind, she must have guessed part of the pitiful story,—she should learn the rest, and perhaps her good counsel might bring the poor sufferer some peace. Yes, Kate resolved to seek Priscilla on the morrow; and with that thought to comfort her, she sank to rest, little dreaming what new trials the morrow was to bring forth.

After a troubled night, Kate Christianson arose, weary and unrefreshed. Though it was still early, yet the grey light of dawn was stealing into the house. Christian was already afield, but the dame was still in her room. Dressing herself with somewhat more than ordinary care, Kate crept downstairs, and set herself to perform her few household duties. Having finished these, she hastily drew on her bonnet and shawl and left the house.

She was obliged to go thus early, for in five minutes more her mother would be down, and would be sure to ply her with a series of questions as to her going forth. But now that she was free and fairly on her road her heart turned sick within her. 'Twas such a sorry errand! Well, it was part of her punishment, and as such it must be bravely borne.

Nevertheless she lingered on her road, choosing the quiet, unfrequented paths, and withdrawing aside whenever a human soul came by, so that when she arrived at Brightlinghead the day was well broken. What was Kate's surprise, however, to find the cottage door closed, the blinds all drawn, and no sign of life about it anywhere!

She walked resolutely up to the door and knocked. No answer. She knocked again: the sound of her knuckles on the door reverberated through the house, but brought no sign of life. At this moment an old coastguardsman happened to pass by.

'What be you wanting there, mistress?' he asked gruffly; and Kate meekly replied,

'I came to seek the preacher's daughter.'

'Mistress Sefton? She be gone away.'

'Gone!'

'Ay; travelled away with her father. They are wanderers always, it seems, and never bide in one place long.'

'Then they are not coming back?'

'Nay; leastways not for many a day!'

Trembling, and more sick at heart than ever, Kate moved from the door, and began to retrace her steps along the road.

What to do now? There was only one plan left, and that was to seek out Richard Orchardson. That he had ceased to care for her, Kate knew only too well; her only hope was that her sorry state might at least arouse his pity. But how to find him, how to speak with him? She might wait all day and never see him, and she dared not go to the Willows. Dared not?— nay but she would! Trouble had made her desperate. If she sent to him he would avoid her—of that she felt sure; the only way was to bring him right before her face. Full of this new determination, yet shrinking fearfully from the task she had to perform, Kate drew her shawl more tightly about her shoulders, and looked around with a shiver. The day was well advanced, but it was cold and dark and sunless. She walked on and on till she was some distance from the Willows, but she knew there was life there, for she could see the smoke issuing from the chimneys, and she could hear the echoing bark of the mastiffs which were always chained in the yard. With flushed cheek and wildly palpitating heart, Kate walked on, never once pausing to think until she came to the lodge gate.

Then good fortune attended her; for she met one of the grooms coming out of the gate.

'Will you tell me,' she asked, in a low trembling voice, 'if Master Richard is at home?'

'Master Richard? Nay!'

'Where is he?'

'Don't 'ee know he's gone away to London?'

'Gone away!'

'Ay, went away a week ago, and he bean't likely to be back here again till winter-tide.'

The man passed on, and left Kate standing cold, trembling, and speechless.

As Kate Christianson returned towards the Fen Farm faint and despairing,—for she felt now that

Richard had abandoned her for ever, and that there was no hope for her in this world,—she saw before her the figure of a man.

He was walking slowly towards the farm, on the road which led to the sea; and though he was too far from her to be distinctly recognised, she knew that he was a stranger. Now and then he paused and looked around him, with the perplexed air of one to whom the surrounding scene was unfamiliar.

Not wishing to come face to face with any person, she held back upon the road, suffering him to pass on out of sight. Listlessly and sadly she wandered down to the mere side, and looked at the dark water wearily, as she had looked upon it that black night before her child was born. Very still and peaceful it looked, in the grey light of the windless, sunless day. Over the shore where she stood several sea-gulls were flying and uttering shrill cries. She stood listening in a dream.

Presently she turned from the water side and walked towards the farm. As she did so, she saw approaching her, with rapid strides, the same man she had previously seen before her on the road.

It was impossible to avoid him now; so she pushed on past him, averting her face as she came near.

As she came up, he looked at her keenly, and made a sign of recognition; but she noted nothing of this, and was passing rapidly by, when his voice arrested her:

'Stop, mistress!'

She turned trembling, and looked at him. He was a middle-aged countrified fellow, dressed like a small farmer, in coat and knee-breeches; and his feet and legs were dirty, as if with a long tramp on the highway.

'Don't 'ee know me, mistress?' he continued, with a forbidding smile. 'Well, some folk ha' short memories. But I know *thee*, and by the same token I ha' found thee. My name's Joe Prittlewell, and I come fro' Harringford, where thy poor ba'rn was born.'

Poor Kate uttered a terrified cry, and clutched him by the arm.

'O speak low! speak low! It they should hear!'

'Nay,' said the man sternly, 'it be too late to speak

low now, for the mischief's out. I ha' spoken wi' thy
mother and wi' thy brother, up yonder at the farm.'

'You have not told them ! No, no ! '

'Bide a bit, and listen. When you did slip away
from my dame's care, with ne'er so much as a " Thank
you, dame," or a parting gift, we was sore puzzled, and
angry enou' at thy ingratitude ; for there was all thy
keep to pay for, and the lying-in, and the buryin' beside,
for the parish would not help us a groat. " Never
mind, dame," says I : " I'll soon find the wench's
friends, an' I had only a bit of a clue." Well, searching
in thy chamber, I finds a ring, a leetle gold keepsake
ring, and inside that ring was printed thy mother's name.
So we worked it out together, my dame and I ; and I
vowed the first free day I had to come along and speak
wi' thy folk ; and so I come.'

Dazed and terrified beyond measure, Kate looked at
the man, scarcely hearing the words that he spoke.
Her secret was out then, once and for ever ; and by
that time, perchance, her mother's door was already
closed against her.

'Did you say you had spoken with my mother ? '
she cried at last.

'Ay, marry ; and ha' given her back her gold ring.'

'And you told her—nay, nay, you did not tell her—
you would not be so cruel—you——'

'I told the dame o' thy lying-in at our house, and
of the buryin', and that we were poor folk, and could
not stand to lose thy keep and thy lodging. Then thy
good brother gave me four silver crowns, and pushed
me fro' the door. " Keep this all to thyself," says he,
" and one day soon I'll ride o'er and talk wi' the dame
at home." " Nay, never fear," says I, " I can keep my
mouth shut ; " and I comed away.'

Kate stood moaning and wringing her hands ; then,
with a sudden impulse, she turned, and began walking
rapidly away from the farm.

The man kept at her side.

'Don't 'ee take on so, my poor wench,' he said
gruffly. 'Thou'rt not the first nor the last as has made
a fool o' thysen' wi' no help fro' parson ; bless 'ee, they
thinks no more o' that in *our* good town than they

does up in Lunnon. Thy folk will forgive thee, never fear!'

'Never, never!' cried Kate.

'Who's thy ba'rn's feyther, tell me that! Won't he stand by thee? He will, if it be true, as I ha' heerd, he be a gentleman born.'

Kate started, with a wild glance at the man.

'Who told thee he was a gentleman?' she asked.

'No man, mistress; but my good dame did gather it fro' thy wild talk, when thou wast lying-in. Nay, I can tell thee thy gallant's name—'twas "Richard," "Richard," ever on thy tongue; and there were another name, too, a long name, beginning with a round "O"; and I knows who owns it, though I be a stranger hereabout.'

As the man spoke, Kate heard footsteps behind her, and turning quickly, she saw her brother running rapidly. Directly her eyes fell upon his face she saw that he knew, or guessed, everything. His eyes looked terrible, and his teeth were set together.

As he came up panting, she shrank back, and lifted up her hands, as if expecting a blow.

'Christian!' she cried imploringly. 'Brother dear!'

'Nay,' answered Christian, in a low voice, 'you have no brother now. You have chosen between us and shame, and we have done with you for ever. I come to you from my mother—to tell you never to darken her door again.'

Kate answered with a moan, hanging her head in hopeless acquiescence.

'God knows our lot was heavy enough,' proceeded Christian. 'God knows our mother's cup of grief was full enough, without this last sorrow. But there—I waste words, 'tis too late for words now. All I want now from you, Kate Christianson, is the villain's name.'

'Oh, Christian, I cannot speak it! Do not ask me!'

He fixed his eyes terribly upon her, and took her by the wrist. She did not shrink or cry; he might have killed her just then, for all she cared.

'No need to speak,' he said; 'I know it—and yet, I would have it from your own lips. Richard Orchard-

son is the father of thy dead child? Answer—yea or
nay?'

She did not answer in words, but her face spoke
plainly enough. Christian threw her from him, and
turned away.

'That is all I sought to know. I am content.'

'Oh, Christian, you will not harm him! I—I love
him! Perchance he will make amends.'

He might have struck her now, so much did her
last words madden him, had not the man interposed.

'Nay, master, keep thy temper! Perchance, as the
poor wench saith, the gentleman will make amends.'

Christian looked at the speaker for a moment with
the ferocity of a wild beast; then, shaking him off contemptuously, again approached his sister.

'You shall not starve. No sister of mine shall
starve. Go with this man, and he will shelter you, till
I have settled with our mother what to do. But you
must not come back—remember that! You have no
home now.'

'Yes, Christian,' said poor Kate, faintly; and
without another word Christian walked rapidly away.

They stood on the road watching his figure until it
disappeared. Then the man turned to Kate, who was
sobbing bitterly, and said,

'Take comfort, wench. Thy folk will forgive thee
sure enow, an you gi'e them time; for after all, 'twas
human nature. Come home along o' me.'

Sad and sick at heart, Christian returned homeward.
The events of that morning had come like a thunder-
clap, leaving him no time to think or plan. Had he
yielded to his own natural impulse, he would have led
his penitent sister back, for he loved her dearly; but all
pity, all compunction, all natural affection, was crushed
beneath the terrible, unbearable weight of one thought
—that his sister's betrayer was Richard Orchardson.

It was almost too much to bear. By what cruel
fatality could it be that the Orchardsons were destined,
at every important turn of his days, to shadow and
blacken his being? First, there were the old traditional wrongs, bred in the wild past and abiding in

the blood; then, there was his father's death, caused, directly or indirectly, by an Orchardson; again, the family ruin and his mother's despair; and last of all, horrible beyond measure, and in all humanity unbearable, this betrayal of his too foolish, feeble, and loving sister. Yes, the cup was indeed full to overflowing, and all his soul now was set on some desperate revenge.

To add to his mad misery, he knew that Richard Orchardson was just then far beyond his reach, pouring his poisoned words, possibly, into the pure ears of Priscilla Sefton. This last thought was wildest of all. Unable to bear its horrible suggestions, he hurried across the marsh, and approached the Fen Farm.

The hall door stood wide open, and the house was quite silent. He entered quickly, and passing into the sitting-room, saw his mother sitting quietly there, in her old attitude, the Bible by her side.

'Well, mother, I have seen her,' he cried, entering the room, 'and, alas! she hath confessed.'

There was no reply. The widow sat nerveless in her chair, with her eyes fixed on vacancy, and one out-stretched hand on the open Bible. The faint light came through the heavily-curtained window, and touched her pale face and snow-white hair.

Christian approached quickly, stooped down before her, and uttered a terrified cry.

She was dead in her chair.

CHAPTER XV.

THE DEAD WOMAN.

So Christian fell at once into that great blackness where the atheist lies, with eyes averted from heaven and his forehead pressed into the hard earth. By no intellectual process, by no succession of bitter doubts and ruthless syllogism, but simply through the utterness of moral despair, there was forced upon his soul the consciousness that the world is without God, and that those who doubted God's very existence were in the right. If there were a God indeed, if the gentle Providence of the preacher were a fact or a possibility, such things could never have been; that at least seemed clear. Or if God existed, he must be on the side of evil; cruel, pitiless, incomprehensible, unblessing and unblest. All was blind fate; anarchy subsisting in the very shadow of death.

Feeling this, in all the tumult of his wild grief, he sat and looked in the eyes of the dead woman, not yet closed reverently, but fixed in horrible contemplation of some sight of terror which only dead eyes see; sat and gazed into her eyes and held her clay-cold hand till his own fingers felt like ice, and the chill of the grave was in his heart. Hours passed thus. Night and death were in the house, with no sound, no stir.

At last he rose, lifted the lamp, and held it close to his mother's marble face. Ah! what a record of hate and pain was written there! The face was fixed in pallor, the eyes were blank, but the weary lines and furrows still remained, and the brows were knitted, and the poor thin hair, parted neatly over the blue-veined temples, kept its snow.

'Mother! mother!' he moaned; but no tears came.

Then his eye fell upon the old Bible, still standing open by the corpse's side.

With trembling hand he took it up, and turning to the flyleaf, read his father's name writ there, and his mother's name, and poor Kate's, and last his own; all their names, and the date of his father's and mother's wedding, and the birthdays of the children, himself and the poor sister whom sorrow had untimely tried. Of all that little household only one now remained—alone in all the world. The rest had faded from him, like dreams that had scarcely been.

His mind went back to the beginning of it all; to the dark feuds between the two houses, begun in blood before he came.

He saw before him, as in a vision, the Orchardsons and Christiansons of tradition, flitting to and fro amid the shadows of civil war and political change, armed, angry, always with their hands against each other. He remembered how one wild deed had avenged another,

'He sat and gazed into her eyes.'

how blow had met blow, how hate had met hate, until the men of both houses were more like devils than human beings. Then he bethought him of his father's death-bed, and the black knavery, for so it seemed, which had hastened the poor man's end; of the hour when, as a boy, he struck his enemy's son, and saw him bleeding at his feet; of the lawsuit which followed and beggared the household already poor. Last and saddest of all came the thought of his sister's shame and his old mother's broken heart; these, too, due to an Orchardson, the wickedest of the race.

Amidst these confused images and memories, one form moved like a celestial vision. At every confused vista of his mad recollection there came up before him the image of Priscilla Sefton, with a look of beautiful admonition. She, too, had vanished from him; she who might have made amends for all, and turned his desolation into some abiding peace. Ah! what would he not have given just then if she could have suddenly appeared before him to touch the rock of his hate with the wand of her Divine compassion, and strike its stone to tears!

As he thought and thought, the silence became too much for him to bear, and passing from his mother's side, he went to the hall door and threw it open.

It was a fine moonlight night of high wind; white clouds were scudding over the moon's face; and the air was full of luminous phosphorescence. The fields and marshes lay so distinct before him, that he could trace the black lines of the ditches and hedges, and the patches of wood, as clearly as if it had been day. The wind was coming from seaward, and, listening intently, he could hear a sound which seemed like the moaning of the sea.

Leaving the door open behind him, he passed out, and hastened across the fields to a neighbouring cottage, where dwelt an aged couple who often did rough work about the farm. He knocked loudly, and the door was opened immediately by an old woman.

'My mother is dead,' he cried quickly. 'Haste to the house and watch by her till I return. I am going up to the village.'

The woman uttered a wail; but before she could assail him with any questions, he was gone.

A strange and sudden thought came over him, and with the fury of a man possessed by a demon, he rushed across the moonlit fields. In a very short time he reached the village; but he did not stop there. Hastening on, he entered the long avenue leading to the Willows, gained the terrace, and pausing there, stood for some minutes panting for breath.

The great house was in darkness; but at last he discovered light in one window, a window opening to the ground. Without hesitating a moment, for his wild thought still possessed him, he pushed the window open, and entered. There was a startled cry, a tall figure sprung up, and he found himself standing face to face with Squire Orchardson.

'Help!' cried the squire in terror. 'Who's there?'

'It is I, Christian Christianson.'

His voice was clear and distinct as he replied, and but for his death-white face, and close-set lips, he would have seemed free of all agitation. Years after that night he remembered his coolness and self-command, and wondered at them. He looked steadily in the squire's face and waited.

For a time the old man seemed overpowered by surprise, glanced nervously towards the bell-rope and at the door.

'What seek you here?' he said at last. 'At this hour——'

'I have come to speak with your son.'

'My son is far away,' answered the squire quickly. 'What do you want with him?'

'Nay,' said Christian, 'the father will do as well. I have come to you from—from my mother.'

His voice faltered a little at the name, but his eye still looked calmly in the other's face.

'Your mother wishes to see *me?*' cried Orchardson in complete astonishment.

Christian answered with a curious inclination of the head.

'If this is indeed so,' said the squire nervously, 'if your mother has any word to say to me that may calm ill blood, God forbid that I should thwart her. I have heard of her trouble, not without compassion. Tell her I will come to her to-morrow.'

'No, to-night! to-night!' cried Christian in the same low voice; and he made a step as if to place his hand upon the old man's arm.

'To-night? Impossible!'

'I tell you I have come to you from her. Will you follow me? or are you afraid?'

The old man drew himself up with a nervous shrug of the shoulders.

'Nay, I am not frightened so easily; and, indeed, what should I fear? But the request is so sudden, so unreasonable.'

'Come and see her,' persisted Christian, 'that is all I ask.'

'Nay, if the dame is ill——'

'Ay, sick unto death,' was the answer. 'She is waiting for you: come!'

The squire looked at his visitor again, and then, after a moment's hesitation, concluded to obey the strange summons. It did not seem altogether extra-ordinary that Dame Christianson, being possibly at the point of death, might have some last request to make, or some final confession. With all his faults, and they were numerous, Orchardson had his human feelings; and he would have been rather relieved than otherwise at a death-bed reconciliation with the woman who had suffered so much from his animosity.

'Wait here a moment,' he said; 'I will go with you.'

So saying, he withdrew from the room; in a few minutes he returned, cloaked, and staff in hand.

Could he have seen the strangely ominous smile which crossed Christian's face as they passed out into the night, he would doubtless have hesitated before leaving his own door.

Even as it was, he kept the young man well before him as they went, and held his hand underneath his cloak, gripping a weapon. For he, better than most men, knew the stuff of which his hereditary adversaries were made, and which rendered them capable of almost any deed of violence.

Christian led the way so rapidly that the old man had some difficulty in keeping up with him. Once or twice the latter paused for breath, or to put further questions, to all of which Christian answered in monosyllables. They passed through the slumbering village, along the brink of the mere, and at last they came in sight of the Fen Farm.

Not far from the door, Orchardson again paused.

'If your mother is very sick,' he said, 'would it not be better to seek holy aid? I should be glad to see some man of God by her bedside.'

Without replying, Christian strode on to the farm door, pointed his companion in, and followed. But the room where he had left his mother lying was empty, and the chair was vacant. He turned and led the way upstairs. On the landing above he encountered the old man and woman his neighbours, and spoke to them in a whisper. Then he pushed open a bedroom door, and entered; Orchardson followed close behind.

The room was dimly lit by an oil lamp, and on the bed, stretched out in white, lay the corpse of Dame Christianson, stiff and cold.

At sight of the bed and its ghastly occupant, the squire recoiled and uttered a cry. In a moment Christian's powerful hand clutched his arm like a vice.

'Look!' said Christian.

'Merciful heaven! she is dead!'

'Yes, she is dead. I have brought you here to look upon your work; yours, and your son's. You killed her. You killed my father first, then her. Nay, you shall not stir.'

Pale as death, and trembling violently, Orchardson tried to shake himself free and leave the room.

'She died to-night,' said Christian, 'before I came to you; and she died cursing you. You did not hear her curse, but you shall hear mine. But first, *where is* Richard your son? Tell me where he is, that I may follow him, and avenge my mother and sister.'

'What do you mean? You talk like a madman. Let me leave this place.'

'Not till you tell me where to find your son.'

'He is far away.'

'Where?'

'I do not know. Release your hold, young man. You are profaning your mother's death-chamber.'

He had struck the right note at last. With a wild look at the dead figure on the bed, and a half-smothered sob, Christian led the old man from the room, and downstairs into the hall; thence into the gloomy chamber, still lighted by a lamp, where his mother had died.

By this time Mr. Orchardson had recovered his self-command. Looking keenly at Christian, and throwing into his manner a certain sympathy of superiority, he said with decision,

'You have brought me here on a fool's errand, but I am sorry for you. God knows I never wished any ill to your mother. I would have been lenient to you all, had you not driven me to desperation. Well, what more have you to say to me?'

'Only this,' answered Christian: 'if you were not an old man, you should not leave this house to-night alive. But you may go. My reckoning shall be with your son.'

Mr. Orchardson walked towards the door; then, as if impelled by a sudden thought, he turned quickly, and fixed his keen eyes on Christian's face.

'My son hath no reason to love you,' he said, quietly; 'but what evil hath he done you, that you should hate him so?'

Christian did not reply, but met the old man's eye with a look of terrible meaning.

'My son is a gentleman,' continued Mr. Orchardson. 'If you are thinking of the lying tales concerning him and your unhappy sister, let me tell you that he is innocent in that matter; nay, I have it from his own lips that he is innocent. And even were he guilty as you believe, 'tis but a boy's folly, and he would make amends.'

With the swiftness and ferocity of a wild animal, Christian crossed the room towards Mr. Orchardson, who shrank back as if apprehending personal violence. But though his clenched hands were raised trembling in the air, he struck no blow.

'Your son hath betrayed my sister, and killed my

mother, who lieth yonder. No matter where he is hiding, I shall find him. No matter how long I may have to wait, I shall kill him ; and I should kill *you* this night for the wrong you did my father, if I did not wish you to live to see my vengeance on your son—to see him lying dead before you, killed by my hand.'

The old man shrank back in horror, less at the words than at the expression on the speaker's face.

'Wretch !' he gasped, 'I will swear the peace against you. The law——'

'No law will save your son from me. It will be life for life, and may God's curse blind me if I do not as I have sworn. Now begone ! '

Christian pointed to the door. With an exclamation, half-angry, half-fearful, Mr. Orchardson shrank away before the outstretched hand, and tottered out into the night, closing the hall door with a crash behind him. Reaching the gate beyond, he paused a moment, and saw the dim light coming from the upper chamber where the woman was lying dead. Then shocked and shaken by what he had heard and seen, he made his way slowly back to the Willows.

Left to himself in the lower room, Christian fell into a chair, and hid his face in his hands. For nearly an hour he remained thus, a prey to his own wild thoughts; then he rose and walked back to the death-chamber, and knelt down by his mother's side.

Early the next morning, after a night of little sleep, Mr. Orchardson rose, and sitting down to his desk, wrote a long letter to his son. The letter contained much general matter; among it all, these warning words:—

'All this is as I have told you. As you love me, keep away from the Willows yet awhile ; for the fool is dangerous, and you can scarce guess the hate which breedeth in his simple heart. He layeth his sister's flight and his mother's death at our door. Look to yourself, my dear Dick, should you meet; but nay, you must not meet. And so, with many fond wishes that your suit may thrive, farewell.'

To make all safe and sure, Mr. Orchardson himself

rode over to the neighbouring town with the letter containing the above warning, and sent it by coach with his own hand.

The next few days were a dreary blank to Christian Christianson. Like one in a dream he heard folk coming and going; saw the wooden coffin borne in at the door; went up afterwards and saw the waxen face lying at peace within it; sat for hours in the solemn room; finally, one sad day, heard the bell tolling, as he followed the hand-bearers with their black burthen up the hillside, through the village, to the green churchyard.

In a dream still, he stood in his black cloak, bareheaded, by the open grave, and heard the loose mould drip heavily on the coffin wood. 'Ashes to ashes, dust to dust; in sure and certain hope of the resurrection to eternal life.' But no sweet pity, no thought of Divine resurrection, filled his soul. All his thoughts were turned one way—how to avenge his mother, how to set right his sister's wrong by some sudden and desperate deed. Then he too might die—the sooner the better.

His plans were all matured. To remain longer in the place of his birth was poison to him. He had an idea that all avoided him, that the story of his sister's disgrace and the family dishonour turned every heart against him; whereas, if the truth must be told, his own sullen suspicion and gloomy reticence were the causes which prevented the neighbours from volunteering help or sympathy. He hated the place, the familiar faces, the common air and sunshine. He would go away, never perhaps to return.

Meantime, while preparing to depart, he inquired high and low, secretly but persistently, the whereabouts of Richard Orchardson; but no one could help him Some said that the young man was upon the Continent; others that he was somewhere in the great city of London. Nor could he gain any tidings whatever of Priscilla and her father; they too had vanished, without leaving any trace.

In those days, when the daily newspaper was not thought of, and when the electric telegraph was not

even a dream, folk had not to wander far away if they
wished to leave their old lives entirely behind them.
Fifty miles was as far away, to all intents and purposes,
as five times fifty is now. Tidings of those he sought
were not likely to be brought to Christian's ears. If
he wished to find them, he must follow them out into
the world, and trace them step by step.

This indeed he resolved to do, being too fiercely im-
patient to wait until his enemy might return home. He
scarcely knew his own heart yet—it was so clouded and
tortured by passion ; but in reality it was possessed by
two spirits—one of hate and the other of love. Come
what might, he had resolved to avenge the family, and
to have it out with Richard Orchardson, even to the
death ; but he was no less firmly bent on finding
Priscilla Sefton, the only vision of beauty and goodness
he had ever had on this dark earth.

CHAPTER XVI.

ON BOARD THE 'MILES STANDISH.'

IN the autumn of the year of which we are writing,
there lay in the harbour basin of Southampton the good
ship *Miles Standish*, a barque of eight hundred tons
burden, laden with goods for the American market,
and having, moreover, accommodation for several cabin
passengers, besides a large party of emigrants bound to
New England. The skipper, Ezekiel Moses Higginbotham, of Salem, Massachusetts, was a shrewd New
Englander, of pious bearings ; and it was with no small
satisfaction that he reflected that the emigrant party
under his care were for the most part religiously dis-
posed agricultural labourers and farm servants, destined
to join a settlement of hard-working Moravians far in
the heart of the colony.

It was the evening before the day fixed for the
sailing of the vessel, and the sun was just setting in
golden splendour, after a day of unusual brightness and

magnificence. Under an awning stretched from stern rail to companion of the vessel, sat two figures—one a tall grey-headed man dressed somewhat like a clergyman, the other a girl in pensive black. They were the Wesleyan preacher, Richard Sefton, and Priscilla his daughter.

As they sat in the shadow, the old man looking down, the girl gazing with hopeful eyes on the sunlit light that covered the sparkling water, the numerous shipping, and the rose-tinted town, there came from the fore part of the ship the sound of an evening hymn, sung by male and female voices to a quaint old tune. Mr. Sefton listened well-pleased, while Priscilla, not raising her voice, sang low in accompaniment, with a happy smile.

When the song ceased, there came straddling to them a long shambling figure, smoking a great cigar. One eyelid was wide open, the other completely shut owing to some injury to the nerve; so that he was one-eyed like Polyphemus; but his countenance, brown as mahogany and tough as leather, was sufficiently good-humoured.

'Good even, captain,' said Priscilla, smiling. 'Shall we set sail early to-morrow?'

Captain E. M. Higginbotham answered with a nod.

'If so be the wind blows fair as it dew to-night, I calculate we shall be out of sight of these shores afore sunset; leastways if we can git a couple more hands aboard, for two of our white men have bolted, and we air short-handed as it is.'

As the skipper spoke, a boat shot alongside, and a voice was heard hailing the vessel. In another minute a light figure leapt on board, and approached the little group near the companion.

With a cry, Priscilla recognised Richard Orchardson, clad in a dark suit of semi-nautical cut, and wearing a broad-brimmed sailor's hat. He approached smiling.

'Father! it is young Mr. Orchardson. He hath kept his promise, and come to bid us farewell.'

By this time Richard's hand was clasped in hers; and as the blind man rose to greet him, he exclaimed eagerly,

L

'Nay, not farewell!'

'But we sail to-morrow,' said Priscilla.

'And, God willing, I will sail in your company, as you once besought me to do.'

Priscilla looked at him in astonishment. More than once, indeed, when they had first discussed their plans for accompanying the little colony to the States, it had been hinted, more in jest than earnest, that young Orchardson's help and company would be welcome; but Priscilla herself had never seriously thought of the possibility. She knew the young man's love for her, yet never calculated that it might lead him so great a length. Not entirely with pleasure now did she look into his eager face.

But Mr. Sefton reached out both hands, and took those of Richard warmly. The young man knew his foibles, and had humoured them so well that he was a prime favourite.

'You are welcome,' he said, 'and I think you have decided wisely. But what saith your worthy father?'

'He hath given me free leave to roam for a year,' replied Richard. 'If you can show me how to help the good cause, how to make myself helpful to the poor folk under your care, I shall be heartily glad; for, indeed, I am sick of an idle life, and would fain be of some use in the world.'

Mr. Sefton nodded approvingly; and it was soon settled, by a reference to the skipper, who stood looking on phlegmatically, that Richard should take passage in the *Miles Standish.* So the seamen hoisted up his luggage from the boat, which still floated alongside, and descending to the skipper's private cabin, he paid his passage-money and received an acknowledgment in writing about as legible as a cuneiform inscription.

Returning to the deck, Richard found Priscilla leaning over the vessel's side, and looking shoreward. Her face was shadowed, and she scarcely turned her eyes towards him as he approached.

'Are you angry that I came?' he asked in a low voice.

'Why should I be angry?'

'I had thought you might be pleased. For mine

own part, I could not dwell content in the land when you were gone.'

She turned her face to his, with a searching look.

'You are not frank with my father,' she said. 'You make him believe that you would serve God, and good Master Wesley's cause, but you care for neither.'

He answered, with a peculiar smile, 'Sweetheart, I care for both—for your dear sake.'

She stamped her little foot upon the deck, in positive anger.

'Go back to your father,' she cried; 'your place is with him, and with your English kinsmen. Why should you follow us? We shall never perchance return to England, and you only waste your time. It is I whom you follow, not my father; and I shall be better content if you do not come.'

So she spoke, with cheek half averted from him; and never had she looked more winsome and fair. The dying light of day lingered upon her cheek and on her hair, while Richard, with dark eyes fixed upon her, leaned upon the bulwark, smiling to himself at her petulance, and feeling certain that it would soon pass away.

There was a pause. Finding she did not speak again, he said quietly,

'If it be a sin to forsake father, country, kinsmen, for the sake of one dearer than all, then in sooth I am to blame. To be near you, Priscilla, I would wander to the world's end. But do not think that I will fret you with my society. Unless you wish it, I will never come near your presence. I shall be content to sail in the same ship, under the same sky, with one so dear; and if God should so will it,—which God Himself forbid!—to sink with you to the same deep rest.'

Priscilla trembled as she listened. Could it be Richard Orchardson who was speaking? The words seemed so unlike any she had heard from him,— more earnest, solemn, and truthful, less flippant and self-confident. Had Christian Christianson been the speaker, she could have understood; for he had often used such language, or language as deeply earnest. But, indeed, Richard Orchardson was for the time in earnest too. Had she known more of the world, she

would have been aware that even light men have their
solemn moods; and that, given time, place, and occasion,
even a hypocrite or a self-lover may be honestly and
unselfishly moved.   Just then, Richard Orchardson,
despite his characteristic self-pride and heartlessness,
felt indeed a lover, who had sacrificed the world for his
mistress' sake, and was ready to follow her in all the
chivalry of fearless manhood.   The girl's beautiful
presence, the dreamy scene, the deepening twilight, the
soft voices of the sea, had all their temporary spell upon
him.   It is idle to think that such things have witchery
for only good men; they influence the bad and ignoble
also; nay, even brute beasts feel them, blindly feeling
upward to speech and soul.

What could Priscilla say?   She could scarcely
blame the man for loving her so much; and there was
something in his devotion which touched her heart.
She made one last appeal to him not to leave England.
'Ask anything but that,' he said; and she yielded per-
force, frankly telling him, however, that if he hoped to
win her love, he hoped in vain.

'Because you love another,' he cried eagerly, thinking of his enemy.

'Because I love no man,' she answered simply; and
with that answer his vanity was quite content.

The Seftons, we may explain at this point, were not
leaving England with the view of never returning.
They were simply accompanying the emigrants, who
were mainly Moravian converts, to the colony, to ex-
amine the ground there, and see how much more good
might be done by sending out further emigrants in the
future.   It was a scheme in which the great Mr. Wesley
was himself interested; and Mr. Sefton had contributed
largely to the necessary funds.   So the blind man and
his daughter were sent, in a quasi-official way, to be the
shepherd and shepherdess of the outgoing flock; and
then, when the work was done, to return for similar
work elsewhere.

That evening, the skipper of the *Miles Standish*
rowed ashore, and, accompanied by his chief mate, a

little hard-grained Yankee, began beating the slums of Southampton, in the hope of making up his crew. But good men were scarce, and even bad ones were not to be had for the mere asking.

'I reckon we shall have to sail short-handed after all,' cried Captain Higginbotham, scratching his head.

He was standing at the door of a dingy public-house on the waterside, surveyed at a respectful distance by divers landsharks and waterside characters, who took no little delight in his dilemma. In company with his mate, he had beaten up every possible lodging-house and drinking den in the town, without any definite result whatever.

As he spoke, there stood before him a tall muscular figure, dressed in a slop seaman's suit, very like those which were dangling for sale over the doors of nearly all the low outfitting shops in the town. On his head he wore a rough seaman's cap, round his throat a rough muffler was loosely thrown. He had a loose shambling gait, characteristic of the waterside loafer, and when he spoke, he shuffled with his feet, and looked upon the ground.

'Waal, where do *you* hail from?' growled the skipper, looking at him contemptuously.

'I've heard as how you're short-handed,' said the man, with a strong country accent, 'and I thought——'

'Waal, what might *you* happen to think?' asked the captain.'

'I thought as how *I* might serve.'

The captain surveyed the speaker leisurely, beginning with his feet, and lifting his gaze slowly, inch by inch, till it met a pair of deep-set eyes, intensely bright and keen. Then he shook his head.

'Don't try it on with *me*, stranger,' he said. '*You* won't suit.'

'Why?'

''Cause *I* guess you're no more a salt-water sailor than that theer pump-handle.'

'How do you know that?' asked the man, with the ghost of a smile on his cheek.

'By the voice of you, by the rigs of you, and by the cut of your precious jib. Let's feel of your hands!

Theer! Call that a sailor's paw! Why, you're a land-lubber, and never smelt green water.'

'And if so be I am,' persisted the man, 'why shouldn't I smell it now? Lookee, skipper! I'm strong and I'm young, I can row and sail a boat, and I'm willing to work my way out for my keep, if so be you'll take me.'

The skipper was about to give another grim negative, when the mate caught him by the sleeve and whispered in his ear. The two talked in a low voice together for some minutes, then the captain turned sharply to the volunteer, and fixed him with his one eye.

'You mean it, stranger?'

'Yes, I want to get out to the colony.'

'Wheer might you be raised, and what's your name?'

'I was born and christened in Essex county, and my name——' here the man hesitated a moment, but continued boldly, 'my name's John Dyson.'

'We sail to-morrow morning, first tide.'

'Soon as you like, skipper.'

'Then I'm your man, John Dyson. I'll hev you, and chaw my head off if I don't make a sailor on you, some-how. Dew you say done?'

'Done.'

'Done it is,' said the captain, and held out his horny hand.

Late that evening, when the town was asleep, the captain, well-primed with liquor and tolerably well con-tented, entered his gig, followed by the new seaman, carrying a small canvas bag of necessaries. As they rowed out through the dark basin, with its twinkling lights, the stranger volunteered a question.

'Skipper?'

'Waal?'

'I've heerd there's a blind man aboard your ship,— a blind man and his daughter.'

'And if there is, yon lubber, what then?'

'Nought; it is no affair of mine, only I thought——'

'Hold your jaw,' growled the captain. 'Guess we don't ship you to think, but to pull ropes. Never you mind my passengers; your job's afore the mast, and you'll hev to look alive aboard any ship of mine.'

A few minutes afterwards the new hand stepped on board, and was roughly ordered off to the forecastle.

As he stood on the fore part of the vessel alone in the darkness, his manner changed, and casting off for the moment his awkward attitude, he stood erect and listened; while from the distant cabin there came the sound of a woman's voice singing.

'I was right after all,' he muttered to himself; 'she is here—he hath followed her: I have only to watch and wait.'

CHAPTER XVII.

OUTWARD BOUND.

EARLY the next day, the good ship *Miles Standish*, with free sheets and all sail set, was slipping with a fair wind down the English Channel, with her bowsprit pointing almost due westward, and the low-lying shores of England lying dark and dim on the starboard side. The breeze was light, yet firm, the smooth billows just darkened by a pleasant ripple, the skies overhead blue and light, and the air sunny.

She was not a brilliant sailer, the *Miles Standish*, and was without splendid accomplishments or beauty of any kind; but she did her work in a sober, settled, business-like fashion, that showed she could be depended upon in all kinds of weather. Though she was well laden, she carried her cargo easily, and there, in the open ocean highway, where vessels of all sorts and sizes were going and coming, she held her own, running with many clippers of her own tonnage, and would have proved a laggard only in the event of a long beat to windward.

Priscilla Sefton stood on deck, and looked with pleased eyes on the radiant scene around her: ponderous merchantmen, beating clumsily homeward towards the silvery mouth of the Thames; fishing-boats and coasting cutters, darting to and fro like happy wildfowl; here and there a snowy-sailed gunboat or formidable man-of-war's man, with closed portholes like clenched teeth; and sail of all degrees and sizes, running with the *Miles Standish* along the smooth watery highway to the west. It was her first real experience of the beauties of the sea; for though she had more than once crossed the narrow Channel in a sailing packet, it had generally been at night, or in such weather as made clear-headed observation impracticable, not to say impossible. So she was like a happy child. She had no such tender ties in England as could make her sad or homesick, and if she thought now of Christian Christianson, it was as of a pleasant friend, whom she might or might not meet again, but whose life in any case was complete without any new contact with her own.

Alas! how little did she know that the blind Sisters were weaving their tangled thread to confuse her pretty dreams and plans! How little did she guess that on board that very ship were lurking the two elements of love and hate, by which her fate was destined to be determined for joy or sorrow!

'Are you sorry to leave England?' asked Richard Orchardson, coming near her as she leant over the bulwarks and looked landward. 'For my part, I should not care if it sank for ever beneath the sea, so that I had the green water to look on, this good ship to sail in, and you to keep me company till the end of time.'

'And your father?' said Priscilla, smiling. 'You forget that he abides in the land and would sink with it.'

'Heaven forbid!' cried Richard quickly. 'I did indeed forget the dear old man! But as for dreary England, for the place where I was born, never did I hate it so much as now.'

'And I *love* it!' returned Priscilla, looking with dreamy eyes at the faint line of the English shore. 'I love England, and English folk. I should not like to die afar. I think my ghost would rise, and speed across the seas to the dear old land.'

'Nay, but all lands are alike, when those we hold dear are with us.'

'I do not think that,' answered Priscilla simply, not heeding the tender tone or noting the warm look with which the words had been accompanied. 'A good man loves his dear ones first, and then his home, how poor soever it be, and then his country ; and he who loves the last best, doth often love the others most.'

Richard flushed nervously, for something in the little speech sounded like a reproach. In Priscilla's presence, deeply as he enjoyed its charm, he was never quite free from the irritation a somewhat ignoble disposition must ever experience beneath the spell of an ingenuous nature. This irritation, instead of generating a noble shame, vented itself in the dark workings of the strong personal passion which filled the young man's soul.

That day passed, and when night came, the weather was still exquisitely calm. The shores of England had faded away into the sea, leaving in their stead, on the dark sea-line, clusters of splendid stars ; and all around, and overhead, the arches of heaven were hung with luminous lamps, and in the west the moon was large and round as a shield, strewing the glassy swell with palpitating beams.

Richard Orchardson had chosen his opportunity well. By joining Priscilla on board ship, by becoming of necessity her constant companion and fellow-passenger, he was likely to find ample means of reaching her heart. And now, on this first night of the voyage, when the very breaking of the sea seemed full of unsatisfied yearning, and the glowing heavens bright with love, Priscilla and he were again alone together. If with the very elements as accomplices he could not gain her sympathetic attention, then surely his suit was hopeless.

Hopeless indeed it seemed. Directly he touched upon the theme of love, Priscilla drew her hand away from his (he had taken it in the fervour of some fond protesting speech) and said, 'Good-night.'

'Good-night!' he repeated.

'Yes ; now you begin again to talk foolishly, I will not stay. I was right, after all. You would have done better to have remained in England.'

'Nay, but hearken!'

'You have broken your promise.'

'How?'

'Not to fret me with speaking as no other man hath dared to speak. Well, I was right. You had better have remained at home.'

So saying, she left him and went below.

Scarcely had she left the deck, when a figure flitted past Richard's side, and disappeared in the direction of the forecastle.

The green hand, John Dyson, found himself among a rough lot forward. The forecastle itself was a foul, ill-smelling hole, dark as a tomb, and impure as a charnel-house, and its occupants were for the most part old sea-dogs, with scarcely an idea in the world beyond seamanship and rum.

At first these choice spirits seemed to resent the intrusion of a green hand among them, evincing their humour by a series of jokes more practical than profound, and in every way the reverse of delicate. On discovering, however, that John Dyson, though a quiet, retiring person, was inclined to resent such liberties, or to retaliate in the same humorous spirit by knocking one or two of the jokers' heads together, the choice spirits thought better of it. They perceived that John Dyson was a very harmless shipmate if let alone, but that he was very far from harmless when strangers encroached too far. In point of physical strength, he was a match for any two men in the ship; in point of determination and courage he was equal in an emergency to the whole crew.

His work lay before the mast, and he seemed to prefer that it should be there. Naturally quick and energetic, he was soon able to hold his own with the other seamen, and his great physical strength gave him an additional advantage. So that the worthy captain and his mate were not long before they congratulated each other on having shipped John Dyson.

One peculiarity of the new hand they could not fail to remark; he was careless to indifference of his life, and whenever there was any dangerous duty to be performed below, or aloft, he was the first to undertake it.

Four days after the ship left port, she was tossing in

an ocean black as ink, and there was heard on every side the ominous sound of rising wind and water. An order was given to double reef topsails, and among those who ran up the rigging like wild cats, John Dyson was foremost.

As he hung out on the extreme edge of the fore-topmast yard, with the sail belching and bellowing and thundering around him, and the wild canvas struggling like a living thing in the clutch of his hand, he saw far below him on the deck the form of Priscilla Sefton, standing near to the companion. The vessel gave a great lurch, and he saw her stagger on the deck, but before she could fall or leave her place, Richard Orchardson had sprung forward and caught her in his arms.

The next minute there was a loud cry forward, 'A man overboard!'

John Dyson heard the cry, as the wild water, with a thunderous roar, surged up around him, stunned him, and sucked him down. In the eagerness of his gaze downward, he had relaxed his hold and fallen—prone into the sea.

For a moment he seemed to lose consciousness. Then he found himself struggling and choking on the summit of a great wave, looking after the ship, which seemed to stand stationary like a cloud, while he was swept away before the waves.

He heard the cry—he saw the faces clustering at the side; among them he recognised, or seemed to recognise, her face, white and fearful; then he sank down into the trough of the sea, and saw nothing but flying foam and roaring water.

Fortunately, he was a strong swimmer. Instinctively he struck out for life. Rising like a cork on the crest of the next wave, he saw the schooner's sails telling out before the wind, and saw her sweeping round. Then the waters sucked him down into the trough again, and he was washed on.

Strangely enough, his head was quite clear. He felt his danger, but was more or less indifferent to it, though the mere instinct of self-preservation made him use what skill he possessed in keeping afloat.

Presently, after he had almost given up the hope of succour, he saw the schooner bearing down towards him under the lightest of canvas. As she came nearer, passing within a ship's length of him, he saw again the faces thronging against her side. A shout rose in the air—faint and far-off it seemed, like a voice from a mountain-top, and he knew that he was seen.

The vessel sped past, and then, having done so, was brought up to the wind to leeward of him. Every wash of the waters now swept him nearer and nearer to it, but he struck out firmly, and partly impelled by his own strength, partly driven by the surging waves, swam for life.

The rest seemed darkness and confusion. He heard the waters roaring, saw the vessel looming above him, while human voices sounded faintly from its decks; then, blinded by the salt surge and choking spray, he clutched a rope which was flung to him and over him— and in another minute was drawn on deck, dripping like a rough-coated water-dog.

Priscilla had been an eyewitness of everything, from the moment that the alarm was raised to the moment when the man was drawn back on deck. She had watched the water wildly, scarcely distinguishing the living shape upon it, until, as the rope was thrown, she had caught the glimpse of a wild wave-washed form, a gasping upturned face, and waving arms. As for the face, it was only dimly perceptible, covered with tangled hair, foam-bespattered, and changed almost beyond recognition.

But when they had drawn the man on board, she would have stepped forward to look at him, and perhaps speak to him, had not Richard interposed.

'You had better stop here,' he said, 'they are a rough lot before the mast.'

'Nay, but the poor man may need succour yet. If I may not go to him, do you go in my place, and tell him——'

Just at that moment the skipper came aft, after having made his inspection of the rescued man. Priscilla questioned him at once, and received from his own lips the assurance that there was no cause for further alarm.

'The man's all right, I calculate,' said the skipper, phlegmatically. 'You see he's a land-lubber, and I guess it's his first salt-water bath, but he can swim like a fish, and he's none the worse. Don't you fret yourself about *him!*'

So Priscilla did not go forward. Had she done so she would have seen John Dyson standing near the fore-castle hatch, wet and bewildered, but otherwise much the same as before he fell into the sea. In one particular only was he changed. The men noted it, whispered about it among themselves, and laughed in a puzzled sort of way.

Before he had fallen into the sea, he had worn a beard. *Now*, curiously enough, no sign of a beard was to be seen.

The sea had washed it away!

It was a noticeable fact that after that day John Dyson grew sullener and stranger than ever. When he came on deck next morning, his face was strangely dis-figured; one of his eyes was terribly blackened, and there was an ugly bruise upon his mouth, obliterating the natural expression entirely.

The mate cocked his eye at him, but made no remark—the marks seemed the natural consequence of the accident; but the men shook their heads, and winked significantly at one another.

Later on in the day the boatswain accosted the mate.

'Queer customer, this green hand. Have you ob-served his figurehead?'

The mate nodded, and the boatswain continued:

'Well, a fall into the sea don't mark like that. He's made those marks hisself.'

'What the thunder do you mean?'

'Wore a false beard when he went overboard, and came back clean shaven. Put those cuts and bruises on with his own hand, I guess.'

The mate cogitated for a moment, then gave a hoarse chuckle.

'What d'ye make of it?' he asked.

'Some one wants him, I s'pose, and he's feared o' being known.'

'Well, it's no consarn of ours. We've shipped him, and he does his work like a sailor. But keep your eye on him, for all that.'

That very night, as Captain Higginbotham issued from below, he saw a figure crouching on the deck, and gazing eagerly down through the skylight—into the cabin where Priscilla, her father, and Richard Orchardson were seated at the evening meal.

'Who's there?' cried the skipper.

Without answering the figure began to move towards the fore part of the ship.

'Who's there—d'ye hear?' repeated the skipper, striding forward and gripping the figure by the shoulder. 'What, John Dyson! What d'ye mean by skulking about aft?'

John Dyson made no reply.

'Jest you go forward, and mind this—your place is before the mast.'

Still silent, John Dyson glided back to his place among the men, while the captain, with a suspicious shake of the head, watched him disappear.

CHAPTER XVIII.

'JOHN DYSON.'

HALF-WAY across the Atlantic, the *Miles Standish* encountered the storm-winds of the autumnal equinox, and for several days and nights captain and crew had all their work before them in keeping the little vessel snug. The small party of Wesleyan emigrants lay sick amidships, Mr. Sefton kept his berth, and Priscilla scarcely left her cabin. During this period, Richard was assiduous in his attentions on both father and daughter.

On the third morning of the storm, Richard went on deck, and found the ship lying-to with just enough canvas set to keep her steady, on a sea as white as

snowdrift, and under skies as black as ink. Dawn was
just breaking, with wild wind and rain.

Clinging to the companion, with the spray breaking
over him, Richard looked along the decks and saw the
watch gathered forward, fresh from taking in more sail.
Apart from them stood a powerful figure, clinging to
the forerigging, and looking to windward.

Richard started. He could not see the man's face,
but something in the figure seemed curiously familiar.
He only knew one man in the world so powerfully
fashioned, and that man was Christian Christianson.

The man turned, and their eyes met.

Richard was troubled anew; for the face, save that
it was greatly disfigured and distorted, bore a certain
resemblance to that of his old enemy. The eyes especially, with their deep determined light, were strangely
like those of Christianson.

After a momentary gaze, the man turned his head
away, and looked again at the sea. Richard smiled
at his own fears. Doubtless there was a strong physical
resemblance between the strange sailor and Christianson; but the latter was in England, safe and far away.
He cast another scrutinising look at the wild, rudely-
dressed figure, then he turned to the captain, who stood
by the man at the wheel.

‘Can you tell me that man's name?’ he inquired
carelessly. ‘The tall man with the bruises upon his
face?’

‘Yes. That's one of our extra hands, John Dyson.’

‘An Englishman?’

‘Yes; and a good sailor he is, though a green hand.
Seems to interest you, I guess?’

Richard glanced forward, and saw that the man,
though seemingly occupied at some of the ropes, was
still looking stealthily in his direction.

‘He is very like some one I used to know, that's all.’

‘Waal,’ said the skipper phlegmatically, ‘I calculate
he ain't much good. My mate tells me queer tales
about him, and I reckon he must be some gaol-bird
that has flown out of the stone cage. But that's no
business of mine; I shipped him, and he does his work
like a man.’

Richard cast another nervous look at the sailor, who still stood in the same position, obviously watchful. Was it possible? Could it indeed be Christian Christianson, masquerading for some dark purpose of his own? The idea seemed preposterous, and Richard soon dismissed it. Nevertheless, the resemblance troubled him, and gave rise to a certain watchful uneasiness.

His first strong impulse was to speak to Priscilla, and direct her attention to the person calling himself John Dyson.

On reflection, however, he felt that it might be unwise, for the sake of a very foolish suspicion, to recall to her the memory of one who had been a dangerous rival. For all he knew, that rival was altogether forgotten, and the longer he remained so the more likely was his own passionate suit to thrive.

At last the equinoctial storm abated, and was succeeded, as is so often the case, by an interval of sunny weather. The troubled sea became smooth as glass and bright as gold, the wind died gradually away, the skies grew cloudless and clear.

Then Priscilla came on deck again, adding sunshine to the sunshine.

No sooner did she do so, than Richard looked for the strange sailor. He was nowhere to be seen.

Nor did Richard fail to remark afterward that whenever Priscilla was on deck John Dyson was invisible. Whether by set design or accident, he invariably happened to be out of the way.

'Sweet is sunshine after storm.'

Those were pleasant days, those now spent upon the sea: pleasant, that is, to Priscilla Sefton. She was able to sit constantly on the deck, look at the sparkling blue water, and dream.

Now for the first time her thoughts scanned the past, and tried to unravel the pleasant mystery of the future. It was the past which troubled her most, however; it was to these many and stormy episodes in the valley of Brightlinghead that her thoughts most persistently returned; and as she did so the face of Christian Christianson, almost forgotten for a space, constantly flashed before her dreamy eyes.

While she had been with him Priscilla had caught too much of the whirlwind of his passion to be able to analyse her own feelings regarding him—she only knew that for his faults she seemed ever ready to make excuses. Then his strange passion had alarmed her, and she had fled, with a quiet prayer upon her lips, that under brighter and happier circumstances the two might some day meet again. Would that prayer ever be answered? would it ever again be her lot to stand as she had stood upon the silent sea-shore—feel his strong hand grasping her own, and hear his voice, saying, 'Priscilla, I love you!'

Love her! ah yes, he did love her very much, she was sure of that; and now she acknowledged to herself, what she had never dared acknowledge to him, that his love had been, in a measure, returned.

One night, during the fine weather, a curious circumstance happened, one which for the time completely shattered Priscilla's dream, and made her even more uneasy as to what might be going on far away.

Evening prayer was over, most of the emigrants had retired for the night, when Priscilla, feeling restless and singularly wakeful, went up on deck to enjoy the fresh air and muse for a few minutes alone.

She walked for a time up and down the deck; then she paused, and, leaning on the bulwarks, looked down into the sea. The night was well advanced, but she could see the glimmering of the waves, deep down, by the light of the moon and a brilliantly starlit sky.

She stood for a time looking down, then her dreaminess passed away; she raised her head, and was about to turn and continue her walk, when a shiver ran through her frame, her hand grasped nervously at the woodwork at her side, and her eyes gazed full into the eyes of an apparition!

Standing a few paces away, with his melancholy eyes fixed on hers, his face deathly pale, was Christian Christianson.

Was it dream or reality? Priscilla could not tell. The shock was so sudden that she completely lost her habitual self-control, and uttered a terrified scream.

The next moment the face and form which the moonlight had revealed to her with such terrible distinctness were nowhere to be seen.

But her scream brought assistance: in a moment she was surrounded with eager inquiries. The captain bent his one eye upon her, and roughly but kindly patted her cold, trembling hand; Richard Orchardson stood by, eager to offer more substantial comfort: but to none of these would Priscilla give a detailed explanation of what had taken place.

'Perchance it was only a fancy,' she said. 'Methought I saw the spirit of one who is far away. But I will go down to my father, and I will not disturb you with my foolish fancies again.'

The captain, who was inclined to make allowances for the hysterical tendencies of women, accepted this explanation and thought of the matter no more; but Richard Orchardson was of a more inquiring mind, and consequently was not so easily satisfied. Long after Priscilla had bidden all a sweet good-night, and shut herself in her cabin, he walked the deck trying to unravel the mystery.

In vain; without Priscilla's aid he could never know what had taken place that night.

All that night, sleep was a stranger to Priscilla Sefton's pillow; now, more than ever, her thoughts wandered back to the village from which she was flying; and her brain conjured up the picture of the pale sad face which she had seen so vividly in vision. How very pale and sad it had looked: how reproachfully the eyes had gazed at her. Even now, as she looked and listened, she seemed to hear his voice calling to her across the sea, and her tender heart was full of self-reproach. 'It was cowardly cruel of me to leave him,' she said; 'if I had stayed, with God's help I might have saved him; but now—nay, the Lord only knows what he may become!'

Though the memory of the strange apparition haunted her, she resolved to speak of it to no one: and for a time she kept her resolve; at length, however, the terror of it—the harassing thoughts of what it might portend, grew so strong upon her, that she felt she could keep silent no longer, and she spoke of it to Richard Orchardson.

The two were seated together during the twilight on a secluded part of the deck. Priscilla had an open book upon her lap. Richard was finishing the perusal of an old letter, which he had received from home just before sailing. Having read it slowly through, he folded up the closely-written sheet, and put it into his pocket. Then bending forward he looked into the girl's pale thoughtful face.

'I must crave your forgiveness,' he said, quietly; 'my father sent many messages to you, and until this day I have forgot to deliver them.'

'Indeed,' answered Priscilla, quietly; 'he was always good and kind to me, and I thank him from my heart. I hope that when he wrote he was well and happy.'

'Yes, he was well, and seeing that he was alone, tolerably happy.'

'He should not be alone,' answered Priscilla, gravely. 'He had only you, you should have stayed with him like a good son—since you had no serious business or holy errand to take you away.'

For a time the two were silent; then the young man spoke again.

'Priscilla, would you like to hear what my good father said ?'

'Assuredly, if it is well for me to hear it.'

'Then listen: "I am dull, dear Dick—very dull and sad; but I would bear it all right gleefully if I could but look forward to the day when you would come back to me, with Priscilla Sefton for my daughter and your wife!"'

'He did not say that!'

'Assuredly, he did.'

'Then you should not have told me. Nay, do not speak of it; if you do, I shall keep my word and never trust you again.'

'Then I will speak of it no more.'

Again they were silent; this time Priscilla was the first to speak.

'Did your father give you no news ?' she asked

quietly; 'hath he not spoken in that letter of any one I know?'

'He has mentioned many; of whom were you thinking most particularly, Mistress Priscilla?'

She paused a moment, then replied,

'Of the Christiansons, of Fen Farm!'

How dark the man's face grew! for a moment he almost hated the little demure figure at his side.

'Why do you ask for *them?*'

'Because I am interested in them, and because I fear that since I left the village some harm hath surely come to them.'

'Why do you think that, Priscilla?'

'I will tell you. You heard me cry out the other night—and I am sure you have since wondered wherefore. Well, you shall know now. 'Twas because I did suddenly see the face of poor Christian Christianson, as plainly as I see yours now!'

'His face! where?'

'On this vessel. The moonlight was strong and bright, it fell full upon the face. It made it so strange and clear, that had I been on land I should have sworn that I had seen the living man.'

'A foolish fancy! Good heavens, you cannot think it more!'

Priscilla smiled quietly.

'That is a strange question,' she said. 'How could it be aught else, when we both know poor Christian to be hundreds of miles away? But the memory of that strange vision troubles me, and makes me think that something terrible may have happened since I came here!'

'Priscilla!'

'Well, my friend.'

'Be advised by me—try to forget Brightlinghead—and, above all, think of Christian Christianson—no more!'

'Why do you tell me to forget my friends?'

'Because I have your welfare at heart—because I wish to shield you from harm.'

'Which might come to me through Christian Christianson?'

'Which *will* come to you, to us both, through him, if we ever cross his path again. He hateth both me and mine with bitter, undying hatred—as meaningless as it is strong. Ever since my boyhood he has made himself terrible to me. He knew he was the stronger of the two, and he used all his strength against me. He persecuted me continually, and to this day I bear the mark of his brute hand. I bore it all because I pitied him, but now all is changed: since we both knew you, he hath known the power of hurting me in a way I cannot bear!'

He paused, and looked into her face—it was very pale; and her hands were clenched convulsively together. It was better than he had anticipated; she was passive, if not pleased; so he went on.

'Priscilla, will you forgive me if I speak?'

'Nay, there is one theme on which I have besought you never to speak to me!'

'And after this day I will try to obey you; but hear me now. Priscilla, Christian Christianson knew I loved you. He knew that by tearing you from me he could blight my life and make me a miserable man. He knew that by poisoning your soul against me, he could hurt me more keenly than ever he had been able to do, and it was thus he tried to strike me. He wooed you from me, and he chilled your heart against me— not that he loved you, but that he hated me! So, God knows, I have cause to hate him in turn; but I would forgive him all he ever did to me, if you would promise me never, God willing, to cross his path again!'

Priscilla did not answer him. Her head was whirl-ing round : her soul was stirred by a wild tumult which she could not quell.

Richard Orchardson watched her. So intent was he that he had not noticed a black figure crawl stealthily along the deck and crouch like a snake behind them.

He looked at Priscilla; she was still silent: he bent forward and took her hand.

'Priscilla,' he said, 'it will be a pitiful day for you if ever you take that man's hand in friendship again. He belongs to an evil race. The father was a beggar and a borrower of my father's bounty. The sister is an outcast, as you know, despised by all good women. For himself, he hath all the taint of the breed, without one redeeming virtue—his father's dishonesty, his mother's stubborn ingratitude, his sister's infirmity of disposition. If I told you all I know of him, you would despise him freely, and banish him for ever from your heart.'

He stopped suddenly—the crouching figure rose, sprang forward, and a hand of iron gripped the slanderer by the throat.

CHAPTER XIX.

FACE TO FACE AGAIN.

RICHARD looked up in horror, while Priscilla uttered a terrified cry.

'Liar!' repeated the man, still gripping Richard by the throat.

There was no more mystery now. It was Christian Christianson in the flesh who stood before them, his face livid and terrible, his eyes burning, his strong frame, wrapt in its sailor's rags, trembling with passion.

'Help!' shrieked Richard; and the next moment the two men were struggling and clinging together in a murderous embrace.

There was a hurried tramp of feet, a quick rush of figures across the deck, and then, at the captain's sudden word of command, the men fell as one man upon the pair, and tore off Christian by sheer force.

Pale as death, half strangled, and terrified to the soul, Richard stood clinging to the bulwarks, and trembling violently.

'What's all this?' cried the skipper, cocking his one eye fiercely at Christian, who still struggled like a wild beast in the grasp of the crew. 'A sailor assaulting one of my passengers! Keep quiet, will you, John Dyson, or I'll hev you knocked on the head with a marling-spike! What's it all about?'

'For God's sake secure that man,' gasped Richard. 'He—he has tried to murder me!'

The skipper turned savagely on Christian, but before he could say another word, Priscilla had stept forward and was looking into the prisoner's face.

'Christian! is it possible? Nay, I can scarce believe mine own eyes. Alas! what brought you here?'

Christian gazed down at her wildly, but did not answer; his fatal homicidal passion still mastered him, and he made another frantic struggle to be free.

'What, you know this man?' cried the skipper, in unaffected astonishment, to Priscilla.

'Yes,' answered Priscilla, 'I know him well.'

'And I know him,' exclaimed Richard, tremulously grasping the captain's arm, 'and I warn you that my life is in danger unless he is safely secured. He hath followed me on board this vessel to kill me, and I demand protection.'

Grim as death now, the skipper walked up to Christian, and looked him sternly in the face.

'Speak *you*, John Dyson! or whatever the 'tarnal your name is. Hev you anything to say for yourself?'

Christian answered between his set teeth,

'Nothing—that man has spoken the truth.'

'What?'

'I came to kill him, and I *shall* kill him, be sure of that.'

An ugly look came into the worthy skipper's face, a baleful light into his one eye.

'So killing's your game, is it?' he said dryly. 'Waal, I'll teach you to try it on board *my* ship. Take him below, and put him in irons at once.'

Before Priscilla could interfere, Christian was dragged forward. He had ceased to struggle now, and walked away quite quietly, but the expression on his firm-set face had not changed.

No sooner had he disappeared, than Priscilla fell swooning upon the deck.

The skipper raised her gently in his arms, while Richard sprinkled water on her face and tried to restore her. When she came to, she looked wildly around her, as if seeking a familiar face.

'Is it *thou*, Christian?'

Richard's white face grew positively livid as he heard the hated name.

Then recollection came to her, in one vivid electrifying flash, and she covered her face with her hands and began to weep hysterically.

The skipper's eye watered, for Higginbotham, despite his Cyclopean physiognomy, was a tender-hearted man when the ladies were in question, and could not bear to see a lovely woman in trouble.

'There's more in this than I thought,' he reflected. 'John Dyson, I calculate, is more than a common sailor, and my name isn't E. M. Higginbotham if missie's pretty face hasn't brought him arter it across the sea.'

Then he said aloud,

'Now look'ee, young mistress! Though your friend John Dyson's in irons, he's all safe and squar', and no harm will come to him as long as he keeps quiet. When he passes his word to carry on like a sensible critter and not like a raging sea-sarpint, I pass *my* word that we'll knock off them irons and set him free.'

Inspired by a new thought, Priscilla raised her pretty pleading face, with the tears still sparkling in her eyes, and stretched out her trembling hand.

'Oh, sir, may I speak to him? He hath a good heart, and I think he will listen to me!'

'Speak to him, and welcome,' answered the skipper, kindly.

But Richard interposed quickly.

'On no account! I tell you the man is a dangerous maniac. Nay! you shall *not* go to him.'

But Priscilla was determined. Her heart was very full, and she yearned to find out what wild and desperate thought had brought Christian there; to speak to him some words of comfort, and perhaps of gentle rebuke and entreaty; to cast out, as far as might be, and as she had done more than once before, the evil demon that possessed him.

So in spite of Richard's renewed protestations she went forward with the captain, and descended, with the help of rough but friendly hands, to the dark forecastle den, where Christian sat a prisoner, hand-cuffed and heavily ironed.

He looked up as she appeared before him, but did not utter a word.

Priscilla looked at him for several minutes before he made any sign of recognition, although he turned his head and looked at her, but he still kept silent.

'Christian, listen to me!'

'Well, Priscilla?'

'I have got the good captain's leave to speak with thee; and I have come to see if you have aught to say?'

She spoke demurely, almost timidly; Christian listened darkly, but moving his head restlessly from side to side, like a beast in physical pain. The thirst for vengeance had at that moment almost supplanted love. Looking at Priscilla, he knew that she had just come from the side of his enemy, and glancing fiercely down at the irons which secured him, he fretted more wildly to be free. As for Priscilla, she was thinking little at that moment of Richard Orchardson, her mind was so sorrowfully sad at the sight before her. She longed to be tender, and that very longing made her manner stranger and colder than it had ever been before.

'Will you not speak to me?' she asked at length. 'Have you nothing to say?'

'Nothing.'

'What hath made you leave your home, your mother, your sister, and come here upon the sea?'

The man uttered a laugh which was painful to hear.

'Home?' he said, 'nay, I have no home. My mother lies in the graveyard, my sister is an outcast, broken-hearted, and I am here with one thought only,—to hunt down the devil who has been the cause of all our woe!'

Priscilla shrank back in terror.

'Christian, talk not so. It is blasphemous.'

'And it is not blasphemous to break an aged woman's heart; to ruin an innocent maid, and bring beggary and destruction on a happy home! Look you, mistress, I am not fit company for you. You had best go back to him who is your choice.'

'It is not like you to talk so—you were not wont to pain me.'

'God alone knows what I was wont to do. The past is dead to me; 'tis with the future I have to do now. My work is cut out before me. I mean to finish it before I die.'

He turned his head as if he wished the conversation to end, but Priscilla did not move away. Once already she had fled from him, and her regret had been so keen as to hold her firm now. She moved a few steps towards him, and laid her hand tenderly upon his arm.

'Good Christian,' she said quietly, 'if I were to listen to the voice of pride within me, I should walk straight back to my cabin yonder, and never seek your presence here again. But I know you better than you know yourself. Come, do not treat me as an enemy or a false friend, for you know well I am neither; but tell me what has brought you here?'

'I have told you already, mistress; I mean to have my just revenge.'

'Upon Mr. Orchardson?'

'Ay,' answered Christian, in a voice so terrible that she shrank back again.

'Alas! you are bitterly to blame. Why are you so bent upon hunting a fellow-creature down?'

'Why?—because he and his have been the scath and scourge of me and mine; because I lay at *his* door the sorrow of my sister, whom he betrayed to shame, the broken heart of my mother, and the miserable shattering of all our lives!'

'No, no!' cried Priscilla, 'you are madly wrong. Your poor sister——'

'*He* betrayed her—with her own lips she told me that he betrayed her.'

'It is not possible!'

'It is certain,' cried Christian. 'But there, talk not of her; hath *he* not told you that her name is unfit to pass your lips? and perchance he spoke the truth; but before God I swear to you, as I swore before, that for every bitter tear she hath shed I will have a drop of his heart's blood!'

His passion was so overmastering that she stood appalled. She saw that words were useless, that they fell like drops of dew upon a flaming brand. So she stood wringing her hands, and weeping for very fear.

Then she cried through her tears:

' Christian ! once—not so long ago—you said you loved me—and you swore for my sake to be a good man. Listen to me, in God's name ! It would be better to die, better to be lying in your grave, than nurse such terrible thoughts ! It is true that you have suffered ; but alas ! to suffer is our lot ; and as God forgives us our trespasses, so should we forgive those that trespass against us. Forgive Richard Orchardson ! You must ! you will ! '

She paused, but Christian did not answer her. Emboldened by his silence, she went on :

' If I could induce you to forget and forgive, to leave all these heartbreaking troubles behind you, and begin a new life, all might yet be well, and with God's blessing——'

' Do not talk of it—I seek not God's blessing ; all I seek is to have vengeance upon my enemy ; for that I'll watch and wait, and though I wait for fifty years the time will come.'

For some little space yet, Priscilla remained and continued her gentle pleading ; but at every word Christian grew more morose, and at last he would answer nothing. At length, with a weary disappointed sigh she left him, saying to him that she would come back again, and vowing in her heart that she would leave no device untried to turn him from the wicked purpose upon which he had set his heart.

For she said to herself, ' It seems to me that sorrow has turned his brain. God help him—and may God help *me* to bring some solace to his soul.'

On the after-deck she met Richard Orchardson ; he paused to speak to her, but Priscilla, with a strange shrinking at her heart, passed silently by, and quickly gained her cabin.

There she sat down to think. She reviewed the story which Christian had unfolded in broken hints, and as she did so her heart was filled with a bitterness almost as strong as that which filled the heart of the

Injured man, while the thought of Richard Orchardson made her sick with shame. So Richard was the girl's betrayer, and yet he had looked on unmoved when she lay almost dying at Priscilla's feet. Priscilla's eyes were opened now. She frankly acknowledged to herself that Christian had bitter cause for hatred, and the pity in her soul strengthened the love which he had already awakened there.

As the night wore on, she felt she could not rest below. Still shocked and agitated beyond measure, she went again on deck.

Close to the cabin companion, she encountered the worthy captain.

'Waal, he said, with a kindly smile, 'how hev you left John Dyson now? Hev you brought that young man to his senses?'

Tears stood in the girl's eyes as she replied, just touching the lappet of the skipper's coat with her little hand.

'O captain dear, you have a kind heart, and I am sure you will pity him, for he hath had much, much trouble. His name is not John Dyson, but Christian Christianson, and great sorrows have made him mad.'

'Ah! I knew from the fust he were no common sailor, his hands were too soft and white, his tongue too civil and free. But I daren't set him loose till he dew come to his senses and promises to behave hisself all squar'. Can I take his word, think you, if he promises that?'

'Yes,' replied Priscilla. 'Whatever he saith, he will fulfil.'

The skipper nodded good-humouredly, and strolled forward. Priscilla was about to follow him, when Richard emerged from the companion, and greeted her with a joyful exclamation. To his renewed surprise, she turned her head away, and tried to pass by without a word.

'What is the matter?' he cried, reaching out his hand to detain her.

She shook off the touch with a shiver of horror, and made another attempt to pass. But he persisted.

'I see,' he said, turning white with agitation; 'it is

as I feared. That villain hath been poisoning your
thoughts against me.'

'He is no villain,' answered Priscilla with sudden
intensity; 'if he hath spoken truth, *you* are the villain,
not he!'

Richard's face went whiter; he trembled from head
to foot with a new and sickening fear.

'What hath he said?'

'He hath justified himself against you—that is
enough.'

'By more lies and calumnies,' cried Richard, while
his face became full of anger and despair. 'And you
have listened to him! *You!* Then God help me, for
I am wronged indeed.'

'You are not wronged—he and his have been wronged
from the beginning.'

'It is false, Priscilla, though you say it.'

'It is true.'

'Tell me what he hath said. At least, let me defend
myself.'

'You cannot,' answered Priscilla.

'Let me try!'

Thus urged, Priscilla told him what she had heard
concerning himself and poor Kate Christianson. At
the first breath of the accusation, Richard shrank like a
guilty thing, while his face went from pale to red, from
red to pale, and his whole frame shook with agitation.
But as she proceeded, scarcely looking in his eyes, for
her sense of the shameful tale made her own cheeks
crimson, he had time to recover his self-possession.

When she ceased, he smiled sadly, and heaved a
heavy sigh.

'It is as I thought,' he said. 'Well, so be it. You
have judged me unheard, and I must submit.'

'I have not judged you,' she returned with a certain
hesitation, 'it is for God to judge you—but is it true or
false?'

'False, every word!' cried Richard fervently.

She started, and looked him in the face. There was
nothing to betray him there—only a deep sorrow, and a
sullen sense of cruel injury.

'Christian would not lie,' she said.

'He would do worse than lie, to injure me in your esteem. To poison your soul against me he would invent—as he hath invented—calumnies as black as hell. Well, since he can do so much, let him do more. Go, set him free. Let him take my wretched life. I do not care now.'

And he turned away as if to hide his face and weep.

At this cunning piece of acting, her certainty was shaken, and her gentle heart was touched. Could it be possible, she thought, that Christian, ever headstrong and prone to err, had been misled? Then she suddenly remembered that the accusation had come, not from idle hearsay, but from Kate Christianson's own lips.

'His sister hath told him,' she said; 'she accused you. Oh it is terrible! God must punish such cruel deeds! His mother lies dead in her grave, of a broken heart.'

Then, with a heavy sob, able no longer to speak or listen, she descended to her cabin, and sank upon her knees in prayer.

CHAPTER XX.

PRISCILLA MAKES HER CHOICE.

RICHARD ORCHARDSON stood on the lonely deck, and looked up wildly to the stars of the night, which were thickly clustering over the quiet sea. Despair and rage were in his soul; for he saw too plainly that Heaven and the girl's heart were against him, and that the last chance was lost, unless he could prove himself innocent in Priscilla's eyes.

And as he looked upward, with many a muttered curse upon his enemy's head, he was troubled by no qualms of conscience for any past misdeed, but rather experienced a gloomy feeling of oppression, a sullen sense of wrong.

No man's soul is unmixed evil; indeed, such a soul would be monstrous, not human; and Richard Orchardson felt that night that he was among the most injured of men. He sincerely loved Priscilla; he had followed her over the high seas with a feeling very like devotion; he felt, moreover, that from day to day her influence wakened and kept alive what was best and noblest in his nature; he had almost forgotten alike the animosities and the follies of his early life; he was, in a word, in the position of the culprit who honestly desires to reform, and who (to quote the moralist) is 'going to turn over a new leaf.' Yet Providence itself seemed against him. Just as the prize of virtue was in his grasp, just as he was growing happy with the dreamy hope of sweet possession, all was changed as by a miracle, and between himself and felicity rose again the human being he hated most.

Yes, it was enough to make a man blaspheme and curse his stars! Why had not a kindly Providence kept this man away, buried him mountain deep under the earth, or sunk him to the bottom of the sea? Why did he live, to darken the sunshine?

There was danger, too. So long as Christian lived, Richard Orchardson knew that his own life might at any moment pay the forfeit. As the thought crossed his mind, he shivered with a sickening sense of dread.

While Orchardson was nervously pacing the a'ter deck, furious with his own thoughts, yet timidly starting at every sound, Captain Higginbotham was below, questioning the prisoner.

Seated on a bunk, face to face with Christian, whose face he saw dimly by the light of a swinging lamp, the skipper tried his hand at cross-examination.

'Waal, how dew you feel now, John Dyson, or whatever else the 'tarnal your name is? Dew you feel like fighting, or dew you feel like giving in? I calculate you're come to your senses by this time; for there's nothing like sitting in ship's irons for cooling a man's idees.'

'You are mistaken, captain,' answered Christian, quietly; 'I am of the same mind still.'

'Then you won't pass your word to keep afore the mast, and dew your work like a man, and let that young randydandy alone?'

'No.'

'You're a bold hand, John Dyson I do calculate.

What's it all about?   Come, tell me slick and squar'.
About a gel?   About young missie there in the cabin?
Waal, she's too good for either of you, she is, and that's
a fact; but theer, young randydandy's a gentleman, and
you're only a common man.'

'Nay, I am as gently born as he,' said Christian
'and by the same token of older blood.   But that is
neither here nor there.   I have sworn to kill him, and
kill him I shall.'

'Not aboard my ship,' cried the skipper, more and
more astonished by the man's quiet determination yet
subdued demeanour.   'If you try it on aboard the *Miles
Standish*, you'll swing from the yardarm as sure as your
name's John Dyson.   But that ain't your name neither,'
he added reflectively; young mistress calls you Christian;
and a precious Christian you air, to be trying to take
the life of a fellow-critter!   Waal, Dyson or no Dyson,
Christian or no Christian, you'll wake and sleep in them
irons till you change your mind.'

So saying, the skipper withdrew, and made his way
on deck.

All that night Christian sat silent in his place, and
never closed his eyes.   Thoughts wild and terrible,
stormy and sad, possessed him, and kept soul and body
wide awake; besides, the physical irritation caused by
the fettering irons was growing keen enough to drive
away all sleep.   So he sat moodily resigned as to the
present, and tried to plan his conduct for the days that
were to come.

But the more he thought, the more moody and
despairing he grew; for it seemed in this, as in everything else, that the hand of God was against him.   He
was sorry now that he had revealed himself; that one
mad act had rendered him helpless.   If he could only
get free; if he could but stand for one day only, and
hold within his hand the life of his enemy, he would
ask no more!

The hours dragged wearily on; night passed away,
and the cold, grey light of dawn streamed down from
the troubled sky, and found the man more pitifully sick
at heart than ever.

'The cold, grey light of dawn streamed down from the troubled sky, and found him more pitifully sick at heart than ever.'

That day the wind freshened; most of the hands were busy on deck, and Christian was left alone. When the day was nearly spent, a figure crept quietly into the forecastle, and a tender, trembling hand was laid upon his arm. Turning quickly, he looked straight into the eyes of Priscilla.

The sight of her face startled him. She looked so pale, so careworn, so different from the happy, pensive little maiden whom he had known, loved, and dreamed of. Was it Priscilla—was he dreaming or waking? for the figure which he saw crept up to his side like a docile child, kissed his hand, and moistened it with tears.

'Priscilla?'

'Yes, Christian, it is I. I have been waiting for hours to come to you, but could not get leave; and I dared not brave the good captain's orders for fear of bringing you to still greater harm; but he consents to the meeting now, and I have come.'

'Priscilla, dear Priscilla!' cried Christian, deeply moved, 'what ails you that you are so pale, so strange?'

'Nay, 'tis nothing,' said the girl, wearily passing her hand across her eyes; 'do not speak of *me*, it is of you I wish to talk. Oh, Christian, Christian, it is breaking my heart!'

'Breaking your heart?'

'The thought of you, the sight of you, with these cruel chains about you—I cannot sleep at night, and I cannot rest all day. Christian, I shall never know a moment's peace till the man I love is free!'

Was he awake or dreaming? Was it all true or possible? Could it be Priscilla who spoke, who uttered the very words which he knew it was life to him to hear? Yes, she had spoken at last, she loved him, and for a moment the terrible darkness which oppressed his soul seemed to pass away.

'My darling!' he murmured; and Priscilla, gazing up at him through her tears, asked quietly,

'Christian, am I right? your heart is not changed— you care for me still?'

'Care for you! merciful God, what a question!'

'Ah, then it is true, and I am glad. Christian, dear,

dear Christian, as you love me, save yourself for me; give one promise to the captain, and he will take off these cruel irons; and when we reach land, we will depart in peace!'

She paused, but he was silent. He knew now what she would have; and though his love for her was strong—ay, stronger a thousandfold than it had ever been—vengeance arose and gained the mastery.

'Christian, answer me. I do not ask you to forgive him, I only ask you to save yourself, and—yes, I will say it—to keep my heart from breaking.'

'God knows, Priscilla, I would give my life to spare you pain. As well ask me to give up my life, Priscilla, as to let that man go free.'

'Oh do not say so! God does not suffer such sins as his to go unpunished; but it is His work, not thine, Christian. Promise me, make me happy for this night at least, and all will yet be well.'

She bent above his hand and kissed it again; then, with a sudden impulse, she cast her arms about his neck, and hid her face upon his bosom.

'My darling!' he murmured; 'Priscilla, don't weep; whatever comes to me, I know that you will be secure from harm.'

'But you will give me your promise?'

'Ask me not to-night, Priscilla; come to me again, my darling; but first before you go, answer me one thing.'

'Yes.'

'If I promise to let this man live, to forget all our house's wrongs, what then—what of yourself, Priscilla?'

'Of myself?'

'Will you become my wife?'

She was silent, looking down and trembling. Presently she answered,

'At least I will promise this: To marry no other living man.'

'You will—you swear it?'

'Yes.'

'My darling, my own brave girl! Now go, Priscilla, for you are weary; but you will come to me again?'

'Oh yes, I will come.'

She laid her gentle head upon his bosom, and suffered him to kiss her cheek. Then, her bosom heaving
with a strange new sense of mingled sorrow and joy,
she crept quietly from the forecastle and left him there
alone.

Priscilla slept soundly that night; and her sleep
was attended by pleasant dreams. She arose in the
morning looking better and prettier than she had done
for days, and asked for an early interview with the
captain.

This she had little difficulty in obtaining; Polypheme, always taken by a pretty face, was unusually
partial to Priscilla.

He received her in his own cabin, and bent his one
eye upon her with a more benign look than ever. How
pretty she looked in her grey gown, with the new-born
light of love in her eyes! She had come to plead her
lover's cause; and the excitement of this, coupled with
a strange bashfulness caused by the memory of the
interview of the preceding night, suffused her cheeks
with colour, and put a tremulous smile upon her lips.

But she spoke so earnestly, and pleaded so well, that
the captain, who at first seemed obdurate, listened with
some attention, and promised at length to go and speak
with Christian again, and so ascertain if it would be
possible for him to grant Priscilla's request.

'All I ask of you,' she said, 'is to set him free.
'Tis cruel to keep him bound and a prisoner, when he
hath committed no offence.'

The captain, who guessed the reason of her pleading, smiled grimly.

'What may be his name, did you say, mistress?'

'Christian Christianson.'

'A good name for one that's slick and squar'; but
I tell you he ain't slick and squar'! He's about as bold
a hand as ever come aboard the *Miles Standish*. He come
aboard as a common sailor, and now I calculate he's a
gentleman who's working his way to the gallows!'

'He was mad with trouble and shame, and knew
not what he did. Be kind to him, captain dear; remember with what measure you mete it shall be meted
to you again!'

The captain rubbed his horny hand over his weather-beaten brow, and sat in sore perplexity.

'Tain't fair for you to tackle *me*. I ought to do my duty, missie; and my duty is to keep the man in irons.'

'No, no.'

'But yes. I don't say I mean to do it, but I tell you it's my duty; and never afore to-day has Ezekiel M. Higginbotham known what 'tis to turn away from duty. Look you here, my dear, if you come here with your pretty face and pleading ways, you'll be the ruin o' me. But say no more. I know what I know. Guess them irons hurt *you* more a precious sight than they hurt the chap that wears them. He's a tough 'un; I take no account of him; but for you, my dear —there, go right away, or Captain Higginbotham won't know the meaning of duty soon.'

So Priscilla, feeling that just at present nothing more was to be done, imprinted a grateful kiss upon the captain's hand and left him.

No sooner had she disappeared than another figure entered without ceremony into the captain's cabin. This was Richard Orchardson. His face was very pale, his brow lowering, his hand twitching nervously; he closed the door before he spoke.

'Captain Higginbotham,' he said, 'do you mean to do what the girl has asked you? do you mean to release the ruffian who is in irons for assaulting me?'

The first surprise of the meeting over, the captain glared upon his visitor with anything but a pleasant light in his eye.

'Eavesdropping,' he muttered. 'Young man, I calculate you'd be better employed in keeping your own berth, than placing your darn'd ear at the keyhole of my cabin door. As for what I do, and what I don't do, it ain't no consarn of yours!'

''Tis my concern this far. That wretch threatened my life and you heard him. You put him in irons, because you knew it was the only means of keeping me from harm. Let him free, and what is the result? I am on board ship, in mid ocean, and unable to defend myself; my enemy, set free by you, will carry out his devilish purpose, and murder me.'

If the expression on the captain's face might be trusted, Polypheme evidently thought that the deed would be well done. He was a rough-and-ready old sailor, but he had knocked about a good deal, and so had gained no little insight into human nature. The little drama which was being enacted about him, he understood by this time tolerably well. He had seen into the hearts of his three passengers: he adored Priscilla; and of the two men he certainly gave the preference to John Dyson. Though at first he had been much irritated at the deception which had been used, the man's rough openness of manner appealed to him infinitely more than did the more polished conduct of his enemy and rival. Still, with all his prejudices, he was obliged to acknowledge the truth; and the truth was, that if he released Christian Christianson to please Priscilla, he certainly rendered himself liable for whatever evil consequences might ensue.

This reflection by no means improved the captain's temper. He turned roughly upon his companion,

'Waal, young man, have you done?'

'Yes; I've warned you, and that is enough for me. Whatever you do, you must answer for before man and God, remember that!'

'Yes, I guess I *will* remember it, my friend,' muttered the captain to himself as Orchardson moved away; 'I guess I'll remember every darn'd word you've uttered, for I like the cut of your jib less than ever. Waal, the little girl had some sense anyhow, when she made sail from such as you!'

Utterly beside himself with passion, Orchardson strode angrily to the after cabin; he had played his trump card; if that failed, what could he do? That the captain, in utter defiance of his wish, would dare to set Christian free he could not for a moment believe; but although he could force him to keep Christian in irons for some little time, he could not force him to forbid Priscilla those stolen interviews to which he had already been a witness. Yes, he had seen her throw her arms around the man's neck, kiss his hand, and wet it with her tears. Here was the gall which was working so bitterly in his soul. He determined, at all hazard, to put an end to this uncertainty. If she would not marry him, she should not marry his enemy; nay, sooner than that, he himself would take the initiative, and kill the man, or take her into his arms and leap with her into the sea.

He sought an interview with Priscilla; and at length he obtained it; but it left him more distraught and agitated than ever. It was clear to him that, so long as Christian lived, there was no room for another in Priscilla's heart.

Then, between jealousy, despair, and fear, the man's nature grew diabolic. A thousand desperate dreams and schemes flitted through his brain; until at last he was ready to draw destruction upon his own head, so long as his enemy's destruction and discomfiture were ensured at the same time.

CHAPTER XXI.

BETWEEN TWO ELEMENTS.

In the dead of the calm autumn night, when all on board the vessel except the watch were sound asleep, and when the captain himself was snoring comfortably in his cabin, there suddenly arose a loud cry of alarm forward, followed by a rush of feet across the decks.

The next minute the mate rushed into the captain's cabin.

'What's the matter?' asked Higginbotham, leisurely opening his one eye.

'Something wrong forrard—for God's sake come, it looks like fire!'

In an instant the captain, who was only partially undressed, was on his feet. Of all alarms that can startle a brave sailor's heart on the high seas, that of fire is surely the most terrible; and the captain, though he was bold as a lion, shook life a leaf.

'I'm coming!' he said, beneath his breath. 'Don't alarm the passengers; and, above all, keep it quiet from the women.'

The night was dark and still, the wind strong but

gentle and fair, the ship, under all her wealth of snowy canvas, gliding smoothly along from billow to billow. On the forward deck the crew were collected in a crowd, some half-dressed, as if newly startled from sleep, all, pale and panic-stricken as frightened sheep, gazing down. The scuttle of the forecastle was off, and from the dark hold a thick black smoke was rising, with a heavy suffocating smell.

'Man the buckets!' cried the skipper. 'Rig the head pump and get ready the hose.'

The men rushed to and fro obeying the order; and soon a steady stream of water was pouring down the scuttle. The main pump was kept going, and buckets of sea water were passed from hand to hand and poured down; but the water seemed only to feed and thicken the smoke which grew momently more sulphurous and black.

'Where's the fire?' gasped the captain. 'How did it begin?'

No one knew. All the watch on deck could tell was that their attention had suddenly been awakened by a burning smell, and the sight of smoke coming from below; and that they had given the alarm and brought their comrades from their berths.

With wild shouts and cries the men continued labouring to get the fire under; but it was obvious by this time that it was unmanageable: the dreadful smoke came thick as lava from the mouth of a volcano, blinding and suffocating the lookers-on.

Suddenly, in the midst of the tumult, the captain saw a white figure standing near to him, and heard a clear voice calling his name. He turned and recognised Priscilla.

'Don't be alarmed, missie!' he said. 'Please God, we'll get it under!'

But with a quick cry of terror she put her hands upon his arm.

'But Christian—is he safe? Oh captain, he was down *there!*'

The skipper staggered as if struck by a bullet. In the terror and agony of the alarm, he had entirely forgotten the prisoner.

'Where's John Dyson?' he cried in a voice of thunder.

No man answered; the men looked wildly at one another; the skipper groaned and waved his arms madly in the air.

'My God, he's below; and with them irons on, he can't escape!'

Then pressing forward in defiance of the smoke, he shrieked down the scuttle,

'Dyson! John Dyson!'

No answer came in words; but at that moment a tongue of sharp flame shot up through the scuttle, in the very heart of the darkness.

Priscilla screamed, and fell upon her knees. Yes, Christian was there, helpless to save himself, stifling, suffocating, perhaps already dead.

'Save him! save him!' she cried.

The skipper hesitated, for he had a wife and little ones ashore; but in a moment his mind was made up; throwing off coat and waistcoat, he stood in his shirt-sleeves, facing the black columns of smoke.

'If there's a man among ye, let him foller me!' he cried, and plunged into the forecastle.

The seamen stood in terror, shrinking back. All at once a black form, naked to the waist, leapt forward and followed. He was a gigantic negro who had once been a plantation slave, and now occupied a subordinate position in the cook's galley.

Blacker and blacker rose the reek; fiercer and more frequent grew the jets of fire, hissing and moaning under the streams of green water that still poured steadily down.

'Don't stop pumping,' cried the mate; it's the only chance!'

A hushed and horrified silence fell upon the groups of men; they moved to and fro silently, and but for the renewed urging of the mate, would have stood paralysed with fear.

At that moment Priscilla saw, standing close to her, the figure of Richard Orchardson. He was leaning against the foremast, as if faint and terror-stricken.

'Where is the captain?' he cried to the mate, who stood by.

'Down below, looking after one of the hands.'

'You should not have suffered him! It will cost him his life.'

As Richard spoke, one wild cheer arose from the crew. Through the forecastle scuttle, amidst the blinding blackness, appeared the skipper; behind him came the negro; and between them, supported in their powerful arms, was seen the insensible form of Christian Christianson.

At this moment the flame belched upward, bright as crimson lightning. Scorched and blinded, the negro let go his hold; but with a wild cheer, mate and crew rushed forward, and dragged the three figures out upon the dripping deck.

The negro fell forward on his knees, charred and wounded by the fire, which had licked round his limbs from below; the body of Christian fell like a log close to the spot where Priscilla was kneeling; while the little skipper, breathless and choking, but otherwise uninjured, began shrieking out his orders to the crew.

The fire now shot up in steady streams, and caught the foresail, which, in a moment, became a sheet of flame, while a crackling roar ascended from below, with wilder bursts of crimson.

It was clear now that the ship was really doomed, and that in a few minutes she would be on fire from stem to stern.

'Lower the boats!' cried Captain Higginbotham. 'Call the passengers!'

There was no need to call them. They were gathered together in a terrified throng at the waist, looking forward in horror; but among them stood the tall form of the blind preacher, the crimson light falling on his sightless orbs, his lips moving in solemn prayer.

The boats were lowered, and floated safely, with the rowers in their places, in the smooth sea on the port side; water kegs and provisions, rapidly gathered together, were placed in each; the ladders were placed, and the captain stood above them, guarding the passage.

'The women first!' he cried; and one by one the women were handed down—some to the long-boat, some to the captain's gig. Then the mate ran aft with Priscilla in his arms; he had found her, half swooning, bending over Christian's insensible form.

She was handed gently down; her father followed; then Richard and the rest.

'Bring along John Dyson!' said the skipper; and at the word Christian was carried aft, and placed in the gig at Richard's very feet.

He did not stir, but he was breathing and alive.

What followed was like a frightful dream to all who had their senses in that dreadful hour. Almost before the boats could be cast free, the flames seized the entire vessel, played like fiery snakes around mast and rigging, caught the sails, which shrivelled up like paper, shrieked and roared and flashed with scorching bloodshot beams and horrible sulphurous fume. The skies above, and the seas below, were crimson with the flame; the air was bright as with the red light of dawn, and the terrified people in the boats could see each other's faces.

The boats pushed off from the vessel's side, Captain Higginbotham standing erect in the stern of the gig, and looking back. Only those who know how a sailor loves his ship can understand what sorrow filled the stout skipper's heart as he looked his last at the *Miles Standish*. He had sailed her for years; he knew every seam and stitch upon her as well as a lover knows the beauty-spots in his mistress's face; and he had, moreover, a large pecuniary share in her ownership. Therefore, something like a tear glittered in his eye as he saw her drifting away between the two elements, one consuming and destroying her above, the other waiting for her below.

In the boat with the captain were Mr. Sefton and Priscilla, Richard Orchardson, Christian, and a number of the emigrants. In the other boat, commanded by the mate, were the remainder of the emigrants and ship's company.

As the gig pushed off, Christian opened his eyes, and saw above him, in the red light, two familiar faces —those of Priscilla and Richard Orchardson. The girl's eyes were fixed on him, watching eagerly for a sign of returning life; the moment he stirred, she uttered a joyful exclamation.

But Richard Orchardson leant over, saying in a low voice to the captain,

' Put that man in the other boat, I beseech you ! '

' Nay, nay, let him stay here ! ' said Priscilla ; ' or if he goes, let me go too.'

The skipper made no sign. He was still too busy looking at the ship. Like a fiery portent, she was drifting away before the wind ; and they were already far enough away to lean on their oars and watch her in safety.

Richard repeated his request. Higginbotham turned at last.

' Silence, and keep your place, young man ! ' he said, sternly. ' This ain't no time for foolish quarrels, now we're all together in the hands o' God.'

And he added, pointing to Christian,

' Take off them irons ! '

Two of the crew leant over at the word of command, and, setting Christian free, raised him to a sitting posture, with his body in the bottom of the boat, and his head resting against the gunwale. He was breathing freely now, but was still dizzy and faint.

' How are you now, John Dyson ? '

Christian turned his head, and murmured something unintelligible. Then he suddenly became conscious of his enemy's white face gazing down upon him, and he staggered to his knees, and tried to spring towards him.

' Keep back,' cried the skipper, ' or, by thunder, over you go into the sea. Listen to me, John Dyson ! I took you out of them flames, and I saved your life, but if you lift a finger agin any soul on board this boat, to the bottom of the sea you go.'

A general murmur from the boat's crew showed that this was no mere empty threat. Several strong hands held Christian back ; but, struggling and panting, he pointed at Orchardson, and cried,

' Then speak to him ! Ask him who set your ship on fire ! '

' What d'ye mean ? ' said Higginbotham, startled at the words.

'I mean that he did it! Look at him—he cannot deny it.'

Pale and trembling, Richard shrank back from Christian's accusing finger.

'The man is mad,' he gasped.

But with a deep, threatening groan, the sailors paused on their oars, and glared at Richard Orchardson, while the skipper cried in a terrible voice,

'Speak, *you!* If that man speaks truth, he's spoken your death-sentence—he has, by the Etarnal!'

'It is false, false!' cried Richard, wildly. 'You must be mad as he to listen to such an accusation. You know he is my mortal enemy—you know he did seek my life; if anyone be guilty, it is he, not I!'

The boats were now close together, rocking on the dark billows of the sea.

A mile away the ship burned brightly, consumed and charred almost to the water's edge.

Suddenly there was a rush of flame heavenward, a heavy, thunderous roar; then darkness. The remains of the ship had sunk like a cinder to the bottom of the sea.

For a moment all eyes were turned that way, and everything was forgotten in the piteous sight. With the last glimpse of the vessel that had borne them so safely and so long, came a horrible sense of desolation.

They were alone in a frail boat, not on the gentle Pacific, where calm like that which surrounded them might last for days and days, but on the Atlantic Ocean of constant storms, where, if the tempest arose, no boat could hope to live.

'Keep your places, all!' said the captain. 'We'll hev all this out soon; and if so be that ship was fired by any living man aboard these boats, the hand of the Lord will point him out to us, never fear! But now we must shape our course, and try for to fall in with some passing ship—guess it's **our last** chance out here on God Almighty's ocean.'

CHAPTER XXII.

CAST AWAY.

As the captain uttered the words, the solemn voice of the blind preacher arose as if in response, and all eyes were turned to the tall figure, sitting with uplifted arms in the midst of the little lines of emigrants gathered together in the boat.

'We are in God's hands, my brethren. Let us pray ! '

Instantly the captain uncovered his head; the other men in the boat followed his example, while, in a perfectly calm voice, Mr. Sefton, who throughout all that night had never for a moment lost his serenity, poured out an extempore prayer for help and guidance. When it was ended, the captain stood up in the stern, and in a loud voice gave his commands to the mate, who was steering the companion boat.

It was arranged that the two boats should keep each other in sight as well as possible; but that, should any unforeseen circumstance come to separate them, attempt should still be made in either case to keep in the line of passing ships. To make for any land was impossible; they were almost in mid-ocean. The only hope was that, before a tempest arose, they might be sighted from the deck of some vessel, and saved.

Only he who has been shipwrecked, and cast away on the great ocean in an open boat, can realise the hopelessness and weariness of the situation; but the tale is one 'twice told;' the circumstances too familiar and common for detailed recapitulation.

It had been about midnight when the first alarm of 'fire' was given; and now, within less than one short hour, the ship had vanished in the consuming flame, and they were all homeless wanderers on the deep. The night was dark and chill. It needed a keen look-out to keep the other boat in view; but ever and anon the crew of one shouted to the crew of the other; and the voices had a strange, supernatural sound.

Dawn broke at last, with chilly gleams of wind and

rain. The sun came out of the sea like an orange globe, and the light crept from ripple to ripple with faint prismatic rays, till the whole stretch of ocean was dimly lit. Then they saw on every side of them, whichever way they turned, the darkly heaving horizon line; but no sail.

The light came on haggard faces, worn with wait-ing and watching. At the tiller sat the captain, quiet and resolute, with a tender eye for the women, and a cheery word, when it was needed, for the men. Near to him was Priscilla and her father; the latter with his eyes closed and his hands clasped, as if praying in sleep; the former very wan and sad, with her eyes ever turned towards Christian, who sat watching her with bloodshot eyes from the bottom of the boat. Priscilla saw now with horror that his face was blackened as with smoke and fire, that his dress was smoke-covered and ragged, and one of his arms, which was bare to the elbow, badly burnt.

Since the captain had spoken in stern reproach, while ordering the prisoner's irons to be knocked off, Christian had scarcely stirred; and, as if to keep his spirit under sweet control, looked only at Priscilla, and never once turned his eyes again towards his enemy. Richard Orchardson sat deathly pale opposite to Pris-cilla, separated from Christian by several men and women. In the agony of those terrible hours, he seemed to have grown years older; so pinched and grey were his features, so lifeless and dead his mien.

All that day the boats sailed on quietly together; nothing happened of any consequence to break the dark monotony of the situation.

Towards nightfall the wind rose slightly; and as the boat became awkward to run in the rough sea, a small sail was set forward, to give her comfortable steering way and keep her trim. She was heavily laden with her human freight, and needed careful management, to avoid foundering in the rough 'jumble' that now began to rise.

Darkness fell; and in its midst the sound of the wind and the surging of the sea became doubly dreadful. Cries and moans began to rise from the women ; and even the men uttered terrified exclamations from time to time.

But when the terror was highest, the voice of the blind preacher was heard again, enjoining prayer and trust in the Lord who made the sea. This man's courage and trust were so absolute, the moral influence of his presence was so great, that the brave skipper, who was brave as a lion, but less serenely pious, looked at him in growing admiration. Nor did he less admire the daughter, who emulated her father's resignation, and at his command led the voices of their people in a tender evening hymn.

And still Christian Christianson kept silent in his place, subdued by the solemnity of the situation, and tranquillised for the time being by the serene presence of her he so passionately loved.

On the morning of the second day, which broke calm and cold, with gusts of fitful wind on a short chopping sea, the look-out man in the captain's boat suddenly pointed to the horizon, and cried, ' A sail ! ' Almost simultaneously, they heard a cry from the companion boat, which was rising and falling a quarter of a mile away, and saw a man standing erect in the bow, straining his eyes towards the same point in the horizon.

And sure enough, all eyes, turning one way, beheld afar off, half lost in flying foam and vapour, now seen, now almost blurred from vision, a dark spot against the background of a grey daylight,—a silhouette, like the sail of a small boat, which, being scrutinised by experienced men, resolved itself presently into the black topsail of a ship.

A wild cry went up from the poor shipwrecked folk, and all, as with one accord, turned to look at the captain.

His eye was fixed on the distant object, and his face was baleful and unexpressive even to stoniness ; but his big heart was beating fast, and it was not without an effort that he concealed his agitation.

Priscilla was the first to break the silence.

' Captain dear, is it a ship ? '

He knew that all were watching and waiting for his answer, but he kept his eye still fixed on the distant object, and replied without turning his head,

'Give me time, missie, give me time! Yes, 'tis a ship sure enough!' and then, as another wild cry went up from the boat, he added in a deep clear voice, 'Yes, 'tis a ship, but what of that? Wait a bit, forrard there! It's one thing for to see a ship, and another thing to be seen *by* a ship; and even once seen 'tis another thing to be *picked up* by a ship. Don't holler yet, but wait and watch!'

They waited patiently enough, because every moment brought the gladsome apparition nearer.

Daylight flamed behind it, while, black and portentous, sail after sail arose, and finally, the black hull itself. Then, as the light increased, and the wind came out of the light, and gladdening ripples danced everywhere upon the morning sea, they saw a goodly brig in full sail, bearing down towards them as fast as she could fly—sailing westward, with windward light behind her. She was coming so straight for them, though doubtless they were as yet unseen, that there was no need to make any signal, save the little shred of sail, or to give any other sign of distress. They must and should be seen, that was certain.

With that certainty, came another deepening terror.

What could the barque be, and what human hearts did it contain? Perhaps it would pass cruelly by, without lending a succouring hand; for in those days, more than these, there were many devils afloat on the high seas. Perhaps those who manned her were wild and desperate men of some foreign nation, who might carry them away to untold sorrows, or nameless tortures of captivity.

'What dew you make of her, William Long?' cried the captain, addressing the look-out in the bow, an old sailor of mighty experience. 'Is she a Yankee or a Britisher? a merchantman or a privateer?'

William Long's opinion was that she looked too small for a merchantman, and too squat for a privateer; that she was not a Yankee nor yet a Britisher, and was, if anything, a petty trader from some foreign port.

Hand over hand, the brig approached them; and at last they could plainly perceive, from the commotion on her decks, that they were seen. Suddenly there was a puff of smoke at her side, followed by a sharp report; she had fired a gun.

'Ready there!' cried the captain, while his face brightened. 'She's going to pick us up.'

Down she came, with dark faces crowding at her side. Then, to the huge joy of all these shipwrecked wayfarers, she squared her yards, came round on the wind, and waited for the boats to run alongside.

'A Dutchman, by the Eternal!' cried the skipper delighted. 'Boys, give her a cheer!'

Straightway sailors and passengers cheered together, and the cheer was echoed instantly from the other boat. In a few minutes more the captain had run his boat alongside, and one by one the wayfarers sprang on deck.

Facing them, on the deck of the brig, was a squat figure in a red cotton nightcap, smoking an enormous wooden pipe, and surrounded by a crew of squat pigmies, in red cotton nightcaps too. His face was broad, weather-beaten, and good-humoured, and he gave a friendly grunt as Higginbotham approached, and seized him by the hand.

An excited colloquy ensued, but as neither skipper understood a word of the language of the other, it led to no very definite result; until one of the Dutch seamen, stepping forward at a nod from his skipper, offered his services as interpreter. It then turned out that the barque was the *Anna* of Rotterdam, commanded by Jan Brock of the same city, and outward bound for Halifax, Nova Scotia. The accommodation on board was limited, especially in the after portions of the vessel, but such as it was, the wayfarers were welcome to share it—as well as the rough fare of the ship's crew, of which the *pièce de résistance* was (as after experience proved) the hardest of Dutch cheese.

But Captain Higginbotham was enraptured. Again and again he wrung his brother skipper's hand, and then, turning to his own passengers and crew, all of whom were now on the *Anna's* deck, he loudly congratulated them on having fallen into the hands of a man and a brother.

The rescued people were distributed over the ship, the crew of the *Miles Standish*, including Christian, going forward to the forecastle, the emigrants finding tolerable quarters amidships, while cramped accommodation was found in the captain's quarters aft for Priscilla and her father, Richard Orchardson, and Captain Higginbotham. Priscilla had a little cabin in the poop all to herself; it was very tiny, and smelt horribly of bilge water and tobacco; but once alone there, she fell upon her knees, and thanked God for His great mercies, and for her fortunate escape.

CHAPTER XXIII.

ICE-DRIFT FROM THE POLAR SEA.

CAPTAIN HIGGINBOTHAM, surveying his new friends leisurely with an eye of profound experience, soon discovered that good seamanship was by no means the characteristic of either skipper or crew; that the former spent a good deal of his time in his berth, pipe in mouth, under the influence of the Indian narcotic and his national liquor, and that the latter sailed the ship pretty much as sweet fancy taught them. Fortunately, the wind was light and fair, the ship a tough and tight one; and for the rest, everybody was grimy, greasy, and very good-humoured.

During the evening following their rescue, while the ship was slipping along quietly before the same steady easterly wind, Higginbotham strolled forward, and saw Christian sitting alone on a coil of rope, with his head resting against the rail.

. ' Waal, John Dyson ? '

Christian looked up without replying. He had washed away the traces of smoke and blood, and his face looked white and strange.

' Hev you come to your cool senses, John Dyson,'

'Once alone there, she fell upon her knees, and thanked God for His great mercies.'

continued the skipper after a pause, 'or air you still
a-hatching mischief? I want to talk to you a bit.
Out theer in the boat you said some one set my poor
old ship afire ?'

'I said it, and I knew it.'

'Speak out your mind. 'Tain't for what I lost in
her, though I had my share in her timber and her
cargo, but Lord knows I loved the old ship, and a
bit of my heart went down in her when she sunk like
a cinder into the sea. Speak out then, John Dyson!
Dew you think she had foul play?'

'I said it, and I think it.'

'Waal, now, your reasons,—come?'

'I will tell you what happened before the alarm
was given. I had fallen asleep, sitting almost as you
see me now. Suddenly I wakened, and saw, close to
me, something like a man's shape. It was dark, but
light enough to see *that*. Then, before I could stir,
or cry, or even think, I smelt the stench o' fire, and
saw black fumes of smoke rising all around. I tried
to spring up, but my irons held me fast from flying,
yet I shrieked to them sleeping around me, and they
gave the alarm.'

'Is that all, John Dyson?'

'Is it not enough? Your good ship perished by
fire, and *he* kindled it. The moment I saw his face
in the boat, the moment I met his eyes, I knew 'twas
he and no other. May hell consume him! May he
answer for it in tenfold flame, when God judgeth quick
and dead!'

The captain's face was black as a thunder-cloud,
as he listened. He said nothing more, but stood in
gloomy meditation ; then, muttering to himself ominously, he went aft, and gazed darkly over the vessel's
side.

But the more he thought, the less method he could
find in Christian's mad accusation. He knew the
hatred between the two men, and he knew likewise
how one would spare no pains to heap confusion upon
the other. Still doubting and wondering, he sought
out Richard Orchardson, and openly taxed him with
the infernal deed—prepared, if he confessed his guilt,

to hand him over to the swift vengeance of the shipwrecked crew.

To his surprise, Richard assumed a high tone of indignant protestation; loudly proclaimed his innocence, and demanded to be brought face to face with his accuser; and finally stormed and wept so like an innocent man foully taxed and troubled, that the captain was completely thrown upon his beam-ends.

'In the name of God,' cried Richard at last, 'what end could I serve by such devilry? The man did threaten my life, and you had him in irons; nay, you yourself could see that he was mad for blood as any wild beast. Do you think, man, that I was as mad as he? Did I hold my life so cheap, and care so little for the beloved companions of my voyage, that I sought to compass my own death, and theirs, by an act worthy of yonder madman, not of me? I am a gentleman of good birth, law-loving and law-abiding. How dare you blacken me so with your base suspicion! How dare you blight my good fame, at the whisper of a gaol-bird, an outcast without a name!'

This bluster overcame the good captain, who indeed saw no tittle of rational evidence to connect the speaker with the loss of his ship. On the very face of it, it seemed utterly improbab'e and inscrutable. Of all men living, Richard Orchardson seemed least likely to imperil his own life so insanely.

So Higginbotham walked forward, and found Christian sitting as he had left him, like the very image of despair.

'You air a liar, John Dyson!' he said, between his set teeth, and turned savagely away.

Meantime, a strange tumult was going on in Christian's soul. Though his body was possessed by a kind of brooding torpor, which caused him to remain for hours in the same position, like a shape of stone, his thoughts were tempestuous enough, but confused and broken, like cloud-phantoms reflected in a mere.

His sister's shame, his mother's death, his own wild flight from home, his life on shipboard, his interview with Priscilla, his attack upon his enemy, the fire by night, the sudden shipwreck,—all seemed like a troubled dream; and lo! there he sat, baffled, disregarded, no nearer to vengeance than before.

For despite the holy influence of his love for Priscilla, the thought of vengeance remained. To forget *that*, under any temptation, would have been to forget his father and his mother, all the sufferings of their house, and above all, his sister's wrong. Not even Priscilla, not even the prospect of her love and divine compassion, could or should obliterate those memories. He had sworn an oath, and he meant to keep it. Richard Orchardson should die.

If his conscience needed stronger justification, it was found in his firm belief that Orchardson had fired the ship. He had no doubt whatever that this was so, though he had no proof that would satisfy any unprejudiced individual. Yes, Orchardson was guilty; another black record in the calendar of his hateful life.

And Christian, though he seemed tamed and unresolved for the time being, was merely accumulating venom and watching till the time came to strike. He saw little or nothing of his enemy; for Captain Higginbotham had contrived to make his brother captain understand that 'John Dyson' was a dangerous lunatic, to be strictly watched, and above all, never suffered to come aft on any pretence whatever.

On first receiving this warning, the Dutch captain was for clapping him into irons immediately, but at Priscilla's intercession he refrained, and merely gave his crew orders to knock the madman on the head, if necessary. So Christian found himself avoided like a leper, as 'dangerous,' by the crew of both vessels. The only friendly face among them was that of the gigantic negro who had assisted to rescue him from the fire. This poor black had taken a fancy to him from the first, and still showed his sympathy to the best of his power.

To Christian, nursing his wrath and sorrow before the mast, Priscilla came once and again. One of their conversations may be taken as a sample of several.

'Oh, Christian, God is good. Let us pray to Him together.'

'Nay, I am not one of the praying kind.'

'But think of His great goodness and mercy. He

held us in the hollow of His hand, and yet He spared us ; think of that.'

'I think rather that He suffered us to be cast away, through the device of a devil.'

'Alas! therein do you show the madness of your hate. You should be just even to your enemy. Mr. Orchardson is innocent as I of the evil you cruelly lay at his door.'

Christian looked up with a strange expression.

'Then the devil hath been again at your ear! Priscilla, it will ever be so, until he is silent for ever.'

'That threat again, and that look which hath made me heart-sick so often! Oh, Christian, I fear you. He is right—you are mad indeed.'

'An eye for an eye, a tooth for a tooth, saith the Lord!'

'But we may not take the Lord's vengeance into our own wicked hands. Christian, promise me to forego your vengeance, or——'

'Go on.'

'Or I shall never again call you friend of mine.'

That gentle warning did not move him now, for all the sullen evil in his nature was awake. So he answered in a low voice,

'Even *that* will not change me. My mother cannot sleep in her grave, my sister cannot look in the face of men, till they are avenged.'

So she left him, returning sad and tearful to her cabin.

Now, in her pretty anxiety to bring those two warring hearts together, she deepened the hate of both; since Richard Orchardson was watching her interviews with his rival, and Christian in his turn knew that she turned back from them to the other's counsel. Knowing Christian's violent disposition, and his readiness to think all evil against his enemy, she did not for a moment entertain his terrible accusation of arson; indeed, the fact that he had made it, to some extent hardened her heart against him—it seemed of a malignity so diabolic.

And during those days after the rescue, Richard Orchardson was so martyr-like and so sad; saying so little in reproach, looking so much ; that more than once meeting his eyes she sighed, and spoke to him gently, till some gentle answer came. In her heart she said, 'Both these men love me, and one methought I loved ; but I would trust my fate to neither ; for the one I could have chosen is dangerous and jealous to madness, and the other is too weak and full of suspicion.' Often in her heart she wished she were free of both.

But our tale must not linger with the thoughts of Priscilla Sefton, nor with the hopes and fears, the jealousy and hate, of the two men who had followed her across these waters. Strange events were to happen, to perplex still further the relations of all three ; and these events were to be determined by the fortunes and misfortunes of the ship that was bearing them westward, to some undiscovered fate.

For several days the fair wind lasted. Then the vessel passed into a great sea-mist, covering troubled tracks of windless calm.

The moment this mist was reached, it became intensely cold ; the sails and cordage became stiff with frost, the decks slippery with ice. Looking over the side, they saw small fragments of broken ice floating upon the sea. Then it became dark ; so dark that all day long the ship's lights were kept burning, and the fog-horn loudly blowing.

At midday, the look-out man sang out that he could hear something like the sound of waters surging, and could see the gleams of breakers. The Dutch skipper rushed forward, and immediately shouted out to the helmsman an order to 'keep away.' The order was obeyed only just in time ; and as the vessel swept round before the faint wind, all saw distinctly the surges thundering round a gigantic iceberg, which rose like a mountain in the midst of the sea. The next minute it was swallowed up in black fog.

It was now evident that they were in a position of some peril. In anticipation of north-west winds, which often prevailed at that season of the year, they had steered too northerly a course, and had consequently fallen in with drifting ice. To what extent they were

surrounded, it was as yet impossible to tell. Shorten·
ing sail, and keeping a sharp look-out, they crept on
through the darkness, waiting for the mist to clear.

All at once the wind began to rise, blowing in fitful
squalls from the south-east, but almost simultaneously
the mist rose. Then they saw, by the light of a sullen
sunset, with great bars of orange and red, like the skin
of some wild beast, the sea on every side of them
covered with loose bergs of all sizes, drifting southward;
some sparkling with all the colours of the rainbow,
others dark and shadowy as floating blocks of cloud.

Priscilla stood on deck, and gazed wonderingly on
the strange sight, thinking only of its loveliness and
novelty.

But Captain Higginbotham, who stood near her,
was otherwise moved; for he saw in the neighbourhood
of drifting ice, and in the rapidly rising wind, a new
danger—not easily to be avoided by the Dutch skipper,
for whose seamanship he had by this time acquired a
supreme contempt.

'Look, captain dear!' cried Priscilla. 'Are they
not beautiful? That one is like a great church, with
blue vaults beneath, and a figure like an angel on the
threshold; and that other like a fair ship, with sails of
crystal and masts of marble, crowded with folk in
shining robes, singing " Holy, Holy!" like the hosts in
the Pilgrim's tale.'

'They're pretty enough to look at, missie,' returned
the captain, ' but nasty customers to come agin when a
ship's making nine knots an hour. I'd rather hev their
room than their company, anyhow.'

So saying, he turned and joined his brother skipper,
who was standing pipe in mouth on the poop, and
regarding the bergs with a grin of total stupidity and
unconcern. Conversation with him was impossible,
and Higginbotham, after in vain trying to discover
what course he meant to steer, left him, with an exclamation expressive of supreme disgust.

Night fell, but fortunately there was a moon, showing itself from time to time through drifts of flying
cloud, and shedding even when itself unseen a faint
atmospheric light. As the wind was still high, it was

soon necessary to shorten more and more sail, until at last the ship was almost bare. At last it was determined to heave-to, which she did for the greater part of the night, with her head to the east and her main-topsail to the mast.

All the night the icebergs loomed on every side, sometimes coming so unpleasantly close that a man might almost have leapt upon them from the slippery decks. The sea all round, far as eye could behold, was black with their shadows.

It was soon obvious, however, that they were not a portion of any large pack, but merely a fleet of loose floes broken off and cast adrift by some storm or other convulsion of nature. As the night advanced they grew less numerous, and before daybreak the nearest was several miles away.

CHAPTER XXIV.

THE STORM.

BUT with daybreak came a new alarm.

The wind died almost completely away, but a tremendous swell was setting from the south-east, and in the same direction the gates of dawn were blocked by huge masses of black and purple cloud, layer on layer, flattened one upon another, while out of the dense mass rose a black vapour, like smoke from a funnel.

The Yankee skipper stood amidships, with William Long and several other of his own seamen, looking to the eastward.

'What dew you make of them clouds, William Long?'

The sage addressed stuck his quid into the corner of his cheek, spat leisurely over the vessel's side, drew his shirt cuff across his mouth, and then replied,

'Gale o' wind from the sou'-east.'

'Right you air, William Long. It's been brewing hell and thunder in that theer witch's caldron ever

since last night, and now, though it ought to be bright
day, there ain't enough light to read a compass by;
and d'ye hear *that?*'

As he spoke, there came from the heaving swell a
heavy roar like thunder—the voice of the sea itself,
ominously moaning.   It was curiously dark; a troubled
sense was in the air,

> 'Like that strange silence which precedes the storm,
> And shakes the forest leaves with ut a breath.'

And now far away, between the layers of cloud, strange
streaks of light were running like quicksilver. Whether
they were day-beams trying to break through the darkness, or flashes of sheet-lightning, it was difficult to
tell.

Meantime the brig was rolling and tossing on the
black billows like a thing in pain; her cordage creaking,
her sails flapping with artillery-peals, her decks opening
and shutting with the strain.

The waves came up smooth and unbroken, like
black mountains rolling down to engulf the vessel,
which was still hove to under the lightest of sail.

Just then the Dutch skipper appeared on deck, and
in a loud voice gave his orders. As the crew flew to
obey them, Higginbotham turned to his own men with
a look of horror.

'Look at that!' he exclaimed. 'If the 'tarnal
Dutch lubber isn't going to clap on canvas!'

Such was indeed the case. Springing up the masts
and into the rigging, the Dutchmen were already busy
preparing to set sail.

Higginbotham rushed aft, confronted the skipper,
and pointed eagerly to windward. The skipper smiled
and nodded, and discharging a thick volume of smoke
from his throat, gave an approving grunt. As he did
so, the air was filled with an ancient and horrible smell,
composed of rank tobacco and Schiedam.

Pale with rage, Higginbotham secured the services
of the sailor who had previously acted as interpreter,
and with his aid expressed an opinion that no one but
a madman would unfurl a yard of canvas in the face of
such weather-signs as confronted them.

Thus warned, the Dutch skipper smiled again, but more disagreeably. Then he said (through the interpreter) that he knew his own business. There was no danger; only a nice little fair wind coming out of the morning red. He knew how to sail a ship better than any 'Englander,' and he was afraid of nothing. Finally, he expressed a request, which the interpreter did not translate, that Higginbotham would go below—either in a narrow sense into the ship's cabin, or in the broad sense to a place that may be nameless, very far below indeed.

Scarcely had the Dutch skipper finished his speech, when a gigantic wave, lifting up the vessel like a cork into the air, swept him off his legs and rolled him into the lee scuppers. There he remained, without attempting to rise, either because the drink had mastered him, or because the shock had stunned him.

Almost simultaneously, the clouds to eastward opened, a flash like sulphurous lightning lit up the dark heavens, and the ocean, a league to windward, appeared as white as milk.

In a moment, Higginbotham sprang on the poop, and shrieked to his own men,

' All hands to shorten sail. If the Dutchmen interfere, chuck 'em into the sea ! Quick, for your lives ! '

Obeying the order as one man, the crew of the *Miles Standish* sprang up into the rigging. One glance to windward showed even the Dutch sailors that it was a matter of life and death. The storm was almost upon them, in all its fury.

Scarcely were the chief sails roughly stowed, than, with a shriek and a roar, the wind struck the vessel, while the water beneath and around her foamed to boiling white. The bare masts bent like reeds, while the topsail, not being quite secured, burst loose, flapped, and was torn to ribbons in a moment and blown away. For a time the vessel hung broadside, with her lee bulwarks under, and the sea almost up to the main hatch.

Without a word Higginbotham sprang to the tiller-ropes, hurled the helmsman aside, took the tiller, and jammed the helm hard over. After a long struggle, the brig began to pay off; then, like a canoe shooting the rapids of some mighty river, she swept away before the blast.

Behind them, a black rift, opening as the mouth of some gigantic caldron, belched forth fire and water; fire and water of the surcharged thunder clouds, piled mass after mass upon each other; while in one portion of the night-black east, the vapours rolled open and showed the bloodshot sun, glaring like a rayless eye upon the desolation. The rain covered the deck in torrents, and on the slippery waters, black from above and green from below, the lightning played in blinding beams.

Meantime the ship, blown bodily as if in the air between wind and water, smothered, choking, struggling, shrieking, like a living thing, the black clouds looming down upon her, the terrific seas surging up to destroy her, flew before the blast.

In the fury of this first onset, several men were washed overboard, and the Dutch skipper, who had risen to his feet, frenziedly gesticulating, would have followed their example, had he not been blown against the backstays, and flapped there like a limp and dripping rag.

'The sea is rising!' cried Higginbotham. 'There, forward! reef the foresail and set it!'

Assisted by the Dutch crew, his men obeyed him. The sea was rising indeed, and threatening to drown the vessel outright; but thanks to the foresail, they managed to heave her to for a little time, and rising and sinking in the tremendous sea, and lying over again almost to the main hatch, the brig fronted the tempest.

Below, Priscilla was on her knees by the side of her blind father; and in the midst of the frightened people, Richard Orchardson stood clinging to his berth, as white as death.

Suddenly there was a blinding flash, a thunderous roar. The vessel was covered in flying foam and fire, like flame and smoke. Then they saw the foresail shrivelling up like a shred of cotton, and blowing away into the darkness; while the vessel, with a wild lurch, came broadside to the sea.

For a minute it seemed as if all was over. She sank like a log into the trough of the sea, and one huge billow swept her from stem to stern, carrying away half-a-dozen shrieking lives. But again Higginbotham, though the water drenched him from head to foot, jammed the helm hard over, and again, with a shock like an earthquake running through her wooden frame, she paid off, and rushed away with the rushing waves before the blast.

There was now nothing for it but to let her run, and trust to chance.

Fortunately there was a ragged piece of foresail still remaining, and this served to keep her from broaching to. Higginbotham clung to the tiller with set teeth, though again and again the water, washing over the stern, smothered him and tried to drag him from his post.

Two long days and nights that gale lasted, blowing the ship they knew not whither, but sweeping her still in a northerly direction. Even after the first day's storm ceased, and the great masses of cloud behind them began to move and come up slowly, like serried legions of some stormy host, the wind increased in violence, the seas still rose, and no sun was seen.

But on the morning of the second day, after they had flown at lightning speed hundreds upon hundreds of miles, the sun burst out through flying billows of cloud, and poured a faint yellow sulphurous spume upon the tossing sea.

The clouds now passed overhead swifter than the ship flew, and by that sign they knew that the force of the gale was broken.

A new foresail was now bent on, and the vessel was able to 'heave-to' comfortably, and wait for the storm to subside.

'It's about time it *did* break!' muttered Captain Higginbotham to himself, as he glared with Cyclopean eye eastward. 'If we hed kep' on running a day and a night longer, guess we should hev come right jam smash agin the North Pole!'

Now that the danger seemed over, the Dutch skipper

was at first inclined to be quarrelsome, and to put his brother skipper in irons for having mutinously taken possession of the management of the ship, but on reflection, after moistening his anger with a bottle of Schiedam, he thought it better to swear eternal friendship—which he did, with many hand-shakes and wild gesticulations.

While things were at this pass, Priscilla and her father tried to come on deck, accompanied by Richard Orchardson. During the fury of the gale, none of the passengers had been allowed to leave their quarters below; and now, at Higginbotham's solicitation, they did not come beyond the cabin companion.

Peeping from thence, Priscilla saw a knot of sailors gathered forward, and among them the powerful form of Christian.

During the tempest he had worked hard with the rest, never shrinking from any post of danger, and again and again putting his life in peril. In the wild tumult of the elements, he seemed for a time to forget his mad purpose,—and indeed he did so, for to think at all was difficult at such a season ; all a man could do was struggle with all his bodily strength against overpowering odds, oblivious of all save the fierce, almost mechanical fight for life.

The light brightened from yellow to pale pink, and the seas came along with slowly surceasing force. Before midday, the gale died away into a strong breeze, and it was possible to set easy sail.

The vessel, still dripping and struggling like a winged bird, had bowled along swiftly for several hours, when a cry arose forward of ' Land ahead ! '

And sure enough, far away on the port bow, they saw the first loom of something black, like a low-lying bank of cloud.

An order was immediately given to take soundings, but no bottom was got with two hundred fathoms of line.

' Sure enough it looks like land,' said Captain Higginbotham, while the order was given to stand off, as close to the wind as possible.

Presently, when the sun began to sink in the western heavens, its light flamed red on what had at first been taken for land, and showed what looked like a mountainous island, forty or fifty miles away. At that moment the old sailor, William Long, strolled aft.

'Waal, William Long, what dew you make of that land ?'

William Long clung to the backstay, and went through the usual formality of clearing his mouth of tobacco juice before he spoke.

'I makes this of it, captain. It's no more land than this here brig is land. It's an iceberg, captain ! and look'ee yonder ! '—(as he spoke he lifted his right hand and swept the horizon to the north). 'If that ain't the *iceblink*, I've never been in these latitoodes afore.'

Far away along the northern horizon line there was a long strip of glimmering white, with occasional patches of dull yellow and quivering blue. William Long was an old whaler, and recognised the phenomenon in a moment.

Scarcely had he spoken, when there came, in corroboration of his words, a sudden crash, as if the vessel had struck upon some sunken rock. The brig trembled through all her timbers; and looking over the side, the seamen saw large fragments of broken ice bobbing up to the surface on each quarter. They had struck against a portion of submerged ice, and shivered it to fragments.

There could be no doubt now that they were in dangerous waters. If any further proof were wanting, they could have told the close proximity of icefields by the rapidly falling temperature.

The sheets were stiffening, and flakes of frost, thin as gossamer, were forming on the sails.

CHAPTER XXV.

BESET BY THE ICE.

RAPIDLY taken observations showed them that they were somewhere in latitude 50°, longitude 55°, and that consequently the iron-bound coast of Labrador could not be far away.   Tempestuous weather and Dutch seamarship had carried them out of their course many hundred miles.

Fortunately the wind now changed into the lightest of breezes, and they were able to steer a more southerly course ; but again and again, after nightfall, they passed masses of floating ice, and several times struck with wild concussion against drifting fragments, but without serious damage to the *Anna's* oaken frame.

All hands of both crews were now on the alert ; two men stood at the helm, extra hands were on the look-out, and the Dutch captain directed the ship's movements from the forecastle deck, passing the word aft to ' port ' or ' starboard ' the helm as occasion rose, and thus avoiding fatal collisions.   Despite all these precautions, the night was so dark, and the weather now so thick, that they were more than once in extreme danger.

When day broke again, they found themselves surrounded on every side by floating bergs and fields, with one green passage, about two miles broad, of comparatively open water.   But right ahead to the westward was a frowning battlement of blackness which looked like land.

Meantime, the passengers below were faring but badly.   Mr. Sefton was prostrate in his berth with symptoms much resembling those of low fever, and Priscilla, worn with sickness and anxiety, looked the merest ghost of herself.

The foul air of the cabin, the coarse food, and the incessant vibration, had all told upon her delicate frame. Richard Orchardson was unceasing in his attentions to both father and daughter, but he too seemed succumbing to the hard and perilous life aboard ship.

To them presently came the Yankee captain, and at his solicitation Priscilla went on deck.   Scarcely had she left the cabin, however, and come out into the chilly morning air, than she fainted away.   Richard caught her in his arms, and gently carried her back to the cabin.

Scarcely had they disappeared, than the tall form of Christian, ragged, haggard, and wild, crept from behind the mainmast, and seemed about to follow, when Captain Higginbotham interposed.

'Waal, John Dyson?' he cried sternly. 'What dew you want here?'

'She is dying,' answered Christian. 'He hath killed her. Yes, it is his doing.'

'Keep back, John Dyson. I have told you often, and I tell you now, your place is afore the mast.'

'And I tell you that we are lost, and that we are lost through *him*. He fired your ship—why do you let him live?'

As he spoke his eyes were full of a light like that of madness; so at least it seemed to the good captain, who stubbornly shook his head.

'Neow you jest take a friend's advice, John Dyson. Go back to your work like a man, and don't think of nought but helping me to get this ship safe to land. As for that young miss, remember she's aboard, and you'll have to answer to Almighty God for her life. Show you're a man, I say, and not a roaring he-b'ar.'

At that moment William Long's voice sounded from the forecastle:

'Land ahead!'

Without another word, the captain took Christian by the arm, and drew him gently to the fore part of the vessel; he made no resistance, but obeyed as if stupefied and dazed.

Clear and distinct, right ahead, the land was now seen—a frowning line of crags and mountains, with black and purple shadows, looming distinct against the background of a pale grey sky. So cold and clear was the air, that this sombre coast seemed quite near, though it could not have been less than fifty or sixty miles away.

Land ahead; on the one side of the vessel fields of ice ever closing in; and on the other—what? More ice, in seemingly impenetrable lines of gigantic bergs rising beyond the drift ice and stretching far as eye could see.

There was a Babel of voices, as the Dutch and English-speaking crew clustered together and looked around. The Dutch skipper stood smoking his eternal pipe, with a look of stupid consternation.

Soundings were again taken. This time they reached the bottom, at a depth of one hundred and fifty fathoms.

Slowly and cautiously the ship worked along the edge of the line of bergs, looking for a lead to the southward. Once or twice she entered the ice, but only to retreat in time to avoid being cracked like a walnut-shell between bergs in motion. So she crept out again into the open water, and hung about like a bewildered bird.

Then it was suggested that she should put about and work back along the open passage by which she had entered the ice—a kind of huge trap, from which, as they soon found, there was no safe return. For no sooner had she turned, and sailed a few miles along the open water, than she found that enormous bergs, like things of life, had drifted down and blocked the passage, waiting with yawning jaws for her to enter among them and be crushed.

Like a duck in the funnel of a decoy, the brig fluttered this way and that way, but found no practicable outlet.

More than once she was in mortal peril.

As she approached one huge berg, a very mountain of shining whiteness, solid as marble, a portion of its side shifted and broke away—when, with a crash like thunder, the mighty mass toppled over, within a hundred yards of the shuddering ship, deluging her with flying foam.

Night found her thus—a chilly, foggy night, in which the stiffened sails became hard as boards, showers of icicles fell from the frozen rigging at every change of position, and the decks became slippery with frost.

Turning again in the darkness, she ran along the edge of the ice ; and now, as night advanced, there was a murmur in the air of rising wind—blowing this time from the northward, and coming so cold from the pole that it cut the cheek like a lash of steel and drew blood.

At daybreak, it was blowing half a gale.

' What dew you think o' this, William Long ? ' asked Captain Higginbotham of that grizzled maritime authority.

'I think as how we're in a trap, captain; and if so be as winter's a-setting in early, there's little chance for that theer ice to clear. Unless we can bore a way through the loose ice yonder, we'll hev to go to bed like the snakes and wait for summer.'

But to attempt to bore southward just then was out of the question, for the northerly gale was still rising. By midday it blew with such fury that it was found necessary to run right in under shelter of the ice, and fix a couple of anchors to a solid berg.

This was done, with no little trouble and peril; and thus anchored to solid masses which seemed drifting to windward, they saw smaller bergs and loose floes sweeping past like ships before the shrieking wind. On one of these loose fragments stood a huge she-bear, shrieking in terror or anger as she floated by.

Creeping again on deck from the solitude of the cabin, Priscilla saw the ship beset, while the ice-fields on every side were dyed crimson by the sun, which, pausing on the level horizon line, hung like a huge drop of liquid blood. Not far distant, to the westward, lay the land they had previously sighted, with thunderous surges breaking on its rocks, while higher up its lurid mountain-heights flashed back the sunset's bloodshot beams. Innumerable terns and kittiwake gulls were hovering over the vessel, many quite fearlessly alighting on its yards, as tame as doves; and in the open water close by, flocks of seals were disporting.

There was a roar in the air above of shrieking wind, and a sound all round of surge and crashing ice, but down on the deck there was comparative shelter from the fury of the gale. Priscilla crept to the Yankee skipper's side, and reaching out her hand, softly touched his arm. She said nothing, but looked around with a strange awe and wonder, mixed with maidenly fear.

Then she shivered, for the air was icy cold.

'You'd best keep below, missie,' said the kindly skipper. 'This air ain't fit for tender lungs to breathe. I've seen the north wind bring blood from a man's chest afore now.'

'Why are we staying here?'

'I'll tell you, missie. We're beset by the ice, and what's more, there's a northerly gale blowing. If them anchors slipt, we should drive down on the bergs to lee'ard, and this ship's shell ain't tough enough to stand *that*, I reckon.'

At this moment Richard came up, and a sharp gust sweeping the deck, Priscilla clung to him. He put his arm around her waist to support her, and in her anxiety she did not attempt to free herself from his hold.

So for a space they stood, while a pair of jealous eyes, gazing from the forecastle, watched them with a new and aching despair.

Then Christian thought, 'She loves him! He hath poisoned her heart against me, and she loves him!'—and he could have killed them both.

'Do you think there is danger?' asked Richard wistfully, still supporting her.

The skipper did not answer. He was never the man to lie, and he did not care to awaken useless fears, especially in the heart of his favourite. He thrust his hands deep into the pockets of his sailor's jacket, and glared with his one eye at the sunset, as if in gloomy speculation.

Then he turned away, and going forward, saw Christian watching, like a wild beast preparing to spring. So the wary skipper placed himself in a convenient attitude, ready to interfere with brute force if the man meant mischief, as he feared.

Now, something in their common danger brought the hearts of the young man and maid together, as they stood there on the chilly deck.

'You are cold,' said R'chard softly. 'Let me fetch you something warm to cover you.'

'Nay, I am not cold,' she answered; then she added, with tears in her voice, 'O Richard, I fear for my father! He is so old, and he seems so ill. If he should die——'

She paused, for the tears choked her.

'He will not die,' returned Richard cheerfully. 'We shall soon escape from this terrible place, and find a haven.

'Pray God it may be so!—but if evil should come

to him, I should die too. Now my dear mother is dead, he is my only friend and protector.'

'Say not so. You have one other.'

'None that I love so much, none to content me if he were gone.'

He held her more closely, and under the inspiration of the moment, whispered eagerly,

'You have one who loves you more than all the world—one who would protect you with his life, one who for your sake has forsaken father and fatherland, is with you now, and will be with you till the end.'

Trembling now, she tried to release herself, but he held her fast.

'Do not hold me!' she cried. 'Let me go back to him!'

'Am I not forgiven?'

'Forgiven—what? Prithee let me go!'

'Stay a little yet,' said Richard; then in a voice of solemn earnestness he continued, 'Sweetheart, we may never leave these cruel shores alive. This ice may be our tomb. Nay, tremble not; for if it were, I for one should die peacefully, if I were certain of your sweet love. Without that, life is nothing; with it, death would be divine.'

She looked at him in wonder. His pale face was shining, his eyes full of overmastering passion.

'This is no time to talk of such things. Rather pray to God, Who holds us in the hollow of His hand;' and again she tried to disengage herself from his circling arm.

'I have prayed—I pray—to God, for one thing only—yourself, Priscilla!'

At last she released herself, but pausing, looked again into his face.

'I shall never marry. If God in His mercy spares us, my place will still be with my father. Do not speak of it again.'

The words were decided enough, but the tone was so gentle, the look so kind, that Richard might well smile to himself as the delicate figure flitted away. Flushed and wild with passion, he hung over the ship's side, and looked at the wintry scene around him.

He did not believe that there was imminent danger, but he had not lied when, in the fervour of passionate feeling, he had sworn that he could face death in Priscilla's company. Still, his dream now was of sunshine and a fair haven, with the maiden's love as his excellent reward.

And all this time the other's eyes were watching, with a feverish desire. Christian did not stir, though the impulse to do so was strong upon him; but his face was set in terrible resolve. In his heart of hearts, he too was praying to God.

'He has robbed me of everything, even her love. His life, O God—give me his life! It is forfeit to me already. God of justice, if there be God indeed, give me his life!'

Night fell; and with night came, borne down in the lap of the gale, whirlwinds of blinding snow, snow so thick that it smothered mast and rigging, drifted in great heaps upon the deck and against the bulwarks, and clothed the shivering seamen with garments of whiteness. And now the wind came in blasts so terrible that again and again the vessel was in danger of being torn away from the shelter of the solid ice, which groaned and crashed around her like mountains upheaved by earthquake.

But as soon as an anchor dragged, the men sprang out, and at peril of their lives made it fast again, digging holes for the fluke with their hatchets, in the firmest portions of the berg. As they worked thus, the snow drifted over and almost smothered them, and two men disappeared into chasms of the ice, never to appear again.

At last the snow ceased, after having fallen for hours, and there came a faint starlight, in which the ship loomed strange and phantomic, shrouded in silver, with half-frozen snow hanging like bearded icicles to its masts and rigging, and its decks spread with a thick carpet of whiteness. Above, the cold heaven glittered as with innumerable points of bluish steel; while the ice all around assumed fantastic shapes, with vast shadows and flying gleams of silver and azure.

But though there was not a cloud in the zenith, the blast blew from the Cold Clime with never-ceasing force.

At midnight, there came other perils, in which all others were forgotten.

All at once, as if at some concerted signal, the whole framework of the solid floe began to move and close in upon the ship.

Sharp reports like those of artillery, but infinitely deeper and more terrible, resounded on every side, while here and there, with a force like that of earthquake, the ice was torn into mighty fissures, up which the blue water spouted and flowed.

Between wind and water the tumult was stupefying.

Then the ice closed in with slow and pitiless strength, till it held the ship as in a vice.

A cry went up from the terrified sailors, for the solid ribs of oak began to crack and yield like the shell of a breaking egg.

Fortunately the pinch came very slowly, and the ship's timber was unusually tough and strong; while, thanks to large portions of yielding floating ice which surrounded her on every side, and acted as a sort of fender, she did not actually come in contact with the main body of the floe.

Preparations were at once made for the worst. Orders were given to get the boats out upon the ice, and to land such provisions as might be necessary in the event of the ship's destruction. Barrels of meal and salt junk, kegs of spirits, bags of biscuits, were passed from hand to hand and thrown out upon the ice. Men shouted, women screamed, but all voices were drowned in the elemental tumult.

Pale as death, Richard Orchardson accosted Captain Higginbotham, who stood directing the movements of his own crew, moving about like shrieking ghosts in the dim light.

'Is the ship doomed?' he cried. 'Must we take to the ice?'

'We're in the Lord's hands,' replied the skipper. 'This ain't no time for talking. If you're a man, lend a hand!'

Thus urged, Richard clambered over the ship's side,

and joined the busy crowd who were passing things from hand to hand across the loose ice. Despair and terror gave him strength; he leapt eagerly to a place, and was soon as busily employed as the rough crew.

Upon them as they were thus busily engaged burst another storm of blinding snow, so thick and heavy, that it became pitch dark, and they could not see each other or even the outline of the ship. The men shrieked to each other in terror, some threw themselves upon their faces to avoid being swept away, others clung wildly to each other.

With a sharp cry of fear, Richard struggled back towards the ship, but as he moved, the solid ice seemed to crumble beneath him, and he heard the roar of surging water.

At this moment he dimly saw standing close to him a white shape, like the shape of a man. In the extremity of his fear, he tottered to it and clutched it wildly.

'Help!' he gasped.

Scarcely had he uttered the cry, when he felt himself lifted as if by superhuman strength and carried rapidly across the ice. His head swam, a new and nameless horror possessed him, but he still clung frantically to the shape which carried him.

Through the blinding drift he was swiftly hurried. As a lioness might carry off a child, or as a mighty polar bear might carry off a small seal, the shape carried him away.

He looked wildly round for the ship, but could see nothing but blinding whiteness. Then he struggled to release himself, but was held in a clutch like that of iron.

'Help!' he shrieked again.

It seemed like some hideous dream. The shape still ran with him across the solid ice, in the teeth of the flying drift, the biting blast

Then, sick with terror, he swooned away.

When he opened his eyes, he was lying prone. The snow had ceased, and the starlight again shone faintly down. He looked up, and saw standing before him, wrapt from head to foot in snow, a tall human shape.

Then a white face was pressed down close to his,
and while a hot breath touched his cheek, a voice
hissed these words:

' At last ! '

CHAPTER XXVI.

'AN EYE FOR AN EYE.'

IN a moment he had recognised his mortal enemy.
With a wild cry he leapt to his feet, and looked round
for the ship. But no ship was visible: only on every
side gigantic hummocks of ice and snow.

He turned and would have flown; but Christian
gript him by the throat.

'Stand and listen ! I could have slain you in your
swoon, but that would have been too merciful. Look
in my face ! quick ! do you know me ? '

' Yes ! '

' Remember my broken-hearted father ! remember
my betrayed sister ! remember my murdered mother !—
remember all these, and remember her whose heart you
have turned against me, before I kill you.'

' Help ! you will not murder me ! '

' Cry, but no one can hear you. The ship lies
yonder, a mile away. I have brought you hither to
make expiation. You hear ? '

' For the love of God—— '

' He has given you into my hands.'

' No, no !—do not harm me ! I will do whatever
you wish—I will abandon my pursuit of Miss Sefton—
yes, I will make amends.'

' Can you bring back the dead to life ? Can you
heal the hearts you and yours have broken ? Devil ! '

As he spoke, he compressed his grip upon the other's
throat, so that he could not speak.

Answer me one thing, before I kill you. Did you
not fire the ship ? Answer ! '

He released his grip, and the answer came in a wild
negative, while Richard fell crying upon his knees——

' No, no !'

' Before God ? '

' Before God.'

Using a fierce oath, Christian struck him in the face with his open hand.   He fell back shrieking.

'Another lie to help sink your soul to the pit of hell ! '

As Christian spoke, there came from the distance the faint report of a gun ; after a moment's interval, it was followed by a second report, and by a third.

' You hear ? ' he cried with a terrible laugh. 'They miss you already, but they cannot save you.   Nothing can save you now.'

But the sound of the gun, and the knowledge that help was not far away, seemed to give Richard strength and speed.   He leapt to his feet, and before the other could touch him, fled in the direction of the sound.

It was a race for life, for Christian followed close behind him, and almost struck him as he ran.   Under ordinary circumstances, he was the fleeter, and terror lent him wings.   He increased the distance between them at every step.

Over the slippery ice, between the frowning hummocks, twisting, turning, he fled for life.   Once he heard his pursuer stumble and fall, but he heard him spring up again in a moment, and follow like a bloodhound.

Another gun from the ship.   He rushed wildly on.

Suddenly, as he fled, he saw before him a long blue line of gleaming water—a fissure like a narrow stream, in the very heart of the ice.   There was no time to turn, so he rushed on towards it ; and as he came near, he saw to his despair that it was too broad to leap.

But Christian was close behind.   Richard flew to the very edge, and pausing there in horror, threw up his hands and turned his face toward his enemy.

As he did so, the loose ice crumbled under his feet, and with a shriek he disappeared.

Christian paused in time, and gazed with wild eyes towards the water.   Then, in the dim light, he distinctly saw the head of Richard re-emerge, while his hands with dying strength clung to the slippery *ice*, and a last wild cry for help rose into the air.

He answered with a horrible laugh, and leaving his enemy to die passed away in the direction of the ship.

As he went, another black cloud came up behind the fields of ice, and another storm of snow came sweeping out of it. But still he groped his way in the right direction ; and at last, as the shower thinned, and the dim light came out again, discerned the vessel in her old position, a quarter of a mile away.

Scarcely had his eyes fallen upon her, when a shock like earthquake ran through the whole body of ice on which he was standing, and simultaneously he saw the portion of the floe to which the ship was fastened detach itself and crumble like a heap of sand.

Nothing was to be seen but blinding ice-smoke.

When it cleared, Christian saw that the ship had broken loose, and was sweeping, amid the flotsam and jetsam of shattered ice, right out into the open water—drifting broadside, without a rag of sail, and careening frightfully to leeward under the pressure of the wind.

He rushed on towards the edge of the ice.

Before he reached it, another cloud came up, with another storm of snow.

He stood blinded, waiting for the fall to cease. When it did so, he gazed with wild eyes out on the open water.

The bergs were flashing and the surge was sounding, but the ship had disappeared.

He was left alone upon the fields of ice !

CHAPTER XXVII.

HERE BEGINS CHRISTIAN CHRISTIANSON'S RECORD, WRIT DOWN BY HIS OWN HAND.

ALTHOUGH I am no scholar, and am, moreover, greatly lacking in those secret spiritual gifts which make certain rude men write and speak as if inspired, I have undertaken, at the request of my dear friend and master, Mr. John Wesley—a good and great man, whom late in life (yet, thank God, not *too* late) I have learned to understand—at his request, I say, I have undertaken to set down certain strange things which occurred to me during what I may term, in all humility, the period of my conversion.

But first, before I begin to tax my brain for these half-vanished memories, and to set forth how marvellously the Lord hath dealt with me, let me avow that I was never one of those who care to make public inquisition of their own souls for the astonishment and edification of foolish creatures agape for spiritual miracles. I was ever, like all men of my race, one caring little for the sympathy of strange folk ; dumb in trouble, loving solitude, dwelling, often sullenly, with my own thoughts ; so that when my heart bled, it bled inwardly, and when I was broken on the wheel of despair I wore a brave front to the world, and when I prayed to God I prayed in a secret place

For a long time, therefore, I have debated within myself whether these things should be written down at all, savouring as they may of foolish vanity, and magnifying unduly God's dealings with myself, the least of His creatures. For though I would speak of events to me miraculous, as evincing His special and providential care for my poor personal salvation, is not this same miraculous intervention taking place also in the lives of innumerable other men ? Is there one poor creature of all the human race—nay, one poor sparrow of the air— of whom He takes not equal heed ?

Knowing well mine own insignificance, and feeling duly the mercies which have been vouchsafed to me, I could have been well content to keep these things to myself, as sacred between my Lord and me.

But having spoken in these strains to Mr. Wesley, who alone of all men knows how God hath dealt with me, he was strongly of opinion that I should write all down : holding, firstly, that God deals in precisely the same measure with no two human souls ; secondly, that the true record of any conversion is a kind of divine testimony ; and, lastly, that there are certain points in my poor experience which may just now, when the world is so filled with the sound of vainglorious battle,

the fume of unbrotherly controversy, be of especial
value to foolish men. He reminded me, furthermore,
of the many spoken and written testimonies of wrathful
men made peaceful, and foul men made clean, all through
some special and heavenly dispensation, and he held
that these testimonies, though so infinitely less precious
than those of the martyrs, could not well have been
spared.

Reasoning of this sort, coming from so learned a
mouth, presently convinced me, the more so as growing
older I perchance grow more garrulous, and have long
had it in my mind to tell something of the marvels I
have known. For few men, if any, have dwelt where I
have dwelt, seen what I have seen, in the realm of the
lonely snow.

Thereupon, having decided to obey his bidding, I
received from Mr. Wesley a promise that he himself
would take this record under his learned care, with a
view either to its suppression or publication, as he should
think fit; and that in the latter event—namely, of
publication—he will with his own hand correct those
lapses of language, faults of verbiage, and general vices
of expression, into which an unlettered man, little used
to composition, is likely to fall. This promise comforts
me, as I begin my task; for of all men living I hold
my dear master best and wisest, not only in those things
which affect our heavenly salvation, but in those others
which pertain to our right living and dying, as reason-
able creatures, here below.

[Following the above preamble, in Christian Christianson's narration, comes the long account of the writer's
birth and other family matters, the great feud between
the Christiansons and the Orchardsons, the coming of
Priscilla Sefton, the sailing of the *Miles Standish*, the
shipwreck in mid-ocean, the rescue by the Dutch vessel,
the great storm, and the trouble among the ice;—with
all of which events the reader is familiar. On the margin of the manuscript are divers notes in Mr. Wesley's
handwriting, made at a time when that holy man in-
tended to publish the whole story, for the benefit of the
faithful. For reasons which were doubtless well weighed

that intention was never carried out, and on Mr. Wesley's decease the manuscript came back into the possession of the Christianson family.

Passing over those matters which have already been explained and pictured, we come to that part of Christianson's narrative which describes him alone, and cast away, with his wild eyes searching the desolate sea, and finding no trace of the ice-beleaguered ship.]

Standing alone on the edge of the great floe, and knowing now certainly that the ship was driven away and perchance destroyed, I did not at first realise the extremity of my situation ; for I was still bewildered by the excess of mine own murderous passion, and was in a measure bereft of reason ; yet I searched the wild sea instinctively, looking in vain on every side for a glimpse of a sail ; then finding none, I gazed up at the lonely sky, with a strange sense of mingled terror and exultation.

For I thought :

' Come what come may, I care not now, since the purpose of my life is fulfilled. If it be God's will that I must die, and never see again my love's face or the green hills of my native land, I am still content; for I have drunk the full sweetness of my just revenge.'

Then arose before me, sweet and terrible, the face of Priscilla—faint and far away as that of an angel. Had I lost her ? Had I, by my own dark deed, parted myself from her for ever ? Even the cold despair of this fear did not quite chill my fiery exultation.

I looked again seaward.

Southward, under a low canopy of mist, stretched drifting ice ; and nearer, the open space of water was tumbling and whitening. I strained my eyes in all directions : I gazed hither and thither, but saw no ship.

More than once, some fragment of ice or cloud in the far distance seemed to assume the shape of the beleaguered vessel, but only to disappoint the sight on closer scrutiny. Yes, the ship was gone !

Could she have foundered in the white squall ? Could she have sunk to the bottom, taking with her the gentle creature who had been sent—and sent, alas ! in vain—to sweeten my life ? As the thought came to

me, I threw my arms into the air, and prayed the Lord
to spare my darling—to bear her safe back to the sunny
land.

How long I remained gazing I cannot tell; it must, I
think, have been for hours, during which space I ran restlessly up and down the edge of the ice, seeking some
new point of vantage for sight of the vanished ship.   At
last I turned away, fearful that I was utterly abandoned.

The fierce squalls of wind and snow still continued,
but they came now less fitfully and at longer intervals;
and in the pauses between their coming a bright frosty
radiance filled the air, making even distant things
distinct as if it were day.   Still, the eye could not
penetrate far, or distinguish with certainty one shape
from another; so that I still hoped, when daylight
came, to discover the ship.

Before daybreak the wind fell, the skies became
cloudless and crystalline.   Then suddenly, as if by
miracle, the fields of ice were flooded with crimson
light.

Shall I ever forget the dawning of that day ?   Such
a dawn, methinks, found Cain standing by his overthrown altar, looking on his own red hands.

It seemed, all at once, as if the world brightened
like blood; the far north shot up crimson beams, the
fields of ice turned to ruby and vermilion hues, the
sea a deep purple, the heavens above like the strange
amethyst stone.   There was no cloud in the sky, no
ripple on the sea.   In the dim south, the glory was
reflected on flake-white clouds, broken with pink and
vermilion bars.

But how shall such a hand as mine describe these
things ?   What can I say, save that the terrible peace-
fulness and loveliness of that new morning found me
standing like a guilty thing—as indeed I was—nay,
like Cain himself ?   As the red light flooded the sea,
and played upon my face and form, I felt as if I too
could hear the voice of God, crying, 'Cain, where is
thy brother ? ' while I replied, not like Cain, but with
shamefuller defiance, '*Thou* hast slain him, O God,
and it is just.'

Flooded with that new brightness, the scene around

looked strangely fair, the fairer for its utter desolation,
for now it was possible to define the prospect clearly,
and distinguish objects in the far distance.

Then I perceived for the first time that the great
floe on which I stood was merely a kind of bank, or
outer-work, lying against a rocky line of coast some
miles away; drifting thither by tempest, it had
grounded, and then clung with frosty talons to the
shore. Looking northward, I saw where ice ended
and water began; whereas I had conceived that the
ocean was frozen as far as the horizon.

Southward was the great open water where our
ship had been beset; but the mass of ice beyond was
not solid, but floating, consisting of bergs of all hues
and sizes, drifting slowly to the south. So it was
possible, after all, that the ship was saved.

Again and again I searched the sea for a glimpse
of her; and so clear was the atmosphere that I could
have plainly discerned even a small sailing boat many
leagues away; but there was no sign of what I sought,
and seeing that no hope lay in that direction, I again
gazed towards the neighbouring line of land.

The coast was rocky and craggy, with wild cliffs,
as it seemed, of basalt, rising to dark slopes and sullen
low-lying hills; and here and there were spots of
sombre greenness, and nowhere was any sign of snow.

At this sight my heart took courage. What land
it was I knew not, but perchance it might contain
human creatures? So I hastened thither across the ice.

I had to pick my way warily, for there were dangerous fissures in the floe, and in some places the ice
was so rotten and thin that it crumbled underfoot.
Here and there were open pools, some many furlongs
wide, others like tiny tarns of pellucid and emerald
greenness; and these I skirted carefully, with ever-
cautious footsteps. At last it seemed that cruel Fate
was against me; for when I was nigh half-way to the
coast, I found myself facing a great water, or green
arm of the ocean, which seemed to interpose a hopeless
barrier between me and the strange haven beyond.

In this green water, numerous seals were disporting,
while others sat on the edge of the ice, sunning them-

selves in the morning rays; and so tame were these last, that they suffered me to come within a few yards before they leapt into the sea; and having dived down, they rose again, and floated quite near, watching me with eyes as soft as those of little children or young maids. Right out in the midst of the water, which was nigh a mile across, a narwhal was spouting; and hovering over this monster of the deep, flew, with sharp cries, innumerable sea-gulls and terns.

Wide as the water was, I might readily have got across, being from youth a skilled swimmer, but the water was bitter cold, and had I stript I should have frozen. So I wandered wearily along the bank, until finally I found, to my great joy, that the water ended and gave place again to ice; whereon, walking cautiously, and oftentimes in peril of my life, I at last reached the land.

This steel-bound coast grew the more strange and sinister to sight as I came nearer; for the crags were of black basalt, with great caves hung with stalactites and icicles, and the crumbling shingle on every side was of a foul brown, like iron-sand. Over my head, as I stood up-gazing and seeking a footpath whereby to climb, hovered a great bird like an eagle, wheeling in circles, as the raven doth when haunting our own English cliffs.

There was no way for it but to climb; so I chose a place where the ascent seemed easiest, and began to scramble upward. Not without peril did I reach the top; more than once my foot slipt, and I had to cling with hands and knees to the jagged rock; but it was not God's will that I should die that way, and at last I came upon the summit, and pausing there, stood panting for my breath.

Then I beheld that the hills which I had seen from the distance were almost wholly fashioned of black and barren stone, and that the green stains I had seen thereon were not sweet growing grass, but a kind of foul moss, very thin and spongy to the tread. Beyond this moss there seemed no other sign of vege-tation; not a tree or bush, however bare; no flower, not even the weedlings of the rock. All was so barren and ominous that my heart sank within me, and I felt for the first time the grievous shadow of my own sin.

Ay me! as the years roll back, like dark vapours, how vividly do I behold that dreary place! While all around seemed so white and fair, in the light of the chill morning, the land alone seemed sinister and forbidding—fit abode, fit grave, for one so stained with sin and sorrow as myself.

I wandered on until I gained the highest elevation I could discover, trusting to spy from thence a fairer prospect inland, and perchance the sign of some savage habitation. Standing thereon, I saw, to my despair, not land at all, but open water, stretching far away into the west.

Then indeed my soul sank in despair, for I knew that God had forsaken me, and cast me away, like Crusoe, upon a desolate ocean isle.*

CHAPTER XXVIII.

THE ISLAND OF DESOLATION.

I SHOULD grow wearisome and over-garrulous if I tried to set down all the strange distempered thoughts that filled my soul that first day of my desolation; for despair is a tedious companion, and at last I despaired indeed; seeing no hope, no haven, no escape, beyond the lonely sea on one hand, and the lonely field of ice, with more sea beyond, upon the other.

This much, however, let me tell: that, although as yet I repented in no measure of the evil I had wrought by my own hand, it was some comfort to remember

* Here on the margin of the old manuscript is a note in Mr. Wesley's handwriting: 'Doubtless this is a mere figure of speech. No man knew better than the writer that God "forsakes" no man, since, by the measure of His grace, not of our deserving, we are saved. Often those whom He seems to "cast away" are nearest to His hand; but in all manners and at all seasons He works darkly, for issues that we cannot comprehend.—J. W.'

that mine enemy had not died directly by my violence, though indirectly his death had come about through my sinful passion. Standing there lonely in the sight of Heaven, I vindicated myself against the voice which still cried in my ear, ' Cain, where is thy brother ? ' Although I rejoiced in his death, *I* had not slain him ; nay, had not God Himself taken the task out of my hands ?

Nevertheless, despite my rejoicing, I was cruelly haunted by the remembrance of his dying face, as it flashed before me on the edge of the ice, while his wild hands clutched the crumbling brink, and his shriek for help rang out on the air.

I might have saved him, then, by reaching out a finger; yet I had left him to die !

But my chief thoughts now were not of him, or of any that I hated or loved in this world, but of mine miserable body—how to preserve it safe in so terrible a place. I had not cared much for life before, when life seemed sure; but now that the chance of escape was so small, my rude spirit rose in a despairing dream of preservation. Perchance rescue would come in some unheard-of way ; and then, if Priscilla lived, I should see her face again, and be forgiven.

The day was now far advanced, and the pinch of hunger within me warned me that I had not eaten food since the previous day. With this sudden sense of hunger came a new and sickening thrill of dread ; so that I shivered to the bone, and gnashed my teeth, with cruel tears. For now I seemed to see the full extremity of my doom. I had no morsel of food with me, and the isle was barren ; so that, unless succour came soon, I must starve to death.

In the pockets of the rude seaman's clothes I wore, I found only a clasp-knife (such as sailors use), some twine, a cotton handkerchief, a wooden pipe, and a piece of coarse tobacco in a tin tobacco box. Fortunately, ere I left the ship, I had put on my thick seaman's jacket and boots, so that I was well clad against the cold ; but alas ! my danger now threatened not from without but from within, where the worm of famine already began to gnaw

But God's mercy is infinite, and it was not written that I should die a dog's death by the slow torture of starvation.

As I walked along the summit of the island, searching the seas and the ice-fields on every side, I saw, miles away (the air of that region being marvellously fine and clear) divers black objects scattered upon the ice ; and I immediately bethonght me of our labour the previous night, when the ship was threatened and we had been casting out provisions to prepare for the event of the vessel's utter destruction. Hope now gave me wings, and, descending the crags again, I hastened across the ice.

The way returning, like the way coming, was long and tedious, nor was it easy to keep the right direction, winding among so many great hummocks and skirting so many pools and lakes ; but at last I gained the place I sought, the very spot where our ship had anchored the previous night, before the force of the tempest drove her away.

Scattered there upon the water's edge I beheld a portion of the goods the seamen had been landing amid the storm. Part of the ice had broken off, carrying with it doubtless much of the loose store, but there remained several small barrels of flour, a sack containing ship's biscuits, some loaves of rye bread, two great Dutch cheeses, and a small keg of rum ; and besides those creature comforts, a small hatchet, a large roll of blankets, some loose planks from the carpenter's room, and a deal box containing flint and steel, some dry tinder, and a tin flask of lamp oil.

It is needless to tell how greatly my heart rejoiced at the sight of these treasures, which seemed sent for my preservation ; but I threw up my arms to the still sky, and, with tears oozing from my sad eyes, I thanked the Sender.

It was now afternoon, and I dreaded lest night should come on, or the calm weather become broken, before I had borne these stores, or a portion of them, to some place of safety on the land ; so without more ado I shouldered as much as I could carry, namely, the sack of ship's biscuits and one barrel of flour, and gripping in my left hand the deal box and the hatchet, I hastened towards the shore.

Laden as I was, I found it a tedious journey, but my natural strength was ever great, and now I was fortified by despair. Again and again, however, I had to sit and rest.

When at last I reached the coast, and threw down my burthen on the shingle, I was so worn out that I could not even break my fast.

Presently, however, I recovered strength, and breaking up some ship's biscuits in my hand, ate eagerly.

But my work was only just begun, for I was resolved to secure all that chance had left me of the ship's goods; so, without resting long, I toiled back over mine own footprints, to seek another load.

This time I carried with me the roll of blankets, which I balanced with one hand upon my head, a great cheese, which I held firmly under mine arm, and the small keg of rum, which I gript in mine hand by a strap of hemp encircling it. My progress this time was slower and wearier than before, for my strength was less. At last, however, I came to land; and by this time, though it was still early in the afternoon, the sun was already beginning to disappear.

This set me thinking where I should pass the night; so I searched along the shore until I found in the crags a hollow, well screened from the wind, and there I spread some of my blankets to make a couch. Scarcely had I done this when darkness came upon me.

It was not so dark, however, that I could not carry up to the rock the goods I had saved from the ice, and pile them near my sleeping-place; having done which, I supped freely on ship's biscuit and some rum from the keg, and wrapping myself up in my blankets fell sound asleep.

Though the air that came from the ice-floes was keen and chill, the night was not cold, for it was not yet winter-tide in that region.

My sleep was heavy, but it was broken by wild dreams.

Methought, as I lay, that Richard Orchardson, clad

all in white, as in his shroud, came and bent over me, and that when I opened my eyes he screamed and fled; and I, rising, sped after him over great fields of ice lit up by the moon, he still shrieking as he went; but suddenly he turned with shrill laughter and faced me, his hands outreaching, and his face like a head of Death, with no flesh thereon, but flame in the sockets of the eyes. Then he cried in a terrible voice, ' Cain, Cain! where is thy brother?' and before I knew it he had me by the throat. In vain I struggled—nay, I could not struggle, for my hands were turned to stone, my feet to lead; and ever his lean fingers strangled my throat, so that my hour seemed come. Then, as I tried to free myself with a scream, mine eyes opened, and I woke: to see the starry heavens glittering above my head, and feel all around me the deep breathing of the night.

As I lay thus waking, I heard from the distance a strange sound like the bellowing of beasts; it seemed to come from the neighbouring ice, and was accompanied by another sound, like the splashing of waves. So I reached out my hand and gript the hatchet, which lay close by me; but after listening for some time, and still gripping the hatchet firmly, I fell to sleep again.

With the first gleam of daylight I awakened, and rose from my bed.

My limbs felt numb and stiff, and I was shivering slightly, but after running to and fro for some minutes upon the strand, I felt quite warm and strong.

Then I drew forth my wooden pipe, and filled it with tobacco, and having taken out the flint and tinder, managed to procure a light. I had never been a great smoker, and now for the first time I felt the true blessing of the Indian weed. Seated on a great stone, pipe in mouth, I sadly reviewed my condition, while the red ball of the sun rolled up out of the ocean, and daylight spread like the slow flame of a newly-kindled fire.

Sleep had partly calmed my troubled pulses, and the tobacco fumes completed what sleep had begun.

I saw now with stolid certainty what I had wildly perceived before: that I was a lost man, unless I could live on upon that place of desolation until some kind of succour came; and I saw, moreover, that in all human probability succour would never come at all.

All men cling to life, even those for whom it has most sorrows; and for mine own part I clung to life still. So I bethought me of other men who had been cast away, and who by their own unaided strength had preserved themselves sound and safe under dire distress, while all the elements were leagued against them. What they had done I perchance might do, since by God's mercy I was at least preserved against famine. My strength had ever been as the strength of ten; and I determined to use it all for my preservation before I yielded to my miserable fate.

After breakfasting on ship's biscuit, I again made my way across the ice; and in the course of three more journeys afoot, I carried safely to land all the rest of the loose stores left by the ship—nor did I leave behind even the carpenter's planks, which I guessed might yet serve me in my need.

When this work was completed, the sun was in mid-heaven.

I now remember how many a man in similar extremity had saved himself from utter despair, and even from madness, by the hard durance of toil; and I determined to think as little as might be of the wretchedness of my condition, but to lull my troubled soul with whatever rough labour I might devise for the body's gain.

My first care was how to store the ship's goods in some safe spot where no harm might come to them from either wild beasts or foul weather. So I searched the island up and down, seeking some spot already fitted by nature to be a place of refuge.

My first search was along the seashore.

Everywhere on the sea level I found basaltic caves, some vast as the great halls of our old manor-houses, and hung with slimy weeds and glittering stalactites; and in many of these, as I entered them, I heard the motion of seals and other great beasts of the sea. In all of them the atmosphere was foul and clammy, and the air bitterly cold.

So I left the shore, and, climbing the crags again, sought the upland slopes.

At last I found, high up on the island, but well sheltered from the ruthless wind, the place I sought— a fissure in the solid hillside, broad enough to hold two or three men standing abreast, some ten feet long and seven feet deep. Its bottom and sides were of bare rock, and all that it lacked, to form a kind of earth cabin ready-made, was a roof against the storm.

Returning towards the eastern shore, I searched along the crags for some place of easy descent and ascent, up which I might succeed in carrying my stores; and after a long search, I found a place where the cliffs had been rent bodily asunder by some convulsion of nature, leaving between them a jagged natural path, perilous in places, but fit for my purpose. Descending here, I walked round to the rocks where I had first slept.

Determined to lose no time, I began at once to transport my goods, and succeeded so well that before nightfall I had carried everything to the top of the island, where I ranged them in a heap within a hundred yards of the spot I had chosen for a habitation. Then, taking my roll of blankets, I spread them deep down in the fissure of the rock, and there, with the clear skies above me, I lay and slept.

Thus passed my second night upon that island of desolation.

CHAPTER XXIX.

CHRISTIAN ROOFS HIS HOUSE.

I WAS awakened by the sound of rushing hail, and by the hard hailstones beating upon my face. Arising and climbing the side of the rock, I saw that it was day-break, and blusterous weather. The wind was blowing from the nor'west, and bringing up at intervals clouds of hail and sleet.

As I stood, I heard from overhead a shrill clangour as of voices high up in the air; and gazing upward I saw a great flight of birds winging southwards, and calling faintly to each other. They flew in a string like wild geese, with a leader in the centre, and the rest forming the two sides of a wedge; and although, from time to time, as the wild gusts blew them about, they changed places with each other, they preserved the wedge-like shape of their flight until they disappeared.

Scarce had these passed, when I heard another sound like the whirr of wings; and gazing upward again, I saw the air clouded with great flights of duck, flying southward too.

Then I knew, partly from old experience, and partly from what I had read in books of travel, that these birds, wiser in their generation than foolish men, were hastening to summer climes, before the approach of winter weather.

As I watched them, my eyes grew dim with tears, and I wept that I lacked wings to fly with them from that dreary clime. And now my heart sank indeed, for I was certain that I could never leave that place alive.

The very extremity of my despair decided me to quick action; for I saw that if heavy snows should come I must certainly be a lost man. So I determined, without delay, to make myself some rude shelter from the storms; and with that view I ran at once to the place where I had left my stores.

Coming to the place, I saw something which filled my heart with fear and consternation.

Although the stores were still there, they were not as I had left them overnight, for the bag of ship's biscuits had been torn open, as if by claws or teeth, and a portion of its contents carried away, as I thought, by some wild beast; and one of the barrels of flour had been rudely broken open, and part of the contents scattered upon the ground.

Only a human being, or some formidable animal, could have done so much; and since the island was uninhabited, and wholly desolate, I at once set the deed down as that of some midnight prowling beast. Therefore I clutched my axe, and looked round on every side, half expecting the monster to spring forth ; but it made no sign, and at last, warily and watchfully, I began the work I had come to do.

Lifting the loose ship's planks one by one in my two arms, I carried them to the side of the fissure of the rock ; and then, having measured them with finger and thumb, began to divide them crossways in twain. It was slow work, as I had no saw, but only my knife and hatchet ; and dividing these three planks took me the better part of that day.

Now, half of one of the planks thus cut in twain would just stretch breadthways across the opening of that natural cavern ; and by ranging the six half-planks parallel to each other, and leaving between each a foot of open space, I had a foundation for the roof I wished to build. Then I took two coarse blankets from beneath, and spread them out upon the planks, separately from each other ; placing upon them great stones, which were plentiful thereabout, to keep them from being blown away by the wind.

All day, as I wrought at this task, I saw more birds passing overhead, all flying to the south ; and more than once my heart failed me, and I cried to myself, 'Of what avail to labour, since I must perish in the end ?' But the stubborn spirit of my race prevailed, and in the very strength of despair I laboured on.

That day I had partially roofed my dwelling in the rock. Stones and fragments of rock were thickly piled upon the planks and blankets I had spread beneath ; and underneath was a dark recess or cave, with only one entrance, just wide enough to admit a man at the lower end. This entrance I devised to protect, later on, with some kind of trap-door or rocky barrier, as a safeguard against the attacks of prowling beasts.

Now, while busy at this work, I made a discovery which was destined in a great measure to lead to my body's preservation. On the western side of the island, where I searched for stones, I found the green ground broken up, and full of rotten vegetation, like the moss-turf to be found in some parts of England. Then remembering that such turf makes excellent fuel, I, with my clasp-knife, cut out squares as large as I could manage, and heaped them ready to carry away. For hours I laboured, and before sunset had gathered a goodly pile; this I arranged stackwise, as I had seen done at home, so that neither snow nor rain could reach the dry portions below.

Not content with these, I cut more squares, and carried them in armfuls into the cave; and I found them so dry after the drought of summer, that they burned almost too quickly.

Then I made in the centre of the cave a small circle of stones, and in the centre I put the fire. I had no chimney, and for a time I was nigh choked with the fuel smoke; but I knew that it was wholesome, and would drive away the clinging damp.

Before resting that night I carried into my cave all the rest of my stores, and ranged them carefully along the bottom of the solid rock; leaving myself just room to stretch my body and limbs at full length.

Taking stock of what God's mercy had left me, I found that I had now remaining, as my security against famine, and for personal uses, the things that follow, viz.:

Two small barrels of flour.

Five loaves of rye bread.

Two Dutch cheeses.

A sack of ship's biscuits.

A small keg of rum, containing about two gallons of the raw spirit.

Four blankets (counting not the twain I had spared to roof my cave).

Flint and steel, with dry tinder.

A flask of lamp oil.

A clasp-knife.

Some coarse twine.

A pipe of wood, and about a quarter of a pound of negro-head tobacco.

Added to these, I wore upon my body as garments: a thick jacket and trousers of woollen woof, a sailor's woven guernsey, a flannel shirt and drawers, thick yarn stockings, strong knee boots with nails, and a seaman's sou'-wester made of oilskin cloth.

In the middle of that third night I was wakened by a noise above my head.

I started up and listened, afraid. At first all I heard was the low moaning of the wind, and the pattering of hail; but suddenly there came another sound, like the heavy tramp of feet.

The sound ceased; then I distinctly heard something breathing heavily, close to the roof of my cave.

I knew it could be no human thing which troubled my rest in such a place, and, unarmed as I was, I did not at first care to face any monster or wild beast; but, at last, summoning courage, I clutched my hatchet, which lay close to my hand, and thrust my head out into the night.

It was pitch dark, and I could see nothing. The thing, whatever it was, had disappeared.

CHAPTER XXX.

A NEW PERPLEXITY.

THE next dawn was dark and cold, with more storms of hail. As I emerged into the dim light, and gazed up at the zenith, I saw five wild swans sailing swiftly overhead.

I watched them with a heavy heart till they disappeared against the southern sky.

After breaking my fast with bread and biscuit, and drinking at a tiny fountain which I had discovered trickling from the solid rock, I wandered down to the western side of the island, carrying the hatchet in my hand, and for many hours I laboured cutting more moss-fuel and setting it in dry stacks. When I could work no more, I wandered down towards the sea.

The western side was quite free of drift ice, and looked on clear and open sea. For several miles out from shore it was thickly sown with reefs, many of them visible even at high tide, and frequented by large numbers of cormorants, of a kind larger than any I had

seen on our own shores. But what pleased my sight
more, and indeed brought the tears to my foolish eyes.
was the sight of a little familiar bird, which I saw in
one of the creeks as I approached.

It was so tame that it only flew away a few yards,
whistling prettily, and then alighted again and stopped
to look at me quite fearlessly as it ran along the sand.
It was a small red-legged sandpiper, like those that are
so plentiful on the shores below the Fen Farm ; and
looking upon it, and listening to its thin sweet call, I
was straightway transported in fancy across the sea, to
the strands where I was born!

All alone it seemed, with no others of its kind, and
doubtless, when winter weather came, it would fly
away southward like the rest—perchance to the far-off
English shores, perchance to the sandy creeks I had so
often haunted as a boy!

As I stood watching it, my spirit turned back sadly
to those happy days! I saw again the familiar sandhills, the low-lying shores, and beyond all the green
slopes, the woods, and the red-tiled roof of the Fen
Farm; and I thought of my dead mother in her
grave, and of my lost sister, and of all the vanished
days; so that my force was broken, and sitting down
upon a rock, I hid my face in my hands and wept most
bitter tears.

Presently I arose, and wandering along the shore
saw many seals, both swimming in the sea and basking
on the edges of the rocks. Then I bethought me of
what certain shipwrecked mariners had written concerning the flesh of this animal and its precious oils,
and I determined, though I had no gun, to slay a seal
if possible.

But though the beasts were tame, they were wary,
and after many attempts to creep upon them unseen
and unheard, I desisted hopelessly ; when, just as I had
given up, I saw one of the beasts lying high and dry on
the shore above me.

The moment it beheld me it tried to make for the
water, but I intercepted it ; seeing which, it flapped
wildly with its fins and barked like a dog, and when I
approached nearer it gathered up stones in its fins and

smote them fiercely in my direction. Then I went to
it, uplifting the hatchet, and it showed its teeth savagely,
but tried to escape me. Now these poor beasts, though
so swift in the water, are made by nature quite helpless
on land, having no legs to run, but only great heavy
bodies (surcharged with oil) and fins and tails ; so
that this one was at my mercy. When I lifted up
the axe to strike it, it growled, and would have bit me ;
but I slipt behind it, and struck it with all my force
upon the head, so that the hatchet was buried in its
skull.

And now my heart misgave me, and it seemed that
I was cruelly murdering some innocent human thing ;
for the poor beast was not yet slain, but cried piteously ;
and when I struck it again, it turned its great soft eyes
up to mine, weeping like a human creature—yea,
weeping, for I could see the great salt drops of rheum.
Yet, willing to put it out of pain, I struck it once more
with all my strength, and the third time I struck it
upon the snout (where only, as I afterwards learned,
these animals are truly vulnerable), and it rolled over
on its belly, dead.

Now, many an one would smile to hear that, when
I had succeeded in killing the seal, I stood over it like
a guilty thing, and hated myself for having taken its
life; and, indeed, I know that these poor beasts are
made only for man's convenience, and look neither
before nor after, but pass like other soulless things.
And yet, methinks, he does great wrong, and mostly
to his own disposition, who uses them ungently ; for
they love their lives, and enjoy greatly the sweet air
and sunshine, even as men and women do ; nay, have
they not, like men and women, great love for one
another and for their young? Have I not seen one
of these same sea-beasts, a female, thrust up its own
body to take the blow aimed at its suckling offspring,
and die cheerfully—kindlier in this instance than many
mortal mothers, who cast their babes away to die ?

These things I write now, being old ; when I was
young, I cared little for the creatures below me. Yet
many of these might read sinful men a lesson, if they
would only heed. Man, in his pride and vainglory,

vaunts himself the fairest and best of things that live,* yet he, too, is only a creature, though he has a seeing soul. Woe to him, if God should so use him as He often uses the other children of God!

My sense of guilt did not last long. Presently I tried to lift the seal upon my back, but finding it heavy, and slippery as ice, I determined to cut it up upon the spot. This I did with my clasp-knife; skinning the beast rapidly, then dividing its flesh into several portions, and casting away only the head and entrails.

While I was thus engaged, there hovered over me, loudly screaming, large numbers of gulls, many of which were so bold that they swooped down from time to time and snatched loose pieces of flesh and blubber from my very feet.

By the time that my task was done, I was bespattered from head to foot with blood and oil; so that had human eyes beheld me, I must have been a sorry sight to see. Then I sheathed my knife, and wrapping the choicest portions of the carcase in the seal's own skin, proceeded to bear them to my cave.

Reaching the place after no little toil, I came to the cave mouth, and threw down my burthen and the hatchet. I then discovered that by some mischance I had dropped my knife, so, without a moment's delay, not stopping to lift even the hatchet, I ran back to the sea-shore.

After a brief search I found the knife, lying near the spot where I had slain the seal, and gripping it joyfully (for to one in my forlorn condition it was of priceless value) I returned as I had come.

And now a thing happened which filled my soul with nameless amazement, a thing quite unforeseen and inconceivable, and so strange that to my foolish mind it looked like devilish magic.

For coming to the mouth of my house or cave, I saw the seal's skin and flesh lying where I had thrown

* 'And so he is, by high prerogative of grace; but a man without this is infinitely lesser than the beasts that die, for these fulfil their uses, while he fulfils no use at all. That grace comes to all men who are willing to make choice of it, I have ever held, in the face of much unchristian opposition. To argue the contrary is to argue that God is unjust—a manifest contradiction, bordering on blasphemy.'—J. W.

them, but the hatchet, which I could have sworn I left beside them, had disappeared!—and though I searched all round the spot, I found no trace of the thing I sought!

Then, in my perplexity, thinking perchance that I had been mistaken, and must have carried the weapon into the interior of the cave, I made search there, with the same result as before. Emerging again into the light, I stood like a man dazed and drunken, uncertain what to think or do.

Presently, growing more and more confused by a thing so unaccountable, and wondering if I had deceived myself after all, and had never brought the hatchet to the place where I sought it, I returned to the sea-shore, searching everywhere as I walked.

But I came back as I went, amazed and terrified.

Then I searched along the rocky ground, looking for any sign of footprints; for I questioned myself, was it possible that some beast, coming to the place in my absence, had borne the thing away in its mouth? Yet this seemed inconceivable; and for the rest, the ground was so hard and stony that even mine own feet left no print perceptible to the eye.

By this time I was truly terrified, and ran up and down like a mad man, searching still.

Then there came into my mind a new but foolish thought, at which I brightened. Was it possible that some boat had landed on the island, and that the hatchet had been found and taken away by some human hand?

To make sure if this were possible, I walked round the island, examining the seas on every side, and every creek and cranny of the shores around. I might as well have rested still. There was no sign of boat or men.

I was now in utter despair, and I sat down at the door of my dwelling, wondering what strange chance would happen next.

CHAPTER XXXI.

THE FACE ON THE CLIFF.

BY this time it was afternoon, and very windy and dark.

To distract my thoughts, I entered my house and lit my fire; then I brought out the train oil I had saved from the ship, and devised how I should make myself a lamp, both for light in the darkness of the cave and for warmth also if snow and frost should come. So I took the twine that I had carried in my pouch, and pouring some of the oil into my tobacco pouch, soaked the twine therein; and afterwards, plaiting two pieces of twine together for stiffness, and mixing with the oil a portion of the soft oily fat of the seal, I made a kind of coarse taper, like the rude rushlights our fishermen fashion in the fens out of dry reeds and tallow. This I carried within, and striking a flame with flint and tinder, tried to make the taper burn; which it did not readily, for I had soaked the twine too thick in oil; but essaying again, I made another of the like, which gave a feeble light and burned even too rapidly.

When I had made a number of these rude lights, I fixed one against the side of the rock, plastering it in its place with seal blubber; and truly I have seen a worse rushlight in country cabins among the Fens, where also such things are home-made.

Having done this, and feeling very hungry, I took a portion of the seal's flesh and heated it over the flame, drawing thence just enough warmth to take off the edge of rawness. This flesh I ate, and found it savoury enough; and with that and some crumbled biscuit, and a palm full of rum to wash them down and quench the taste of oiliness upon the lips, I made a good meal.

Yet all this while I never ceased to perplex my brain as to what had become of the missing hatchet; whether it had been taken from me by wild beasts, or by some devilish agency, or whether, my wits somehow

failing me (how I knew not), I had through sheer folly
mislaid, or lost, or cast it away? Think over it as I
might, the thing was wholly unaccountable. All my
ignorance could do was to devise a long and still more
careful search for the morrow, when perchance better
memory might come to me, or the thing be recovered by
some new chance.

Darkness came early upon me; for now each day
was growing shorter and each night darker.

It was many hours before I could sleep, for I was
sorely troubled.

I was awakened by a horrible vision—to comprehend
which rightly, he who reads must picture to himself
clearly the abode in which I lay.

The rocky cavity which I had roofed over for my
house, and which was of the length, breadth, and depth
I have already written down, was shapen like a huge
kist or coffin, large enough to hold several men side by
side, and with some little space to spare at the feet.
Above the narrow end was the entrance, which I now
covered at night with a flat piece of loose rock, nearly
large enough to fill the opening well, when I gript it
from below and pulled it over.

Now, on this night of which I speak, I had fixed
against the wall another of my newly-fashioned lights;
and while the dim flame was flickering on the walls of
my house (I had almost written my sepulchre, for such
it seemed) and my fire dimly burning, I fell asleep.

I wakened suddenly, in strange terror, as men sometimes awake from nightmare, with the cold sweat
standing on my forehead, and mine eyes staring wide;
and then I saw, by the light of the taper which was just
flickering out, and by the red ray of the fire, a face
gazing wildly into mine.

It appeared in the aperture at the lower end of
the cave, looking down, and even in that dim light I
recognised it.

The face of Richard Orchardson, horrible, and white
as death!

For a space I could not speak. The blood froze in
my veins, my heart stood still, and then I think I must
have partly swooned, and closed mine eyes.

When I opened them again, the face was gone.

I sprang up with a cry. At that moment the light went out, and I was left in darkness.

With no small difficulty, and many unsuccessful attempts, for I was shaking like a reed, I succeeded in procuring flame and igniting another rushlight; and all this time I was shivering and shrinking, dreading to feel some ghostly touch upon my shoulder. Again and again I shrank in dread, fancying I saw the face again.

I went to the aperture, and found it closed, with the rock there as I left it overnight; and I said to myself, ' It was his spirit! He has come to haunt me, and he will haunt me till I die!'

Ah! the horror of those dark hours! The vision had been so real, so vivid, that I could not set it down as only a dream; nay, I was certain that the man's ghost was walking the watches of the night!

In my terror I prayed, kneeling on my bed with clasped hands.

With the first peep of day I left the cave.

It was a strange, blood-red dawn. Great clouds were piled up northward and westward, and through a hollow in their centre, round like the mouth of a cannon, poured fumes and blood-red flame.

The seas all round the island were dark, save for one smooth crimson track, like a red road through Hell's blackness, leading up to that great hollow. There was a chill wind, with a strange moaning high in the air.

I stood gazing at the dawn.

Presently, as the light increased, I climbed to the highest ascent of the island, and thence, as was my wont many times a day, searched the ocean on every side for a sail.

No sail; no sign; no hope, was there!

The vision of the night had left me sick with terror, and I cried to myself:

' It is better that I should die. Of what avail to linger on, when there is no hope this side of death; when to live on is weariness and despair by day, and horror by night; when, if I live, I shall go mad and haunted, and end like a wild beast of the field, with no glimmer of light, or hope, or sweet memory, in the brain? Yes, better to die!'

So I thought I might die swiftly and easily if I chose one of the high crags and leapt therefrom to the rocks beneath.

Full of this thought, I ran thither, not wishing to think, or pause, or even pray, till it was done.

But as I descended the hillside, and hastened towards the high crags, which were rather more than a mile away, I saw something which made me pause in wonder and in fear.

On the edge of the tallest crag a form was visible, with its back to me, looking downward!

At first I thought it was a great stone, but as I gazed it moved, and I saw that it lived. What could it be? A beast of the sea, come thither to sun itself, or some huge bird, or some unknown monster of the land?

I ran nearer and looked again. Then again my heart gave a leap, and I staggered like one sunstruck—for I saw plainly that the shape was human.

Strange and savage it seemed, with ragged raiment, wild dishevelled locks, and bare head.

Scarce knowing now what I did, I ran on and came close upon the shape, and at last I clearly discerned it to be the shape of a man.

Suddenly he heard me, looked round, and saw me; then, as I kept rushing towards him, he leapt to his feet with a startled scream.

Then I recognised him indeed!

It was Richard Orchardson, living, and brandishing my lost hatchet in his hand, as if to keep me at bay.

CHAPTER XXXII.

THE TWO MEN.

I shrank back in horror, thinking at first that I looked upon a ghost; while he, with a faint cry, brandished the hatchet, and struck feebly at the air.

Methinks I see him now as I saw him then—his face ghastly and foul, his cheeks sunken, his hair and beard wild and unclean, his raiment torn, and his whole form stained with rain and the moisture of weedy caves. Spectral he seemed, and hideous, like one risen from the dead.

But I saw quickly that he was no dead man, but Richard Orchardson himself, saved by some miracle from a watery death; and straightway I understood clearly that the face I had seen in the loneliness of night was no vision, but the face of the very man.

At the mere sight of what I had hated so much, all my old hate returned, and therewith a wicked loathing such as we feel for unclean things. These thoughts must have flashed up like fire into my face, for I saw him shrink and tremble, looking round which way to fly.

I sprang towards him, and he brandished the hatchet to strike me back; but I closed with him, and found him feeble as a reed in my fierce grasp.

I wrenched the hatchet from his feeble grip; he shrieked and fell prone upon the ground. Then I stood over him, with the hatchet raised, and with hands uplifted to shield him from the blow, he shrieked again.

'Mercy!' he cried. 'Do not kill me!'

There was murder in my heart, and I was mad to see him living, but something stayed my hand. My God, I thank Thee! It was Thy touch that made me afraid!

'Speak!' I said. 'How came you here?'

He murmured some broken words in answer, and pointed wildly out to sea. Then he cried again for me to spare his life.

Twice was the weapon raised to strike, and twice did my arm pause and my hand fall. I dared not slay him.

'Do not kill me!' he moaned again. 'I am perishing for lack of food and shelter. The hand of death is on me already, as you may see!'

What he said was piteous truth. He had no strength left, being spent with cold and famine.

Seeing me hesitate, he clung around me, dumbly beseeching pity; but I shuddered at his touch, and spurned him from me with a cruel, mocking laugh. For I saw that there was no need of violence, and that, without putting the sin upon my soul, my vengeance was still sure.

'Take off your hands!' I cried. 'Take them off, or——'

And as with an oath I raised the hatchet, he obeyed.

Then, without another word, another look, I turned from him, and left him lying helpless on the ground.

My wit is too rude, my skill too small, to record rightly the emotions that filled my soul that day; for my soul was a wild chaos of wonder and hate, pain and loathing, surprise and fear—all strangely blended in a confusion of troubled thought.

And yet, amid all this mental tumult, this stormy darkness of the disposition, there came, as a thin ray of light creeping among stormy cloud, a certain curious comfort—that I was not alone in my desolation.

As I went to the high places of the island, and looked around me, thinking as usual to see some glimpse of a sail, the place seemed somewhat less solitary—I knew not why.

I glanced back for assurance that I had not been dreaming, and there the man was where I had left him; but he had risen to his feet, and was gazing up my way. Then my hate took me, and I cursed him; but he was far away, and could not hear. I turned a corner of the rocks, and shut him from my sight.

Then I paused, trying to think it all over; but dreams came instead of thoughts. I dreamed of all the old feud—of my father's death-bed, of my dead mother, of all the sorrow and all the shame; I remembered my oath to kill the enemy of our house; and how I had followed him from land to sea, as a wolf follows a goat, seeking for his life.

Thus dreaming, I sprang again to my feet.

'I was a fool!' I cried to myself. 'I prayed to God to give him into my hands, and God hath answered my prayer. I will go back, and end it all!'

But I went not back. The wild murderous mood passed away again, as quickly as it had come; and like a man troubled and confused, having seen some supernatural and inconceivable thing, I wandered to my cave in the rocks.

Sitting at the mouth of my cave, with the cold heaven above my head, and nothing but the sad rocks and the distant sea before mine eyes, I pondered again over what had taken place; and the more I pondered the more strange and inconceivable it all grew. All that seemed certain was that Richard Orchardson had survived, and that, thus far, my deep scheme of vengeance had been in vain. There did we both lie outcast, in a lonely land, with small chance of ever seeing green England again; while, far away from both, Priscilla was perchance sailing upon a sunny sea, or stepping on some flowery strand.

For I could not think but the ship was saved, knowing now that there was no solid ice, but only floating bergs, in the path she had taken. By which I am reminded to tell a thing I have not yet told, viz., that on that very morning, looking southward, I saw that all the great bergs had disappeared below the horizon, and that the sea southward was quite open and free.

So what had I done? In the mad fury of my hate I had parted from that sweet face which was my heaven on earth (and which *now*, God help me! is my heaven up yonder), and had cast myself away incontinent, for revenge's sake, and had gained nothing but trouble, deep shame, and unutterable despair. I had left mine enemy to die; and lo! he had risen, as it were, out of the very grave. We had been face to face, and I had not slain him; so I was no nearer my revenge than I had been of old.

It was not that I hated him less that I fell sick of mine own revenge, and loathed the earth I looked on, and the heaven overhead. All had been poisoned to me, all made unprofitable, by the existence of this man; and yet, though his existence was a poison to me still, I felt that I dared not lay violent hands upon him again.

Then I remembered, with sudden exultation, how,

in that lonely island, there was no morsel of human food save that which I had stored for mine own preservation; and this being so, and no help nigh, the man was certainly doomed to a wretched death. If hunger did not slay him from within, cold must slay him from without; for he had no place to shelter his evil head when tempest and coldness came.

'God is just, after all,' I thought; 'and though He has spared this man, it is for slower torture and more dreadful death;' and I laughed to myself, seeing how, after all, my righteous vengeance must come about.

As I sat musing, I saw more swans and geese passing overhead, and several large birds, winged like the albatross, but jet black, flying low over the island This reminded me again of the dark days coming; but I no longer cared or feared. So long as my vengeance was completed, I heeded not myself. God might then deal with me as He pleased.

This made me hasten to prepare more fuel from the rocks, which I carried in armfuls into my cave, and stacked against the walls.

That afternoon there was a thin fall of snow, covering all the island with a thin carpet-like fleecy lawn. At nightfall the flakes grew large as fragments of wool, and fell unceasingly; and when I entered my cave, and drew the rock down over me, they were still falling.

I slept little that night, for my soul was too greatly troubled.

Again and again I rose, looked out, and saw snow still falling, so that the whiteness was piled thick upon my rude roof; falling in among the crannies of the stones, the flakes froze there, and became as a firm mortar to hold the stones together.

It was bitter cold without; yet the narrow space within, being closely sealed against the weather, was warmed with the smoke from the fire, and with my breath, and with the heat of my body. Yet I was glad to have the thick blankets to wrap around me, and twice to drink a little spirit from the keg—which sent through my frame a warmth like liquid fire.

Then I thought: 'He is well-nigh spent already,

and if he lives through this night I shall be amazed. Well, our places are changed; he is the weak, I the strong; he homeless and hungry, I sheltered and well nourished. God is just.'

Yet even with this thought to cheer me I could not sleep; for I could not cease from wondering what might become of him, where he was taking shelter, whether he was perishing from cold? So I shifted uneasily upon my bed, and ofttimes looked out again through the falling snow, thinking I might espy him.

But I saw only blankness, and the dark snow shining with a strange silent motion, like a shroud shaken before the eyes.

Now, so strangely and foolishly are we men fashioned, that we comprehend little or nothing by our imagination, but everything by the habit of the sense. Speak to a man of twenty thousand folk just buried by earthquake, or of hundreds shipwrecked cruelly at sea, and he is little moved; but show that same man one single creature crushed beneath a fallen wall, or drowning in a swift river, and he will weep for pity. Now, by the same token, I who had devised mine enemy all manner of suffering and cruel tortures, was secretly troubled to think of him that night shivering, perchance dying, in the wintry snow. Not that I would have stretched out a hand to save him, even in direst extremity; not that I forgot my hate, and turned my heart to pity; not that I doubted the justice of his punishment, the righteousness of his doom; nay, it was not that, but this: that we two men were all alone on the island, and that one of us was doomed to die.

In the world, where human beings throng, we hear with composure of death and sorrow; and if one comes to us saying, 'Such and such a man, who shamefully wronged you, is suffering, or sick, or dead,' we are well content, realising little of the event in detail, but feeling a certain sense of God's universal justice.

Had there been on that island one hundred men cast away—nay, had there been twenty, or even ten—besides the man my enemy, I should not have vexed my heart for him, or cast one thought towards him, or pictured to myself his dying face. But God had so

answered my prayer for vengeance that He had given
the man to me utterly; made that lonely isle our world,
with only our two souls upon it, until the end should
come.

'Give me this man!' I had prayed. He was given
me. 'Put his life into my hand, let my mercy be the
measure of his woe!' This too God had done. Could
my vengeance be completer? Could I doubt my God
again?

I *did* doubt Him.

Why had not the man died? Why had he risen up
like a ghost from the grave? Why was I haunted by
the thought of him, listening for his footsteps, dreading
to hear his voice? It was surely just for God to punish
him, but could He not have done His torture cunningly,
without vexing me with the sight?

But the world had receded from us like a sea, leaving
us alone as upon a solitary shore, with no life near us,
and nothing watching us but the open Eye of God.

What was to happen? I knew not; but all that
night I saw the Eye above me, waiting the event.

CHAPTER XXXIII.

IN THE SHADOW OF THE CAVE.

THE next dawn was dim and dark; the heavens were
blotted with grey cloud, and the snow still fell. When
I thrust back the rock, the drift fell in and almost
smothered me; but I clambered out, and saw that the
island was smothered in the snowy whiteness.

Then I thought I would go down to the shore and
slay another seal; but in this I was deceiving myself,
for my true bent was to discover what fate had overtaken Richard Orchardson during the night. So I took
my hatchet, and walked through the snow towards the
place where I had last beheld him—over against the
western shore.

I looked everywhere, but saw no sign of him, nor

'"Finish your work!" he cried. "Kill me, I say, and finish your work."'

any trace of footprints. Then I passed down to the sea-shore, and making believe to be on some other errand (lest his eye should discover me, and I be caught seeking what I most despised), I looked high and low.

Presently I heard a cry, and saw, tottering out of a great weed-hung cave, the very man I sought. Beholding him, I turned away, as if he were the last thing I dreamed to find, or cared to seek; and I would have hastened thence.

But he came staggering after me, reaching out his thin hands ; and I saw that he was shivering and half-frozen, and that his eyes were wild.

'Christian !' he cried, 'Christian Christianson !'

I started to hear my name, and my heart leapt that he of all men should dare to speak it. While I stood aghast, he came up, and tottering, clutched me to keep himself from falling.

'Let me go!' I said, trying to shake him off. 'Let me go, or——'

And I raised the hatchet, as I had done the previous day.

But his hold only became the tighter.

'Yea, kill me!' he gasped, thrusting up his thin face to mine, so that I could feel his hot breath. 'I am dying, but it is so slow! I do not wish to live; I shall never quit this place alive. For God's sake, kill me !'

'Loose your hold,' I said, 'and promise never to cross my path again !'

But he still held me, and though his touch sickened me, my strength was paralysed, and I could not do him harm.

His teeth chattered in his head, and his face was full of a desperate and frenzied desire.

'Finish your work !' he cried. 'You brought me here; yes, *you !* Kill me, I say, and finish your work !'

'You lie! I did not bring you here.'

'You did—God curse you for it ! You were ever a thorn in my side, a shadow in my path, and now you have brought me here to die !'

As he spoke, he moaned despairingly, and fell upon his knees as if half swooning. Then did I bend over him, and cry, gazing fiercely into his eyes :

' Remember Kate Christianson ! Remember my mother, who died broken-hearted ! Remember my father, whom your father betrayed ! '

Even as I spake, he fainted at my feet.

I left him lying where he fell, and took the path which led to the crags. I did not wish to look back, but when I gained the height something held and drew me, and I gazed down.

He lay there still, even as one dead.

Straightway I would have departed, but I could not for my life. I stood watching and waiting, sick at the sight I saw, sick at myself, sick of earth and heaven.

At last I saw him stir.

Presently he rose to his knees, and then I think he must have been praying; for his hands were clasped, and his face was raised to the cold sky.

I looked no more, but passed across the island to the western shore, and there fortune befriended me, for among the rocks I fell upon another seal, which I slew with one blow upon the snout. It was smaller than the one I had slain before, and I could lift it easily upon my shoulders. This I did, and carrying it up the heights threw it down beside my cave.

Then, eager to forget myself in any kind of toil, I set to work, skinning the beast, and cutting up its flesh as before. While I sat thus employed, the snow fell lightly, covering me like a garment, but I paid no heed.

Presently I saw a shape coming towards me. He came up close, and stood gazing. I kept my eyes fixed down upon my knife.

At last I looked up.

' Did I not bid you never cross my path ? ' I said between my set teeth.

' I am starving,' he replied.

At this I laughed to myself, with my heart full of hate and exultation; but even yet I did not look him in the face.

' I am starving,' he repeated. ' Since you would not kill me, give me food.'

I laughed again. There was a brief silence; he kept his place, and I knew that his eyes were fixed upon my face.

Presently he spoke again.

'Why should you hate me so much ?   I would have used you well, but you had ever a stubborn heart.   We shall never quit this place alive. Give me food, and God will requite you.'

His voice was so faint and weak that I hardly knew it ; none the less I pitied him not, no more than I might have pitied a starving hound. Nay, to the hound I would have cast some shred of help, some fragment of my store ; but my heart was shut to him.

'It was your turn once,' I said quietly—'it is my turn now.'

As I spoke he moved past me, to the entrance of my cave.

'Since you will not give me food, I will take it !' he murmured, half to himself, half to me.

Then I rose, still bloody with the work I had been doing, and gripping my knife :

'Keep back!' I said, fixing my eyes for the first time upon his white face. 'There is nothing here for you !'

'It is mine as much as yours,' he answered feebly. 'I tell you I am starving!'

'Starve!'

'Give me but one morsel of bread !'

'Not one.'

'I am frozen—let me shelter from the snow.'

'Not *here*.'

Uttering a despairing cry, he flung himself upon me, and struck at me with his feeble hands ; but with one hand I held him, feeling him like a straw in my strong grasp, and shook him as an eagle shakes a lamb.

Then I said :

'Let there be an end to this between us. You get no help from me. What I have is mine, and rather than share one fragment with such as you I would cast all into the sea. You hear ? And do you wonder, man, why I have not killed you ? This is why—you are not worth killing—I leave you to a dog's death, such as you deserve.'

So saying, I threw him off, and he sank moaning on a fragment of rock ; then he hid his face in his hands, and I saw the tears streaming through his cold fingers. This made me hate him none the less, but despise him the more. But suddenly, as he lingered thus, he stretched out his arms to the empty air, and cried, as if crying to one who stood in the flesh before him, this one word twice repeated:

'Priscilla!　Priscilla!'

I started and looked round, half dreaming indeed to see her standing between us; but I was a fool for my pains, and saw nothing. Then I strode over to him, and struck him on the shoulder with my clenched hand.

'Why do you call on *her?*　How dare you name her name?　Do you think she can help you?　Do you think that she would help you if she could?'

His answer came fearlessly, though his voice was so weak.

'I think she is an angel, and you are a devil!'

'How dare you think of her at all?　Think rather of your grave!　Listen, Richard Orchardson. You will die here, but I shall live—I shall be saved. I shall bide safe till succour comes, for I have a place to shelter me and food to eat. Then I shall go back into the world and find Priscilla, and tell her how I had my revenge. And then——'

'And then,' he interposed, looking up at me, 'what will she say to you?'

'She will say, as she has said before, " I love you," and I shall make her my wife. You hear?—my wife!'

He still kept his dim eyes fixed upon my face as he said:

'You will tell her that you left me to die?'

'Yes.'

'That though you had plenty, you denied me a morsel of bread?'

'Yes.'

'Then she will say as I say—that you are a devil!'

Maddened by his defiance, I struck him in the face with my open hand. No sooner had I done so than I hated myself for the deed. He uttered no word, but rising feebly to his feet with a faint moan, began to totter away. Then suddenly, as I beheld him going, watched the feeble form, the ragged, trembling limbs, the bowed and tempest-beaten head, my hard rocky heart felt a strange pang of pain, and in that moment was distilled one drop of the heavenly dew, which men name Mercy.

I would have called him back, but I was ashamed.

Suddenly, as I watched him, he stumbled and fell forward upon his face. I waited for him to rise, but he lay still; and at last, eager to see if he were living, I went over and raised him up.

But when I beheld him living, and his eyes wide open gazing strangely into mine, I released my hold and was ashamed, scarce knowing what to say.

'Get up!' I cried fiercely, though there was no fierceness left in my heart. 'Why are you lying here?'

'Begone,' he answered faintly. 'Leave me to die.'

And he turned over on his face again.

Much troubled, angry with him and with myself, hating myself for a kind of feverish pity which I could not quite subdue, I walked back to the mouth of the cave; and there I stood thinking. Should I leave him to die indeed? Should I, having plenty, see him, even my enemy, perish of cruel starvation?

Then I thought of *her*, whose dear name he had uttered in a pleading tone of prayer. Was the man right? and would she, whose holy approval I cherished secretly more than all else in earth or heaven, deem me a devil indeed? I remembered how often she had tried to play the peacemaker; how she had chid my violent passion, scorned my unreasoning hate—how sweetly, with innocent maidenly rebuke, she had touched the hard rock of my hate, in hopes to bring from thence the living waters of charity and love.

Then I looked around me, on the cold heaven and on the frosty sea. If that island of desolation were to be my grave (as indeed seemed probable), could I die in peace, or in any heavenly hope, if I had denied to any poor starving creature a little morsel of bread?

My mind being at last made up, I returned to the place where the man still lay, and standing over against him said:

'Get up—and listen.'

He did not stir, but by a low moaning sound gave sign that he heard.

'You shall not say that I took everything, and left you nothing; but remember, what you take is no gift of mine, and that I hate you none the less though I suffer you to take it. Go to my cave yonder, and select what you need—God knows I care not if you take all; but having taken it, find a place for yourself; cross not my path, but choose your own dwelling and your own grave—no matter where, if they are far from mine.'

Without waiting to hear his answer, I walked away, and passing over the stony heights sought the loneliest shores of the island. There I remained for hours, wondering and pondering. God could surely not blame me now? I had left all I possessed in the world to the man I hated; and I was indifferent (as I had said) had he used it. All I asked was to be spared the sight of him, the horrible torture of his near neighbourhood. Surely God would now spare me *that?*

It was not to be. I had prayed to the Maker to place the man in my power, wholly, unreservedly, to do with as I willed; to give him up to me for torture, for sorrow, and for death. My prayer was answered, but not to the full measure. The rest was yet to come.

At last I returned across the island. Returning to the mouth of my cave, and looking in, the first sight I saw was Richard Orchardson, lying with his head against the rocky wall, in a heavy sleep! In his hand he held a piece of hard rye bread, which he had been gnawing, and a portion of dried seal's flesh lay by his side, also partly consumed; but what sickened me as I bent over him was a sickly stench of rum.

Close to him was the keg of raw spirit, and the piece of hollow stone which I had used for a cup; and some of the rum was spilt upon the ground, and upon the sleeper's ragged clothes.

I shook him, but he did not waken; when I shook him yet more violently, he opened his glazed eyes, saw me, and grinned like an ape—then, muttering to himself, tumbled off again to slumber.

Then I knew, by the signs around him, by his frail condition, and by his stinking breath, that he had made himself drunken with the raw spirit; and seeing this, all my rage of hate returned, and I pushed his body fiercely with my feet, bidding him arise and depart. But he was drugged and stupefied, and paid no heed.

Thereon I would have raised him in my arms and cast him forth, but looking up I saw the snow again beginning to fall, and I knew that if I cast him forth he would perish of cold. So after trying again to arouse him from his stupor, I let him sleep on.

Presently he began to murmur in his sleep, and I knew by his words that he was dreaming wild dreams. Anon he threw up his arms as if to shield himself from a blow.

'Sweetheart, keep him away! . . . he is coming to kill me. Look, look at the axe! . . . Ah, devil, devil!'

And he clutched at the air, as if struggling with some foe unseen. Suddenly with a cry he awakened, and opening his eyes, saw me sitting over against him, in the shadow of the cave.

CHAPTER XXXIV.

'COME BACK WITH ME!'

Now, the fumes of the fierce spirit not having faded from his brain, and his whole mind being clouded and fevered from sleep, he gazed at me wildly, yet with no sign of fear; then, to my amaze, began to laugh feebly, and point at me with a skinny forefinger.

'Priscilla, come!' he whispered, as if to some one at his side. 'They have put him in irons, and he cannot stir. Give me your hand, sweetheart—quick! quick! the ship's afire!'

Then, though I saw that his wits were wandering, his words brought back the memory of that wild night when the ship went down, and remembering my suspicion that his hand had fired the vessel, I loathed him the more. Presently his words grew wilder, and I saw that he was going over in his thought all the horrors of our shipwreck; and ever, as he fancied, Priscilla was at his side, he comforting her with loving words.

Sick to hear him rave, yet still without the heart to cast him forth, I rose to leave the cave. As I passed him, he clutched at me feebly, yet hardly seemed to know me when I turned and shook off his hold.

So I went forth, and found the snow still falling, and the sun just sunken behind the sea.

Wildly troubled, I walked along through the drift, which in places was knee-deep, and tried to think it all o'er; and the more I thought, the more my trouble grew; and when it was quite dark, I sat bareheaded on a rock, bewildered in the misty perplexity of mine own thought. For it seemed strange beyond measure, and beyond measure cruel and unbearable, that this man I loathed most should haunt me like a ghost, and mock me with the memory of my life-long, unreasoning hate; that the same fate should pursue us both, until the same roof sheltered us and the same death awaited us not far away; that all my dream of vengeance should have come to naught but foolish piteousness and a dreary sense of unutterable despair.

Then I thought to myself that, since fate had willed all this for my confusion, I would at least escape the man's presence, and avoid the place till he was dead; or if I should perish first, and be buried beneath the snow, so much the better, since I began to loathe my life.

Presently it grew so bitterly cold that if I had remained still I should have frozen; and lacking courage to die that way, I ran to and fro to keep myself warm. And now a great wind began to rise, howling and shrieking from the north, and thick snow, falling and driven, covered me, so that I could hardly breathe.

Then I laughed at mine own folly in yielding up my warm shelter to another, and such another; and without more ado, casting all my late resolves to the winds, I ran back to the cave, leapt down, and groping my way over the man's body (for the place was black dark), felt about till I found my smouldering fire, and procured a light.

When I had lit one of my rushlights and fixed it against the rock, I saw Richard Orchardson lying where I had left him, sleeping fast with his eyes wide open; and indeed I should have deemed him dead had I not heard his troubled sterturous breath.

Twice or thrice the wind rushed in and extinguished my light; so I went to the aperture, and carefully drew down upon it the rock I used for a door; and after that I put fuel on the fire, though the place remained bitter cold.

Thus it befell, after all, that I lay under the same roof with my enemy—an event that, but a little while before, I should have deemed impossible and laughed to scorn. His life had been in my hands, and I had not taken it; he had asked me for food and shelter, and I had denied him neither: and there, almost touching me, he lay and lived. Looking upon him as he slept, I despised myself for my weakness, since I had spared him, not out of loving-kindness, but from feebleness and fear.

Ah, well! hate is easy, God knoweth, out in the world where men battle with one another; but it is hard, as I have proven, when two men are all alone with God.

All night the wind wailed terribly, with violent gusts, but Richard Orchardson slept sound. For myself, I scarcely rested at all, but whenever I dozed would wake suddenly, with a nameless terror in my heart.

No ray of light from without penetrated our place of shelter; the fumes of the moss-fuel rose up in red clouds and filled the cave with dimness; and in that dimness I lay restless, till the cold day came.

From time to time I lifted the rock and looked out, and at last, after many weary hours, I saw the dim rays of wintry dawn.

Then I threw back the rock, and the blast blew in, with heavy drifts of loosened snow; whereon I saw him waken, with eyes of terror gazing up at me. His face was ghastly, his cheeks sunken, and he shivered like one with an ague, chattering his teeth.

I stood erect, with my face averted from his, while
I said :

'Listen, man ! Are you listening ?'

After a pause I heard him answer,

'Yes.'

'You were drunken last night, and I let you lie
where you fell ; but this place is mine. Your presence
poisons it ; you have no right here. Find yourself
another shelter.'

He rose, shivering, as I spoke, and prepared to leave
the cavern.

Then I continued :

'You shall not say that I left you to starve. Take
what I offered you yesterday—a portion of what I saved
from the ship ; take it, and go ; all I wish is never to
see your face again.'

So saying, I leapt out into the snow, and without
once turning to look back, walked rapidly away.

And now, as I went through the deep snow, and
sought my point of vantage on the highest part of the
island (whence it was my daily custom to search the
seas for a sail), I saw that winter had come indeed ;
for not only was the island itself one mass of whiteness, from the highest land down to the very brink
of the sea, but the great floe to the eastward was
smothered in drifts of snow, and far away northward,
where the dawn was burning duskily, like a sullen brand,
there was the blink of innumerable anchored bergs.
Southward and eastward only the seas were clear, save for
one or two loose icebergs drifting towards the horizon ;
and one of these was so like a ship with all sails set
that my heart leaped into my mouth, and I uttered a
joyful cry. Alas! I soon discovered that what I saw
was a floating iceberg only, and no ship at all.

Descending the crags on the westward side of the
island, I roamed along the shore ; and here the breath
of the sea was so fresh and warm that it seemed more
like summer than winter-tide. But save only a few
gulls and terns, and some seals swimming among the
creeks, there was no sign of life. The little friendly
bird which had so reminded me of my home, and which
I had noticed nigh every day chirping about the sands,

was nowhere to be seen; and even the flocks of green cormorants had left their roosts upon the outlying reefs.

So I wandered along the lonely shore, listening to the sad surging sound of the sea.

I noted that day that the sun, which was constantly obscured by black clouds, kept low down upon the horizon, circling westward, but never rising up into the open heaven; so that the day was very brief, and, almost before I knew it, it was afternoon. For hours I struggled with the pangs of hunger, not having yet broken my fast; but at last, finding the gnawing within too much to bear any longer, I returned to the cavern in the heights.

As I approached, I saw Richard Orchardson standing at the cavern's mouth; and any heart but mine would have pitied him—so haggard did he look, and woe-begone, so gray and old.

Now, the moment he saw me coming, he began to move away; but I came up to him, and called to him to stand.

So he paused, gazing at me sadly, with an expression of utter despair.

'Have you taken your share of the ship's goods?' I asked sternly.

'I have taken nothing,' he replied, in a faint voice.

'I gave you leave to take food and find yourself another shelter. I did this, not because you deserve succour, but that you might not come begging to me again. Since you have let the chance slip, begone!'

'I am going,' he replied.

'Remember that I warned you,' I continued violently. 'My soul sickens at the sight of you, but I would not stain my hands with your miserable blood. By right your life belongs to me. If you cross me again I shall take it, though I have spared it hitherto.'

As I ceased, he turned his great sunken eyes upon me, and I no longer saw in them any sign of fear. Despair will give courage even to timorous men and to beasts that startle at their own shadows.

'You have done your worst,' he said, in the same

faint, hollow voice. ' Why did you not kill me, as I
prayed ? '

' Did I not tell you? Because you are not worth
killing. Because you cannot escape from this place,
and must die without any touch of mine.'

He looked around on the snow-clad island, and on
the desolate sky and sea; his eyes grew dim and wet,
though no tears fell; and dropping his head like a
death-struck beast, as he turned away he uttered his
whole sad soul in one faint, despairing cry,

' O God! my God!'

Now, had the man fallen upon his knees and
asked piteously for mercy, or had he fled from me in
guilty fear, I know my heart would have hardened
against him as it had done before; but seeing him so
desolately resigned, and feeling how little he cared for
life, I was moved to a secret compassion. His agonised
cry to heaven rang through my heart; it was so hopeless and so sad.

' Stay,' I said, ' I have not done with you yet!'

He turned again, and gazed upon me.

' Answer me one question before we part. Did you
fire the ship? '

I saw his face change, while his lips were set
convulsively.

' No,' he said, fixing his eyes full on mine.

' You swear it ? '

' Of what avail would it be to swear? I tell you
—no.'

' Are you lying to me ? Yes, I see it in your face.
You are lying! Do you think I am fool enough to
believe you ? '

' I care not what you believe. Now let me go.'

' No, you shall stay !'

And reaching out my hands, I held his arm in the
vice of my strong grip. Why I did this I knew not,
only I was angry with my own compassion, and tried
to lash myself into a fury I did not feel.

' What do you want with me ? ' he cried, helpless in
my grasp as a sick child.

And I knew not how to answer him. My whole
mind was clouded with doubt, and I was fearful lest

he should guess my weakness of purpose. Only I felt that I could not let him depart desolate, to die in some secret place.

'If I let you go, will you promise never to return?'

'I will promise.'

'Never to come my way, to beg sustenance from me, to let me see your face?'

'You need not be afraid,' he replied: 'I shall not trouble you again.'

'What will you do?'

'God knows. Die—the sooner the better.'

'You wish to die?'

'Yes.'

I looked at him fixedly for some moments, as if to read his very heart, before I spoke again.

'Then you shall live. You shall not have your wish. Come back with me!'

So saying, I forced rather than led him towards the cave. He seemed enraged at first, but afterwards, seeing his helplessness, he made no resistance, but walked feebly with me the way I led him; his head dropping heavily forward on his breast, and his limbs trembling beneath him.

When we came to the cave, I bade him enter. After a moment's hesitation, he obeyed, and sank shivering on the spot where he had lain the previous night.

Then I entered the place also, and feeling again the pinch of hunger, cut off with my clasp-knife a portion of dried seal's flesh, and with that and some crumbled biscuits began to break my fast. I ate ravenously, until my hunger was appeased; then, looking up, I saw him, with his head resting against the rock, and his eyes half closed.

I took some seal's flesh and a biscuit, and threw them to him, as I might have thrown them to a dog.

'There is food,' I said. 'Eat!'

He did not stir, but opened his eyes quietly, as he replied

'I am not hungry.'

'Eat, I tell you!'

And with an oath that shall not be written here, I brandished the knife before his eyes.

I do not think he was afraid; perchance he by this time knew my heart better than I knew it myself; but be that as it may, he reached out his thin white hands, and taking what I had so roughly given him, put a morsel to his lips.

CHAPTER XXXV.

THE AURORA.

I WAS ever a simple man, little given to book-reading or analysing (as wise men love to do) their own thoughts; and when I led Richard Orchardson back to my cave, and gave him food to eat, I knew no more what spirit moved me than I know why the winds blow divers ways, and why stars ofttimes shoot from yonder sky. This only I remember, that my mood was so mingled and confused, that while I threw him food with one hand I could have struck him fiercely with the other.

This too was very strange to me then, though I understand it better now: that in proportion to the man's helplessness grew his mastery over me. In his very weakness lay his strength against me. When he sank down powerless before me, careless how I used him, indifferent alike to my wrath and to my compassion, I seemed to hear a voice crying in mine ear, 'Ah! coward! coward!'—but at every cry of this voice I steeled my heart the more.

Then I tried to persuade myself that what I did was done in cruelty, not in feebleness; that I had brought him there and forced him to eat, not because I cared whether he lived or died, but because I took pleasure in his extremity, and could leisurely feast mine eyes upon his pain. It was something, after all, to hold his life in my hand—to watch him as a wild beast or bird watches its prey—to feel that he was utterly, hopelessly, fatally, within my power. Yes, that made amends. I had dragged him out of the sunshine of the

world; I held him down as in an open grave, and
whenever I pleased the earth would cover him. Surely
I had accomplished my revenge.

Night came again; and found us lying close to one
another, in the darkness of the cave.

I slept heavily for some hours; and then, full of
restlessness, I rose and looked out. Then I saw that
the wind had fallen, and that the sky above was
beautifully clear.

I glanced down at him, and saw him lying still,
with his head against the rock; sleeping, as I thought,
for I could hear his heavy breathing.

In my fevered watchfulness I loathed to remain in
the place poisoned to me (as it seemed) by his breath;
so I left the cave, and wandered out into the night.

Then I beheld for the first time a wonder which
many and many a time afterwards filled my soul with
awe, and which even now, as I sit in this land of
dark skies and greyness, seems like the memory of a
beautiful dream. As I came out upon the height, and
looked around me, I saw the heavens to the northward
sparkling, as through a veil of the thinnest lawn, with
innumerable constellations. All was still as death:
the snow-clad island, the darkly glimmering sea on
every side.

Then suddenly, as I gazed northward, there appeared
spanning the heavens a great broad bow of phosphorescent light; out of this bow began to fall sparkling
streams of clearest blood-red fire; and in an instant,
shooting up from the horizon, rose flames of all the
rainbow's hues, but infinitely brighter, darting up with
quivering tongues to meet the flames of the bow—till
all the heavens seemed afire.

Then, a great awe fell upon me, beholding so
wonderful a thing.

As I gazed, shapes like living forms, nay, like
angels in their overpowering brightness, seemed coming
and going among the flames; which rushing presently
together, as if by enchantment, fashioned themselves
into a glorious cupola of splendour, filling the whole
heaven, and overflowing like a fountain in streams of
vari-coloured light, amber yellow at the top (where

the fountain feathers itself and turns to fall), bright emerald and amethystine lower down, and blood-crimson closer to the horizon ; and all these hues so flashing and changing, so sparkling and intermingling one with another, that the eyes were dazzled, and the soul seemed gazing on the tremulous fabric of a dream.

Now, had the heavens opened, and the very face of God appeared in the midst of that supernatural brightness, I could not have wondered more ; for Divine the vision seemed, and of more than earthly glory, like the glory of the celestial City of God.

Underneath the many-coloured heaven, the sea now lay black as ink, and the snow-fields assumed a ghastly whiteness, like the cerements of the dead ; for it seemed a splendour in which the dark earth had no share, and for which the sea had no reflection ; a thing, indeed, wholly Divine, supernatural, and unaccountable.

I know not how long the vision lasted, but it must have been for hours, and while it shone and changed I did not cease to watch. But at last it began to die away out of the heavens ; and soon, like a picture fading from the eye, it was almost gone, all that remained being a few straggling beams (like the little blue flames that run along burning spirit) low down upon the horizon.

I did not know then that this beautiful phenomenon of the aurora is in no sense extraordinary in this region, but common, and wholly in the way of Nature. Afterwards I learned to become familiar with it, and to marvel less. And yet, what am I saying? What is this same Nature that surrounds us but a perpetual miracle and matter for marvel? Should the coming and going of the sun, the motions of the celestial bodies, the changeful seasons, with all their mysterious changes, awaken our wonder less because they are familiar as the fields where we were born ?*

---

* ‘Our writer here, good man, gets out of his depth, and flounders into mysticism, a mode of thought ever to be distrusted. Nothing can be more simple and methodical than the machinery of Nature—nothing clearer than its lessons of punctual duty ; and the Creator cares far less that we should marvel at His Glory than that we should comprehend plainly His teachings, as a law for life. Our Lord, by that token, was the plainest and least visionary of men.’—J. W.

Nay, indeed, but what simple fools are men? Those who scarce heed the miracles of sunrise and sunset will gape with awe at a rick on fire. Folk who take no heed how the kingfisher builds his nest, or how the cuckoo rears her callow young, will find endless delight in a screaming parroquet, brought home by some sailor in a cage.

'Tis the unfamiliar that charms the fool; whereas to the wise man the nearest thing is oft the most Divine.

Be that as it may, my stormy spirit was by this manifestation of superhuman power and loveliness sensibly subdued and softened. I walked back to my cave like one that has seen a spirit passing before his face; nay, rather, for a closer similitude, like Moses when he beheld the presence of God in the midst of the Burning Bush.

The man still lay as I had left him, but as I entered he started, and cried out in terror.

Then I said:

'Are you awake? I wish to speak with you, for the last time.'

He said nothing, but I knew that he was listening, and I continued:

'I have thought it all over, and I shall leave God to deal with you as you deserve. We are cast away together, and in all human likelihood we shall perish on this island. Well, if you leave this place, you will cast your death at my door; and you shall not have that consolation. Now, attend.'

'Go on,' he replied.

'Since there is no other shelter on the island, you may remain; and since there is no other sustenance but the ship's stores, you shall share them; but on these conditions: During the daytime, if I come here, you will go forth, and when I go forth, you may return. During the night-time, when to go forth is impossible, you will keep your place, I mine. But if at any time you utter one word, if you attempt in any way to break the eternal silence of hate that should exist between us, our compact is broken: I shall kill you, or drive you forth, never to return.'

I paused again, and his voice murmured in the darkness:

'As you will.'

'Understand me well,' I continued. 'This is my last word to you, Richard Orchardson. There must be no communion between us by speech or look. I shall avoid you, and take heed that you avoid me. Henceforth I shall be no more conscious of your presence than of a stone or a piece of rock-weed. I shall blot you for ever from my sight, from my thought, from my memory—from this night forth. You will be to me as a thing dead. You understand?'

'Yes.'

'You swear to keep these conditions?'

'Yes.'

So it was sworn; and from that moment darkness and silence like death came between us, though we were alone together in all the world.

CHAPTER XXXVI.

THE DEAR.

THUS it befell that we two abode together in the same dwelling, if I may call that a dwelling which, with Nature helping me, I fashioned with my rude hands: so near to each other that we could hear each other breathing, yet so far from each other that we never exchanged look or word. As far as might be, I averted my soul as a man averts his face—avoiding him in the daytime, forgetting him in the silence of the night; yet all in vain; for I was conscious of him unceasingly, and his shadow darkened my most secret thoughts.

I have read somewhere, in some old book or newspaper, of two poor sisters who, full of an unnatural hate, dwelt together like this in the same room in a great town; being too poor to take separate lodgings, they divided their wretched room by a line made with chalk across the floor; and so, with that chalk line only between them, abode in silence for a score of weary years; until one was carried out feet foremost, and the other, still cruel and unforgiving, was left alone. Of such hard stuff, I know, some hearts are made; of rock instead of flesh, and hard as the upper and nether millstone. Yet these foolish women had busy sounds of life all round to cheer them—the tramp of feet, voices, and all the motion of a great city; while we, whose hearts were no less hard, and whose condition was surely as sorry in the sight of God, had only the naked heavens, and the troubled sea, and the punctual changes of darkness and of light.

Stubborn and unforgiving, grudging the mercy I had shown (which was no true mercy, but feebleness and fear), I came and went. The days were now briefer than ever, and the nights very long and dreary; but though winter had surely set in, the temperature was not yet too cold to bear with patience, and even with comfort. For the soft swell of the southern ocean, which is ever warm like living breath, greatly subdues the violence of the climate of the islands in that region; so that neither man nor beast need perish, as they must needs do under like conditions a few degrees nearer to the north.

Nevertheless, the cold was sharp and keen, the life beyond measure unseasonable and hard to bear. The island was draped in whiteness, and far away to the north stretched the vast fields of silent ice; while to southward and westward, where the seas thundered unfrozen, great chill mists, like steam from a caldron, were constantly arising. Nowhere was any sign of life; nay, not even a withered tree, a leafless bush, to mimic summer greenery with leaves and flowers of hueless ice. No sign, no similitude, of that green world which I had lost, never, perchance, to find again!

There was but one way to defy the loneliness of Nature and the sad monotony of the elements, and that was to discover some vigorous occupation to fatigue the frame while light lasted. This occupation I found in chasing and killing the poor seals of the sea; and although I was without firearms or any kind of projectile, I contrived by cunning and stratagem to slay full many of them, as I had slain the first.

'Twas a wild beast's life, but it kept me from perishing. From morn to night I would prowl and crawl and watch, or swiftly run, as the simple quarry led me; crafty, cruel-eyed, swift, stealthy, as any predatory beast.

The foolish seals, which swarmed in the creeks and caves of those lonely shores, were of divers breeds; some large as sheep that graze on our downs, others small as the otters of our rivers. I saw none of the great-tusked species which some mariners tell of; great as bulls, and as savage when assailed. Some had coarse rough skins, which would have been worthless even in the hands of a skilful tanner; others had hair as long and coarse as wool; and others, again, were smooth, red, and silken, glistening like oil in the sun.

My best sport was out upon the ice, where I was wont, by watchfulness and strategy, to intercept the beasts when they came from the water holes to bask in the sun. Being asleep, they are easily surprised by one who is careful to seek them up the wind; for their hearing is dull in proportion to the keenness of their scent, as I have very frequently proved.

Besides these animals, and now and then a shoal of white whales out in the sea southward, there were few signs of life. Most of the seabirds had disappeared, with the exception of some solitary gulls, and from time to time a lonely gannet, or sea goose, driven northward by some ocean storm.

The flesh and oil of the seals I thus slew kept me well supplied with fresh food and light; and presently, to beguile the weariness of the long nights, I set to work and fashioned myself a rude covering, or overcoat, of the skins; which covering I would wear when the wind blew cold, or when much snow fell. I also wove several coverlets of warm skin to draw over me at night.

Meantime, how fared the companion of my cave?

Well, he kept the conditions, and spake not, neither looked my way; while I, with face averted, toiled close by. And ever in the daytime, when I entered he would creep out, and crawl like a forlorn thing about the island. But he made no effort to hunt for himself, seeming altogether too feeble and faint of heart.

Now one night, when the cold was strangely keen, even within the cave, I heard him breathing hard and shivering; and after a sharp struggle within of shame and pity, I took several of my warm skins, roughly sewn together, and threw them unto him.

He started and looked up, so that our eyes met. Then, without speaking, I made a sign to him to take the skins, which he forthwith drew over him, and presently fell to sleep.

I had taken no strict count of the flight of days, and had no kind of reckoner or guide in that dreary place; but, so far as I could guess, we were now midway in the month of December. For it was early in November when the Dutch ship was beset among the ice, and several long weeks had passed since then.

To me, thus miserably cast away, one day was so like another that I almost failed to distinguish each from each; nor did I discern the six days from the seventh, but laboured without a Sabbath—-the gracious day which to weary and heavy-hearted men is so full of rest and blessing.

And yet, being ever a profane man, little given to prayer and church-going, I missed not that consecration of one day out of seven; nor did my thoughts any day turn heavenward, either for strength or consolation.

But now I am about to record a thing which at the time moved me strangely; and of which I cannot think even now without a curious stirring of the heart.

One day, which might have been a Sabbath-day indeed, so still and sweet were earth and heaven and sea, I wandered forth as usual. Not a breath stirred, the air was full of a pleasant and balmy chillness, and the sun circled along the horizon with mild and gentle beams.

Seeing it so fair, I paused at the mouth of the cave, and drawing off my sealskin overcoat, threw it back upon my bed; then I took my hatchet, which I used ever as a weapon, and wandered away.

First I roamed along the western cliffs, searching the creeks for anything alive; but all I saw was swarms of seal swimming out at sea, and basking upon the distant reefs. Far off, in a patch of violet calm, a whale was spouting; and so still was the air, that I conld hear the roar of his blow-hole from where I stood.

Then I clambered down to the western shore, and found nothing there.

Returning over the island, I made straight for the fields of ice; for although from the heights I could discern no sign of life upon them, I knew that the water-holes and the ice in their close vicinity were favourite haunts of the beasts I sought.

I rambled about the ice for hours, and although, as I had expected, I saw many seals, none were foolish enough to let me come nigh; till at last, as I was returning dissatisfied, I fell upon one of the small silken-coated species, fast asleep upon the floe. Coming round a great hummock, I was close upon it ere I knew, and ere it could reach the neighbouring water I killed it with a dexterous blow.

Now the beast was so light and small that I threw it bodily upon my shoulder, and carried it easily away; when, as I approached the gloomy shore, I was startled by a wild shriek as of a human being in mortal fear.

The next moment I saw, running swiftly towards me, the wild figure of a man, no other indeed than Richard Orchardson; and well might he shriek in terror, for behind him at a gallop was a huge white bear—the first beast of the kind I had seen in these regions.

These animals are indeed fatal to man, having the lion's swiftness, the fierceness of the wild cat, and the sinuousness of the snake; and this that I beheld was a true monster of the breed, with huge shaggy paws, mighty talons, and horrible crimson jaws.

Even as I gazed, the man sped towards me, but before he could reach me, as was clearly his intent, slipped, and fell upon his face.

The bear, which was some thirty yards behind, paused a moment, seeing him fall, and beholding me for the first time; then, without hesitation, it came bounding on—with just the same wavy sinuous motion, just the same cruel swiftness, though it was so great a monster, as hath the lissom weazel of our English woods and fields.

Then my heart leapt in my mouth, for I saw that the man was lost.

As I write, it all comes back to me—the lonely field of ice, the fallen man, the horrible hungry beast approaching with open mouth; and I see the man now, as I saw him then, turn up his white face with one wild look of horror and despair.

I had no time to think, to pause; in another minute the beast's fangs would have been at his throat, its tongue lapping his blood. Before I knew what I was doing, I had thrown down the dead seal, and, bounding forward, placed myself between the beast and the fallen man.

There, hatchet in hand, with set teeth, I stood, half-a-dozen yards from the bear.

Now, before such a mighty animal as that, an unarmed man is helpless; and I had only my hatchet, which, in such a struggle, would have been useless as a straw. But, as God willed it, something in my erect and defiant attitude made the beast pause in his career.

He paused, looked at me, sniffed with his nostrils, and uttered an ominous growl.

For one moment my fate hung in the balance, and surely, had I now retreated a step, or shown any sign of fear, I should have perished; but instead of retreating I advanced steadily, my eyes fixed firmly on those of the bear, the hatchet raised as if to strike, and out of my very desperation I uttered a savage cry!

As I advanced, the bear retreated sideways, still growling terribly; and at last, to my great joy, began to creep rapidly away.

Running in a circle, it avoided me. Thrice it turned, hesitated, and thrice I advanced as if to the attack. Then, to my astonishment, I saw it rise on its hind legs, sniffing the air; then, with its nose close to the ice, it galloped round to the spot where I had left the dead seal.

As it did so, Richard Orchardson, who had been looking on in wonder, ran towards me, and again put my body between him and the bear; which now, seizing the seal with teeth and talons, tore it piecemeal and devoured its flesh eagerly, only pausing now and then to throw up its head and utter fierce growls of gluttonous delight.

I saw that we were saved, and for the first time felt a sense of overmastering terror, feeling what manner of horrible death I had escaped; so without more delay I hastened away to the shore, leaving the savage beast to the meal I had procured for it.

As I went, Richard Orchardson followed me, so near that he might have touched me with his hand.

It was not till some hours afterwards that I clearly realised what I had done; nay, perhaps if the truth were told, I did not wholly realise it till after many years.

But be that as it may, the thing was done. I had preserved, at the risk of my own life, the life of the man I hated most in all the world.

CHAPTER XXXVII.

VIGIL.

I REACHED the shore, and climbed the cliff until I gained the snow-clad height. Pausing there, I turned and saw Richard Orchardson standing close by me, with his eyes on mine.

Then a foolish kind of anger seized me, for I loathed myself for having done what I had done; and without remembering our pact, I broke the silence that had dwelt so long between us.

'Why do you follow me?' I cried. 'Did I not warn you?'

He gazed at me sadly, as he replied, in another question:

'Why did you save my life?'

I could have struck him in the face. I turned from him with a gesture of loathing and dislike.

'Why did you save my life?' he repeated, following me. 'I did not wish to live.'

I turned and faced him.

'Do not think I saved you out of pity. I saw you were a coward, and I thought to myself, "He shall not die yet"; that was all. Now, go—keep your miserable life, and let us part here.'

I would have left him, but he still persisted. His manner was so desolate, so despairing, his voice so hollow and sad, that I listened in spite of myself.

'Why can there not be peace between us? I have as much cause for hate as you, and yet I am willing to forget the past. Since we shall never leave this place alive, why need we quarrel still? You must have a hard heart, to hate so bitterly and so long.'

'Begone!' I said, between my set teeth. 'I will not be judged by *you*. I shall never forget, or forgive.'

'As you will,' he answered bitterly, 'but methinks, hate is foolish, seeing we are so utterly cast away. And your acts belie your words. Had you not given me food and shelter, I should have been a dead man long ere this. Had you not interposed, I should have died by the bear.'

I knew not what to reply, for his words were true enough, and although I was ashamed of my own benefactions (which sprang not out of true compassion, but a feebleness and infirmity of will), I had indeed saved him again and again from death.

Seeing me hesitate, and misconceiving perchance the emotions of mingled shame and rage which then possessed me, he reached out his thin hands and touched me. I shuddered as if I had been stung.

'Since I owe my life to you,' he said, 'let me owe you something more. It has long been upon my mind to utter the request which I am now about to speak. I think I shall die here, but you are strong, and help may come. Well, when I die, do not let the wild beasts devour me, but bury me in the ground, like a Christian man.'

'Ask nothing from me,' I said, repulsing him.

'Ah! but promise!' he cried, his eyes full of feeble tears. 'And promise one thing more! If you are saved, if you return to England, as indeed may be, go to my poor father, and tell him how I died; yet break it to him gently, for the old man loves me, and he is the only living soul to mourn me when I am gone.'

I gazed at him in wonder, for I could scarce believe mine ears. Did he think I was made of wax, that I had no bitterness of memory, no fortitude of hate, when he asked such charity from me? Did he think I would spare an Orchardson one drop of pain, one pang of the sorrow he had given to me and mine?

'Will you promise?' he pleaded. 'Then I can die in peace.'

And he sobbed like a child, hiding his face in his hands.

I did not answer him, but with one fierce look, into which I sought to concentrate all my long life of loathing, I left him to his tears.

Night came, and I lay alone in the cave.

Several hours had passed since I had left Richard Orchardson on the cliff, and when at sunset I had returned to my place of shelter, he had not returned. After making up my fire, I busied myself making candles of dry seal-fat and rough twine.

But when darkness fell, I could not help wondering why the man did not return. Could any fresh evil have overtaken him? Although I was angry with myself for the solicitude, and although I was persuaded myself that I was cruelly indifferent, I could not help listening from time to time for the sound of his coming. Yet he came not, and suddenly, so perverse is our human disposition, I began reproaching myself for having left him so cruelly.

I had risen to my feet, and was moving towards the entrance of the cave, thinking to look out in search of him, when I heard a strange sound above me, and the next instant he sprang down, wild with terror, and covered with snow.

'Help!' he shrieked, and pointed to the opening by which he had entered. 'It has followed me again. Look!'

And he fell upon his knees, clinging with his arms around me.

Then, gazing towards the aperture above us (which,

as I have elsewhere explained, was just large enough to admit the body of a man), I saw two fierce glittering lights, which I knew to be the eyes of the bear.

The monster was standing over against our cave, and, surprised at the strange brilliance within, was gazing curiously down. By the dim ray which issued forth from the fire and the lights fixed against the wall, I could dimly see the great shaggy head and the savage mouth.

For a moment terror seized me; but speedily recovering my courage, I snatched down from the wall one of the burning lights, and holding it in my hand, approached the aperture. For I remembered having read that certain wild beasts have a terror of fire, and that even fierce wolves of the forest, swarming to destroy some hapless voyager, had been scattered by the waving of a burning brand.

I shouted aloud, and thrust out the light full at the face of the bear. To mine own amaze the stratagem answered, and the great beast, startled and blinded by the flame, suddenly withdrew.

Then I reached up my hand, and drew down the stone, closing the opening to the cave.

Turning to Richard Orchardson, I saw him still on his knees, as if praying. The moment he met mine eyes, he spake.

'I was returning hither across the height,' he said, 'when I heard the bear behind me, and I fled, for fear.'

I answered him straightway, using the mocking thought that came uppermost:

'And yet you craved to die?'

'Not that way! not that way!'

As he spake, I heard above us the sound of the bear passing hither and thither, and scraping in the snow. The sound continued for some minutes, during which I hearkened intently; then it ceased and all was still.

The night passed, and the monster did not return; even had he done so, he could not readily have reached us to do us injury, protected as we were by the stony covering of the cave, which was now hard-welded together by frost and snow. But I guessed, no doubt rightly, that the beast, being glutted with flesh of the seal, had followed Orchardson, not from savage hunger, but from foolish curiosity, never perchance having seen a man before that day; so that when the flame was flashed into his brute face, he withdrew fearfully, puzzled by a thing unmatched and unaccountable in his cold experience.

Be that as it may, he returned not, and methinks he wandered far away northward, for next day I tracked his great footprints over the island, across the shore, and thence back among the fields of ice. Doubtless he was a straggler from the chillier regions to the north, for during the whole time I remained upon the island of desolation I never saw another beast of that monstrous breed.

I know not how it happened, but despite all my cruel antipathy for my companion, the experience of that day and night insensibly loosened the hard barrier of bitterness between us. Once or twice we exchanged speech, though roughly and sullenly, and, as before, I let him share my food and shelter; so that presently it seemed quite natural that he should partake equally of my cruel fortune, and my daily hope and fear.

Every day I searched the seas for a sail, the ice for some sign of living folk; and every day when I returned, his pale face questioned mine for some sign to soften his despair. But surely it was now hoping against hope; for winter had set in fixedly, and the days were brief and dim, and the breath of the Cold Clime was coming southward like an exhalation, wrapping tho island in a constant shroud of frost and fog.

We had thus much in common, despite our life-long hate: that we were equally cast away and abandoned, that we had each the same hope and the same despair, that we had both the same dark thoughts for company, the same sad cause for fear. Thus alike were our conditions, save that I was the stronger, having in my youth been tempered like iron by exposure to cold and storm. Thanks to my fierce yeoman blood, I throve where he failed, even in that intemperate and fatal air

Now, before many days had passed, I saw the face of my companion, which I watched furtively from time to time, grow thinner and paler, while great veins hardened on his delicate brow, and his breath came heavy and slow, as if from a painful chest. I noted, moreover that he ate little, and that with a sore effort, ever sighing heavily between the mouthfuls, and moving his head from side to side.

Every day he left the cave, and moved feebly about the heights, but presently he scarcely moved at all, but would sit, with my coat of skins wrapped round him, upon a stone, looking wearily at the sea; then when the cold seized him, and the teeth chattered in his head, he would creep back again to the cheerless warmth within.

Meantime the rayless sun circled slowly along the horizon, never rising into the dim zenith of the heaven ; and sometimes for days together it was like a pure ball of blood, with neither heat nor rays. Then sheeted shapes of white mist and cold fog would float across the ice, and cover the forlorn island, while the skies above were sadly veiled.

It was brightest at night-time, in the silence of the night; for often, out of the very heart of the darkness, which was truly ‘ darkness visible,’ the wonderful aurora would arise, till the melancholy heavens seemed afire; and looking fearfully from that cold cave, I would see the phosphorescent boreal iris gleam and sparkle, dripping all colours of the prism, till methought that I beheld the miraculous splendours of the far-off Gates of God.

I should grow wearisome to dulness if I sought to write down all the record of that long and painful vigil, of that daily life without change, without event, of that dull mechanical round of unbroken, desolate despair.

We watched and waited, hoped and prayed ; but no succour came.

Then, feeling the terrible desolation of that silent and ghastly companionship with one a stranger and an enemy, I knew that, without such companionship, I

should have sickened or gone mad. It was something,
at least, not to be utterly alone. It was something, in
the infinite dreariness of the long nights, to awaken,
listen, and hear a heavy breathing close at hand. It
was something to feel that, so near to me, another man
might be dreaming, as I had just dreamed, of brightness,
of the green fields of dear England, of a home in the far-
off happy Fens.

O God of Mysteries, Fashioner of all wonders under
the illimitable heaven, whose will made all creatures,
and made of all creatures most pitiful Thy servant
Man! Thou hadst taken us into the hollow of Thy
hand! Thou hadst lifted us out of the shadows of this
low life, into the air that angels breathe!

My spirit swoons, my hand trembles, as I try to
record what is yet to come.

CHAPTER XXXVIII.

OUT IN THE SNOW.

ALL one night, every time I did awaken, I heard him
moaning in his sleep, and moving uneasily upon his
hard bed.

His mind was wandering, and again and again I
heard him murmur familiar names; and once indeed
he called my name aloud, in a tone so shrill and pitiful
that my heart leapt into my mouth, and I felt afraid.

But when the dark morning came, and I looked
over to his sleeping-place, he was not there!

Looking up, I saw that the cave was open, and
through the narrow aperture a sullen redness was
creeping in.

I waited for some time, thinking he would return;
but when he came not, I cast my skins around me (for
it was bitter cold) and crept out into the air.

A cold fog covered the island, faintly tinged by the
sinister redness of the morning sun; and so thick was
the vapour all around, I that I could only distinguish

things that were quite near, and even these looked large and phantasmal, being magnified by the clinging mist.

All was still as death, save for the strange thunder of the calm sea, which came upon the sense like a low reverberation within the ears, and deepened the stillness with its mysterious and ominous chime.

As one wakens in the dead of night, suddenly conscious of some supernatural visitation, and waits shiveringly for something that is about to happen, while the pulses shut sharp upon the beating heart, and the clammy sweat-drops hang upon the pallid brow— so did I waken and listen. A curious terror possessed me, I knew not wherefore, a sickening sense of dreadful anticipation.

Leaving the cave, I crept out among the chill and sheeted mists.

Suddenly, as I walked, I started in wonder; for I saw quite close to me, poised over the snow-clad island, a dull red ball like an eye watching me ; and so near did it seem, that it seemed partly resting on the crags close at hand. This ball was no other than the round disc of the sun itself, made startling and phenomenal by some curious effect of the intervening fog ; yet even when I knew its nearness to be only a delusion of the sense, the appearance troubled me, and I shrank like one who sees a supernatural vision.

I was now perplexed beyond measure to account for Richard Orchardson's disappearance. For days past he had scarcely left the cave, and even when he ventured forth, he had remained close at hand, walking feebly, or sitting in a dream. So it seemed strange that he should have left his couch so early, and in weather so dangerous, since the heights were full of dangerous cavities and precipices, and one false step might take him to his death. Nor could I conceive what errand could have taken him forth.

I searched this way and that, but found no trace of him ; and at last, casting off all shame in my new wonder, I shouted aloud. There came strange ghostly echoes out of the fog, and murmurs from the distant sea, but no reply of any human voice.

Then, half alarmed, half wroth with myself for heeding what might become of him, I returned to the cave and broke my fast; then busied myself in putting my fire in order, whistling for the sake of forgetfulness, and trying not to think at all. An hour passed thus; and presently, looking forth, I saw that the fogs had cleared a little, and that the heights were not so dark.

Then, reasoning with myself, I reproached myself for the uneasiness which possessed me, reminding my soul of its righteous hate, and of the broad river of blackness between my life and his. If he was dead, why, it was well; his punishment had come.

But this mood did not last long. As the day advanced, I grew more uneasy, and by-and-by forth I went again, picking my way carefully from place to place, from mist to mist. More than once I lost my way, and came near to death on the edges of the slippery crags, on the brink of which the sun still rolled, like a thin and rayless ball.

At last I found him.

I had turned my face from the cliffs, and was ascending the stony hillside, when I stumbled against a body stretched prone on the ground, and looking down in terror, I saw him stretched upon his face, ragged, half-naked, and to all appearance, dead.

Why he had come there I know not till this hour; but he must have wandered thither, awake or asleep, and stumbling over the rocky ground, fainted where he fell.

Then I thought, 'He is dead at last,' and straightway a great awe fell upon me, so that I could scarce breathe or move; and the thought of all my hardness came back upon me, and I hated myself more bitterly than ever I had hated him.

Recovering from this first terror, and forgetting all my threats and all my vows, I knelt down by his side, and turned his face upward; when greater awe fell upon me, for the eyes were fixed and glazed, and the features white as marble, with one stain of red blood upon the lips.

I see him now as I saw him then; so white and worn and thin, his cheeks deep sunken, his hair, which

had grown long and unkempt since his sojourn upon
the island, flowing grey upon his shoulders; his mouth
wide open, his eyes staring, his throat thin and shrunken
like an old man's. Like an old man indeed he seemed,
worn out with years; he who was once so young and
bright !

As a murderer looks on the man that he hath slain,
I looked upon him, while a voice cried in mine ear that
by a little more charity, a little more tenderness, a few
kind words, I might have saved him. And there he
lay ! all the light and health gone that make a living
man, leaving only instead silence and a face of stone.

And yet, even then, with swift thoughts I justified
myself. I had helped him beyond his deserving, I had
spared and sheltered him; all I had denied to him was
kindliness and gentle words. What was he to me that
I should pity him; I who owed him such a life-long
grudge of hate ?

I bent down my head, and listened for his breath;
no breath came. Then I opened his garment and put
my hand upon his heart; but I could feel no beat. As
I touched him so, a shiver ran through my frame, and
my head went round.

Then I took his hands in mine and chafed them, for
they were cold as stone. As I did so, methought I felt
him stir.

I felt for his heart again, and for the first time I
seemed to detect a faint warmth, a tremulous beat,
feeble as the flutter of the tiniest leaf.

Then a thought came to me, and I ran swiftly away
in the direction of the cave; for the air was clearer
now, and I could just see my way. Leaping down, I
found the keg of raw spirit, which was as yet half full,
and by its side my cup of hollow stone; this I quickly
filled, and then, creeping forth carefully, not to spill the
spirit on the ground, hastened back to the man's side.

I found him lying as I had left him, face upward.

Bending by him, I took his head upon my knee, and
dipping in the spirit with my finger gently wet his lips;
and presently, to my surprise and joy, he stirred feebly,
while a faint sound came from his mouth.

Then I knew that if he remained there he would be

frozen—the ground being covered with snow, and the air being so bitter cold; and when I saw at last that he might live, I took him up gently in my two arms (alas! he was so thin and light that I felt his weight no more than that of a little sickly child), and carried him towards my cave.

As I went, he moaned, and I felt his body tremble against me, which made me hasten the more quickly, not looking down into his face, lest he should open his eyes and behold me. The air was so dim and fog-enwrapped, and the snow so deep under-foot, that my passage was slow; but at last I reached the cave, set him down at its mouth, and entering first, drew him softly in.

By this time he was breathing heavily, with full signs of life, though his sight seemed still glazed and dark, and his face set in pain.

I laid him down full length upon mine own bed of blankets and skins, and pillowed up his head, with his feet to the fire; then I felt his hands, and finding them still very cold, rubbed them gently with mine own.

All these things I did like one in a dream, not rightly comprehending what I did; my dread now being that the man might die, leaving me alone with God in that desolate place.

CHAPTER XXXIX.

THE SICK MAN'S DREAMS.

BEFORE night came, the superficial chill of hands and body passed away, and the fiery flush of fever, which had been burning all the while within, broke out upon his face; and the film fading from his eyes, was succeeded by a gaze of strange wildness, with neither true consciousness nor recognition.

Then I saw him struggling for his breath, moaning inarticulately, tossing from side to side, in the dire extremity of a mortal sickness.

It was well, I think, that he was more or less unconscious, for methinks I could not have borne, at first, his knowledge of my tenderness; but finding him thus helpless, and as it were sightless, I continued to minister to him, using all my poor care and skill.

I fetched cold water in my cup, and set it ready by his side to cool his lips, and now and then, when he seemed very faint, I moistened his lips with water and spirit mixed together.

Then, having no kerchief, I took the neck-cloth from my throat, and tearing it into several pieces, moistened one piece, and laid it upon his brow for coolness, changing it from time to time.

Presently, fearing that he might sink from lack of food, I crumbled a biscuit in water, and when I had softened it to a sop, put some to his mouth; but he would not swallow, and spat the fragments forth.

Then, having closed the mouth of the cave, and fixed two of my lights against the wall, I took my coat of skins and threw over him, because a sharp shivering seized him from time to time.

This done, I could do no more, but sat in the shadow, and watched, as a nurse watches her sick charge.

That night I slept not, but remained ever ready to minister to his wants when he started and cried.

See, now, how strangely God had dealt with me! My great fear now was lest this man should perish, and leave me without a living soul, without one sign of humanity, in that place. With him for neighbour, though without any sweetness of companionship, I had been able to bear my desolation.

But all night long I thought with terror on what would be my lot if he should die, and I be left utterly alone. The cruel sky, the lonely sea, the changeless ice and snow, would then become too terrible to bear.

I have often in my rude way wondered how mortals would fare if death were no common burthen (as it is, through God's blessing), but only the lot of a certain portion of men that live; if, I would say, not all creatures, but only some, were fated to die like the beasts. Out of this inequality of evil, what bitterness would come, what revilings and cursings of an ungenerous Providence! But since all must die alike, we are resigned. What all must bear, many can bear right cheerfully, knowing the hour of each must surely come.

By the same token, suffering becomes easier when it is shared by any other living soul; nay, I can well believe that even a poor dumb hound, patiently enduring some pang with its master, may, by speechless community of sorrow, lighten that master's load. And I, with even my mortal enemy for company, had been saved from utter extremity of weariness; for while he, too, felt the pinch of cold, the pang of hunger, and the shadow of a common loneliness, I could not hold myself quite solitary in suffering or in despair.

As I sat and watched that night by the sick man, I thought much of Priscilla, much of that sweet counsel which she had been wont to give me in the days when we were loving friends; and methought, from time to time, that I saw her very presence before me, as the shining of an angel in white robes. Tears rose in mine eyes as I reflected how cruelly, yet how strangely, God had dealt with me, and how perchance I should never behold that gentle maid again.

Then, looking at Richard Orchardson, so white and wan, so worn with the suffering I had brought him, I said to myself: 'He, too, loved her, and he too hath lost her;' and straightway the very memory of our common love softened me to him the more, and awoke in my heart an inconceivable tenderness and pity. Yes, it was surely a new bond between us, in the sad surcease of hate, that we had both lifted eyes of yearning to that gentle maiden, who with all holy arts had sought to bring us together.

We had both lost her; both lost the world. We were alone with God. What remained but to wait patiently, to taste the cup of pain in common, and then to die?

With thoughts like these, so new, so pitiful, I watched him through the night.

The next day he remained in the same condition. Towards night-time he began to rave.

I saw that the fever, or whatever disease it was that possessed him, was at its height; for his face grew crimson, his eyes filmy and moist, while blood and foam began oozing from his mouth. Then I noted that his breath was foul, as with scurvy; that the skin upon his hands was scaly, and loosened at a touch; and that there were foul sores bursting upon his neck.

So I moistened pieces of cloth in water and laid them upon the sores, and with fresh water I rinsed his lips and gums; doing for the sick man, moreover, other offices that may be nameless here.

Presently, seeing his head greatly oppressed by its long thick locks, and remembering how they do in hospitals with folk in fever, I took my sailor's knife, and cut off a large portion of his hair, as close as might be to the head; after which he seemed easier, and rested better upon his pillow.

But all this time I tried in vain to get him to swallow a few moist crumbs of food; he would take nothing save a little weak spirit and water, which I forced him to swallow now and again; so that every hour he grew manifestly weaker, till his poor remains of strength were well-nigh spent.

Meantime, he did not cease to rave; and listening to him I distinguished many a well-known name, and oftentimes mine own; but the name that was uppermost upon his lips was, as before, that of Priscilla. Sometimes his thoughts were among the green fens of England, at others they were sailing on the great sea; but Priscilla seemed ever with them, wheresoe'er they went.

I pitied him none the less when he prattled of Priscilla, for I knew he had no hope of her this side of death's darkness; but when he murmured another name dear to me, the shadow of my old hate came back.

'Kate! Kate!' he whispered suddenly, as I moistened his brow with the wet rag; and I shrank back as if I had been stung.

Then suddenly opening his eyes and gazing vacantly upon me, he moaned again:

'Kate! Kate Christianson!'

I left his side and withdrew to the further side of

the cave; there I sat sullenly brooding over the memory
his words had awakened, and for a long space I neither
looked at him nor offered him any aid.

Presently he called for water, and at first I hesitated, cursing him in my heart; but my conscience
stinging me, I arose and gave him a draught, which he
drank with feverish eagerness, as if he were all afire
within.

CHAPTER XL.

'OUR FATHER.'

IT was on the evening of the third day, while I sat
watching him as he lay in a heavy sleep, that he suddenly opened his eyes and looked at me; and I saw to my
surprise that the vacant film had left his gaze, and that
there came into the face a quiet light of recognition.

'Is it *thou*, Christian Christianson?' he said, so
faintly that I could scarcely hear.

I could not answer, for a great lump rose in my
throat, but half-averting my face I inclined my head.

I knew that his eyes were still watching me, and
presently I heard him say:

'What hath happened?   Why am I lying here?'

I answered him, in a low voice:

'I found you lying in the snow, and I carried you
back into the cave.'

A sharp moan came from his lips.

'Then it is all true, and we are not saved, as I was
dreaming.   Methought we were on shipboard, sailing
back to England.'

There was a long silence.   I turned my face and
gazed at him; he was lying with his eyes closed, feebly
breathing, but while I looked at him he opened his eyes
and spoke again.

'After all, it doth not matter, since I am so nearly
spent.'

I could not answer him at first, but taking the hot
rag from his forehead, I moistened it with fresh water,
and returned it to its place.   As I did so he looked up,
and our eyes met.

'Thank you,' he said; adding softly, 'I shall not trouble you long.'

And the thin furrows of his cheeks grew moist with tears.

A little while after this he rambled again, but not so wildly, and now his fancy seemed in sunny places ; so that when he came to himself his look was more peaceful.

I went to his side, and tried, dumbly, to make him eat a portion of the sop I had prepared ; but he pushed it gently away.

'Eat,' I said, 'or you will die!'

He gazed at me with a strange, long, searching look.

'I am a dead man,' he answered wearily; 'nothing can save me.'

Then sinking his head back upon his pillow, he continued :

'Save for your care, I should ne'er have lived so long. Why do you keep me alive? Is it because you love to see me suffer pain?'

The question went through my heart like a knife, but how could I reply? He little knew the pity stirring in my heart's core.

'If you have any mercy,' he said presently, 'promise to give me Christian burial. Do not leave my poor body to the ravenous beasts?'

I remembered how he had craved this promise before, and how I had not answered. I answered now, eager to give him comfort.

'If I survive you, I will do as you wish.'

'Will you swear it?' he said.

'I swear it,' I replied.

He closed his eyes as if relieved, and presently began to sleep again. After a little time he lay so silent that I could not hear him breathe, and I thought with a cold shudder that he might be dead ; but bending over him, I perceived that he was still alive, though his breathing made no sound.

Yet indeed, as he lay stretched there, he seemed as one fallen into his last sleep ; and the sacredness of death seemed upon him, on his worn sad face, his forehead pencilled with blue veins, his closed eyelids, his lips just flecked with foam. One thin hand lay beneath his cheek, the other hung like wax upon the sealskin coverlet, and over him brooded a solemn silence, like the silence of the cold grave.

I lifted his hand, and it was icy cold. I touched him on the shoulder, and spoke to him, but he did not hear.

Then, fearing that his time was come, and that he would never speak again, I grew more than ever terrified; and at last, in the fulness of my fear and self-pity, I sank upon my knees by his side.

Holding his cold hand, I prayed aloud to God that he might live; that I should not be left wholly desolate and forlorn.

'Spare him, O God!' I prayed. 'Of all living things, he is the sole creature that remains to me, and if he goeth, where shall I look for the light of a human face, the touch of a human hand? He has shared my shelter, eaten my substance, and his sorrow has been harder to bear than mine. Spare him, O God! Leave me not utterly alone.'

Now, even as I prayed, his strength revived again, like the rising of a weak ocean-wave; and as I knelt with head bowed, I heard the faint sound of his voice.

'Christian Christianson!'

I started and looked up wildly at the sound of my name. His chill hand fluttered like a leaf in mine, as he murmured:

'I have your promise?'

I pressed his hand for answer, for I could not speak.

'And you will bear the news to my dear father? Tell him I died blessing him, and remembering how much he loved me. Tell him, moreover, that I died in the hope of the blessed resurrection, through Jesus Christ our Lord.'

As he spake, he drew his hand softly from mine, and putting both hands feebly together on his breast, murmured the first words of the Lord's Prayer:

'Our Father which art in Heaven . . . hallowed be Thy name . . . Thy kingdom come.'

Then he paused suddenly, for, still keeping on my knees, I was sobbing audibly, choked and stifled with tears which would not flow.

He reached out his hand, and touched me.

'Shake hands,' he said.

I took his hand in both of mine, and touched it with my trembling lips.

'Pray for me again,' he whispered. 'Pray for me, and I shall know that we part in peace.'

God help me, I knew no prayer but that which he had just begun; but this I well remembered, having been taught by my mother to say it night and morn; so straightway I said 'Our Father' in as clear a voice as I could command, and gazing reverently upwards; and as I prayed my force was broken, and my warm tears flowed as from the living rock, bedewing the hand I clasped within mine own. I had no shame now; it had left me for ever, with my bitter hate; and as I knelt there, it seemed as if the heavens were opened above me, and I could hear the singing of angels from some heavenly clime.

When the prayer was ended, and I still knelt weeping, he turned his face to me and said:

'Before I die, there is yet another thing upon my mind that I must speak.'

'Speak, then,' I whispered.

He turned his eyes full on mine, like one sadly seeking forgiveness.

''Twas I that fired the ship!'

CHAPTER XLI.

THE LAST LOOK.

Now, although I had known this thing from the first, having never in mine own mind doubted that his hand had done that deed of darkness, though he had so constantly denied it, I shrank from him in horror, and would have dropt his hand.

But his cold fingers held me, while his wild eyes read my face.

'God help me, I knew not what I did, for I was mad! I saw her heart was yours, and I thought to stifle you where you were chained. But **God** has punished me, as you see.'

I was silent, with a cold chill and shrinking upon me; and presently he moaned, still clutching my fingers in his:

'Have you nothing to say to me? Can you forgive me now?'

Then the cloud of my old hate passed from me for ever, as I replied:

'May God forgive us both! He hath dealt with us as we deserved.'

Though all that time the shadow of Death was in the cave, Richard Orchardson lived through that long night, and far into the morrow morn.

Now that the fatal barrier of pride was cast down from between us, now that our eyes could meet in the sorrow of that last farewell, my heart seemed strangely lightened of its load; and though I still looked forward with an overmastering dread to the moment when I must be left alone, I could pray now as never in my lifetime I had prayed before.

Sitting by the side of my dying companion, in the long intervals of piteous speech and more piteous silence, my thoughts again, like homeward wavering birds, went back across the years; and as I called to mind the bitter ancestral feud, the bloody lifelong strife, there came back to me my poor father's dying words of gentleness and forgiveness. He, poor man, had suffered more than I, and yet he had been patient and gentle to the last!

Then I thought, 'We are nurtured in evil and bitter blame; we sit and feed our sense of wrong apart, when with a gentle word we might make all well; and knowing not our brother's heart, we think it cruel and abominable, at the very moment when the dews of mercy and human kindness are making it sweet.' For I remembered the time just after my father's death, when Squire Orchardson had ridden over to our house door on a peaceful errand; and our hearts had shut against him, though he surely meant us well. How much evil had been spared us all had my mother list'ned that day! But afterwards, through evil blood between two mere children, who knew not what they did, what calamity had come!

As I sat thus musing, and looking at Richard Orchardson, the cave faded away, the years rolled back, and I was standing on the Fen Farm with clenched hands, looking at a pale boy stretched bleeding at my feet; while in mine ears rang the cry of little Kate—'O Christian, what have you done?' And little Kate, where was she? Dead, perchance; or still, a weary woman, wandering about the world. After all, she had loved this man, and had she not out of fear of us kept her love a secret, happiness might have come to her even through him. I had closed my hard heart sternly against her pleading, and had driven her forth cruelly, when she might have been saved, perchance, by one gentle word.

And so the end had come; and the end was the same as the beginning, yet how different!

There lay Richard Orchardson, helpless, grey, and old before his time; and I was still the stronger, as I had been in that struggle when we were boys. There lay he whose being I had embittered, and who had embittered mine; whose death I had prayed for; whose life I had sought to take with murderous hands. We had struck each other with all our might, and he . . . he had fallen; yet now I would have given away the world if I could have raised him up, saying 'Live, and be forgiven'; if I could have seen him again walking erect and happy in the sun; nay, if I could have kept him with me a little while, to lighten my desolate despair.

It was not to be.

God was to fill my cup full measure, even to the very running o'er. I had prayed for this man's life; it was to be given me. Alas! when God answers our passionate pleading, even to the fruition of our wickedest desire, He is inexorable to the end.

He had been restless all the night, but towards the morning he slept soundly, almost peacefully; but about the middle of the day he woke and (to my amazement) asked for food.

I looked at him in wonder. He had sat up on his couch, with a strange flush upon his face, and smiled.

'I am hungry,' he said. 'Prithee let me eat.'

Alas! I knew not what to give him. I had only the seal's flesh (which was too rank for the stomach of a sick man), some loose flour, and coarse biscuit. But I brought him a little spirit and water, while I soaked some biscuit, as I had done before; and my hand shook for joy, since I saw him so brightly changed.

He ate some of the sop eagerly, and with an evident relish.

'You are better to-day,' I said gently.

'Yes, much better,' he replied, smiling still. 'Nay, I feel quite strong.'

Had God answered my prayer? Had the disease departed, and would the companion of my loneliness be spared to me after all? Alas! I had little skill in nursing or in leech-craft; or I would have known, as I know now, how dying men often rally a little space, while the last gleam of life shoots up shiningly, like to the last flash upon the blackening brand.

When he had eaten he lay back upon his pillow and closed his eyes, and in a moment was sound asleep; but this time his sleep was troubled, and he tossed feverishly from side to side.

An hour later he awoke suddenly, and sprang up in bed.

'Look!' he cried, pointing eagerly; then he added in a loud voice, 'Mother! mother!'

I knelt by his side, and took his head upon my shoulder, but he still kept his eyes wide open, as if he gazed upon a vision.

'Mother, who is that by your side? Is it Priscilla? . . . Why are you crying? Nay, tell my father to be comforted, for I am coming home. Hark, what's that? Do you hear, sweetheart? 'Tis our wedding bells?'

Alas! those bells were ringing not on earth, but far away in heaven. Even as he spake a strange shiver ran through his frame, the coldness of death stole from his heart to mine, and, with one last moan, his spirit passed away.

At first I could not believe that he was dead.

I placed his head gently back upon his pillow, and gazed upon him; and there was no change. He seemed just resting wearily, as he had rested so many days.

But even as I looked upon his poor wasted face, and listened for his living breath, there stole upon my soul that sacredness and mysterious stillness which never come till the shadow of Death is present; and over the form I watched fell the chilly consecration of the dust. It was as if some pale angel stood there, stooping darkly, touching brow and cheeks and hands in turn with a frosty finger, till they changed into the whiteness of the lily, then into the chillness of icy stone; till of the thing that was a living creature a few minutes before, only a marble mask remained.

There lay Richard Orchardson, or what had once been he; his feeble frame, his wasted flesh, his haggard face, all changed—no longer old nor young, but beautiful even to terror; covered with peace as with a garment, clothed with the loveliness of Death. For Death crowns all alike. There is no creature so frail, so wretched—nay, there is not even a little child—to whom he denies this royalty of the last repose. We enter the last sleeping-place of a dead beggar, and his rags have become regal, and we stand before him in reverence, like subjects in the presence of a King.

CHAPTER XLII.

' SNOW TO SNOW!'

WHEN I knew that he was dead indeed, I bent over him reverently, placed his arms down by his side, and seeing his eyes wide open, drew down the waxen lids over the sightless orbs. Then I held a little water in the palm of my hand and cleansed the dead face; afterwards with careful fingers arranging his hair and beard.

Lastly, I took one of my rude lights, and set it at the corpse's head, like the death-lights we burn round dead folk in the Fens.

All this I did mechanically, not yet feeling the full

horror of my desolation; but when there was no more
to do, when I had ordered all in Christian cleanliness
and reverence, I sat and gazed upon mine enemy, as if
mine own hour had also come.

What followed seems now, as it was then, like a dream
within a dream.

After the first stony sense of loss, during which I
remained strangely stern and cold, I think I must have
begun to wander in my mind; for I have a dim memory
of sitting there in the cave, with the dead man before
me, and talking wildly to myself; then of passing forth
and wandering up and down the island, through the
drifted snow, like a witless man; of creeping back, and
peering in, as into a tomb, and seeing him still there,
with the corpse-lights at his head; so that I was afraid
to enter, till the bitter cold drave me in.

But God was merciful, and even in those dark hours
of loneliness and fear He kept me from going wholly
mad. Though my mind wandered for a time, my reason
was not quite shattered; amid the darkness of my
despair, when all the winds of terror rushed upon me,
that light within which makes a living soul, though it
trembled in the blast, was not blown out for ever.

And methinks one thing helped me; and this was
the promise I had made the man before he died.

I had sworn that he should have Christian burial,
and that oath I now determined to fulfil.

I kept him with me in the cave for several nights
and days, until the change in him became so dreadful
that I shuddered to look upon his face.

Then knowing that the time had come, I chose a
place not far off, where there was a hollow in the rocky
ground, filled up with snow; and here, out of a hard
drift, I scooped a shallow grave.

To bury him in that hard ground was impossible;
yet I did the best for his poor dust that my wild
thoughts could devise.

I had no coffin for him, and no shroud. He lay in
the garments that he had died in, completely clad; but
instead of cerements, I wrapt the sealskin coverlet
around him, leaving only his face bare.

'*Snow to snow!*'

Then, one still morn, when the air was bright for the place and time of year, I lifted in my arms and carried him slowly forth, across the snow.

I had the rude grave all ready, and now I laid him down within it, with his white face to the sky. As I stood above him, and took my last look of him, more snow began to fall.

Lightly, thinly, delicately, fell the soft flakes on the cold body and on the white, cold, marble face. It seemed as if the Lord Himself were stretching out His hand, and gently covering up the dead!

Then, standing bareheaded, eager still to keep my pledge to him, I repeated, as far as I could remember, the words of the old sweet Burial Service out of our English Book of Prayer; and when I could remember no more, I stretched out my arms in blessing, commending my enemy's soul to God.

Before I had ended, his face had faded away in the falling whiteness; and seeing it vanish utterly, I sobbed like a little child.

' Forasmuch as it hath pleased Almighty God of His great mercy to take unto Himself the soul of my dear brother here departed, I therefore commit his body to the ground, earth to earth, ashes to ashes, dust to dust; in sure and certain hope of the Resurrection to eternal life, through Jesus Christ our Lord.'

Nay, not ashes to ashes, or dust to dust; but snow to snow!

As the sexton of the graveyard draws down the loosened mould, pressing it firm upon the coffin lid, so did I with the drift, till it lay thick and firm above him as any earth; and over and above all I worked the snow into a barrow of the dead, not green, but white; and when all was done as I had promised, I turned away.

And now for the first time I felt the full extremity of my desolation.

For when I entered the cave, there was no face, not even that of my poor dead enemy, to meet me; and the place was forlorn beyond measure. Even in the dead body there had been companionship, so long as it remained.

I sat down in my empty dwelling and wept.

But presently, filled with a new thought of blessed

tenderness, I took two pieces of wood, and tied them together in the shape of a cross; and all that afternoon I wrought upon the cross with my clasp-knife, till I had rudely carved upon it these words:—

> ' HERE LIETH RICHARD ORCHARDSON.
> '*May he rise again!*'

Night had fallen when my task was done. But passing forth, I found the new-made grave, and set the cross upon it, as my last token of forgiveness and goodwill.

As I stood gazing down, the crimson flame of the aurora arose suddenly out of the northern sky, and all the heavens were miraculously illumined. Was it my sad fancy only, that the glory of that vision had never been so strangely bright? Higher and higher towards the zenith rose the prismatic cupola of splendour, fairer and infinitely brighter than any rainbow of promise, with flames of inconceivable brightness, and a glory as of summer dawn, lighting heaven and earth and sea!

At last the wonder faded; deep darkness followed; and I was alone in all the world.

CHAPTER XLIII.

FROM THE LOG OF THE WHALER ' NAUTILUS.'

In the late hairst of 17—, I, Captain John Macintosh, commanding the *Nautilus* brig, of 150 tons, and one of the whaling fleet from Dundee, sprang a leak during an easterly gale while on my way southward, was driven far away to the west, and, putting into Clarence Harbour, ten leagues to the west of Cape Chidley, for repairs, was there beleaguered by the ice, and compelled to pass the winter months in that uncannie clime.

Fortunately, we were well prepared for such an emergency, and being sheltered in a safe creek, we roofed the ship with canvas against the snow; and so, with land on every side of us, plenty of moss fuel ashore, a good stock of provisions, and firearms for hunting, we tholed our trouble, and passed the snell season without the loss of a single soul aboard.

Of our troubles and privations, our sports on ice and land, and our many grand devices to pass away tho eerie time, I have told at large in my log, which I kept carefully from Sabbath to Sabbath, scarce missing a single day; for when I was a-bed one week with a touch of scurvy, my mate, Robert Johnstone, a good scholar, and like myself a native of Bucklyvie, Fife, set all things fairly down.

At last the winter broke, the sun rose up into tho lift, and to our great joy we saw the ice splitting and loosening, with gleams like fire-flaught, and shocks like thunder reverberating far out to sea. Having first cannily overhauled our ship's bottom, which our carpenters reached easily, as she was lifted clean out of the water by the ice, and having made all snug and taut aboard, we prepared to get her afloat: a task we achieved with no little difficulty, having to cut a pathway for her with our hatchets for a distance of nearly two Scots miles, before we could reach the open water of Clarence Harbour.

When this was done, and the *Nautilus* was once more afloat in the deep sea, we shouted like daft men, and prepared at once to set sail. The lift was growing clearer and clearer every hour, and though there was thick damp reek, caused by the evaporation from the surface of the ice, floating about the sea, we determined to linger no longer, so eager were we to reach bonnie Scotland again, and to see those that loved us—parents, sweethearts, wives, or bairns.

Out of the middle of Clarence Harbour ran a channel of salt sea, two miles wide, and shut in on each side by impenetrable ice; this channel, though deep, was discoloured like a great river with melting snow, and sprinkled everywhere by small pieces of broken ice, which floated along like flotsam and jetsam on a river in full spate. There was only just enough wind to steer by, but we drifted along fast enough, with the ice rattling against the old ship's timbers like fragments of broken glass, and the water the colour of oatmeal porridge on every side.

As we went the channel widened, until we had plenty of sailing room, but finding no lead out to the open sea, on account of the solid floes that closed us in to larboard, we drifted past Cape Chidley in a south-westerly direction, with the drift of the main thaw, or current.

Before long, we had our work cut out for us, for before a day had passed we got among drift ice, freshly loosened from the solid floes. Many a sharp rap did the old ship get as she snooved along, with the great blue bergs towering on every side of her, and land fogs making the daytime as mirk as midnight.

Four days and nights we played at this game among the bergs, but at last we reached open water—a clear calm lead to the southward, with never a blink of ice in sight.

On the evening of the fifth day there blew such a spring gale from the north-east as I never wish to see again; as Rob Johnstone said, it was the De'il of the Pole giving us his last cuff on the lugs before he let us go for good; and with the gale came snow, and sleet, and hail, blinding and smothering the ship.

We lay to under a rag of canvas all that night.

At break of day the wind changed, and just in time; for hard under our lee lay the loom of black land, set round with ice as sharp and ugly as sharks' teeth, the edge of which was scarce a mile away.

But the breeze changing into a mild puff from the west, with just a gentle pussie-claw on the deep green water, we prepared to set all sail; when suddenly some of the men, who stood looking over the side towards the land, uttered a cry, and began to blether among themselves.

'What's the matter, lads?' I said, going up to them.

Then old Koll Sanderson, our chief harpooner, and a Shetland man, replied:

'They're saying they see something oot yonner on the ice.'

'What is it, lads?' I asked.

'Saints preserve us a'!' said a young hand from Leith. 'It leuks like a *mon!*'

A man on the ice in that desolate region! I smiled to myself at the notion; but when they cried again, I went to the side and looked, and sure enough I saw, far away, a black shape running on the ocean's edge.

'Give me the glass!' I cried, and Rob Johnstone, who had the telescope under his oxter, handed it to me.

No longer had I clapt it to my eye than I started, and felt a thread go through my heart. The figure was a man's, no doubt, and he was waving his arms in the air, and making signs to us aboard the ship.

'Lower a boat!' I said. 'It's a living creature, though the Lord kens what brought him *there.*'

When the boat was lowered and manned, I stepped into the stern, and leaving Johnstone in command on board, took the tiller. The lads were as curious and eager as myself, and they rowed with a will; and soon I could see plainly with my own een, without the aid of a glass, a great lean figure like a wraith, stretching out his arms to us, and dancing about like a daft body on the edge of the ice!

But, Lord! such a sight as the poor soul presented I never saw before, and hope never to see again! He was wrapt all round with dirty skins, and on his legs were a pair of broken seaman's boots, his frame was like a skeleton's, his hair hung down to his shoulders and over his forehead, while his beard was a foot long, and matted like tow. But the face of him, the looks of him! He looked like Death himself, with sunken checks and hollow een, and his jaw hanging like the jaw of an idiot man.

When he saw us coming near, he fell upon his knees as if praying; and kneeling so, waited till the boat touched the ice.

Then, while the men looked on in wonder, I sprang out and approached him. At that, he sprang to his feet, and though I am myself a tall man, six feet in my boots, he was taller.

When I questioned him he did not seem to understand. His eyes looked vacantly, and he murmured something to himself, but seemed to have lost the use of speech.

Then he began to wave his arms again, laughing

and greeting in the same breath, so that I thought to myself that some great trouble had made him daft indeed.

I pointed to the boat, and made signs for him to go aboard the ship. He understood that right well, I'm thinking, but instead of leaping into the boat, he began running towards the land, making signs for us to follow.

While I stood perplexed, he pointed up to the cliffs, which lay about a mile away across the ice, and I saw by his beckoning that he wished us to follow him up yonder.

At first I hesitated, till it flashed across my mind that maybe he was not alone, and that there were others not far away, cast away like himself, and in some dire trouble. So I took with me two of the men, namely, William Forsyth and Wattie Hetherington, and leaving the other two in the boat, followed him across the ice.

Though he was so worn and thin, and looked like a wraith, he ran so swiftly that it took us all our breath to follow ; and whenever we paused, he stopped and beckoned again.

At last we reached the land—a black line of rugged cliffs, whitened with great patches of ice and snow, and with clear falling streams of melting thaw glittering in the sun.

Passing along the shore, the strange man at last came to a rocky ascent, up which he swiftly ran ; and we following, came out upon the braes of a snowy island, as bare of all vegetation as the palm of my hand.

At last he paused, looking down.

Then, coming up and standing by his side, we beheld to our amaze a mound of hard snow shapen like a grave, and on this mound a rude wooden cross, on which was carven these words that follow :—

> ' HERE LIETH RICHARD ORCHARDSON.
> ' *May he rise again!* '

Even as we gazed, the man knelt upon the snow as if praying dumbly to himself; then, rising quietly, looked down again upon the grave, and wept.

I put my hand upon his shoulder.

'Answer me now,' I said. 'Are there any more folk on the island?'

He understood me, and now for the first time answered, in the English tongue.

'No more; no more!' he cried, in a hollow voice.

Then I asked him if he wished to sail away with us from that dreary place.

'Take me away,' he answered in the same strange tone; 'take me away!'

I wondered in my own mind why he had brought us up here only to stand by a dead man's grave, and I wonder still—for I know not to this hour what spirit moved him.

He stood looking at the cross like one in a dream.

'Come, my man,' I said, touching him again.

He started, and followed us quietly. So we went down again to the shore, and crossing the ice, entered the boat. I placed him beside me in the stern. He did not speak, but sat like one bewildered, with his face ever turned backward to the land we had left behind.

Three weeks after that the *Nautilus*, with the man on board, was in sight of the shores of Scotland, sailing with a fair wind for the port of Dundee.

CHAPTER XLIV.

AT THE SAILORS' HOME.

A few miles from the great city of Newcastle-upon-Tyne stands the town of Tynemouth: which, over a hundred years ago, was little more than a small sea-shore village, inhabited by fishermen, river-pilots, and other rough hard-labouring men and women who get their bread by the sea.

In an open space near the sea-shore of Tynemouth stood (and perchance stands) a small two-storied building of red brick, in front of which was a flagstaff flying the Union Jack. Every piece of timber used in the erection of this building was made of drift-wood

cast up by the sea; the pathway leading to the door
was laid with sand and shells; at the door itself was a
wooden seat, made out of the sternpost of a wrecked
vessel; and along the window-sills were coloured pieces
of stone and large shells, all gathered on the neighbouring shore.

Fifty years before, an old sea captain, born and bred
in the place, had returned to Tynemouth a wealthy
man, and having plenty of money to spare, had built
this house for a mere whim; afterwards, finding it too
large for his own occupation, he had let it out to a
captain of the coastguard; but finally, having quarrelled
with the executive on some question of smuggling or
free trade, he had turned the place into a sort of sailors'
home for unfortunate wayfarers, endowing it with a
small sum of money per annum, terminable at his
death, to be supplemented by small weekly payments
from such inmates as could afford to pay a trifle for
bed and board. From that day forth till the day of
his death, the old gentleman, who had a little cottage
close by, might have been seen almost daily in front of
the Home, in conversation with certain weatherbeaten
veterans, who were enjoying their siesta in the sun,
and repaying their benefactor by retailing to him their
experiences, their grievances, and their adventures,
afloat and ashore.

This son of Neptune, dying suddenly, in the very act
of enjoying a sailor's yarn of more than usual length
and breadth, left all his little property to a degenerate
nephew, who hated salt water, and kept a small hosiery
establishment in Newcastle. The Home was about to
be put up to the hammer, when a benevolent gentleman
interfered, and bought it in for a small sum. Now,
the gentleman was a friend and disciple of the famous
Mr. Wesley, and it occurred to him as a happy thought
that the establishment, instead of being delivered to the
secular arm, should remain a Sailors' Home still, but
more particularly a Home for pious sailors of the Methodist persuasion. By his endeavours a liberal sum was
soon collected, one of the most liberal contributors
being a certain Mr. Sefton, of London; and presently a
new wing was added, to be used as a Convalescent

Hospital, where food, physic, medical attendance, and seasonable prayer were liberally provided for mariners and fishermen in bad health.

On the wooden bench in front of the Home sat, one sunny autumn day, a gaunt tall man in rough sailor's clothes. He might have been old and he might have been young; for none could tell whether Time had made him so woe-begone, or merely Sorrow. He had not long left his sick bed, and as he sat he leant heavily upon an oaken staff.

Standing before him was a plump, motherly-looking woman, in cotton gown and widow's cap; nurse and cook at the Home, and wife to the old ex-coastguardsman, who was its official custodian.

'How do you feel now, good man?' she was saying. 'Better, surely. Nay, this brave weather will soon make you strong again, and fit to travel home.'

The man raised his head wearily, and looked her in the face.

'Home!' he repeated, vacantly.

'Ay, indeed; for sure, now, you have a home, and mayhap a wife and bairns?'

He looked at her again, sighed heavily, and shook his head.

'Then you have kinsmen at least?' continued the woman, with the curiosity of her sex. 'Do they bide far away? Belike you have friends somewhere to whom you can go?'

'No kinsmen. No friends.'

'That is bad,' said the woman. 'Poor man! what will you do? Go again to sea?'

The man did not reply. His eyes were fixed drearily on the quiet ocean, which sparkled beyond the green cliff whereon he sat. Presently, without turning his face from that fixed object of contemplation, he demanded:

'How came I here?'

'To the Mariners' Haven, mean you? Ah, dear, don't you remember? They found you in the streets of Newcastle, all in rags, with a kind of fever upon you, and since doctor said 'twas not catching, the good Methodists sent you down here. I've nursed you, good man, three long months; and sometimes I thought your wits were gone, for you did talk such strange things; but praise be to God, we've brought you round.'

She added, as he did not reply:

'And no one knows your name, or where you come from, though you've been here so long.'

'My name is Christian Christianson,' said the man.

'A right good name for a Christian man, as I pray you are!'

Something in the words, like a fiery spark, seemed to fall upon the man and rouse him from his lethargy. New light came into his eyes, his lips trembled, his frame shook.

'*Her* words,' he murmured, '*her* words, long ago.'

'Your wife, good man?'

'Nay, I have no wife.'

'Then your sweetheart, belike?'

'Maybe,' he answered, nodding his head; and he added sadly, 'Yes, her very words. "A good name for a Christian man."'

'Is she living still, good man?'

'Alas! I know not,' said Christian. 'We parted long ago, out upon the sea, and though I have sought I have not found her; perchance I shall never find her, this side the grave.'

Even as he spoke there came from a room within the sound of rough voices singing a hymn; suddenly, from the very midst of those voices, there shot up another and a sweeter voice, clear as a bell, with soft and silver tones of plaintive tenderness.

As he listened Christian started, trembling; the staff fell from his hand, his face went ghastly pale, and he trembled as with a palsy.

'My God!' he cried. 'What sound is that?'

'''Tis the mariners singing their morning hymn,' said the woman.

'But that voice! that voice! I know it, I know it! O God, can it be?'

'''Tis the young lady-missionary from London. She came yestereven to Tynemouth. She is stopping with good Mr. Lincoln, the hosier, at the sign of the Silver Stocking in Newcastle.'

'Let me see her! let me speak to her!' cried Christian, staggering to his feet.

Just then the hymn ceased.

'Bide a bit,' said the nurse; 'she will come forth directly, and then you may speak to her, if you will. She has a kind heart, and loves poor mariners.'

Exhausted with his agitation, Christian sank upon his seat, with his head against the wall of the portico. Sitting thus, he looked so gaunt, so weatherworn and sad, that you would have taken him for an old man.

A sound of light feet in the lobby within, the murmur of a sweet voice; then out into the sunshine tript a fair shape clad in deep black, holding a hymnbook in her hand.

The edge of her dress touched Christian as she passed by, but he did not stir; he lay back with his eyes closed. Scarcely looking at him, the young missionary passed on.

But the nurse interposed with a respectful curtsey.

'Bide a moment, if you please, unless your ladyship is in haste. This poor man——'

As she spoke she bent over Christian and touched him on the arm.

'Now, master, here be the young lady waiting to speak to you.' Then seeing his condition, she added quickly, 'Poor soul, he has fainted away!'

So it was indeed. But as the young lady and the nurse bent over him, he began to stir.

'He has just risen from his sick bed,' explained the nurse; 'and he was sitting here in the sun when he heard your hymn and began to weep. He is some poor castaway, without a friend.'

The lady's face was lit with divine compassion, but no recognition, as she softly touched Christian's wasted hand with her own. The touch was electric; he opened his eyes wildly, and looked into her face.

'Priscilla!' he cried.

She started in amaze.

'Do you not know me, Priscilla? I am Christian Christianson.'

It was as if the grave had opened, and given up its dead.

Priscilla stood paralysed, and for the moment seemed about to swoon. Recovering herself, she gazed at the wasted shape before her in wonder, sorrow, and even fear.

'Yes, it is I,' he continued faintly. 'I have only stayed for this—to see you, to know you live. Now I can die in peace.'

The words stirred the fountain of love and pity in her heart; so that her eyes filled with tears.

'O Christian,' she cried, 'I can scarce believe that 'tis your living self. I thought—alas! I thought you dead! But is it *you?* How strange, how strange!'

And she continued to look upon him, reading every line and lineament of his form and face. He was changed indeed, but the powerful outline of the Christianson race remained.

'And you?' he asked after a pause. 'How did you escape?'

'God was good,' she replied; 'we drave away southward, and as if by miracle the ice opened to let us go. I would have had them return to search for you; I begged them on my knees to do so, but even Captain Higginbotham said that it was impossible. Then we came to Boston harbour, where we landed, I heartbroken, as you may guess. I went up with my father to the Moravian village, and scarce had we settled there when—when——'

She paused, the tears streaming down her face; then she added with a great sob:

'O Christian, he is gone!'

'Your father?'

'My dear, dear father! God has taken him.'

She turned her face away in the fulness of her sorrow. He reached out his hand and took hers, pressing it tenderly.

'He died blessing me,' she continued, in a broken voice. '"I am going to my dear Master," he said smiling, "where I shall *see*, at last."'

'Then you came back?'

'Some good friends brought me home to my country; and *now* I try to be worthy of him through helping the poor he loved; for I know that our parting is not for ever, but only for a little while.'

So speaking, she raised her eyes to heaven, and looked like an angel already, in the sweet intent gaze of her perfect faith.

Silence followed. Both hearts were very full. The nurse, seeing so strange a meeting, had withdrawn respectfully into the house, and they were alone together.

At last Christian raised his head, which he had bent forward, with his eyes upon the ground.

'Priscilla!'

'Yes, Christian.'

'You have not asked for *him?*'

She started, trembling, and their eyes met. Pale as death, she regarded him, in a new and nameless dread.

'Of him who was also cast away?'

'Yes; Richard Orchardson.'

'It was in my heart to speak of him, but I was afraid, remembering the bitterness between you. Oh, Christian, is he saved, too? You were together—you must know.'

It was now Christian's turn to look upward, which he did reverently, as he replied:

'He is up yonder with your father, among the angels of God!'

'Alas! is he dead?'

'His body lies buried in the snow. Yes, he is dead.'

The terror did not leave her face, for as yet she dimly understood. With a quick, appealing gesture, and a look of increasing suspicion, she exclaimed:

'Not through *you?* Christian, tell me, it was not through *you?*'

'Not through me.'

'You—you did not—kill him?'

'I did not; and yet . . . what am I saying? . . . he perished through my hate. That guilt is on me. Had I not borne him from the ship, he might have been living now.'

'Alas!'

'Do not weep. It has all come about as you prayed. We were with each other to the end, we forgave each other, and ere he died God joined our hands.'

Presently he told her all—the weary vigil, the long suffering, the final reconciliation; and as she listened she wept, for pity, not for sorrow, still with her little hand in his.

When all was told, he pressed her hand softly, saying:

'He forgave me. Can you forgive me, too?'

'Forgive you?' she answered, looking at him through her tears. 'Alas! what have I to forgive?'

'I came but as a shadow on your life. Better had you never known me, for I brought you much sorrow. And yet . . . I loved you, Priscilla!'

'Yes, Christian,' she said, simply, looking down.

'See what God has made of me—a poor waif, who was once a strong man; a weary sinner, who was once puffed out with pride. You did not know me; no man would know me—I am the ghost of my old self.'

Hopeless and desolate beyond measure was the ring of his voice. She drew nearer to him, and with a perfect grace and modesty rested her hand upon his hair.

'You will soon be yourself again, dear Christian,' she said.

'Never, never.'

She drew a little nearer still.

'Not if *I* nurse you? Not if *I* bid you be your old dear self, for Priscilla's sake?'

He looked up wildly, and reached out his hands.

'Priscilla, can it be? You—you——'

She crept into his outstretched arms, crying to herself, and still smoothing his hair tenderly with her trembling fingers, as she said:

'I have no one left but you. Let us remain together till the end.'

'You love me, Priscilla?'

'I have loved you since the hour we first met!'

The hush of a great joy fell upon them; the air grew golden, all the world was changed and glorified, as it ever is in those divine moments when loving souls are blent together.

Presently, she stirred from his arms, where she had

been nestling in the shadow of the porch, and said, smiling:

'Are you happy now?'

'Quite happy.'

'And you have no anger in your heart for any creature alive?'

'None, dearest.'

'You are quite, quite sure?'

'Yes.'

'Then I will give you some good news that I have lately learned. Your poor sister Kate——'

He started eagerly.

'Your poor sister Kate is alive and well; she is waiting for you in the old Fen Farm.'

EPILOGUE.

THE bells of Yuletide were ringing joyfully, the upland slopes were white with snow, and the mere was frozen an inch thick, when Christian Christianson was wedded to Priscilla Sefton; and their hands were joined together by no less a person than the great Mr. Wesley himself, who came post-haste from London to bless the wedding of a maiden he loved full well.

They were married at Brightlinghead: Kate Christianson was there, looking prettier though sadder than in former happier days; and when all was done, they drove quietly home to the door of the Fen Farm.

Sitting up at the Hall, the old squire heard the bells, and looking out upon terrace and lawn, all white and cold, thought sadly of his dear son, who was lying so far away, asleep under the snow. For Christian had kept his word, and had entered the lonely house, standing before the squire bareheaded, and had told his tale. When he had done, his heart ached within him, for the old man sat and looked at him, pale as death, but without a tear; and from that day forth he had scarcely spoken, but sat desolate in the great house, waiting for his time to come.

For many a day the weight of a dark experience, a sorrowful awe, dwelt upon the soul of Christian Christianson. He looked old far beyond his years, and seldom smiled ; but went about his daily work with a grave gentleness, like a man who is thinking of another world. But peace had surely come to him, and he was happy beyond measure in his Priscilla's love. And in due season, when time had softened the memory of his trial, and when the sound of children was heard in the old dwelling, he became a prosperous man, famed for his blameless life and his good deeds for many miles around.

So it happened in the end that out of evil came good, the old feud was forgotten, the spirit of the dead man brought blessing to all that remembered him, and chiefly to him that had hated him most; and presently it came about, after all, that a Christianson wedded an Orchardson, so that the two houses became happily united, by blood that is thicker than water, and love that is stronger than death.

Thus was the heart of Christian Christianson made whole, and the lives of him and his generation made peaceful, through faith in Divine Love. Yet what were such faith worth if this low earth were all, if the tangled threads of our strange human experience were not to be gathered up again, after death's asundering, by the God that made man in His likeness, yea, immortal like Himself? Without that certainty of a divine explanation, without that last hope of heavenly meeting and eternal reconciliation, the life we live would be profitless—as a book left unfinished, as a song half unsung, as a tale just begun.

THE END.

PRINTED BY
SPOTTISWOODE AND CO., NEW-STREET SQUARE
LONDON

A List of Books

PUBLISHED BY

CHATTO & WINDUS,

214, Piccadilly, London, W.

Sold by all Booksellers, or sent post-free for the published price by the Publishers.

ABOUT.—THE FELLAH: An Egyptian Novel. By EDMOND ABOUT. Translated by Sir RANDAL ROBERTS. Post 8vo, illustrated boards, **2s.**

ADAMS (W. DAVENPORT), WORKS BY.
A DICTIONARY OF THE DRAMA. Being a comprehensive Guide to the Plays, Playwrights, Players, and Playhouses of the United Kingdom and America. Crown 8vo, half-bound, **12s. 6d.** [*Preparing.*
QUIPS AND QUIDDITIES. Selected by W. D. ADAMS. Post 8vo, cloth limp, **2s. 6d.**

ADAMS (W. H. D.).—WITCH, WARLOCK, AND MAGICIAN: Historical Sketches of Magic and Witchcraft in England and Scotland. By W. H. DAVENPORT ADAMS. Demy 8vo, cloth extra, **12s.**

AGONY COLUMN (THE) OF "THE TIMES," from 1800 to 1870. Edited, with an Introduction, by ALICE CLAY. Post 8vo, cloth limp, **2s. 6d.**

AIDE (HAMILTON), WORKS BY. Post 8vo, illustrated boards, **2s.** each.
CARR OF CARRLYON. | CONFIDENCES.

ALBERT.—BROOKE FINCHLEY'S DAUGHTER. By MARY ALBERT. Post 8vo, picture boards, **2s.**; cloth limp, **2s. 6d.**

ALEXANDER (MRS.), NOVELS BY. Post 8vo, illustrated boards, **2s.** each.
MAID, WIFE, OR WIDOW? | VALERIE'S FATE.

ALLEN (GRANT), WORKS BY. Crown 8vo, cloth extra, **6s.** each.
THE EVOLUTIONIST AT LARGE. | COLIN CLOUT'S CALENDAR.
VIGNETTES FROM NATURE.

Crown 8vo, cloth extra, **6s.** each; post 8vo, illustrated boards., **2s.** each
STRANGE STORIES. With a Frontispiece by GEORGE DU MAURIER.
THE BECKONING HAND. With a Frontispiece by TOWNLEY GREEN.

Crown 8vo, cloth extra, **3s. 6d.** each; post 8vo, illustrated boards, **2s.** each.
PHILISTIA. | FOR MAIMIE'S SAKE. | THIS MORTAL COIL.
BABYLON. | IN ALL SHADES. | THE TENTS OF SHEM.
| THE DEVIL'S DIE. |

THE GREAT TABOO. Crown 8vo, cloth extra, **3s. 6d.** :
DUMARESQ'S DAUGHTER. Three Vols., crown 8vo. [*Shortly.*

AMERICAN LITERATURE, A LIBRARY OF, from the Earliest Settlement to the Present Time. Compiled and Edited by EDMUND CLARENCE STEDMAN and ELLEN MACKAY HUTCHINSON. Eleven Vols., royal 8vo, cloth extra. A few copies are for sale by Messrs. CHATTO & WINDUS (published in New York by C. L. WEBSTER & Co.), price **£6 12s.** the set.

ARCHITECTURAL STYLES, A HANDBOOK OF. By A. ROSENGARTEN. Translated by W. COLLETT-SANDARS. With 639 Illusts. Cr. 8vo, cl. ex., **7s. 6d.**

ART (THE) OF AMUSING: A Collection of Graceful Arts, GAMES, Tricks, Puzzles, and Charades. By FRANK BELLEW. 300 Illusts. Cr. 8vo, cl. ex., **4s. 6d.**

ARNOLD (EDWIN LESTER), WORKS BY.
THE WONDERFUL ADVENTURES OF PHRA THE PHŒNICIAN. With Introduction by Sir Edwin Arnold, and 12 Illusts. by H. M. Paget. Cr. 8vo, cl., **3s. 6d.**
BIRD LIFE IN ENGLAND. Crown 8vo, cloth extra, **6s.**

ARTEMUS WARD'S WORKS: The Works of Charles Farrer Browne, better known as Artemus Ward. With Portrait and Facsimile. Crown 8vo, cloth extra, **7s. 6d.**—Also a Popular Edition, post 8vo, picture boards, **2s.**
THE GENIAL SHOWMAN: Life and Adventures of Artemus Ward. By Edward P. Hingston. With a Frontispiece. Crown 8vo, cloth extra **3s. 6d.**

ASHTON (JOHN), WORKS BY. Crown 8vo, cloth extra, **7s. 6d.** each.
HISTORY OF THE CHAP-BOOKS OF THE 18th CENTURY. With 334 Illusts.
SOCIAL LIFE IN THE REIGN OF QUEEN ANNE. With 85 Illustrations.
HUMOUR, WIT, AND SATIRE OF SEVENTEENTH CENTURY. With 82 Illusts.
ENGLISH CARICATURE AND SATIRE ON NAPOLEON THE FIRST. 115 Illusts.
MODERN STREET BALLADS. With 57 Illustrations.

BACTERIA.— A SYNOPSIS OF THE BACTERIA AND YEAST
FUNGI AND ALLIED SPECIES. By W. B. Grove, B.A. With 87 Illustrations.
Crown 8vo, cloth extra, **3s. 6d.**

BARDSLEY (REV. C. W.), WORKS BY.
ENGLISH SURNAMES: Their Sources and Significations. Cr. 8vo, cloth, **7s. 6d.**
CURIOSITIES OF PURITAN NOMENCLATURE. Crown 8vo, cloth extra, **6s.**

BARING GOULD (S., Author of "John Herring," &c.), **NOVELS BY.**
Crown 8vo, cloth extra, **3s. 6d.** each; post 8vo, illustrated boards, **2s.** each.
RED SPIDER. | EVE.

BARRETT (FRANK, Author of "Lady Biddy Fane,") **NOVELS BY.**
Post 8vo, illustrated boards, **2s.** each; cloth, **2s. 6d.** each.
FETTERED FOR LIFE. | BETWEEN LIFE AND DEATH.

BEACONSFIELD, LORD: A Biography. By T. P. O'Connor, M.P.
Sixth Edition, with an Introduction. Crown 8vo, cloth extra, **5s.**

BEAUCHAMP.—GRANTLEY GRANGE: A Novel. By Shelsley
Beauchamp. Post 8vo, illustrated boards, **2s.**

BEAUTIFUL PICTURES BY BRITISH ARTISTS: A Gathering of
Favourites from our Picture Galleries, beautifully engraved on Steel. With Notices of the Artists by Sydney Armytage. M.A. Imperial 4to, cloth extra, gilt edges, **21s.**

BECHSTEIN.—AS PRETTY AS SEVEN, and other German Stories.
Collected by Ludwig Bechstein. With Additional Tales by the Brothers Grimm, and 98 Illustrations by Richter. Square 8vo, cloth extra, **6s. 6d.**; gilt edges, **7s. 6d.**

BEERBOHM.—WANDERINGS IN PATAGONIA; or, Life among the
Ostrich Hunters. By Julius Beerbohm. With Illusts. Cr. 8vo, cl. extra, **3s. 6d.**

BESANT (WALTER), NOVELS BY.
Cr. 8vo, cl. ex., **3s. 6d.** each; post 8vo, illust. bds., **2s.** each; cl. limp, **2s. 6d.** each.
ALL SORTS AND CONDITIONS OF MEN. With Illustrations by Fred. Barnard.
THE CAPTAINS' ROOM, &c. With Frontispiece by E. J. Wheeler.
ALL IN A GARDEN FAIR. With 6 Illustrations by Harry Furniss.
DOROTHY FORSTER. With Frontispiece by Charles Green.
UNCLE JACK, and other Stories. | CHILDREN OF GIBEON.
THE WORLD WENT VERY WELL THEN. With 12 Illustrations by A. Forestier.
HERR PAULUS: His Rise, his Greatness, and his Fall.
FOR FAITH AND FREEDOM. With Illustrations by A. Forestier and F. Waddy.

Crown 8vo, cloth extra, **3s. 6d.** each.
TO CALL HER MINE, &c. With 9 Illustrations by A. Forestier.
THE BELL OF ST. PAUL'S.
ARMOREL OF LYONESSE: A Romance of To-day. With 12 Illusts. by F. Barnard.
THE HOLY ROSE, &c. With Frontispiece by F. Barnard.

ST. KATHERINE'S BY THE TOWER. With 12 full-page Illustrations by C. Green. Three Vols., crown 8vo.
FIFTY YEARS AGO. With 137 Plates and Woodcuts. Demy 8vo, cloth extra, **16s.**
THE EULOGY OF RICHARD JEFFERIES. With Portrait. Cr. 8vo, cl. extra, **6s.**
THE ART OF FICTION. Demy 8vo, **1s.**

BESANT (WALTER) AND JAMES RICE, NOVELS BY.

Cr. 8vo, cl. ex., 3s. 6d. each ; post 8vo, illust. bds., 2s. each. cl. limp, 2s. 6d. each.

READY-MONEY MORTIBOY.	BY CELIA'S ARBOUR.
MY LITTLE GIRL.	THE CHAPLAIN OF THE FLEET.
WITH HARP AND CROWN.	THE SEAMY SIDE.
THIS SON OF VULCAN.	THE CASE OF MR. LUCRAFT, &c.
THE GOLDEN BUTTERFLY.	'TWAS IN TRAFALGAR'S BAY, &c.
THE MONKS OF THELEMA.	THE TEN YEARS' TENANT, &c.

*** There is also a LIBRARY EDITION of the above Twelve Volumes, handsomely set in new type, on a large crown 8vo page, and bound in cloth extra. 6s. each.

BENNETT (W. C., LL.D.), WORKS BY. Post 8vo, cloth limp, 2s. each.
A BALLAD HISTORY OF ENGLAND. | SONGS FOR SAILORS.

BEWICK (THOMAS) AND HIS PUPILS. By AUSTIN DOBSON. With
95 Illustrations. Square 8vo, cloth extra, 6s.

BLACKBURN'S (HENRY) ART HANDBOOKS.
ACADEMY NOTES, separate years, from 1875-1887, 1889, and 1890, each 1s.
ACADEMY NOTES, 1891. With Illustrations. 1s.
ACADEMY NOTES, 1875-79. Complete in One Vol., with 600 Illusts. Cloth limp, 6s.
ACADEMY NOTES, 1880-84. Complete in One Vol., with 700 Illusts. Cloth limp, 6s.
GROSVENOR NOTES, 1877. 6d.
GROSVENOR NOTES, separate years, from 1878 to 1890, each 1s.
GROSVENOR NOTES, Vol. I., 1877-82. With 300 Illusts. Demy 8vo, cloth limp, 6s.
GROSVENOR NOTES, Vol. II., 1883-87. With 300 Illusts. Demy 8vo, cloth limp, 6s.
THE NEW GALLERY, 1889-1890. With numerous Illustrations, each 1s.
THE NEW GALLERY, 1891. With Illustrations. 1s.
ENGLISH PICTURES AT THE NATIONAL GALLERY. 114 Illustrations. 1s.
OLD MASTERS AT THE NATIONAL GALLERY. 128 Illustrations. 1s. 6d.
ILLUSTRATED CATALOGUE TO THE NATIONAL GALLERY. 242 Illusts. cl., 3s.

THE PARIS SALON, 1891. With Facsimile Sketches. 3s.
THE PARIS SOCIETY OF FINE ARTS, 1891. With Sketches. 3s. 6d.

BLAKE (WILLIAM) : India-proof Etchings from his Works by WILLIAM
BELL SCOTT. With descriptive Text. Folio, half-bound boards, 21s.

BLIND.—THE ASCENT OF MAN : A Poem. By MATHILDE BLIND.
Crown 8vo, printed on hand-made paper. cloth extra, 5s.

BOURNE (H. R. FOX), WORKS BY.
ENGLISH MERCHANTS : Memoirs in Illustration of the Progress of British Commerce. With numerous Illustrations. Crown 8vo, cloth extra, 7s. 6d.
ENGLISH NEWSPAPERS: The History of Journalism. Two Vols., demy 8vo, cl., 25s.
THE OTHER SIDE OF THE EMIN PASHA RELIEF EXPEDITION. Crown 8vo cloth extra, 6s.

BOWERS' (G.) HUNTING SKETCHES. Oblong 4to, hf.-bd. bds., 21s. each.
CANTERS IN CRAMPSHIRE. | LEAVES FROM A HUNTING JOURNAL.

BOYLE (FREDERICK), WORKS BY. Post 8vo, illustrated boards, 2s. each.
CHRONICLES OF NO-MAN'S LAND. | CAMP NOTES.

SAVAGE LIFE. Crown 8vo, cloth extra, 3s. 6d.; post 8vo, picture boards, 2s.

BRAND'S OBSERVATIONS ON POPULAR ANTIQUITIES ; chiefly
illustrating the Origin of our Vulgar Customs, Ceremonies, and Superstitions. With the Additions of Sir HENRY ELLIS, and Illustrations. Cr. 8vo. cloth extra, 7s. 6d.

BREWER (REV. DR.), WORKS BY.
THE READER'S HANDBOOK OF ALLUSIONS, REFERENCES, PLOTS, AND STORIES. Fifteenth Thousand. Crown 8vo, cloth extra, 7s. 6d.
AUTHORS AND THEIR WORKS, WITH THE DATES: Being the Appendices to "The Reader's Handbook," separately printed. Crown 8vo. cloth limp, 2s.
A DICTIONARY OF MIRACLES. Crown 8vo. cloth extra, 7s. 6d.

BREWSTER (SIR DAVID), WORKS BY. Post 8vo, cl. ex., 4s. 6d. each.
MORE WORLDS THAN ONE : Creed of Philosopher and Hope of Christian. Plates.
THE MARTYRS OF SCIENCE: GALILEO, TYCHO BRAHE, and KEPLER. With Portraits.
LETTERS ON NATURAL MAGIC. With numerous Illustrations.

BRET HARTE, WORKS BY.

LIBRARY EDITION, Complete in Six Volumes, crown 8vo, cloth extra, **6s.** each.

BRET HARTE'S COLLECTED WORKS. Arranged and Revised by the Author.

Vol. I. COMPLETE POETICAL AND DRAMATIC WORKS. With Steel Portrait.
Vol. II. LUCK OF ROARING CAMP—BOHEMIAN PAPERS—AMERICAN LEGENDS.
Vol. III. TALES OF THE ARGONAUTS—EASTERN SKETCHES.
Vol. IV. GABRIEL CONROY.
Vol. V. STORIES—CONDENSED NOVELS, &c.
Vol. VI. TALES OF THE PACIFIC SLOPE.

THE SELECT WORKS OF BRET HARTE, in Prose and Poetry. With Introductory Essay by J. M. BELLEW, Portrait of Author, and 50 Illusts. Cr. 8vo, cl. ex., **7s. 6d.**
BRET HARTE'S POETICAL WORKS. Hand-made paper & buckram. Cr. 8vo, **4s. 6d.**
THE QUEEN OF THE PIRATE ISLE. With 25 original Drawings by KATE GREENAWAY, reproduced in Colours by EDMUND EVANS. Small 4to, cloth, **5s.**

Crown 8vo, cloth extra, **3s. 6d.** each.

A WAIF OF THE PLAINS. With 60 Illustrations by STANLEY L. WOOD.
A WARD OF THE GOLDEN GATE. With 59 Illustrations by STANLEY L. WOOD.
A SAPPHO OF GREEN SPRINGS, &c. With Two Illustrations by HUME NISBET.
COLONEL STARBOTTLE'S CLIENT, &c. With Front. by F. BARNARD. [*Preparing*

Post 8vo, illustrated boards, **2s.** each.

GABRIEL CONROY.	**THE LUCK OF ROARING CAMP,** &c.
AN HEIRESS OF RED DOG, &c.	**CALIFORNIAN STORIES.**

Post 8vo, illustrated boards, **2s.** each; cloth limp, **2s. 6d.** each.

FLIP.	**MARUJA.**	**A PHYLLIS OF THE SIERRAS.**

Fcap. 8vo picture cover, **1s.** each.

THE TWINS OF TABLE MOUNTAIN. | **JEFF BRIGGS'S LOVE STORY.**

BRILLAT-SAVARIN.—GASTRONOMY AS A FINE ART. By BRILLAT-SAVARIN. Translated by R. E. ANDERSON, M.A. Post 8vo, half-bound, **2s.**

BRYDGES.—UNCLE SAM AT HOME. By HAROLD BRYDGES. Post 8vo, illustrated boards, **2s.**; cloth limp, **2s. 6d.**

BUCHANAN'S (ROBERT) WORKS. Crown 8vo, cloth extra, **6s.** each.

SELECTED POEMS OF ROBERT BUCHANAN. With Frontispiece by T. DALZIEL.
THE EARTHQUAKE; or, Six Days and a Sabbath.
THE CITY OF DREAM: An Epic Poem. With Two Illustrations by P. MACNAB.
THE OUTCAST: A Rhyme for the Time. With 12 Full-page Illustrations and numerous Vignettes. Crown 8vo, cloth extra, **8s.**
ROBERT BUCHANAN'S COMPLETE POETICAL WORKS. With Steel-plate Portrait. Crown 8vo, cloth extra, **7s. 6d.**

Crown 8vo, cloth extra, **3s. 6d.** each; post 8vo, illustrated boards, **2s.** each.

THE SHADOW OF THE SWORD.	**LOVE ME FOR EVER.** Frontispiece.
A CHILD OF NATURE. Frontispiece.	**ANNAN WATER.** | **FOXGLOVE MANOR.**
GOD AND THE MAN. With 11 Illustrations by FRED. BARNARD.	**THE NEW ABELARD.**
	MATT: A Story of a Caravan. Front.
THE MARTYRDOM OF MADELINE.	**THE MASTER OF THE MINE.** Front.
With Frontispiece by A. W. COOPER.	**THE HEIR OF LINNE.**

BURTON (CAPTAIN).—THE BOOK OF THE SWORD: Being a History of the Sword and its Use in all Countries, from the Earliest Times. By RICHARD F. BURTON. With over 400 Illustrations. Square 8vo, cloth extra, **32s.**

BURTON (ROBERT).

THE ANATOMY OF MELANCHOLY: A New Edition, with translations of the Classical Extracts. Demy 8vo, cloth extra, **7s. 6d.**
MELANCHOLY ANATOMISED: Being an Abridgment, for popular use, of BURTON'S ANATOMY OF MELANCHOLY. Post 8vo, cloth limp, **2s. 6d.**

CAINE (T. HALL), NOVELS BY. Crown 8vo, cloth extra, **3s. 6d.** each; post 8vo, illustrated boards, **2s.** each; cloth limp, **2s. 6d.** each.

SHADOW OF A CRIME. | **A SON OF HAGAR.** | **THE DEEMSTER.**

CAMERON (COMMANDER).—THE CRUISE OF THE "BLACK PRINCE" PRIVATEER. By V. LOVETT CAMERON, R.N., C.B. With Two Illustrations by P. MACNAB. Crown 8vo, cloth extra, **5s.**; post 8vo, illustrated boards, **2s.**

CAMERON (MRS. H. LOVETT), NOVELS BY.

Crown 8vo, cloth extra, **3s. 6d.** each; post 8vo, illustrated boards, **2s.** each.

JULIET'S GUARDIAN. | **DECEIVERS EVER.**

CARLYLE (THOMAS) ON THE CHOICE OF BOOKS. With Life
by R. H. Shepherd, and Three Illustrations. Post 8vo, cloth extra, 1s. 6d.
THE CORRESPONDENCE OF THOMAS CARLYLE AND RALPH WALDO
EMERSON, 1834 to 1872. Edited by Charles Eliot Norton. With Portraits.
Two Vols., crown 8vo. cloth extra, 24s.

CARLYLE (JANE WELSH), LIFE OF. By Mrs. Alexander Ireland.
With Portrait and Facsimile Letter. Small demy 8vo, cloth extra, 7s. 6d.

CHAPMAN'S (GEORGE) WORKS. Vol. I. contains the Plays complete,
including the doubtful ones. Vol. II., the Poems and Minor Translations, with an
Introductory Essay by Algernon Charles Swinburne. Vol. III., the Translations
of the Iliad and Odyssey. Three Vols., crown 8vo, cloth extra, 6s. each.

CHATTO AND JACKSON.—A TREATISE ON WOOD ENGRAVING,
Historical and Practical. By William Andrew Chatto and John Jackson. With
an Additional Chapter by Henry G. Bohn, and 450 fine Illusts. Large 4to, hf.-bd., 28s.

. CHAUCER FOR CHILDREN: A Golden Key. By Mrs. H. R. Haweis.
With 8 Coloured Plates and 30 Woodcuts. Small 4to, cloth extra, 6s.
CHAUCER FOR SCHOOLS. By Mrs. H. R. Haweis. Demy 8vo, cloth limp, 2s. 6d.

CLARE.—FOR THE LOVE OF A LASS: A Tale of Tynedale. By
Austin Clare. Post 8vo, picture boards, 2s.; cloth limp, 2s. 6d.

CLIVE (MRS. ARCHER), NOVELS BY. Post 8vo, illust. boards, 2s. each.
PAUL FERROLL. ‖ WHY PAUL FERROLL KILLED HIS WIFE.

CLODD (EDW., F.R.A.S.).—MYTHS AND DREAMS. Cr. 8vo, cl. ex., 5s.

COBBAN.—THE CURE OF SOULS: A Story. By J. Maclaren
Cobban. Post 8vo, illustrated boards, 2s.

COLEMAN (JOHN), WORKS BY.
PLAYERS AND PLAYWRIGHTS I HAVE KNOWN. Two Vols., 8vo, cloth, 24s.
CURLY: An Actor's Story. With 21 Illusts. by J. C. Dollman. Cr. 8vo, cl., 1s. 6d.

COLLINS (C. ALLSTON).—THE BAR SINISTER. Post 8vo, 2s.

COLLINS (MORTIMER AND FRANCES), NOVELS BY.
Crown 8vo, cloth extra, 3s. 6d. each : post 8vo, illustrated boards, 2s. each.
SWEET ANNE PAGE. ‖ FROM MIDNIGHT TO MIDNIGHT. ‖ TRANSMIGRATION.
BLACKSMITH AND SCHOLAR. ‖ YOU PLAY ME FALSE. ‖ VILLAGE COMEDY.
Post 8vo, illustrated boards, 2s. each.
A FIGHT WITH FORTUNE. ‖ SWEET AND TWENTY. ‖ FRANCES.

COLLINS (WILKIE), NOVELS BY.
Cr. 8vo, cl. ex., 3s. 6d. each ; post 8vo, illust. bds., 2s. each; cl. limp, 2s. 6d. each.
ANTONINA. With a Frontispiece by Sir John Gilbert, R.A.
BASIL. Illustrated by Sir John Gilbert, R.A., and J. Mahoney.
HIDE AND SEEK. Illustrated by Sir John Gilbert, R.A., and J. Mahoney.
AFTER DARK. With Illustrations by A. B. Houghton.
THE DEAD SECRET. With a Frontispiece by Sir John Gilbert, R.A.
QUEEN OF HEARTS. With a Frontispiece by Sir John Gilbert, R.A.
THE WOMAN IN WHITE. With Illusts. by Sir J. Gilbert, R.A., and F. A. Fraser.
NO NAME. With Illustrations by Sir J. E. Millais, R.A., and A. W. Cooper.
MY MISCELLANIES. With a Steel-plate Portrait of Wilkie Collins.
ARMADALE. With Illustrations by G. H. Thomas.
THE MOONSTONE. With Illustrations by G. Du Maurier and F. A. Fraser.
MAN AND WIFE. With Illustrations by William Small.
POOR MISS FINCH. Illustrated by G. Du Maurier and Edward Hughes.
MISS OR MRS.? With Illusts. by S. L. Fildes, R.A., and Henry Woods, A.R.A.
THE NEW MAGDALEN. Illustrated by G. Du Maurier and C. S. Reinhardt.
THE FROZEN DEEP. Illustrated by G. Du Maurier and J. Mahoney.
THE LAW AND THE LADY. Illusts. by S. L. Fildes, R.A., and Sydney Hall.
THE TWO DESTINIES.
THE HAUNTED HOTEL. Illustrated by Arthur Hopkins.
THE FALLEN LEAVES. ‖ HEART AND SCIENCE. ‖ THE EVIL GENIUS.
JEZEBEL'S DAUGHTER. ‖ "I SAY NO." ‖ LITTLE NOVELS.
THE BLACK ROBE. ‖ A ROGUE'S LIFE. ‖ THE LEGACY OF CAIN.
BLIND LOVE. With Preface by Walter Besant, and Illusts. by A. Forestier.

COLLINS (CHURTON).—A MONOGRAPH ON DEAN SWIFT. By
J. Churton Collins. Crown 8vo, cloth extra, 8s. 　　　　　[Shortly.

COLMAN'S HUMOROUS WORKS: "Broad Grins," "My Nightgown and Slippers," and other Humorous Works of GEORGE COLMAN. With Life by G. B. BUCKSTONE, and Frontispiece by HOGARTH. Crown 8vo. cloth extra, **7s. 6d.**

COLQUHOUN.—EVERY INCH A SOLDIER: A Novel. By M. J. COLQUHOUN. Post 8vo, illustrated boards, **2s.**

CONVALESCENT COOKERY: A Family Handbook. By CATHERINE RYAN. Crown 8vo, **1s.**; cloth limp. **1s. 6d.**

CONWAY (MONCURE D.), WORKS BY.
DEMONOLOGY AND DEVIL-LORE. With 65 Illustrations. Third Edition. Two Vols., demy 8vo. cloth extra, **28s.**
A NECKLACE OF STORIES. 25 Illusts. by W. J. HENNESSY. Sq. 8vo, cloth, **6s.**
PINE AND PALM: A Novel. Two Vols., crown 8vo, cloth extra, **21s.**
GEORGE WASHINGTON'S RULES OF CIVILITY Traced to their Sources and Restored. Fcap. 8vo, Japanese vellum, **2s. 6d.**

COOK (DUTTON), NOVELS BY.
PAUL FOSTER'S DAUGHTER. Cr. 8vo, cl. ex., **3s. 6d.**; post 8vo, illust. boards, **2s.**
LEO. Post 8vo, illustrated boards, **2s.**

CORNWALL.—POPULAR ROMANCES OF THE WEST OF ENG-LAND; or, The Drolls, Traditions, and Superstitions of Old Cornwall. Collected by ROBERT HUNT, F.R.S. Two Steel-plates by GEO. CRUIKSHANK. Cr. 8vo, cl., **7s. 6d.**

CRADDOCK.—THE PROPHET OF THE GREAT SMOKY MOUN-TAINS. By CHARLES EGBERT CRADDOCK. Post 8vo, illust bds., **2s.**; cl. limp, **2s. 6d.**

CRUIKSHANK'S COMIC ALMANACK. Complete in TWO SERIES: The FIRST from 1835 to 1843; the SECOND from 1844 to 1853. A Gathering of the BEST HUMOUR of THACKERAY, HOOD, MAYHEW, ALBERT SMITH, A'BECKETT, ROBERT BROUGH, &c. With numerous Steel Engravings and Woodcuts by CRUIK-SHANK, HINE, LANDELLS, &c. Two Vols., crown 8vo, cloth gilt, **7s. 6d.** each.
THE LIFE OF GEORGE CRUIKSHANK. By BLANCHARD JERROLD. With 84 Illustrations and a Bibliography. Crown 8vo, cloth extra, **7s. 6d.**

CUMMING (C. F. GORDON), WORKS BY. Demy 8vo, cl. ex., **8s. 6d.** each.
IN THE HEBRIDES. With Autotype Facsimile and 23 Illustrations.
IN THE HIMALAYAS AND ON THE INDIAN PLAINS. With 42 Illustrations.
VIA CORNWALL TO EGYPT. With Photogravure Frontis. Demy 8vo, cl., **7s. 6d.**

CUSSANS.—A HANDBOOK OF HERALDRY; with Instructions for Tracing Pedigrees and Deciphering Ancient MSS., &c. By JOHN E. CUSSANS. With 408 Woodcuts, Two Coloured and Two Plain Plates. Crown 8vo, cloth extra, **7s. 6d.**

CYPLES (W.)—HEARTS of GOLD. Cr. 8vo, cl., **3s. 6d.**; post 8vo, bds., **2s.**

DANIEL.—MERRIE ENGLAND IN THE OLDEN TIME. By GEORGE DANIEL. With Illustrations by ROBERT CRUIKSHANK. Crown 8vo, cloth extra, **3s. 6d.**

DAUDET.—THE EVANGELIST; or, Port Salvation. By ALPHONSE DAUDET. Crown 8vo, cloth extra, **3s. 6d.**; post 8vo, illustrated boards, **2s.**

DAVENANT.—HINTS FOR PARENTS ON THE CHOICE OF A PRO-FESSION FOR THEIR SONS. By F. DAVENANT, M.A. Post 8vo. **1s.**; cl., **1s. 6d.**

DAVIES (DR. N. E. YORKE-), WORKS BY.
Crown 8vo, **1s.** each; cloth limp, **1s. 6d.** each.
ONE THOUSAND MEDICAL MAXIMS AND SURGICAL HINTS.
NURSERY HINTS: A Mother's Guide in Health and Disease.
FOODS FOR THE FAT: A Treatise on Corpulency, and a Dietary for its Cure.
AIDS TO LONG LIFE. Crown 8vo, **2s.**; cloth limp, **2s. 6d.**

DAVIES' (SIR JOHN) COMPLETE POETICAL WORKS, including Psalms I. to L. in Verse, and other hitherto Unpublished MSS., for the first time Collected and Edited, with Memorial-Introduction and Notes, by the Rev. A. B. GROSART, D.D. Two Vols., crown 8vo. cloth boards, **12s.**

DAWSON.—THE FOUNTAIN OF YOUTH: A Novel of Adventure. By ERASMUS DAWSON, M.B. Edited by PAUL DEVON. With Two Illustrations by HUME NISBET. Crown 8vo, cloth extra, **3s. 6d.**

DE MAISTRE.—A JOURNEY ROUND MY ROOM. By XAVIER DE
MAISTRE. Translated by HENRY ATTWELL. Post 8vo, cloth limp, 2s. 6d.

DE MILLE.—A CASTLE IN SPAIN. By JAMES DE MILLE. With a
Frontispiece. Crown 8vo, cloth extra, 3s. 6d.; post 8vo, illustrated boards, 2s.

DERBY (THE).—THE BLUE RIBBON OF THE TURF: A Chronicle
of the RACE FOR THE DERBY, from Diomed to Donovan. With Notes on the Winning Horses, the Men who trained them, Jockeys who rode them, and Gentlemen to
whom they belonged; also Notices of the Betting and Betting Men of the period, and
Brief Accounts of THE OAKS. By LOUIS HENRY CURZON. Cr. 8vo, cloth extra, 6s.

DERWENT (LEITH), NOVELS BY. Cr. 8vo cl., 3s. 6d. ea.; post 8vo, bds., 2s. ea.

OUR LADY OF TEARS. | CIRCE'S LOVERS.

DICKENS (CHARLES), NOVELS BY. Post 8vo, illustrated boards, 2s. each.

SKETCHES BY BOZ. | NICHOLAS NICKLEBY.
THE PICKWICK PAPERS. | OLIVER TWIST.

    THE SPEECHES OF CHARLES DICKENS, 1841-1870. With a New Bibliography.
    Edited by RICHARD HERNE SHEPHERD. Crown 8vo, cloth extra, 6s.—Also a
    SMALLER EDITION, in the Mayfair Library, post 8vo, cloth limp, 2s. 6d.

    ABOUT ENGLAND WITH DICKENS. By ALFRED RIMMER. With 57 Illustrations
    by C. A. VANDERHOOF, ALFRED RIMMER, and others. Sq. 8vo, cloth extra, 7s. 6d.

DICTIONARIES.

    A DICTIONARY OF MIRACLES: Imitative, Realistic, and Dogmatic. By the Rev
    E. C. BREWER, LL.D. Crown 8vo, cloth extra, 7s. 6d.

    **THE READER'S HANDBOOK OF ALLUSIONS, REFERENCES, PLOTS, AND
    STORIES.** By the Rev. E. C. BREWER, LL.D. With an ENGLISH BIBLIOGRAPHY.
    Fifteenth Thousand. Crown 8vo, cloth extra, 7s. 6d.

    AUTHORS AND THEIR WORKS, WITH THE DATES. Cr. 8vo, cloth limp, 2s.

    FAMILIAR SHORT SAYINGS OF GREAT MEN. With Historical and Explana-
    tory Notes. By SAMUEL A. BENT, A.M. Crown 8vo, cloth extra, 7s. 6d.

    SLANG DICTIONARY: Etymological, Historical, and Anecdotal. Cr. 8vo, cl., 6s. 6d.

    WOMEN OF THE DAY: A Biographical Dictionary. By F. HAYS. Cr. 8vo, cl., 5s.

    WORDS, FACTS, AND PHRASES: A Dictionary of Curious, Quaint, and Out-of-
    the-Way Matters. By ELIEZER EDWARDS. Crown 8vo, cloth extra, 7s. 6d.

DIDEROT.—THE PARADOX OF ACTING. Translated, with Annotations, from Diderot's "Le Paradoxe sur le Comédien," by WALTER HERRIES POLLOCK.
With a Preface by HENRY IRVING. Crown 8vo, parchment, 4s. 6d.

DOBSON (AUSTIN), WORKS BY.

    THOMAS BEWICK & HIS PUPILS. With 95 Illustrations. Square 8vo, cloth, 6s.

    FOUR FRENCHWOMEN: MADEMOISELLE DE CORDAY; MADAME ROLAND; THE
    PRINCESS DE LAMBALLE; MADAME DE GENLIS. Fcap. 8vo, hf.-roxburghe, 2s. 6d.

DOBSON (W. T.), WORKS BY. Post 8vo, cloth limp, 2s. 6d. each.

LITERARY FRIVOLITIES, FANCIES, FOLLIES, AND FROLICS.
POETICAL INGENUITIES AND ECCENTRICITIES.

DONOVAN (DICK), DETECTIVE STORIES BY.
    Post 8vo illustrated boards, 2s. each; cloth limp, 2s. 6d. each.

THE MAN-HUNTER. | TRACKED AND TAKEN.
CAUGHT AT LAST! | WHO POISONED HETTY DUNCAN?
      A DETECTIVE'S TRIUMPHS. [Preparing.

    THE MAN FROM MANCHESTER. With 23 Illustrations. Crown 8vo, cloth, 6s.;
    post 8vo, illustrated boards, 2s.

DOYLE (A. CONAN, Author of "Micah Clarke"), NOVELS BY.

    THE FIRM OF GIRDLESTONE. Crown 8vo, cloth extra, 6s.

    STRANGE SECRETS. Told by CONAN DOYLE, PERCY FITZGERALD, FLORENCE
    MARRYAT, &c. Cr. 8vo, cl. ex., Eight Illusts., 6s.; post 8vo, illust. bds., 2s.

DRAMATISTS, THE OLD. With Vignette Portraits. Cr. 8vo, cl. ex., 6s. per Vol.

    BEN JONSON'S WORKS. With Notes Critical and Explanatory, and a Bio-
    graphical Memoir by WM. GIFFORD. Edited by Col. CUNNINGHAM. Three Vols.

    CHAPMAN'S WORKS. Complete in Three Vols. Vol. I. contains the Plays
    complete; Vol. II., Poems and Minor Translations, with an Introductory Essay
    by A. C. SWINBURNE; Vol. III., Translations of the Iliad and Odyssey.

    MARLOWE'S WORKS. Edited, with Notes, by Col. CUNNINGHAM. One Vol.

    MASSINGER'S PLAYS. From Gifford's Text. Edit. by Col. CUNNINGHAM. One Vol.

DUNCAN (SARA JEANNETTE), WORKS BY.
A SOCIAL DEPARTURE: How Orthodocia and I Went round the World by Ourselves. With 111 Illustrations by F. H. TOWNSEND. Crown 8vo, cloth, 7s. 6d.
AN AMERICAN GIRL IN LONDON. With 80 Illustrations by F. H. TOWNSEND. Crown 8vo, cloth extra, 7s. 6d. [*Preparing.*

DYER.—THE FOLK-LORE OF PLANTS. By Rev. T. F. THISELTON DYER, M.A. Crown 8vo, cloth extra, 6s.

EARLY ENGLISH POETS. Edited, with Introductions and Annotations, by Rev. A. B. GROSART, D.D. Crown 8vo, cloth boards, 6s. per Volume.
FLETCHER'S (GILES) COMPLETE POEMS. One Vol.
DAVIES' (SIR JOHN) COMPLETE POETICAL WORKS. Two Vols.
HERRICK'S (ROBERT) COMPLETE COLLECTED POEMS. Three Vols.
SIDNEY'S (SIR PHILIP) COMPLETE POETICAL WORKS. Three Vols.

EDGCUMBE.—ZEPHYRUS : A Holiday in Brazil and on the River Plate. By E. R. PEARCE EDGCUMBE. With 41 Illustrations. Crown 8vo, cloth extra, 5s.

EDWARDES (MRS. ANNIE), NOVELS BY:
A POINT OF HONOUR. Post 8vo, illustrated boards, 2s.
ARCHIE LOVELL. Crown 8vo, cloth extra, 3s. 6d. ; post 8vo, illust. boards, 2s.

EDWARDS (ELIEZER).—WORDS, FACTS, AND PHRASES : A Dictionary of Curious, Quaint, and Out-of-the-Way Matters. By ELIEZER EDWARDS. Crown 8vo, cloth extra, 7s. 6d.

EDWARDS (M. BETHAM-), NOVELS BY.
KITTY. Post 8vo, illustrated boards, 2s. ; cloth limp, 2s. 6d.
FELICIA. Post 8vo, illustrated boards, 2s.

EGGLESTON (EDWARD).—ROXY : A Novel. Post 8vo, illust. bds., 2s.

EMANUEL.—ON DIAMONDS AND PRECIOUS STONES : Their History, Value, and Properties ; with Simple Tests for ascertaining their Reality. By HARRY EMANUEL, F.R.G.S. With Illustrations, tinted and plain. Cr. 8vo, cl. ex., 6s.

ENGLISHMAN'S HOUSE, THE : A Practical Guide to all interested in Selecting or Building a House ; with Estimates of Cost, Quantities, &c. By C. J. RICHARDSON. With Coloured Frontispiece and 600 Illusts. Crown 8vo, cloth, 7s. 6d.

EWALD (ALEX. CHARLES, F.S.A.), WORKS BY.
THE LIFE AND TIMES OF PRINCE CHARLES STUART, Count of Albany (THE YOUNG PRETENDER). With a Portrait. Crown 8vo, cloth extra, 7s. 6d.
STORIES FROM THE STATE PAPERS. With an Autotype. Crown 8vo, cloth, 6s.

EYES, OUR : How to Preserve Them from Infancy to Old Age. By JOHN BROWNING, F.R.A.S. With 70 Illusts. Eighteenth Thousand. Crown 8vo, 1s.

FAMILIAR SHORT SAYINGS OF GREAT MEN. By SAMUEL ARTHUR BENT, A.M. Fifth Edition, Revised and Enlarged. Crown 8vo, cloth extra, 7s. 6d.

FARADAY (MICHAEL), WORKS BY. Post 8vo, cloth extra, 4s. 6d. each
THE CHEMICAL HISTORY OF A CANDLE: Lectures delivered before a Juvenile Audience. Edited by WILLIAM CROOKES, F.C.S. With numerous Illustrations.
ON THE VARIOUS FORCES OF NATURE, AND THEIR RELATIONS TO EACH OTHER. Edited by WILLIAM CROOKES, F.C.S. With Illustrations.

FARRER (J. ANSON), WORKS BY.
MILITARY MANNERS AND CUSTOMS. Crown 8vo, cloth extra, 6s.
WAR: Three Essays, reprinted from "Military Manners." Cr. 8vo, 1s.; cl., 1s. 6d.

FICTION.—A CATALOGUE OF NEARLY SIX HUNDRED WORKS OF FICTION published by CHATTO & WINDUS, with a Short Critical Notice of each (40 pages, demy 8vo), will be sent free upon application.

FIN-BEC.—THE CUPBOARD PAPERS : Observations on the Art of Living and Dining. By FIN-BEC. Post 8vo, cloth limp, 2s. 6d.

FIREWORKS, THE COMPLETE ART OF MAKING ; or, The Pyrotechnist's Treasury. By THOMAS KENTISH. With 267 Illustrations. Cr. 8vo, cl., 5s.

FITZGERALD (PERCY, M.A., F.S.A.), WORKS BY.
THE WORLD BEHIND THE SCENES. Crown 8vo, cloth extra, 3s. 6d.
LITTLE ESSAYS: Passages from Letters of CHARLES LAMB. Post 8vo, cl., 2s. 6d.
A DAY'S TOUR: Journey through France and Belgium. With Sketches. Cr. 4to, 1s.
FATAL ZERO. Crown 8vo, cloth extra, 3s. 6d.; post 8vo, illustrated boards, 2s.

Post 8vo, illustrated boards, 2s. each.
BELLA DONNA. | LADY OF BRANTOME. | THE SECOND MRS. TILLOTSON.
POLLY. | NEVER FORGOTTEN. | SEVENTY-FIVE BROOKE STREET.

LIFE OF JAMES BOSWELL (of Auchinleck). With an Account of his Sayings,
Doings, and Writings; and Four Portraits. Two Vols., demy 8vo, cloth extra,
24s.
[Preparing.

FLETCHER'S (GILES, B.D.) COMPLETE POEMS: Christ's Victorie
in Heaven, Christ's Victorie on Earth, Christ's Triumph over Death, and Minor
Poems. With Notes by Rev. A. B. GROSART, D.D. Crown 8vo, cloth boards, 6s.

FLUDYER (HARRY) AT CAMBRIDGE: A Series of Family Letters.
Post 8vo, picture cover, 1s.; cloth limp, 1s. 6d.

FONBLANQUE (ALBANY).—FILTHY LUCRE. Post 8vo, illust. bds., 2s.

FRANCILLON (R. E.), NOVELS BY.
Crown 8vo, cloth extra, 3s. 6d. each; post 8vo, illustrated boards, 2s. each.
ONE BY ONE. | QUEEN COPHETUA. | A REAL QUEEN. | KING OR KNAVE?
OLYMPIA. Post 8vo, illust. bds., 2s. | ESTHER'S GLOVE. Fcap. 8vo, pict. cover. 1s.
ROMANCES OF THE LAW. Crown 8vo, cloth, 6s.; post 8vo, illust. boards, 2s.

FREDERIC (HAROLD), NOVELS BY.
SETH'S BROTHER'S WIFE. Post 8vo, illustrated boards, 2s.
THE LAWTON GIRL. With Frontispiece by F. BARNARD. Cr. 8vo, cloth ex., 6s.;
post 8vo, illustrated boards, 2s.

FRENCH LITERATURE, A HISTORY OF. By HENRY VAN LAUN.
Three Vols., demy 8vo, cloth boards, 7s. 6d. each.

FRENZENY.—FIFTY YEARS ON THE TRAIL: Adventures of JOHN
Y. NELSON, Scout, Guide, and Interpreter. By HARRINGTON O'REILLY. With 100
Illustrations by PAUL FRENZENY. Crown 8vo, cloth extra, 3s. 6d.

FRERE.—PANDURANG HARI; or, Memoirs of a Hindoo. With Preface by Sir BARTLE FRERE. Crown 8vo, cloth, 3s. 6d., post 8vo, illust. bds., 2s.

FRISWELL (HAIN).—ONE OF TWO: A Novel. Post 8vo, illust. bds., 2s.

FROST (THOMAS), WORKS BY. Crown 8vo, cloth extra, 3s. 6d. each.
CIRCUS LIFE AND CIRCUS CELEBRITIES. | LIVES OF THE CONJURERS.
THE OLD SHOWMEN AND THE OLD LONDON FAIRS.

FRY'S (HERBERT) ROYAL GUIDE TO THE LONDON CHARITIES.
Showing their Name, Date of Foundation, Objects, Income, Officials, &c. Edited
by JOHN LANE. Published Annually. Crown 8vo, cloth, 1s. 6d.

GARDENING BOOKS. Post 8vo, 1s. each; cloth limp, 1s. 6d. each.
A YEAR'S WORK IN GARDEN AND GREENHOUSE: Practical Advice as to the
Management of the Flower, Fruit, and Frame Garden. By GEORGE GLENNY.
OUR KITCHEN GARDEN: Plants, and How we Cook Them. By TOM JERROLD.
HOUSEHOLD HORTICULTURE. By TOM and JANE JERROLD. Illustrated.
THE GARDEN THAT PAID THE RENT. By TOM JERROLD.

MY GARDEN WILD, AND WHAT I GREW THERE. By FRANCIS G. HEATH.
Crown 8vo, cloth extra, gilt edges, 6s.

GARRETT.—THE CAPEL GIRLS: A Novel. By EDWARD GARRETT.
Crown 8vo, cloth extra, 3s. 6d.; post 8vo, illustrated boards, 2s.

GENTLEMAN'S MAGAZINE, THE. 1s. Monthly. In addition to the
Articles upon subjects in Literature, Science, and Art, for which this Magazine has
so high a reputation, "TABLE TALK" by SYLVANUS URBAN appears monthly.
. Bound Volumes for recent years kept in stock, 8s. 6d. each. Cases for binding, 2s.

GENTLEMAN'S ANNUAL, THE. Published Annually in November. 1s.

GERMAN POPULAR STORIES. Collected by the Brothers GRIMM and Translated by EDGAR TAYLOR. With Introduction by JOHN RUSKIN, and 22 Steel Plates by GEORGE CRUIKSHANK. Square 8vo, cloth, 6s. 6d.; gilt edges, 7s. 6d.

GIBBON (CHARLES), NOVELS BY. Crown 8vo, cloth extra, 3s. 6d. each; post 8vo, illustrated boards, 2s. each.
ROBIN GRAY. | LOVING A DREAM. | OF HIGH DEGREE.
THE FLOWER OF THE FOREST. | IN HONOUR BOUND.
THE GOLDEN SHAFT.

Post 8vo, illustrated boards, 2s. each.
THE DEAD HEART. | IN LOVE AND WAR.
FOR LACK OF GOLD. | A HEART'S PROBLEM.
WHAT WILL THE WORLD SAY? | BY MEAD AND STREAM.
FOR THE KING. | THE BRAES OF YARROW.
QUEEN OF THE MEADOW. | FANCY FREE. | A HARD KNOT.
IN PASTURES GREEN. | HEART'S DELIGHT. | BLOOD-MONEY.

GIBNEY (SOMERVILLE).—SENTENCED! Cr. 8vo, 1s.; cl., 1s. 6d.

GILBERT (WILLIAM), NOVELS BY. Post 8vo, illustrated boards, 2s. each.
DR. AUSTIN'S GUESTS. | JAMES DUKE, COSTERMONGER.
THE WIZARD OF THE MOUNTAIN. |

GILBERT (W. S.), ORIGINAL PLAYS BY. In Two Series, each complete in itself, price 2s. 6d. each.
The FIRST SERIES contains: The Wicked World—Pygmalion and Galatea—Charity—The Princess—The Palace of Truth—Trial by Jury.
The SECOND SERIES: Broken Hearts—Engaged—Sweethearts—Gretchen—Dan'l Druce—Tom Cobb—H.M.S. "Pinafore"—The Sorcerer—Pirates of Penzance.

EIGHT ORIGINAL COMIC OPERAS written by W. S. GILBERT. Containing, The Sorcerer—H.M.S. "Pinafore"—Pirates of Penzance—Iolanthe—Patience—Princess Ida—The Mikado—Trial by Jury. Demy 8vo, cloth limp, 2s. 6d.
THE "GILBERT AND SULLIVAN" BIRTHDAY BOOK: Quotations for Every Day in the Year, Selected from Plays by W. S. GILBERT set to Music by Sir A. SULLIVAN. Compiled by ALEX. WATSON. Royal 16mo, Jap. leather, 2s. 6d.

GLANVILLE (ERNEST), NOVELS BY.
THE LOST HEIRESS: A Tale of Love, Battle and Adventure. With 2 Illusts. by HUME NISBET. Cr. 8vo, cloth extra, 3s. 6d.
THE FOSSICKER. With a Frontispiece. Crown 8vo, cloth extra, 3s. 6d.

GLENNY.—A YEAR'S WORK IN GARDEN AND GREENHOUSE: Practical Advice to Amateur Gardeners as to the Management of the Flower, Fruit, and Frame Garden. By GEORGE GLENNY. Post 8vo, 1s.; cloth limp, 1s. 6d.

GODWIN.—LIVES OF THE NECROMANCERS. By WILLIAM GODWIN. Post 8vo, cloth limp, 2s.

GOLDEN TREASURY OF THOUGHT, THE: An Encyclopædia of QUOTATIONS. Edited by THEODORE TAYLOR. Crown 8vo, cloth gilt, 7s. 6d.

GOWING.—FIVE THOUSAND MILES IN A SLEDGE: A Midwinter Journey Across Siberia. By LIONEL F. GOWING. With 30 Illustrations by C. J. UREN, and a Map by E. WELLER. Large crown 8vo, cloth extra, 8s.

GRAHAM. — THE PROFESSOR'S WIFE: A Story. By LEONARD GRAHAM. Fcap. 8vo, picture cover, 1s.

GREEKS AND ROMANS, THE LIFE OF THE, described from Antique Monuments. By ERNST GUHL and W. KONER. Edited by Dr. F. HUEFFER. With 545 Illustrations. Large crown 8vo, cloth extra, 7s. 6d.

GREENWOOD (JAMES), WORKS BY. Cr. 8vo, cloth extra, 3s. 6d. each.
THE WILDS OF LONDON. | LOW-LIFE DEEPS.

GREVILLE (HENRY), NOVELS BY:
NIKANOR. Translated by ELIZA E. CHASE. With 8 Illusts. Cr. 8vo, cl. extra, 6s.
A NOBLE WOMAN. Translated by ALBERT D. VANDAM. Crown 8vo, cloth extra, 5s.; post 8vo, illustrated boards, 2s.

HABBERTON (JOHN, Author of "Helen's Babies"), NOVELS BY. Post 8vo, illustrated boards 2s. each; cloth limp, 2s. 6d. each.
BRUETON'S BAYOU. | COUNTRY LUCK.

HAIR, THE : Its Treatment in Health, Weakness, and Disease. Translated from the German of Dr. J. Pincus. Crown 8vo, 1s.; cloth limp, 1s. 6d.

HAKE (DR. THOMAS GORDON), POEMS BY. Cr. 8vo, cl. ex., 6s. each.
NEW SYMBOLS. | LEGENDS OF THE MORROW. | THE SERPENT PLAY.
MAIDEN ECSTASY. Small 4to, cloth extra, 8s.

HALL.—SKETCHES OF IRISH CHARACTER. By Mrs. S. C. Hall. With numerous Illustrations on Steel and Wood by Maclise, Gilbert, Harvey, and George Cruikshank. Medium 8vo, cloth extra, 7s. 6d.

HALLIDAY (ANDR.).—EVERY-DAY PAPERS. Post 8vo, bds., 2s.

HANDWRITING, THE PHILOSOPHY OF. With over 100 Facsimiles and Explanatory Text. By Don Felix de Salamanca. Post 8vo, cloth limp, 2s. 6d.

HANKY-PANKY : A Collection of Very Easy Tricks, Very Difficult Tricks, White Magic, Sleight of Hand, &c. Edited by W. H. Cremer. With 200 Illustrations. Crown 8vo, cloth extra, 4s. 6d.

HARDY (LADY DUFFUS). — PAUL WYNTER'S SACRIFICE. By Lady Duffus Hardy. Post 8vo, illustrated boards, 2s.

HARDY (THOMAS). — UNDER THE GREENWOOD TREE. By Thomas Hardy, Author of "Far from the Madding Crowd." Post 8vo, illust. bds., 2s.

HARWOOD.—THE TENTH EARL. By J. Berwick Harwood. Post 8vo, illustrated boards, 2s.

HAWEIS (MRS. H. R.), WORKS BY. Square 8vo, cloth extra, 6s. each.
THE ART OF BEAUTY. With Coloured Frontispiece and 91 Illustrations.
THE ART OF DECORATION. With Coloured Frontispiece and 74 Illustrations.
CHAUCER FOR CHILDREN. With 8 Coloured Plates and 30 Woodcuts.

THE ART OF DRESS. With 32 Illustrations. Post 8vo, 1s.; cloth, 1s. 6d.
CHAUCER FOR SCHOOLS. Demy 8vo, cloth limp, 2s. 6d.

HAWEIS (Rev. H. R., M.A.). —AMERICAN HUMORISTS : Washington Irving, Oliver Wendell Holmes, James Russell Lowell, Artemus Ward, Mark Twain, and Bret Harte. Third Edition. Crown 8vo, cloth extra, 6s.

HAWLEY SMART.—WITHOUT LOVE OR LICENCE : A Novel. By Hawley Smart. Crown 8vo, cloth extra, 3s. 6d.

HAWTHORNE. —OUR OLD HOME. By Nathaniel Hawthorne. Annotated with Passages from the Author's Note-Book, and Illustrated with 31 Photogravures. Two Vols., crown 8vo, buckram, gilt top, 15s.

HAWTHORNE (JULIAN), NOVELS BY.
Crown 8vo, cloth extra, 3s. 6d. each ; post 8vo, illustrated boards, 2s. each.
GARTH. | ELLICE QUENTIN. | BEATRIX RANDOLPH. | DUST.
SEBASTIAN STROME. | DAVID POINDEXTER.
FORTUNE'S FOOL. | THE SPECTRE OF THE CAMERA.

Post 8vo, illustrated boards, 2s. each.
MISS CADOGNA. | LOVE—OR A NAME.
MRS. GAINSBOROUGH'S DIAMONDS. Fcap. 8vo, illustrated cover, 1s.
A DREAM AND A FORGETTING. Post 8vo, cloth limp, 1s. 6d.

HAYS.—WOMEN OF THE DAY : A Biographical Dictionary of Notable Contemporaries. By Frances Hays. Crown 8vo, cloth extra, 5s.

HEATH.—MY GARDEN WILD, AND WHAT I GREW THERE. By Francis George Heath. Crown 8vo, cloth extra, gilt edges, 6s.

HELPS (SIR ARTHUR), WORKS BY. Post 8vo, cloth limp, 2s. 6d. each.
ANIMALS AND THEIR MASTERS. | SOCIAL PRESSURE.

IVAN DE BIRON : A Novel. Cr. 8vo, cl. extra, 3s. 6d. ; post 8vo, illust. bds., 2s.

HENDERSON.—AGATHA PAGE : A Novel. By Isaac Henderson. Crown 8vo, cloth extra, 3s. 6d.

HERMAN.—A LEADING LADY. By Henry Herman, joint-Author of " The Bishops' Bible." Post 8vo, cloth extra, 2s. 6d.

HERRICK'S (ROBERT) HESPERIDES, NOBLE NUMBERS, AND COMPLETE COLLECTED POEMS. With Memorial-Introduction and Notes by the Rev. A. B. GROSART, D.D.; Steel Portrait, &c. Three Vols., crown 8vo, cl. bds., 18s.

HERTZKA.—FREELAND: A Social Anticipation. By Dr. THEODOR HERTZKA. Translated by ARTHUR RANSOM. Crown 8vo, cloth extra, 6s.

HESSE-WARTEGG.—TUNIS: The Land and the People. By Chevalier ERNST VON HESSE-WARTEGG. With 22 Illustrations. Cr. 8vo, cloth extra, 3s. 6d.

HINDLEY (CHARLES), WORKS BY.
TAVERN ANECDOTES AND SAYINGS: Including the Origin of Signs, and Reminiscences connected with Taverns, Coffee Houses, Clubs, &c. With Illustrations. Crown 8vo, cloth extra, 3s. 6d.
THE LIFE AND ADVENTURES OF A CHEAP JACK. By ONE OF THE FRATERNITY. Edited by CHARLES HINDLEY. Crown 8vo, cloth extra, 3s. 6d.

HOEY.—THE LOVER'S CREED. By Mrs. CASHEL HOEY. Post 8vo, illustrated boards, 2s.

HOLLINGSHEAD (JOHN).—NIAGARA SPRAY. Crown 8vo, 1s.

HOLMES.—THE SCIENCE OF VOICE PRODUCTION AND VOICE PRESERVATION: A Popular Manual for the Use of Speakers and Singers. By GORDON HOLMES, M.D. With Illustrations. Crown 8vo, 1s.; cloth, 1s. 6d.

HOLMES (OLIVER WENDELL), WORKS BY.
THE AUTOCRAT OF THE BREAKFAST-TABLE. Illustrated by J. GORDON THOMSON. Post 8vo, cloth limp, 2s. 6d.—Another Edition, in smaller type, with an Introduction by G. A. SALA. Post 8vo, cloth limp, 2s.
THE PROFESSOR AT THE BREAKFAST-TABLE. Post 8vo, cloth limp, 2s.

HOOD'S (THOMAS) CHOICE WORKS, in Prose and Verse. With Life of the Author, Portrait, and 200 Illustrations. Crown 8vo, cloth extra, 7s. 6d.
HOOD'S WHIMS AND ODDITIES. With 85 Illustrations. Post 8vo, printed on laid paper and half-bound, 2s.

HOOD (TOM).—FROM NOWHERE TO THE NORTH POLE: A Noah's Arkæological Narrative. By TOM HOOD. With 25 Illustrations by W. BRUNTON and E. C. BARNES. Square 8vo, cloth extra, gilt edges, 6s.

HOOK'S (THEODORE) CHOICE HUMOROUS WORKS; including his Ludicrous Adventures, Bons Mots, Puns, and Hoaxes. With Life of the Author, Portraits, Facsimiles, and Illustrations. Crown 8vo, cloth extra, 7s. 6d.

HOOPER.—THE HOUSE OF RABY: A Novel. By Mrs. GEORGE HOOPER. Post 8vo, illustrated boards, 2s.

HOPKINS.—"'TWIXT LOVE AND DUTY:" A Novel. By TIGHE HOPKINS. Post 8vo, illustrated boards, 2s.

HORNE. — ORION: An Epic Poem. By RICHARD HENGIST HORNE. With Photographic Portrait by SUMMERS. Tenth Edition. Cr. 8vo, cloth extra, 7s.

HORSE (THE) AND HIS RIDER: An Anecdotic Medley. By "THORMANBY." Crown 8vo, cloth extra, 6s.

HUNT.—ESSAYS BY LEIGH HUNT: A TALE FOR A CHIMNEY CORNER, and other Pieces. Edited, with an Introduction, by EDMUND OLLIER. Post 8vo, printed on laid paper and half-bd., 2s. Also in sm. sq. 8vo, cl. extra, at same price.

HUNT (MRS. ALFRED), NOVELS BY.
Crown 8vo, cloth extra, 3s. 6d. each; post 8vo, illustrated boards, 2s. each.
THE LEADEN CASKET. | SELF-CONDEMNED. | THAT OTHER PERSON.
THORNICROFT'S MODEL. Post 8vo, illustrated boards, 2s

HYDROPHOBIA: An Account of M. PASTEUR'S System. Containing a Translation of all his Communications on the Subject, the Technique of his Method, and Statistics. By RENAUD SUZOR, M.B. Crown 8vo, cloth extra, 6s.

INGELOW (JEAN).—FATED TO BE FREE. With 24 Illustrations by G. J. PINWELL. Cr. 8vo, cloth extra, 3s. 6d.; post 8vo, illustrated boards, 2s.

INDOOR PAUPERS. By ONE OF THEM. Crown 8vo, 1s.; cloth, 1s. 6d.

IRISH WIT AND HUMOUR, SONGS OF. Collected and Edited by A. PERCEVAL GRAVES. Post 8vo, cloth limp, 2s. 6d.

JAMES.—A ROMANCE OF THE QUEEN'S HOUNDS. By CHARLES JAMES. Post 8vo, picture cover, 1s.; cloth limp, 1s. 6d.

JANVIER.—PRACTICAL KERAMICS FOR STUDENTS. By CATHERINE A. JANVIER. Crown 8vo, cloth extra, 6s.

JAY (HARRIETT), NOVELS BY. Post 8vo, illustrated boards, 2s. each.
THE DARK COLLEEN. | **THE QUEEN OF CONNAUGHT.**

JEFFERIES (RICHARD), WORKS BY. Post 8vo, cloth limp, 2s. 6d. each.
NATURE NEAR LONDON. | **THE LIFE OF THE FIELDS.** | **THE OPEN AIR.**
THE EULOGY OF RICHARD JEFFERIES. By WALTER BESANT. Second Edition. With a Photograph Portrait. Crown 8vo, cloth extra, 6s.

JENNINGS (H. J.), WORKS BY.
CURIOSITIES OF CRITICISM. Post 8vo, cloth limp, 2s. 6d.
LORD TENNYSON: A Biographical Sketch. With a Photograph. Cr. 8vo, cl., 6s.

JEROME.—STAGELAND: Curious Habits and Customs of its Inhabitants. By JEROME K. JEROME. With 64 Illustrations by J. BERNARD PARTRIDGE. Sixteenth Thousand. Fcap. 4to, cloth extra, 3s. 6d.

JERROLD.—THE BARBER'S CHAIR; & THE HEDGEHOG LETTERS. By DOUGLAS JERROLD. Post 8vo, printed on laid paper and half-bound, 2s.

JERROLD (TOM), WORKS BY. Post 8vo, 1s. each; cloth limp, 1s. 6d. each.
THE GARDEN THAT PAID THE RENT.
HOUSEHOLD HORTICULTURE: A Gossip about Flowers. Illustrated.
OUR KITCHEN GARDEN: The Plants we Grow, and How we Cook Them.

JESSE.—SCENES AND OCCUPATIONS OF A COUNTRY LIFE. By EDWARD JESSE. Post 8vo, cloth limp, 2s.

JONES (WILLIAM, F.S.A.), WORKS BY. Cr. 8vo, cl. extra, 7s. 6d. each.
FINGER-RING LORE: Historical, Legendary, and Anecdotal. With nearly 300 Illustrations. Second Edition, Revised and Enlarged.
CREDULITIES, PAST AND PRESENT. Including the Sea and Seamen, Miners, Talismans, Word and Letter Divination, Exorcising and Blessing of Animals, Birds, Eggs, Luck, &c. With an Etched Frontispiece.
CROWNS AND CORONATIONS: A History of Regalia. With 100 Illustrations.

JONSON'S (BEN) WORKS. With Notes Critical and Explanatory, and a Biographical Memoir by WILLIAM GIFFORD. Edited by Colonel CUNNINGHAM. Three Vols., crown 8vo, cloth extra, 6s. each.

JOSEPHUS, THE COMPLETE WORKS OF. Translated by WHISTON. Containing "The Antiquities of the Jews" and "The Wars of the Jews." With 52 Illustrations and Maps. Two Vols., demy 8vo, half-bound, 12s. 6d.

KEMPT.—PENCIL AND PALETTE: Chapters on Art and Artists. By ROBERT KEMPT. Post 8vo, cloth limp, 2s. 6d.

KERSHAW. — COLONIAL FACTS AND FICTIONS: Humorous Sketches. By MARK KERSHAW. Post 8vo, illustrated boards, 2s.; cloth, 2s. 6d.

KEYSER. — CUT BY THE MESS: A Novel. By ARTHUR KEYSER. Crown 8vo, picture cover, 1s.; cloth limp, 1s. 6d.

KING (R. ASHE), NOVELS BY. Cr. 8vo, cl., 3s. 6d. ea.; post 8vo, bds., 2s. ea.
A DRAWN GAME. | **"THE WEARING OF THE GREEN."**
PASSION'S SLAVE. Post 8vo, illustrated boards, 2s.
BELL BARRY. 2 vols., crown 8vo.

KINGSLEY (HENRY), NOVELS BY.
OAKSHOTT CASTLE. Post 8vo, illustrated boards, 2s.
NUMBER SEVENTEEN. Crown 8vo, cloth extra, 3s. 6d.

KNIGHTS (THE) OF THE LION: A Romance of the Thirteenth Century. Edited, with an Introduction, by the MARQUESS of LORNE, K.T. Cr. 8vo, cl. ex., 6s.

KNIGHT.—THE PATIENT'S VADE MECUM: How to Get Most Benefit from Medical Advice. By WILLIAM KNIGHT, M.R.C.S., and EDWARD KNIGHT, L.R.C.P. Crown 8vo, 1s.; cloth limp, 1s. 6d.

LAMB'S (CHARLES) COMPLETE WORKS, in Prose and Verse. Edited, with Notes and Introduction, by R. H. SHEPHERD. With Two Portraits and Facsimile of a page of the "Essay on Roast Pig." Cr. 8vo, cl. ex., 7s. 6d.

THE ESSAYS OF ELIA. Post 8vo, printed on laid paper and half-bound, 2s.

LITTLE ESSAYS: Sketches and Characters by CHARLES LAMB, selected from his Letters by PERCY FITZGERALD. Post 8vo, cloth limp, 2s. 6d.

LANDOR.—CITATION AND EXAMINATION OF WILLIAM SHAKS-PEARE, &c., be ore Sir THOMAS LUCY, touching Deer-stealing, 19th September, 1582. To which is added, **A CONFERENCE OF MASTER EDMUND SPENSER** with the Earl of Essex, touching the State of Ireland, 1595. By WALTER SAVAGE LANDOR. Fcap. 8vo, half-Roxburghe, 2s. 6d.

LANE.—THE THOUSAND AND ONE NIGHTS, commonly called in England THE ARABIAN NIGHTS' ENTERTAINMENTS. Translated from the Arabic, with Notes, by EDWARD WILLIAM LANE. Illustrated by many hundred Engravings from Designs by HARVEY. Edited by EDWARD STANLEY POOLE. With a Preface by STANLEY LANE-POOLE. Three Vols., demy 8vo, cloth extra, 7s. 6d. each.

LARWOOD (JACOB), WORKS BY.
THE STORY OF THE LONDON PARKS. With Illusts. Cr. 8vo, cl. extra, 3s. 6d.
ANECDOTES OF THE CLERGY: The Antiquities, Humours, and Eccentricities of the Cloth. Post 8vo, printed on laid paper and half-bound, 2s.

Post 8vo, cloth limp, 2s. 6d. each.

| FORENSIC ANECDOTES. | THEATRICAL ANECDOTES. |

LEIGH (HENRY S.), WORKS BY.
CAROLS OF COCKAYNE. Printed on hand-made paper, bound in buckram, 5s.
JEUX D'ESPRIT. Edited by HENRY S. LEIGH. Post 8vo, cloth limp, 2s. 6d.

LEYS (JOHN).—THE LINDSAYS: A Romance. Post 8vo, illust. bds., 2s.

LIFE IN LONDON; or, The History of JERRY HAWTHORN and COR-INTHIAN TOM. With CRUIKSHANK's Coloured Illustrations. Crown 8vo, cloth extra, 7s. 6d.   *[New Edition preparing.*

LINSKILL.—IN EXCHANGE FOR A SOUL. By MARY LINSKILL. Post 8vo, illustrated boards, 2s.

LINTON (E. LYNN), WORKS BY. Post 8vo, cloth limp, 2s. 6d. each.

| WITCH STORIES. | OURSELVES: ESSAYS ON WOMEN. |

Crown 8vo, cloth extra, 3s. 6d. each; post 8vo, illustrated boards, 2s. each.

SOWING THE WIND.	UNDER WHICH LORD?
PATRICIA KEMBALL.	"MY LOVE!" IONE.
ATONEMENT OF LEAM DUNDAS.	PASTON CAREW, Millionaire & Miser.
THE WORLD WELL LOST.	

Post 8vo, illustrated boards, 2s. each.

| THE REBEL OF THE FAMILY. | WITH A SILKEN THREAD. |

LONGFELLOW'S POETICAL WORKS. With numerous Illustrations on Steel and Wood. Crown 8vo, cloth extra, 7s. 6d.

LUCY.—GIDEON FLEYCE: A Novel. By HENRY W. LUCY. Crown 8vo, cloth extra, 3s. 6d.; post 8vo, illustrated boards, 2s.

LUSIAD (THE) OF CAMOENS. Translated into English Spenserian Verse by ROBERT FFRENCH DUFF. With 11 Plates. Demy 8vo, cloth boards, 18s.

MACALPINE (AVERY), NOVELS BY.
TERESA ITASCA, and other Stories. Crown 8vo, bound in canvas, 2s. 6d.
BROKEN WINGS. With 6 Illusts. by W. J. HENNESSY. Crown 8vo, cloth extra, 6s.

MACCOLL (HUGH), NOVELS BY.
MR. STRANGER'S SEALED PACKET. Second Edition. Crown 8vo, cl. extra, 3s.
EDNOR WHITLOCK. Crown 8vo cloth extra 6s.

McCARTHY (JUSTIN, M.P.), WORKS BY.

A HISTORY OF OUR OWN TIMES, from the Accession of Queen Victoria to the General Election of 1880. Four Vols. demy 8vo, cloth extra, 12s. each.—Also a POPULAR EDITION, in Four Vols., crown 8vo, cloth extra, 6s. each.—And a JUBILEE EDITION, with an Appendix of Events to the end of 1886, in Two Vols., large crown 8vo, cloth extra, 7s. 6d. each.

A SHORT HISTORY OF OUR OWN TIMES. One Vol., crown 8vo, cloth extra, 6s.
—Also a CHEAP POPULAR EDITION, post 8vo, cloth limp, 2s. 6d.

A HISTORY OF THE FOUR GEORGES. Four Vols. demy 8vo, cloth extra, 12s. each. [Vols. I. & II. ready

Crown 8vo, cloth extra, 3s. 6d. each; post 8vo, illustrated boards, 2s. each.

THE WATERDALE NEIGHBOURS.	MISS MISANTHROPE.
MY ENEMY'S DAUGHTER.	DONNA QUIXOTE.
A FAIR SAXON.	THE COMET OF A SEASON.
LINLEY ROCHFORD.	MAID OF ATHENS.
DEAR LADY DISDAIN.	CAMIOLA: A Girl with a Fortune.

"THE RIGHT HONOURABLE." By JUSTIN McCARTHY, M.P., and Mrs. CAMPBELL-PRAED. Fourth Edition. Crown 8vo, cloth extra, 6s.

McCARTHY (JUSTIN H., M.P.), WORKS BY.

THE FRENCH REVOLUTION. Four Vols., 8vo, 12s. each. [Vols. I. & II. ready.
AN OUTLINE OF THE HISTORY OF IRELAND. Crown 8vo, 1s.: cloth, 1s. 6d.
IRELAND SINCE THE UNION: Irish History, 1798–1886. Crown 8vo, cloth, 6s.
ENGLAND UNDER GLADSTONE, 1880-85. Crown 8vo, cloth extra, 6s.
HAFIZ IN LONDON: Poems. Small 8vo, gold cloth, 3s. 6d.
HARLEQUINADE: Poems. Small 4to, Japanese vellum, 8s.
OUR SENSATION NOVEL. Crown 8vo, picture cover, 1s.; cloth limp, 1s. 6d.
DOOM! An Atlantic Episode. Crown 8vo, picture cover, 1s.
DOLLY: A Sketch. Crown 8vo, picture cover, 1s.; cloth limp, 1s. 6d.
LILY LASS: A Romance. Crown 8vo, picture cover, 1s.; cloth limp, 1s. 6d.

MACDONALD (GEORGE, LL.D.), WORKS BY.

WORKS OF FANCY AND IMAGINATION. Ten Vols., cl. extra, gilt edges, in cloth case. 21s. Or the Vols. may be had separately, in grolier cl., at 2s. 6d. each.

Vol. I. WITHIN AND WITHOUT.—THE HIDDEN LIFE.
„ II. THE DISCIPLE.—THE GOSPEL WOMEN.—BOOK OF SONNETS.—ORGAN SONGS.
„ III. VIOLIN SONGS.—SONGS OF THE DAYS AND NIGHTS.—A BOOK OF DREAMS.—ROADSIDE POEMS.—POEMS FOR CHILDREN.
„ IV. PARABLES.—BALLADS.—SCOTCH SONGS.
„ V. & VI. PHANTASTES: A Faerie Romance. | Vol. VII. THE PORTENT.
„ VIII. THE LIGHT PRINCESS.—THE GIANT'S HEART.—SHADOWS.
„ IX. CROSS PURPOSES.—THE GOLDEN KEY.—THE CARASOYN.—LITTLE DAYLIGHT.
„ X. THE CRUEL PAINTER.—THE WOW o' RIVVEN.—THE CASTLE.—THE BROKEN SWORDS.—THE GRAY WOLF.—UNCLE CORNELIUS

THE COMPLETE POETICAL WORKS OF DR. GEORGE MACDONALD. Collected and arranged by the Author. Crown 8vo, buckram, 6s. [Shortly.

MACDONELL.—QUAKER COUSINS : A Novel. By AGNES MACDONELL.
Crown 8vo, cloth extra, 3s. 6d.; post 8vo, illustrated boards 2s.

MACGREGOR. — PASTIMES AND PLAYERS: Notes on Popular
Games. By ROBERT MACGREGOR. Post 8vo, cloth limp, 2s. 6d.

MACKAY.—INTERLUDES AND UNDERTONES; or, Music at Twilight.
By CHARLES MACKAY, LL.D. Crown 8vo, cloth extra, 6s.

MACLISE PORTRAIT GALLERY (THE) OF ILLUSTRIOUS LITER-
ARY CHARACTERS: 85 PORTRAITS; with Memoirs — Biographical, Critical, Bibliographical, and Anecdotal—illustrative of the Literature of the former half of the Present Century, by WILLIAM BATES, B.A. Crown 8vo, cloth extra, 7s. 6d.

MACQUOID (MRS.), WORKS BY. Square 8vo, cloth extra, 7s. 6d. each.

IN THE ARDENNES. With 50 Illustrations by THOMAS R. MACQUOID.
PICTURES AND LEGENDS FROM NORMANDY AND BRITTANY. With 34 Illustrations by THOMAS R. MACQUOID.
THROUGH NORMANDY. With 92 Illustrations by T. R. MACQUOID, and a Map.
THROUGH BRITTANY. With 35 Illustrations by T. R. MACQUOID, and a Map.
ABOUT YORKSHIRE. With 67 Illustrations by T. R. MACQUOID.

Post 8vo, illustrated boards, 2s. each.

THE EVIL EYE, and other Stories. | **LOST ROSE.**

MAGIC LANTERN, THE, and its Management: including full Practical Directions for producing the Limelight, making Oxygen Gas, and preparing Lantern Slides. By T. C. HEPWORTH. With 10 Illustrations. Cr. 8vo. 1s.; cloth. 1s. 6d.

MAGICIAN'S OWN BOOK, THE: Performances with Cups and Balls, Eggs, Hats, Handkerchiefs, &c. All from actual Experience. Edited by W. H. CREMER. With 200 Illustrations. Crown 8vo, cloth extra, 4s. 6d.

MAGNA CHARTA: An Exact Facsimile of the Original in the British Museum, 3 feet by 2 feet, with Arms and Seals emblazoned in Gold and Colours, 5s.

MALLOCK (W. H.), WORKS BY.
THE NEW REPUBLIC. Post 8vo, picture cover, 2s.; cloth limp, 2s. 6d.
THE NEW PAUL & VIRGINIA: Positivism on an Island. Post 8vo, cloth, 2s. 6d.
POEMS. Small 4to, parchment, 8s.
IS LIFE WORTH LIVING? Crown 8vo, cloth extra, 6s.

MALLORY'S (SIR THOMAS) MORT D'ARTHUR: The Stories of King Arthur and of the Knights of the Round Table. (A Selection.) Edited by B. MONTGOMERIE RANKING. Post 8vo, cloth limp, 2s.

MARK TWAIN, WORKS BY. Crown 8vo, cloth extra, 7s. 6d. each.
THE CHOICE WORKS OF MARK TWAIN. Revised and Corrected throughout by the Author. With Life, Portrait, and numerous Illustrations.
ROUGHING IT, and INNOCENTS AT HOME. With 200 Illusts. by F. A. FRASER.
THE GILDED AGE. By MARK TWAIN and C. D. WARNER. With 212 Illustrations.
MARK TWAIN'S LIBRARY OF HUMOUR. With 197 Illustrations.
A YANKEE AT THE COURT OF KING ARTHUR. With 220 Illusts. by BEARD.

Crown 8vo, cloth extra (illustrated), 7s. 6d. each; post 8vo, illust. boards, 2s. each.
THE INNOCENTS ABROAD; or New Pilgrim's Progress. With 234 Illustrations.
(The Two-Shilling Edition is entitled MARK TWAIN'S PLEASURE TRIP.)
THE ADVENTURES OF TOM SAWYER. With 111 Illustrations.
A TRAMP ABROAD. With 314 Illustrations.
THE PRINCE AND THE PAUPER. With 190 Illustrations.
LIFE ON THE MISSISSIPPI. With 300 Illustrations.
ADVENTURES OF HUCKLEBERRY FINN. With 174 Illusts. by E. W. KEMBLE.

THE STOLEN WHITE ELEPHANT, &c. Cr. 8vo, cl., 6s.; post 8vo, illust. bds., 2s.

MARLOWE'S WORKS. Including his Translations. Edited, with Notes and Introductions, by Col. CUNNINGHAM. Crown 8vo, cloth extra, 6s.

MARRYAT (FLORENCE), NOVELS BY. Post 8vo, illust. boards, 2s. each.
A HARVEST OF WILD OATS. | WRITTEN IN FIRE. | FIGHTING THE AIR.
OPEN! SESAME! Crown 8vo, cloth extra, 3s. 6d.; post 8vo, picture boards, 2s.

MASSINGER'S PLAYS. From the Text of WILLIAM GIFFORD. Edited by Col. CUNNINGHAM. Crown 8vo, cloth extra, 6s.

MASTERMAN.—HALF-A-DOZEN DAUGHTERS: A Novel. By J. MASTERMAN. Post 8vo, illustrated boards, 2s.

MATTHEWS.—A SECRET OF THE SEA, &c. By BRANDER MATTHEWS. Post 8vo, illustrated boards, 2s.; cloth limp, 2s. 6d.

MAYHEW.—LONDON CHARACTERS AND THE HUMOROUS SIDE OF LONDON LIFE. By HENRY MAYHEW. With Illusts. Crown 8vo, cloth, 3s. 6d.

MENKEN.—INFELICIA: Poems by ADAH ISAACS MENKEN. With Biographical Preface, Illustrations by F. E. LUMMIS and F. O. C. DARLEY, and Facsimile of a Letter from CHARLES DICKENS. Small 4to, cloth extra, 7s. 6d.

MEXICAN MUSTANG (ON A), through Texas to the Rio Grande. By A. E. SWEET and J. ARMOY KNOX. With 265 Illusts. Cr. 8vo, cloth extra, 7s. 6d.

MIDDLEMASS (JEAN), NOVELS BY. Post 8vo, illust. boards, 2s. each.
TOUCH AND GO. | MR. DORILLION.

MILLER.—PHYSIOLOGY FOR THE YOUNG; or, The House of Life: Human Physiology, with its application to the Preservation of Health. By Mrs. F. FENWICK MILLER. With numerous Illustrations. Post 8vo, cloth limp, 2s. 6d.

MILTON (J. L.), WORKS BY. Post 8vo, 1s. each; cloth, 1s. 6d. each.
THE HYGIENE OF THE SKIN. With Directions for Diet, Soaps, Baths, &c.
THE BATH IN DISEASES OF THE SKIN.
THE LAWS OF LIFE, AND THEIR RELATION TO DISEASES OF THE SKIN.
THE SUCCESSFUL TREATMENT OF LEPROSY. Demy 8vo, 1s.

MINTO (WM.)—WAS SHE GOOD OR BAD? Cr. 8vo, 1s. ; cloth, 1s. 6d.

MOLESWORTH (MRS.), NOVELS BY.
HATHERCOURT RECTORY. Post 8vo, illustrated boards, 2s.
THAT GIRL IN BLACK. Crown 8vo, picture cover, 1s. ; cloth, 1s. 6d.

MOORE (THOMAS), WORKS BY.
THE EPICUREAN; and ALCIPHRON. Post 8vo, half-bound, 2s.
PROSE AND VERSE, Humorous, Satirical, and Sentimental, by THOMAS MOORE:
    with Suppressed Passages from the MEMOIRS OF LORD BYRON. Edited by R.
    HERNE SHEPHERD. With Portrait. Crown 8vo, cloth extra, 7s. 6d.

MUDDOCK (J. E.), STORIES BY.
STORIES WEIRD AND WONDERFUL. Post 8vo, illust. boards, 2s. ; cloth, 2s. 6d.
THE DEAD MAN'S SECRET; or, The Valley of Gold: A Narrative of Strange
    Adventure. With a Frontispiece by F. BARNARD. Crown 8vo, cloth extra, 5s. ;
    post 8vo, illustrated boards, 2s.

MURRAY (D. CHRISTIE), NOVELS BY.
    Crown 8vo, cloth extra, 3s. 6d. each ; post 8vo, illustrated boards, 2s. each.
A LIFE'S ATONEMENT. | A MODEL FATHER. | A BIT OF HUMAN NATURE.
JOSEPH'S COAT. | HEARTS. | FIRST PERSON SINGULAR.
COALS OF FIRE. | THE WAY OF THE | CYNIC FORTUNE.
VAL STRANGE. | WORLD. |

BY THE GATE OF THE SEA. Post 8vo, picture boards, 2s.
OLD BLAZER'S HERO. With Three Illustrations by A. McCORMICK. Crown 8vo,
    cloth extra, 6s. ; post 8vo, illustrated boards, 2s.

MURRAY (D. CHRISTIE) & HENRY HERMAN, WORKS BY.
    Crown 8vo, cloth extra, 6s. each ; post 8vo, illustrated boards, 2s. each.
ONE TRAVELLER RETURNS.
PAUL JONES'S ALIAS. With 13 Illustrations by A. FORESTIER and G. NICOLET.
THE BISHOPS' BIBLE. Crown 8vo, cloth extra, 3s. 6d.

MURRAY.—A GAME OF BLUFF: A Novel By HENRY MURRAY.
Post 8vo, picture boards, 2s. ; cloth limp, 2s. 6d.

NISBET (HUME), BOOKS BY.
"BAIL UP!" A Romance of BUSHRANGERS AND BLACKS. Cr. 8vo, cl. ex., 3s. 6d.
LESSONS IN ART. With 21 Illustrations. Crown 8vo, cloth extra, 2s. 6d.

NOVELISTS.—HALF-HOURS WITH THE BEST NOVELISTS OF
THE CENTURY. Edit. by H. T. MACKENZIE BELL. Cr. 8vo, cl., 3s. 6d. [Preparing.

O'CONNOR. — LORD BEACONSFIELD: A Biography. By T. P.
O'CONNOR, M.P. Sixth Edition, with an Introduction. Crown 8vo, cloth extra, 5s.

O'HANLON (ALICE), NOVELS BY. Post 8vo, illustrated boards, 2s. each.
THE UNFORESEEN. | CHANCE? OR FATE?

OHNET (GEORGES), NOVELS BY.
DOCTOR RAMEAU. Translated by Mrs. CASHEL HOEY. With 9 Illustrations by
    E. BAYARD. Crown 8vo, cloth extra, 6s. ; post 8vo, illustrated boards, 2s.
A LAST LOVE. Translated by ALBERT D. VANDAM. Crown 8vo, cloth extra, 5s. ;
    post 8vo, illustrated boards, 2s.
A WEIRD GIFT. Translated by ALBERT D. VANDAM. Crown 8vo, cloth, 3s. 6d.

OLIPHANT (MRS.), NOVELS BY. Post 8vo, illustrated boards, 2s. each.
THE PRIMROSE PATH. | THE GREATEST HEIRESS IN ENGLAND.
WHITELADIES. With Illustrations by ARTHUR HOPKINS and HENRY WOODS,
    A.R.A. Crown 8vo, cloth extra, 3s. 6d. ; post 8vo, illustrated boards, 2s.

O'REILLY (MRS.).—PHŒBE'S FORTUNES. Post 8vo, illust. bds., 2s.

O'SHAUGHNESSY (ARTHUR), POEMS BY.
LAYS OF FRANCE. Crown 8vo, cloth extra, 10s. 6d.
MUSIC AND MOONLIGHT. Fcap. 8vo, cloth extra, 7s. 6d.
SONGS OF A WORKER. Fcap. 8vo, cloth extra, 7s. 6d.

OUIDA, NOVELS BY. Cr. 8vo, cl., **3s. 6d.** each; post 8vo, illust. bds., **2s.** each.

HELD IN BONDAGE.	FOLLE-FARINE.	MOTHS.
TRICOTRIN.	A DOG OF FLANDERS.	PIPISTRELLO.
STRATHMORE.	PASCAREL.	A VILLAGE COMMUNE.
CHANDOS.	TWO LITTLE WOODEN	IN MAREMMA.
CECIL CASTLEMAINE'S	SHOES.	BIMBI.
GAGE.	SIGNA.	WANDA.
IDALIA.	IN A WINTER CITY.	FRESCOES.
UNDER TWO FLAGS.	ARIADNE.	PRINCESS NAPRAXINE.
PUCK.	FRIENDSHIP.	OTHMAR.	GUILDEROY.

Crown 8vo, cloth extra, **3s. 6d.** each.

SYRLIN. | RUFFINO.

WISDOM, WIT, AND PATHOS, selected from the Works of OUIDA by F. SYDNEY MORRIS. Post 8vo, cloth extra, **5s.**—CHEAP EDITION, illustrated boards, **2s.**

PAGE (H. A.), WORKS BY.
THOREAU: His Life and Aims. With Portrait. Post 8vo, cloth limp, **2s. 6d.**
ANIMAL ANECDOTES. Arranged on a New Principle. Crown 8vo, cloth extra, **5s.**

PASCAL'S PROVINCIAL LETTERS. A New Translation, with Historical Introduction and Notes by T. M'CRIE, D.D. Post 8vo, cloth limp, **2s.**

PAUL.—GENTLE AND SIMPLE. By MARGARET A. PAUL. With Frontispiece by HELEN PATERSON. Crown 8vo, cloth, **3s. 6d.**; post 8vo, illust. boards, **2s.**

PAYN (JAMES), NOVELS BY.
Crown 8vo, cloth extra, **3s. 6d.** each; post 8vo, illustrated boards, **2s.** each.

LOST SIR MASSINGBERD.	A GRAPE FROM A THORN.
WALTER'S WORD.	FROM EXILE.
LESS BLACK THAN WE'RE	SOME PRIVATE VIEWS.
PAINTED.	THE CANON'S WARD.
BY PROXY.	THE TALK OF THE TOWN.
HIGH SPIRITS.	HOLIDAY TASKS.
UNDER ONE ROOF.	GLOW-WORM TALES.
A CONFIDENTIAL AGENT.	THE MYSTERY OF MIRBRIDGE.

Post 8vo, illustrated boards, **2s.** each.

HUMOROUS STORIES.	THE CLYFFARDS OF CLYFFE.
THE FOSTER BROTHERS.	FOUND DEAD.
THE FAMILY SCAPEGRACE.	GWENDOLINE'S HARVEST.
MARRIED BENEATH HIM.	A MARINE RESIDENCE.
BENTINCK'S TUTOR.	MIRK ABBEY.
A PERFECT TREASURE.	NOT WOOED, BUT WON.
A COUNTY FAMILY.	TWO HUNDRED POUNDS REWARD.
LIKE FATHER, LIKE SON.	THE BEST OF HUSBANDS.
A WOMAN'S VENGEANCE.	HALVES.
CARLYON'S YEAR.	CECIL'S TRYST.	FALLEN FORTUNES.
MURPHY'S MASTER.	WHAT HE COST HER.
AT HER MERCY.	KIT: A MEMORY.	FOR CASH ONLY.

Crown 8vo, cloth extra, **3s. 6d.** each.

IN PERIL AND PRIVATION: Stories of MARINE ADVENTURE Re-told. With 17 Illustrations.
THE BURNT MILLION. | THE WORD AND THE WILL.
SUNNY STORIES, and some SHADY ONES. With a Frontispiece by FRED. BARNARD.

NOTES FROM THE "NEWS." Crown 8vo, portrait cover **1s.**; cloth, **1s. 6d.**

PENNELL (H. CHOLMONDELEY), WORKS BY. Post 8vo, cl., **2s. 6d.** each.
PUCK ON PEGASUS. With Illustrations.
PEGASUS RE-SADDLED. With Ten full-page Illustrations by G. DU MAURIER.
THE MUSES OF MAYFAIR. Vers de Société, Selected by H. C. PENNELL.

PHELPS (E. STUART), WORKS BY. Post 8vo, **1s.** each; cloth, **1s. 6d.** each.
BEYOND THE GATES. By the Author | AN OLD MAID'S PARADISE.
of "The Gates Ajar." | BURGLARS IN PARADISE.

JACK THE FISHERMAN. Illustrated by C. W. REED. Cr. 8vo, **1s.**; cloth, **1s. 6d.**

PIRKIS (C. L.), NOVELS BY.
TROOPING WITH CROWS. Fcap. 8vo, picture cover, **1s.**
LADY LOVELACE. Post 8vo, illustrated boards, **2s.**

PLANCHE (J. R.), WORKS BY.
THE PURSUIVANT OF ARMS; or, Heraldry Founded upon Facts. With Coloured Frontispiece, Five Plates, and 209 Illusts. Crown 8vo, cloth, 7s. 6d.
SONGS AND POEMS, 1819-1879. Introduction by Mrs. MACKARNESS. Cr. 8vo, cl., 6s.

PLUTARCH'S LIVES OF ILLUSTRIOUS MEN. Translated from the
Greek, with Notes Critical and Historical, and a Life of Plutarch, by JOHN and WILLIAM LANGHORNE. With Portraits. Two Vols., demy 8vo, half-bound, 10s. 6d.

POE'S (EDGAR ALLAN) CHOICE WORKS, in Prose and Poetry. Intro-
duction b. CHAS. BAUDELAIRE, Portrait, and Facsimiles. Cr 8vo, cloth, 7s. 6d.
THE MYSTERY OF MARIE ROGET, &c. Post 8vo, illustrated boards, 2s.

POPE'S POETICAL WORKS. Post 8vo, cloth limp, 2s.

PRICE (E. C.), NOVELS BY.
Crown 8vo, cloth extra, 3s. 6d. each; post 8vo, illustrated boards, 2s. each.
VALENTINA. | THE FOREIGNERS. | MRS. LANCASTER'S RIVAL.
GERALD. Post 8vo, illustrated boards, 2s.

PRINCESS OLGA.—RADNA; or, The Great Conspiracy of 1881. By
the Princess OLGA. Crown 8vo, cloth extra, 6s.

PROCTOR (RICHARD A., B.A.), WORKS BY.
FLOWERS OF THE SKY. With 55 Illusts. Small crown 8vo, cloth extra, 3s. 6d.
EASY STAR LESSONS. With Star Maps for Every Night in the Year, Drawings of the Constellations, &c. Crown 8vo, cloth extra, 6s.
FAMILIAR SCIENCE STUDIES. Crown 8vo, cloth extra, 6s.
SATURN AND ITS SYSTEM. With 13 Steel Plates. Demy 8vo, cloth ex., 10s. 6d.
MYSTERIES OF TIME AND SPACE. With Illustrations. Cr. 8vo, cloth extra, 6s.
THE UNIVERSE OF SUNS. With numerous Illustrations. Cr. 8vo, cloth ex., 6s.
WAGES AND WANTS OF SCIENCE WORKERS. Crown 8vo, 1s. 6d.

PRYCE.—MISS MAXWELL'S AFFECTIONS. By RICHARD PRYCE,
Author of "The Ugly Story of Miss Wetherby," &c. 2 vols., crown 8vo. [Shortly.

RAMBOSSON.—POPULAR ASTRONOMY. By J. RAMBOSSON, Laureate
of the Institute of France. With numerous Illusts. Crown 8vo, cloth extra, 7s. 6d.

RANDOLPH.—AUNT ABIGAIL DYKES: A Novel. By Lt.-Colonel
GEORGE RANDOLPH, U.S.A. Crown 8vo, cloth extra, 7s. 6d.

READE (CHARLES), NOVELS BY.
Crown 8vo, cloth extra, illustrated, 3s. 6d. each; post 8vo, illust. bds., 2s. each.
PEG WOFFINGTON. Illustrated by S. L. FILDES, R.A.—Also a POCKET EDITION, set in New Type, in Elzevir style, fcap. 8vo, half-leather, 2s. 6d.
CHRISTIE JOHNSTONE. Illustrated by WILLIAM SMALL.—Also a POCKET EDITION, set in New Type, in Elzevir style, fcap. 8vo, half-leather, 2s. 6d.
IT IS NEVER TOO LATE TO MEND. Illustrated by G. J. PINWELL.
THE COURSE OF TRUE LOVE NEVER DID RUN SMOOTH. Illustrated by HELEN PATERSON.
THE AUTOBIOGRAPHY OF A THIEF, &c. Illustrated by MATT STRETCH.
LOVE ME LITTLE, LOVE ME LONG. Illustrated by M. ELLEN EDWARDS.
THE DOUBLE MARRIAGE. Illusts. by Sir JOHN GILBERT, R.A., and C. KEENE.
THE CLOISTER AND THE HEARTH. Illustrated by CHARLES KEENE.
HARD CASH. Illustrated by F. W. LAWSON.
GRIFFITH GAUNT. Illustrated by S. L. FILDES, R.A., and WILLIAM SMALL.
FOUL PLAY. Illustrated by GEORGE DU MAURIER.
PUT YOURSELF IN HIS PLACE. Illustrated by ROBERT BARNES.
A TERRIBLE TEMPTATION. Illustrated by EDWARD HUGHES and A. W. COOPER.
A SIMPLETON. Illustrated by KATE CRAUFURD.
THE WANDERING HEIR. Illustrated by HELEN PATERSON, S. L. FILDES, R.A., C. GREEN, and HENRY WOODS, A.R.A.
A WOMAN-HATER. Illustrated by THOMAS COULDERY.
SINGLEHEART AND DOUBLEFACE. Illustrated by P. MACNAB.
GOOD STORIES OF MEN AND OTHER ANIMALS. Illustrated by E. A. ABBEY, PERCY MACQUOID, R.W.S., and JOSEPH NASH.
THE JILT, and other Stories. Illustrated by JOSEPH NASH.
READIANA. With a Steel-plate Portrait of CHARLES READE.
BIBLE CHARACTERS: Studies of David, Paul, &c. Fcap. 8vo, leatherette, 1s.

SELECTIONS FROM THE WORKS OF CHARLES READE. With an Introduction by Mrs. ALEX. IRELAND, and a Steel-Plate Portrait. Crown 8vo, buckram, 6s.

RIDDELL (MRS. J. H.), NOVELS BY.
Crown 8vo, cloth extra, **3s. 6d.** each; post 8vo, illustrated boards, **2s.** each.
HER MOTHER'S DARLING. | WEIRD STORIES.
THE PRINCE OF WALES'S GARDEN PARTY.
Post 8vo, illustrated boards, **2s.** each.
UNINHABITED HOUSE. | FAIRY WATER. | MYSTERY IN PALACE GARDENS.

RIMMER (ALFRED), WORKS BY. Square 8vo, cloth gilt, **7s. 6d.** each.
OUR OLD COUNTRY TOWNS. With 55 Illustrations.
RAMBLES ROUND ETON AND HARROW. With 50 Illustrations.
ABOUT ENGLAND WITH DICKENS. With 58 Illusts. by C. A. VANDERHOOF, &c.

ROBINSON CRUSOE. By DANIEL DEFOE. (MAJOR'S EDITION.) With 37 Illustrations by GEORGE CRUIKSHANK. Post 8vo, half-bound, **2s.**

ROBINSON (F. W.), NOVELS BY.
Crown 8vo, cloth extra, **3s. 6d.** each; post 8vo, illustrated boards, **2s.** each.
WOMEN ARE STRANGE. | THE HANDS OF JUSTICE.

ROBINSON (PHIL), WORKS BY. Crown 8vo, cloth extra, **7s. 6d.** each.
THE POETS' BIRDS. | THE POETS' BEASTS.
THE POETS AND NATURE: REPTILES, FISHES, INSECTS.   [Preparing.

ROCHEFOUCAULD'S MAXIMS AND MORAL REFLECTIONS. With Notes, and an Introductory Essay by SAINTE-BEUVE. Post 8vo, cloth limp, **2s.**

ROLL OF BATTLE ABBEY, THE: A List of the Principal Warriors who came from Normandy with William the Conqueror, and Settled in this Country, A.D. 1066-7. With Arms emblazoned in Gold and Colours. Handsomely printed. **5s.**

ROWLEY (HON. HUGH), WORKS BY. Post 8vo, cloth, **2s. 6d.** each.
PUNIANA: RIDDLES AND JOKES. With numerous Illustrations.
MORE PUNIANA. Profusely Illustrated.

RUNCIMAN (JAMES), STORIES BY.
Post 8vo, illustrated boards, **2s.** each; cloth limp, **2s. 6d.** each.
SKIPPERS AND SHELLBACKS. | GRACE BALMAIGN'S SWEETHEART.
SCHOOLS AND SCHOLARS.

RUSSELL (W. CLARK), BOOKS AND NOVELS BY:
Crown 8vo, cloth extra, **6s.** each; post 8vo, illustrated boards, **2s.** each.
ROUND THE GALLEY-FIRE. | A BOOK FOR THE HAMMOCK.
IN THE MIDDLE WATCH. | MYSTERY OF THE "OCEAN STAR."
A VOYAGE TO THE CAPE. | THE ROMANCE OF JENNY HARLOWE.
ON THE FO'K'SLE HEAD. Post 8vo, illustrated boards, **2s.**
AN OCEAN TRAGEDY. Cr. 8vo, cloth extra, **3s. 6d.**; post 8vo, illust. bds., **2s.**
MY SHIPMATE LOUISE. Crown 8vo, cloth extra, **3s. 6d.**

SAINT AUBYN (ALAN), NOVELS BY.
A FELLOW OF TRINITY. With a Note by OLIVER WENDELL HOLMES and a Frontispiece. Crown 8vo, cloth extra, **3s. 6d.**; post 8vo, illust. boards, **2s.**
THE JUNIOR DEAN. 3 vols., crown 8vo.   [Shortly.

SALA.—GASLIGHT AND DAYLIGHT. By GEORGE AUGUSTUS SALA. Post 8vo, illustrated boards, **2s.**

SANSON.—SEVEN GENERATIONS OF EXECUTIONERS: Memoirs of the Sanson Family (1688 to 1847). Crown 8vo, cloth extra, **3s. 6d.**

SAUNDERS (JOHN), NOVELS BY.
Crown 8vo, cloth extra, **3s. 6d.** each; post 8vo, illustrated boards, **2s.** each.
GUY WATERMAN. | THE LION IN THE PATH. | THE TWO DREAMERS.
BOUND TO THE WHEEL. Crown 8vo, cloth extra, **3s. 6d.**

SAUNDERS (KATHARINE), NOVELS BY.
Crown 8vo, cloth extra, **3s. 6d.** each; post 8vo, illustrated boards, **2s.** each.
MARGARET AND ELIZABETH. | HEART SALVAGE.
THE HIGH MILLS. | SEBASTIAN.
JOAN MERRYWEATHER. Post 8vo, illustrated boards, **2s.**
GIDEON'S ROCK. Crown 8vo, cloth extra, **3s. 6d.**

SCIENCE-GOSSIP: An Illustrated Medium of Interchange for Students and Lovers of Nature. Edited by Dr. J. E. TAYLOR, F.L.S., &c. Devoted to Geology, Botany, Physiology, Chemistry, Zoology, Microscopy, Telescopy, Physiography Photography, &c. Price **4d.** Monthly; or **5s.** per year, post-free. Vols. I. to XIX. may be had, **7s. 6d.** each; Vols. XX. to date, **5s.** each. Cases for Binding, **1s. 6d.**

SECRET OUT, THE: One Thousand Tricks with Cards; with Entertaining Experiments in Drawing-room or "White Magic." By W. H. CREMER. With 300 Illustrations. Crown 8vo, cloth extra, **4s. 6d.**

SEGUIN (L. G.), WORKS BY.
THE COUNTRY OF THE PASSION PLAY (OBERAMMERGAU) and the Highlands of Bavaria. With Map and 37 Illustrations. Crown 8vo, cloth extra, **3s. 6d.**
WALKS IN ALGIERS. With 2 Maps and 16 Illusts. Crown 8vo, cloth extra, **6s.**

SENIOR (WM.).—BY STREAM AND SEA. Post 8vo, cloth, **2s. 6d.**

SHAKESPEARE, THE FIRST FOLIO.—MR. WILLIAM SHAKESPEARE'S COMEDIES, HISTORIES, AND TRAGEDIES. Published according to the true Originall Copies. London, Printed by ISAAC IAGGARD and ED. BLOUNT. 1623.— A reduced Photographic Reproduction. Small 8vo, half-Roxburghe, **7s. 6d.**
SHAKESPEARE FOR CHILDREN: LAMB'S TALES FROM SHAKESPEARE. With Illustrations, coloured and plain, by J. MOYR SMITH. Crown 4to, cloth, **6s.**

SHARP.—CHILDREN OF TO-MORROW: A Novel. By WILLIAM SHARP. Crown 8vo, cloth extra, **6s.**

SHELLEY.—THE COMPLETE WORKS IN VERSE AND PROSE OF PERCY BYSSHE SHELLEY. Edited, Prefaced, and Annotated by R. HERNE SHEPHERD. Five Vols., crown 8vo, cloth boards, **3s. 6d.** each.
POETICAL WORKS, in Three Vols.:
Vol. I. Introduction by the Editor; Posthumous Fragments of Margaret Nicholson; Shelley's Correspondence with Stockdale; The Wandering Jew; Queen Mab, with the Notes; Alastor, and other Poems; Rosalind and Helen; Prometheus Unbound; Adonais, &c.
Vol. II. Laon and Cythna; The Cenci; Julian and Maddalo; Swellfoot the Tyrant; The Witch of Atlas; Epipsychidion; Hellas.
Vol. III. Posthumous Poems; The Masque of Anarchy; and other Pieces.
PROSE WORKS, in Two Vols.:
Vol. I. The Two Romances of Zastrozzi and St. Irvyne; the Dublin and Marlow Pamphlets; A Refutation of Deism; Letters to Leigh Hunt, and some Minor Writings and Fragments.
Vol. II. The Essays; Letters from Abroad; Translations and Fragments, Edited by Mrs. SHELLEY. With a Bibliography of Shelley, and an Index of the Prose Works.

SHERARD.—ROGUES: A Novel. By R. H. SHERARD. Crown 8vo, picture cover, **1s.**; cloth, **1s. 6d.**

SHERIDAN (GENERAL). — PERSONAL MEMOIRS OF GENERAL P. H. SHERIDAN. With Portraits and Facsimiles. Two Vols., demy 8vo, cloth, **24s.**

SHERIDAN'S (RICHARD BRINSLEY) COMPLETE WORKS. With Life and Anecdotes. Including his Dramatic Writings, his Works in Prose and Poetry, Translations, Speeches, Jokes, &c. With 10 Illusts. Cr. 8vo, cl., **7s. 6d.**
THE RIVALS, THE SCHOOL FOR SCANDAL, and other Plays. Post 8vo, printed on laid paper and half-bound, **2s.**
SHERIDAN'S COMEDIES: THE RIVALS and THE SCHOOL FOR SCANDAL. Edited, with an Introduction and Notes to each Play, and a Biographical Sketch, by BRANDER MATTHEWS. With Illustrations. Demy 8vo, half-parchment, **12s. 6d.**

SIDNEY'S (SIR PHILIP) COMPLETE POETICAL WORKS, including all those in "Arcadia." With Portrait, Memorial-Introduction, Notes, &c. by the Rev. A. B. GROSART, D.D. Three Vols., crown 8vo, cloth boards, **18s.**

SIGNBOARDS: Their History. With Anecdotes of Famous Taverns and Remarkable Characters. By JACOB LARWOOD and JOHN CAMDEN HOTTEN. With Coloured Frontispiece and 94 Illustrations. Crown 8vo, cloth extra, **7s. 6d.**

SIMS (GEORGE R.), WORKS BY.
Post 8vo, illustrated boards, **2s.** each; cloth limp, **2s. 6d.** each.
ROGUES AND VAGABONDS. | MARY JANE MARRIED.
THE RING O' BELLS. | TALES OF TO-DAY.
MARY JANE'S MEMOIRS. | DRAMAS OF LIFE. With 60 Illustrations.
TINKLETOP'S CRIME. With a Frontispiece by MAURICE GREIFFENHAGEN.
Crown 8vo, picture cover, **1s.** each; cloth, **1s. 6d.** each.
HOW THE POOR LIVE; and HORRIBLE LONDON.
THE DAGONET RECITER AND READER: being Readings and Recitations in Prose and Verse, selected from his own Works by GEORGE R. SIMS.
DAGONET DITTIES. From the *Referee*.
THE CASE OF GEORGE CANDLEMAS.

SISTER DORA: A Biography. By MARGARET LONSDALE. With Four Illustrations. Demy 8vo, picture cover, **4d.**; cloth, **6d.**

SKETCHLEY.—A MATCH IN THE DARK. By ARTHUR SKETCHLEY. Post 8vo, illustrated boards, **2s.**

SLANG DICTIONARY (THE): Etymological, Historical, and Anecdotal. Crown 8vo, cloth extra, **6s. 6d.**

SMITH (J. MOYR), WORKS BY.
THE PRINCE OF ARGOLIS. With 130 Illusts. Post 8vo, cloth extra, **3s. 6d.**
TALES OF OLD THULE. With numerous Illustrations. Crown 8vo, cloth gilt, **6s.**
THE WOOING OF THE WATER WITCH. Illustrated. Post 8vo, cloth, **6s.**

SOCIETY IN LONDON. By A FOREIGN RESIDENT. Crown 8vo, **1s.**; cloth, **1s. 6d.**

SOCIETY IN PARIS: The Upper Ten Thousand. A Series of Letters from Count PAUL VASILI to a Young French Diplomat. Crown 8vo, cloth, **6s.**

SOMERSET. — SONGS OF ADIEU. By Lord HENRY SOMERSET. Small 4to, Japanese vellum, **6s.**

SPALDING.—ELIZABETHAN DEMONOLOGY: An Essay on the Belief in the Existence of Devils. By T. A. SPALDING, LL.B. Crown 8vo, cloth extra, **5s.**

SPEIGHT (T. W.), NOVELS BY.
Post 8vo, illustrated boards, **2s.** each.

THE MYSTERIES OF HERON DYKE.	THE GOLDEN HOOP.
BY DEVIOUS WAYS, and A BARREN TITLE.	HOODWINKED; and THE SANDY-CROFT MYSTERY.

Post 8vo, cloth limp, **1s. 6d.** each.

A BARREN TITLE.	WIFE OR NO WIFE?

THE SANDYCROFT MYSTERY. Crown 8vo, picture cover, **1s.**

SPENSER FOR CHILDREN. By M. H. TOWRY. With Illustrations by WALTER J. MORGAN. Crown 4to, cloth gilt, **6s.**

STARRY HEAVENS (THE): A POETICAL BIRTHDAY BOOK. Royal 16mo, cloth extra, **2s. 6d.**

STAUNTON.—THE LAWS AND PRACTICE OF CHESS. With an Analysis of the Openings. By HOWARD STAUNTON. Edited by ROBERT B. WORMALD. Crown 8vo, cloth extra, **5s.**

STEDMAN (E. C.), WORKS BY.
VICTORIAN POETS. Thirteenth Edition. Crown 8vo, cloth extra, **9s.**
THE POETS OF AMERICA. Crown 8vo, cloth extra, **9s.**

STERNDALE. — THE AFGHAN KNIFE: A Novel. By ROBERT ARMITAGE STERNDALE. Cr. 8vo, cloth extra, **3s. 6d.**; post 8vo, illust. boards, **2s.**

STEVENSON (R. LOUIS), WORKS BY. Post 8vo, cl. limp, **2s. 6d.** each.
TRAVELS WITH A DONKEY. Eighth Edit. With a Frontis. by WALTER CRANE.
AN INLAND VOYAGE. Fourth Edition. With a Frontispiece by WALTER CRANE.

Crown 8vo, buckram, gilt top, **6s.** each.
FAMILIAR STUDIES OF MEN AND BOOKS. Fifth Edition.
THE SILVERADO SQUATTERS. With a Frontispiece. Third Edition.
THE MERRY MEN. Second Edition. | UNDERWOODS: Poems. Fifth Edition.
MEMORIES AND PORTRAITS. Third Edition.
VIRGINIBUS PUERISQUE, and other Papers. Fifth Edition. | BALLADS.

NEW ARABIAN NIGHTS. Eleventh Edition. Crown 8vo, buckram, gilt top, **6s.**; post 8vo, illustrated boards, **2s.**
PRINCE OTTO. Post 8vo, illustrated boards, **2s.**
FATHER DAMIEN: An Open Letter to the Rev. Dr. Hyde. Second Edition. Crown 8vo, hand-made and brown paper, **1s.**

STODDARD. — SUMMER CRUISING IN THE SOUTH SEAS. By C. WARREN STODDARD. Illustrated by WALLIS MACKAY. Cr. 8vo, cl. extra, **3s. 6d.**

STORIES FROM FOREIGN NOVELISTS. With Notices by HELEN and ALICE ZIMMERN. Crown 8vo, cloth extra, **3s. 6d.**; post 8vo, illustrated boards, **2s.**

STRANGE MANUSCRIPT (A) FOUND IN A COPPER CYLINDER.
With 19 Illustrations by GILBERT GAUL.   Third Edition. Crown 8vo, cloth extra, 5s.

STRUTT'S SPORTS AND PASTIMES OF THE PEOPLE OF ENGLAND; including the Rural and Domestic Recreations, May Games, Mummeries, Shows, &c., from the Earliest Period to the Present Time.   Edited by WILLIAM HONE. With 140 Illustrations. Crown 8vo, cloth extra, 7s. 6d.

SUBURBAN HOMES (THE) OF LONDON : A Residential Guide.   With a Map, and Notes on Rental, Rates, and Accommodation Crown 8vo, cloth, 7s. 6d.

SWIFT'S (DEAN) CHOICE WORKS, in Prose and Verse. With Memoir, Portrait, and Facsimiles of the Maps in "Gulliver's Travels." Cr. 8vo, cl., 7s. 6d.
GULLIVER'S TRAVELS, and **A TALE OF A TUB.**   Post 8vo, printed on laid paper and half-bound, 2s.
A MONOGRAPH ON SWIFT. By J. CHURTON COLLINS. Cr. 8vo, cloth, 8s. [*Shortly.*

SWINBURNE (ALGERNON C.), WORKS BY.

SELECTIONS FROM POETICAL WORKS OF A. C. SWINBURNE. Fcap. 8vo, 6s.
ATALANTA IN CALYDON. Cr. 8vo, 6s.
CHASTELARD: A Tragedy. Cr. 8vo. 7s.
NOTES ON POEMS AND REVIEWS. Demy 8vo, 1s.
POEMS AND BALLADS. FIRST SERIES. Crown 8vo or fcap. 8vo, 9s.
POEMS AND BALLADS. SECOND SERIES. Crown 8vo or fcap. 8vo, 9s.
POEMS AND BALLADS. THIRD SERIES. Crown 8vo, 7s.
SONGS BEFORE SUNRISE. Crown 8vo, 10s. 6d.
BOTHWELL: A Tragedy. Crown 8vo, 12s. 6d.
SONGS OF TWO NATIONS. Cr. 8vo, 6s.

GEORGE CHAPMAN. (*See* Vol. II. of G. CHAPMAN'S Works.) Crown 8vo, 6s.
ESSAYS AND STUDIES. Cr. 8vo, 12s.
ERECHTHEUS: A Tragedy. Cr. 8vo, 6s.
SONGS OF THE SPRINGTIDES. Crown 8vo, 6s.
STUDIES IN SONG. Crown 8vo, 7s.
MARY STUART: A Tragedy. Cr. 8vo. 8s.
TRISTRAM OF LYONESSE. Cr. 8vo, 9s.
A CENTURY OF ROUNDELS. Sm. 4to, 8s.
A MIDSUMMER HOLIDAY. Cr. 8vo, 7s.
MARINO FALIERO: A Tragedy. Crown 8vo, 6s.
A STUDY OF VICTOR HUGO. Cr. 8vo, 6s.
MISCELLANIES. Crown 8vo, 12s.
LOCRINE: A Tragedy. Cr. 8vo, 6s.
A STUDY OF BEN JONSON. Cr. 8vo, 7s.

SYMONDS.—WINE, WOMEN, AND SONG : Mediæval Latin Students' Songs. With Essay and Trans. by J. ADDINGTON SYMONDS. Fcap. 8vo, parchment, 6s.

SYNTAX'S (DR.) THREE TOURS : In Search of the Picturesque, in Search of Consolation, and in Search of a Wife. With ROWLANDSON'S Coloured Illustrations, and Life of the Author by J. C. HOTTEN. Crown 8vo, cloth extra, 7s. 6d.

TAINE'S HISTORY OF ENGLISH LITERATURE.   Translated by HENRY VAN LAUN. Four Vols., medium 8vo, cloth boards, 30s.—POPULAR EDITION, Two Vols., large crown 8vo, cloth extra, 15s.

TAYLOR'S (BAYARD) DIVERSIONS OF THE ECHO CLUB : Burlesques of Modern Writers. Post 8vo, cloth limp, 2s.

TAYLOR (DR. J. E., F.L.S.), WORKS BY. Cr. 8vo, cl. ex., 7s. 6d. each.
THE SAGACITY AND MORALITY OF PLANTS: A Sketch of the Life and Conduct of the Vegetable Kingdom. With a Coloured Frontispiece and 100 Illustrations.
OUR COMMON BRITISH FOSSILS, and Where to Find Them. 331 Illustrations.
THE PLAYTIME NATURALIST. With 366 Illustrations. Crown 8vo, cloth, 5s.

TAYLOR'S (TOM) HISTORICAL DRAMAS. Containing "Clancarty," "Jeanne Darc," "'Twixt Axe and Crown," "The Fool's Revenge," "Arkwright's Wife," "Anne Boleyn," "Plot and Passion." Crown 8vo, cloth extra, 7s. 6d.
. The Plays may also be had separately, at 1s. each.

TENNYSON (LORD): A Biographical Sketch.   By H. J. JENNINGS. With a Photograph-Portrait. Crown 8vo, cloth extra, 6s.

THACKERAYANA : Notes and Anecdotes.   Illustrated by Hundreds of Sketches by WILLIAM MAKEPEACE THACKERAY, depicting Humorous Incidents in his School-life, and Favourite Characters in the Books of his Every-day Reading. With a Coloured Frontispiece. Crown 8vo, cloth extra, 7s. 6d.

THAMES. — A NEW PICTORIAL HISTORY OF THE THAMES. By A. S. KRAUSSE. With 340 Illustrations   Post 8vo, 1s.; cloth, 1s. 6d.

THOMAS (BERTHA), NOVELS BY. Cr. 8vo, cl., 3s. 6d. ea.; post 8vo, 2s. ea.

CRESSIDA.	THE VIOLIN-PLAYER.	PROUD MAISIE.

THOMSON'S SEASONS, and CASTLE OF INDOLENCE. Introduction by ALLAN CUNNINGHAM, and Illustrations on Steel and Wood. Cr. 8vo, cl., 7s. 6d.

THORNBURY (WALTER), WORKS BY. Cr. 8vo, cl. extra, 7s. 6d. each.

THE LIFE AND CORRESPONDENCE OF J. M. W. TURNER. Founded upon Letters and Papers furnished by his Friends. With Illustrations in Colours.

HAUNTED LONDON. Edit. by E. WALFORD, M.A. Illusts. by F. W. FAIRHOLT, F.S.A.

Post 8vo, illustrated boards, 2s. each.

OLD STORIES RE-TOLD.	TALES FOR THE MARINES.

TIMBS (JOHN), WORKS BY. Crown 8vo, cloth extra, 7s. 6d. each.

THE HISTORY OF CLUBS AND CLUB LIFE IN LONDON: Anecdotes of its Famous Coffee-houses, Hostelries, and Taverns. With 42 Illustrations.

ENGLISH ECCENTRICS AND ECCENTRICITIES: Stories of Wealth and Fashion, Delusions, Impostures, and Fanatic Missions, Sporting Scenes, Eccentric Artists, Theatrical Folk, Men of Letters, &c. With 48 Illustrations.

TROLLOPE (ANTHONY), NOVELS BY.

Crown 8vo, cloth extra, 3s. 6d. each; post 8vo, illustrated boards, 2s. each.

THE WAY WE LIVE NOW.	MARION FAY.
KEPT IN THE DARK.	MR. SCARBOROUGH'S FAMILY.
FRAU FROHMANN.	THE LAND-LEAGUERS.

Post 8vo, illustrated boards, 2s. each.

GOLDEN LION OF GRANPERE. | JOHN CALDIGATE. | AMERICAN SENATOR

TROLLOPE (FRANCES E.), NOVELS BY.

Crown 8vo, cloth extra, 3s. 6d. each; post 8vo, illustrated boards, 2s. each.

LIKE SHIPS UPON THE SEA. | MABEL'S PROGRESS. | ANNE FURNESS.

TROLLOPE (T. A.).—DIAMOND CUT DIAMOND. Post 8vo, illust. bds., 2s.

TROWBRIDGE.—FARNELL'S FOLLY: A Novel. By J. T. TROWBRIDGE. Post 8vo, illustrated boards, 2s.

TYTLER (C. C. FRASER-).—MISTRESS JUDITH: A Novel. By C. C. FRASER-TYTLER. Crown 8vo, cloth extra, 3s. 6d.; post 8vo, illust. boards, 2s.

TYTLER (SARAH), NOVELS BY.

Crown 8vo, cloth extra, 3s. 6d. each; post 8vo, illustrated boards, 2s. each.

THE BRIDE'S PASS.	BURIED DIAMONDS.
NOBLESSE OBLIGE.	THE BLACKHALL GHOSTS.
LADY BELL.	

Post 8vo, illustrated boards, 2s. each.

WHAT SHE CAME THROUGH.	BEAUTY AND THE BEAST.
CITOYENNE JACQUELINE.	DISAPPEARED.
SAINT MUNGO'S CITY.	THE HUGUENOT FAMILY.

VILLARI.—A DOUBLE BOND. By LINDA VILLARI. Fcap. 8vo, picture cover, 1s.

WALT WHITMAN, POEMS BY. Edited, with Introduction, by WILLIAM M. ROSSETTI. With Portrait. Cr. 8vo, hand-made paper and buckram, 6s.

WALTON AND COTTON'S COMPLETE ANGLER; or, The Contemplative Man's Recreation, by IZAAK WALTON; and Instructions how to Angle for a Trout or Grayling in a clear Stream, by CHARLES COTTON. With Memoirs and Notes by Sir HARRIS NICOLAS, and 61 Illustrations. Crown 8vo, cloth antique, 7s. 6d.

WARD (HERBERT), WORKS BY.

FIVE YEARS WITH THE CONGO CANNIBALS. With 92 Illustrations by the Author, VICTOR PERARD, and W. B. DAVIS. Third ed. Roy. 8vo, cloth ex., 14s.

MY LIFE WITH STANLEY'S REAR GUARD. With a Map by F. S. WELLER, F.R.G.S. Post 8vo, 1s.; cloth, 1s. 6d.

WARNER.—A ROUNDABOUT JOURNEY. By CHARLES DUDLEY WARNER. Crown 8vo, cloth extra, 6s.

WALFORD (EDWARD, M.A.), WORKS BY.
WALFORD'S COUNTY FAMILIES OF THE UNITED KINGDOM (1891). Containing the Descent, Birth, Marriage, Education, &c., of 12,000 Heads of Families, their Heirs, Offices, Addresses, Clubs, &c. Royal 8vo, cloth gilt, 50s.
WALFORD'S SHILLING PEERAGE (1891). Containing a List of the House of Lords, Scotch and Irish Peers, &c. 32mo. cloth, 1s.
WALFORD'S SHILLING BARONETAGE (1891). Containing a List of the Baronets of the United Kingdom, Biographical Notices, Addresses, &c. 32mo, cloth, 1s.
WALFORD'S SHILLING KNIGHTAGE (1891). Containing a List of the Knights of the United Kingdom, Biographical Notices, Addresses, &c. 32mo, cloth, 1s.
WALFORD'S SHILLING HOUSE OF COMMONS (1891). Containing a List of all Members of Parliament, their Addresses, Clubs, &c. 32mo, cloth, 1s.
WALFORD'S COMPLETE PEERAGE, BARONETAGE, KNIGHTAGE, AND HOUSE OF COMMONS (1891). Royal 32mo, cloth extra, gilt edges, 5s.
WALFORD'S WINDSOR PEERAGE, BARONETAGE, AND KNIGHTAGE (1891). Crown 8vo, cloth extra, 12s. 6d.
TALES OF OUR GREAT FAMILIES. Crown 8vo, cloth extra, 3s. 6d.
WILLIAM PITT: A Biography. Post 8vo, cloth extra, 5s.

WARRANT TO EXECUTE CHARLES I. A Facsimile, with the 59 Signatures and Seals. Printed on paper 22 in. by 14 in. 2s.
WARRANT TO EXECUTE MARY QUEEN OF SCOTS. A Facsimile, including Queen Elizabeth's Signature and the Great Seal. 2s.

WEATHER, HOW TO FORETELL THE, WITH POCKET SPECTROSCOPE. By F. W. Cory. With 10 Illustrations. Cr. 8vo, 1s.; cloth, 1s. 6d.

WESTROPP.—HANDBOOK OF POTTERY AND PORCELAIN. By Hodder M. Westropp. With Illusts. and List of Marks. Cr. 8vo, cloth, 4s. 6d.

WHIST.—HOW TO PLAY SOLO WHIST. By Abraham S. Wilks and Charles F. Pardon. Crown 8vo, cloth extra, 3s. 6d.

WHISTLER'S (MR.) TEN O'CLOCK. Cr. 8vo, hand-made paper, 1s.

WHITE.—THE NATURAL HISTORY OF SELBORNE. By Gilbert White, M.A. Post 8vo, printed on laid paper and half-bound, 2s.

WILLIAMS (W. MATTIEU, F.R.A.S.), WORKS BY.
SCIENCE IN SHORT CHAPTERS. Crown 8vo, cloth extra, 7s. 6d.
A SIMPLE TREATISE ON HEAT. With Illusts. Cr. 8vo, cloth limp, 2s. 6d.
THE CHEMISTRY OF COOKERY. Crown 8vo, cloth extra, 6s.
THE CHEMISTRY OF IRON AND STEEL MAKING. Crown 8vo, cloth extra, 9s.

WILLIAMSON.—A CHILD WIDOW. By Mrs. F. H. Williamson. Three Vols., crown 8vo.

WILSON (DR. ANDREW, F.R.S.E.), WORKS BY.
CHAPTERS ON EVOLUTION. With 259 Illustrations. Cr. 8vo, cloth extra, 7s. 6d.
LEAVES FROM A NATURALIST'S NOTE-BOOK. Post 8vo, cloth limp, 2s. 6d.
LEISURE-TIME STUDIES. With Illustrations. Crown 8vo, cloth extra, 6s.
STUDIES IN LIFE AND SENSE. With numerous Illusts. Cr. 8vo, cl. ex., 6s.
COMMON ACCIDENTS: HOW TO TREAT THEM. Illusts. Cr. 8vo, 1s.; cl., 1s. 6d.
GLIMPSES OF NATURE. With 35 Illustrations. Crown 8vo, cloth extra, 3s. 6d.

WINTER (J. S.), STORIES BY. Post 8vo, illustrated boards, 2s. each.
CAVALRY LIFE. | REGIMENTAL LEGENDS.

WISSMANN.—MY SECOND JOURNEY THROUGH EQUATORIAL AFRICA, from the Congo to the Zambesi, in 1886, 1887. By Hermann von Wissmann. With a Map and 92 Illustrations. Demy 8vo, cloth extra, 16s.

WOOD.—SABINA: A Novel. By Lady Wood. Post 8vo, boards, 2s.

WOOD (H. F.), DETECTIVE STORIES BY. Crown 8vo, cloth extra, 6s. each; post 8vo, illustrated boards, 2s. each.
PASSENGER FROM SCOTLAND YARD. | ENGLISHMAN OF THE RUE CAIN.

WOOLLEY.—RACHEL ARMSTRONG; or, Love and Theology. By Celia Parker Woolley. Post 8vo, illustrated boards, 2s.; cloth, 2s. 6d.

WRIGHT (THOMAS), WORKS BY. Crown 8vo, cloth extra, 7s. 6d. each.
CARICATURE HISTORY OF THE GEORGES. With 400 Pictures, Caricatures, Squibs, Broadsides, Window Pictures, &c.
HISTORY OF CARICATURE AND OF THE GROTESQUE IN ART, LITERATURE, SCULPTURE, AND PAINTING. Illustrated by F. W. Fairholt, F.S.A.

YATES (EDMUND), NOVELS BY. Post 8vo, illustrated boards, 2s. each.
LAND AT LAST. | THE FORLORN HOPE. | CASTAWAY.

LISTS OF BOOKS CLASSIFIED IN SERIES.

, *For full cataloguing, see alphabetical arrangement, pp. 1-25.*

THE MAYFAIR LIBRARY. Post 8vo, cloth limp, 2s. 6d. per Volume.

A Journey Round My Room. By Xavier de Maistre.
Quips and Quiddities. By W. D. Adams.
The Agony Column of "The Times."
Melancholy Anatomised: Abridgment of "Burton's Anatomy of Melancholy."
The Speeches of Charles Dickens.
Literary Frivolities, Fancies, Follies, and Frolics. By W. T. Dobson.
Poetical Ingenuities. By W. T. Dobson.
The Cupboard Papers. By Fin-Bec.
W. S. Gilbert's Plays. First Series.
W. S. Gilbert's Plays. Second Series.
Songs of Irish Wit and Humour.
Animals and Masters. By Sir A. Helps.
Social Pressure. By Sir A. Helps.
Curiosities of Criticism. H. J. Jennings.
Holmes's Autocrat of Breakfast-Table.
Pencil and Palette. By R. Kempt.

Little Essays: from Lamb's Letters.
Forensic Anecdotes. By Jacob Larwood.
Theatrical Anecdotes. Jacob Larwood.
Jeux d'Esprit. Edited by Henry S. Leigh.
Witch Stories. By E. Lynn Linton.
Ourselves. By E. Lynn Linton.
Pastimes & Players. By R. Macgregor.
New Paul and Virginia. W. H. Mallock.
New Republic. By W. H. Mallock.
Puck on Pegasus. By H. C. Pennell.
Pegasus Re-Saddled. By H. C. Pennell.
Muses of Mayfair. Ed. H. C. Pennell.
Thoreau: His Life & Aims. By H. A. Page.
Puniana. By Hon. Hugh Rowley.
More Puniana. By Hon. Hugh Rowley.
The Philosophy of Handwriting.
By Stream and Sea. By Wm. Senior.
Leaves from a Naturalist's Note-Book. By Dr. Andrew Wilson.

THE GOLDEN LIBRARY. Post 8vo, cloth limp, 2s. per Volume.

Bayard Taylor's Diversions of the Echo Club.
Bennett's Ballad History of England.
Bennett's Songs for Sailors.
Godwin's Lives of the Necromancers.
Pope's Poetical Works.
Holmes's Autocrat of Breakfast Table.

Holmes's Professor at Breakfast Table.
Jesse's Scenes of Country Life.
Leigh Hunt's Tale for a Chimney Corner.
Mallory's Mort d'Arthur: Selections.
Pascal's Provincial Letters.
Rochefoucauld's Maxims & Reflections.

THE WANDERER'S LIBRARY. Crown 8vo, cloth extra, 3s. 6d. each.

Wanderings in Patagonia. By Julius Beerbohm. Illustrated.
Camp Notes. By Frederick Boyle.
Savage Life. By Frederick Boyle.
Merrie England in the Olden Time. By G. Daniel. Illustrated by Cruikshank.
Circus Life. By Thomas Frost.
Lives of the Conjurers. Thomas Frost.
The Old Showmen and the Old London Fairs. By Thomas Frost.
Low-Life Deeps. By James Greenwood.

Wilds of London. James Greenwood.
Tunis. Chev. Hesse-Wartegg. 22 Illusts.
Life and Adventures of a Cheap Jack.
World Behind the Scenes. P. Fitzgerald.
Tavern Anecdotes and Sayings.
The Genial Showman. By E. P. Hingston.
Story of London Parks. Jacob Larwood.
London Characters. By Henry Mayhew.
Seven Generations of Executioners.
Summer Cruising in the South Seas. By C. Warren Stoddard. Illustrated.

POPULAR SHILLING BOOKS.

Harry Fludyer at Cambridge.
Jeff Briggs's Love Story. Bret Harte.
Twins of Table Mountain. Bret Harte.
A Day's Tour. By Percy Fitzgerald.
Esther's Glove. By R. E. Francillon.
Sentenced! By Somerville Gibney.
The Professor's Wife. By L. Graham.
Mrs. Gainsborough's Diamonds. By Julian Hawthorne.
Niagara Spray. By J. Hollingshead.
A Romance of the Queen's Hounds. By Charles James.
The Garden that Paid the Rent. By Tom Jerrold.
Cut by the Mess. By Arthur Keyser.
Our Sensation Novel. J. H. McCarthy.
Doom! By Justin H. McCarthy, M.P.
Dolly. By Justin H. McCarthy, M.P.
Lily Lass. Justin H. McCarthy, M.P.

Was She Good or Bad? By W. Minto.
That Girl in Black. Mrs. Molesworth.
Notes from the "News." By Jas. Payn.
Beyond the Gates. By E. S. Phelps.
Old Maid's Paradise. By E. S. Phelps.
Burglars in Paradise. By E. S. Phelps.
Jack the Fisherman. By E. S. Phelps.
Trooping with Crows. By C. L. Pirkis.
Bible Characters. By Charles Reade.
Rogues. By R. H. Sherard.
The Dagonet Reciter. By G. R. Sims.
How the Poor Live. By G. R. Sims.
Case of George Candlemas. G. R. Sims.
Sandycroft Mystery. T. W. Speight.
Hoodwinked. By T. W. Speight.
Father Damien. By R. L. Stevenson.
A Double Bond. By Linda Villari.
My Life with Stanley's Rear Guard. By Herbert Ward.

MY LIBRARY.

Choice Works, printed on laid paper, bound half-Roxburghe, 2s. 6d. each.

Four Frenchwomen. By Austin Dobson.
Citation and Examination of William Shakspeare. By W. S. Landor.

Christie Johnstone. By Charles Reade. With a Photogravure Frontispiece.
Peg Woffington. By Charles Reade.

THE POCKET LIBRARY.   Post 8vo, printed on laid paper and hf.-bd., 2s. each.

The Essays of Elia. By Charles Lamb.
Robinson Crusoe. Edited by John Major. With 37 Busts by George Cruikshank.
Whims and Oddities. By Thomas Hood. With 85 Illustrations.
The Barber's Chair, and The Hedgehog Letters. By Douglas Jerrold.
Gastronomy as a Fine Art. By Brillat-Savarin. Trans. R. E. Anderson, M.A.

The Epicurean, &c. By Thomas Moore.
Leigh Hunt's Essays. Ed. E. Ollier.
The Natural History of Selborne. By Gilbert White.
Gulliver's Travels, and The Tale of a Tub. By Dean Swift.
The Rivals, School for Scandal, and other Plays by Richard Brinsley Sheridan.
Anecdotes of the Clergy. J. Larwood.

THE PICCADILLY NOVELS.

Library Editions of Novels by the Best Authors, many Illustrated, crown 8vo, cloth extra, 3s. 6d. each.

By GRANT ALLEN.

Phillistia.
Babylon
In all Shades.
The Tents of Shem.

For Maimie's Sake.
The Devil's Die.
This Mortal Coil.
The Great Taboo.

By ALAN ST. AUBYN.

A Fellow of Trinity.

By Rev. S. BARING GOULD.

Red Spider. | Eve.

By W. BESANT & J. RICE.

My Little Girl.
Case of Mr. Lucraft.
This Son of Vulcan.
Golden Butterfly.
Ready-Money Mortiboy.
With Harp and Crown.
'Twas in Trafalgar's Bay.
The Chaplain of the Fleet.

By Celia's Arbour.
Monks of Thelema.
The Seamy Side.
Ten Years' Tenant.

By WALTER BESANT.

All Sorts and Conditions of Men.
The Captains' Room.
All in a Garden Fair
The World Went Very Well Then.
For Faith and Freedom.
Dorothy Forster.
Uncle Jack.
Children of Gibeon.
Herr Paulus.
Bell of St. Paul's.

To Call Her Mine.
The Holy Rose.
Armorel of Lyonesse.

By ROBERT BUCHANAN.

The Shadow of the Sword.
A Child of Nature.
The Martyrdom of Madeline.
God and the Man.
Love Me for Ever.
Annan Water.
Matt.

The New Abelard.
Foxglove Manor.
Master of the Mine.
Heir of Linne.

By HALL CAINE.

The Shadow of a Crime.
A Son of Hagar. | The Deemster.

MORT. & FRANCES COLLINS.

Sweet Anne Page. | Transmigration.
From Midnight to Midnight.
Blacksmith and Scholar.
Village Comedy. | You Play Me False

By Mrs. H. LOVETT CAMERON.

Juliet's Guardian. | Deceivers Ever.

By WILKIE COLLINS.

Armadale.
After Dark.
No Name.
Antonina. | Basil.
Hide and Seek.
The Dead Secret.
Queen of Hearts.
My Miscellanies.
Woman in White.
The Moonstone.
Man and Wife.
Poor Miss Finch.
Miss or Mrs?
New Magdalen.

The Frozen Deep.
The Two Destinies.
Law and the Lady.
Haunted Hotel.
The Fallen Leaves.
Jezebel's Daughter.
The Black Robe.
Heart and Science.
"I Say No."
Little Novels.
The Evil Genius.
The Legacy of Cain
A Rogue's Life.
Blind Love.

By DUTTON COOK.

Paul Foster's Daughter.

By WILLIAM CYPLES.

Hearts of Gold.

By ALPHONSE DAUDET.

The Evangelist; or, Port Salvation.

By JAMES DE MILLE.

A Castle in Spain.

By J. LEITH DERWENT.

Our Lady of Tears. | Circe's Lovers.

By Mrs. ANNIE EDWARDES.

Archie Lovell.

By PERCY FITZGERALD.

Fatal Zero.

By R. E. FRANCILLON.

Queen Cophetua.
One by One.

A Real Queen.
King or Knave?

Pref. by Sir BARTLE FRERE.

Pandurang Hari.

By EDWARD GARRETT.

The Capel Girls

THE PICCADILLY (3/6) NOVELS—*continued.*

By CHARLES GIBBON.

Robin Gray. | The Golden Shaft.
In Honour Bound. | Of High Degree.
Loving a Dream.
The Flower of the Forest.

By JULIAN HAWTHORNE.

Garth. | Dust.
Ellice Quentin. | Fortune's Fool.
Sebastian Strome. | Beatrix Randolph.
David Poindexter's Disappearance.
The Spectre of the Camera.

By Sir A. HELPS.

Ivan de Biron.

By ISAAC HENDERSON.

Agatha Page.

By Mrs. ALFRED HUNT.

The Leaden Casket. | Self-Condemned.
That other Person.

By JEAN INGELOW.

Fated to be Free.

By R. ASHE KING.

A Drawn Game.
"The Wearing of the Green."

By HENRY KINGSLEY.

Number Seventeen.

By E. LYNN LINTON.

Patricia Kemball. | Ione.
Under which Lord? | Paston Carew.
"My Love!" | Sowing the Wind.
The Atonement of Leam Dundas.
The World Well Lost.

By HENRY W. LUCY.

Gideon Fleyce.

By JUSTIN McCARTHY.

A Fair Saxon. | Donna Quixote.
Linley Rochford. | Maid of Athens.
Miss Misanthrope. | Camiola.
The Waterdale Neighbours. .
My Enemy's Daughter.
Dear Lady Disdain.
The Comet of a Season.

By AGNES MACDONELL.

Quaker Cousins.

By FLORENCE MARRYAT.

Open! Sesame!

By D. CHRISTIE MURRAY.

Life's Atonement. | Coals of Fire.
Joseph's Coat. | Val Strange.
A Model Father. | Hearts.
A Bit of Human Nature.
First Person Singular.
Cynic Fortune.
The Way of the World.

By MURRAY & HERMAN.

The Bishops' Bible.

By GEORGES OHNET.

A Weird Gift.

THE PICCADILLY (3/6) NOVELS—*continued.*

By Mrs. OLIPHANT.

Whiteladies.

By OUIDA.

Held in Bondage. | Two Little Wooden
Strathmore. | Shoes.
Chandos. | In a Winter City.
Under Two Flags. | Ariadne.
Idalia. | Friendship.
CecilCastlemaine's | Moths. | Ruffino.
Gage. | Pipistrello.
Tricotrin. | Puck. | A Village Commune
Folle Farine. | Bimbi. | Wanda.
A Dog of Flanders. | Frescoes.
Pascarel. | Signa. | In Maremma.
Princess Naprax- | Othmar. | Syrlin.
ine. | Guilderoy.

By MARGARET A. PAUL.

Gentle and Simple.

By JAMES PAYN.

Lost Sir Massingberd.
Less Black than We're Painted.
A Confidential Agent.
A Grape from a Thorn.
Some Private Views.
In Peril and Privation.
The Mystery of Mirbridge.
The Canon's Ward.
Walter's Word. | Talk of the Town.
By Proxy. | Holiday Tasks.
High Spirits. | The Burnt Million.
Under One Roof. | The Word and the
From Exile. | Will.
Glow-worm Tales. | Sunny Stories.

By E. C. PRICE.

Valentina. | The Foreigners.
Mrs. Lancaster's Rival.

By CHARLES READE.

It is Never Too Late to Mend.
The Double Marriage.
Love Me Little, Love Me Long.
The Cloister and the Hearth.
The Course of True Love.
The Autobiography of a Thief.
Put Yourself in his Place.
A Terrible Temptation.
Singleheart and Doubleface.
Good Stories of Men and other Animals.
Hard Cash. | Wandering Heir.
Peg Woffington. | A Woman-Hater.
ChristieJohnstone. | A Simpleton.
Griffith Gaunt. | Readiana.
Foul Play. | The Jilt.

By Mrs. J. H. RIDDELL.

Her Mother's Darling.
Prince of Wales's Garden Party.
Weird Stories.

By F. W. ROBINSON.

Women are Strange.
The Hands of Justice.

By W. CLARK RUSSELL.

An Ocean Tragedy.
My Shipmate Louise.

By JOHN SAUNDERS.

Guy Waterman. | Two Dreamers.
Bound to the Wheel.
The Lion in the Path.

THE PICCADILLY (3/6) NOVELS—*continued.*

By KATHARINE SAUNDERS.
Margaret and Elizabeth.
Gideon's Rock. | Heart Salvage.
The High Mills. | Sebastian.

By HAWLEY SMART.
Without Love or Licence.

By R. A. STERNDALE.
The Afghan Knife.

By BERTHA THOMAS.
Proud Maisie. | Cressida.
The Violin-player.

By FRANCES E. TROLLOPE.
Like Ships upon the Sea.
Anne Furness. | Mabel's Progress.

THE PICCADILLY (3/6) NOVELS—*continued.*

By ANTHONY TROLLOPE.
Frau Frohmann. | Kept in the Dark.
Marion Fay. | Land-Leaguers.
The Way We Live Now.
Mr. Scarborough's Family.

By IVAN TURGENIEFF &c.
Stories from Foreign Novelists.

By C. C. FRASER-TYTLER.
Mistress Judith.

By SARAH TYTLER.
The Bride's Pass. | Lady Bell.
Noblesse Oblige. | Buried Diamonds.
The Blackhall Ghosts.

CHEAP EDITIONS OF POPULAR NOVELS.
Post 8vo, illustrated boards, 2s. each.

By ARTEMUS WARD.
Artemus Ward Complete.

By EDMOND ABOUT.
The Fellah.

By HAMILTON AIDE.
Carr of Carrlyon. | Confidences.

By MARY ALBERT.
Brooke Finchley's Daughter.

By Mrs. ALEXANDER.
Maid, Wife, or Widow ? | Valerie's Fate.

By GRANT ALLEN.
Strange Stories. | The Devil's Die.
Philistia. | This Mortal Coil.
Babylon. | In all Shades.
The Beckoning Hand.
For Maimie's Sake. | Tents of Shem.

By ALAN ST. AUBYN.
A Fellow of Trinity.

By Rev. S. BARING GOULD.
Red Spider. | Eve.

By FRANK BARRETT.
Fettered for Life.
Between Life and Death.

By SHELSLEY BEAUCHAMP.
Grantley Grange.

By W. BESANT & J. RICE.
This Son of Vulcan. | By Celia's Arbour.
My Little Girl. | Monks of Thelema.
Case of Mr. Lucraft. | The Seamy Side.
Golden Butterfly. | Ten Years' Tenant.
Ready-Money Mortiboy.
With Harp and Crown.
'Twas in Trafalgar's Bay.
The Chaplain of the Fleet.

By WALTER BESANT.
Dorothy Forster. | Uncle Jack.
Children of Gibeon. | Herr Paulus.
All Sorts and Conditions of Men.
The Captains' Room.
All in a Garden Fair.
The World Went Very Well Then.
For Faith and Freedom.

By FREDERICK BOYLE.
Camp Notes. | Savage Life.
Chronicles of No-man's Land.

By BRET HARTE.
Flip. | Californian Stories
Maruja. | Gabriel Conroy.
An Heiress of Red Dog.
The Luck of Roaring Camp.
A Phyllis of the Sierras.

By HAROLD BRYDGES.
Uncle Sam at Home.

By ROBERT BUCHANAN.
The Shadow of the | The Martyrdom o
  Sword. | Madeline.
A Child of Nature. | Annan Water.
God and the Man. | The New Abelard.
Love Me for Ever. | Matt.
Foxglove Manor. | The Heir of LI
The Master of the Mine.

By HALL CAINE.
The Shadow of a Crime.
A Son of Hagar. | The Deemster.

By Commander CAMERON.
The Cruise of the "Black Prince."

By Mrs. LOVETT CAMERON
Deceivers Ever. | Juliet's Guardian

By AUSTIN CLARE.
For the Love of a Lass.

By Mrs. ARCHER CLIVE.
Paul Ferroll.
Why Paul Ferroll Killed his Wife.

By MACLAREN COBBAN.
The Cure of Souls.

By C. ALLSTON COLLINS.
The Bar Sinister.

MORT. & FRANCES COLLINS
Sweet Anne Page. | Transmigration.
From Midnight to Midnight.
A Fight with Fortune.
Sweet and Twenty. | Village Comedy.
Frances. | You Play me False.
Blacksmith and Scholar.

Two-Shilling Novels—*continued*.

By WILKIE COLLINS.

Armadale.	My Miscellanies.
After Dark.	Woman in White.
No Name.	The Moonstone.
Antonina. | Basil.	Man and Wife.
Hide and Seek.	Poor Miss Finch.
The Dead Secret.	The Fallen Leaves.
Queen of Hearts.	Jezebel's Daughter
Miss or Mrs?	The Black Robe.
New Magdalen.	Heart and Science.
The Frozen Deep.	"I Say No."
Law and the Lady.	The Evil Genius.
The Two Destinies.	Little Novels.
Haunted Hotel.	Legacy of Cain.
A Rogue's Life.	Blind Love.

By M. J. COLQUHOUN.
Every Inch a Soldier.

By DUTTON COOK.
Leo. | Paul Foster's Daughter.

By C. EGBERT CRADDOCK.
Prophet of the Great Smoky Mountains.

By WILLIAM CYPLES.
Hearts of Gold.

By ALPHONSE DAUDET.
The Evangelist; or, Port Salvation.

By JAMES DE MILLE.
A Castle in Spain.

By J. LEITH DERWENT.
Our Lady of Tears. | Circe's Lovers.

By CHARLES DICKENS.
Sketches by Boz. | Oliver Twist.
Pickwick Papers. | Nicholas Nickleby.

By DICK DONOVAN.
The Man-Hunter. | Caught at Last!
Tracked and Taken.
Who Poisoned Hetty Duncan?
The Man from Manchester.
A Detective's Triumphs.

By CONAN DOYLE, &c.
Strange Secrets.

By Mrs. ANNIE EDWARDES.
A Point of Honour. | Archie Lovell.

By M. BETHAM-EDWARDS.
Felicia. | Kitty.

By EDWARD EGGLESTON.
Roxy.

By PERCY FITZGERALD.
Bella Donna. | Polly.
Never Forgotten. | Fatal Zero.
The Second Mrs. Tillotson.
Seventy-five Brooke Street.
The Lady of Brantome.

ALBANY DE FONBLANQUE.
Filthy Lucre.

By R. E. FRANCILLON.
Olympia. | Queen Cophetua.
One by One. | King or Knave?
A Real Queen. | Romances of Law.

By HAROLD FREDERIC.
Seth's Brother's Wife.
The Lawton Girl.

Pref. by Sir BARTLE FRERE.
Pandurang Hari.

Two-Shilling Novels—*continued*.

By HAIN FRISWELL.
One of Two.

By EDWARD GARRETT.
The Capel Girls.

By CHARLES GIBBON.

Robin Gray.	In Honour Bound.
Fancy Free.	Flower of Forest.
For Lack of Gold.	Braes of Yarrow.
What will the World Say?	The Golden Shaft.
	Of High Degree.
In Love and War.	Mead and Stream.
For the King.	Loving a Dream.
In Pastures Green.	A Hard Knot.
Queen of Meadow.	Heart's Delight.
A Heart's Problem.	Blood-Money.
The Dead Heart.	

By WILLIAM GILBERT.
Dr. Austin's Guests. | James Duke.
The Wizard of the Mountain.

By HENRY GREVILLE.
A Noble Woman.

By JOHN HABBERTON.
Brueton's Bayou. | Country Luck.

By ANDREW HALLIDAY.
Every-Day Papers.

By Lady DUFFUS HARDY.
Paul Wynter's Sacrifice.

By THOMAS HARDY.
Under the Greenwood Tree.

By J. BERWICK HARWOOD.
The Tenth Earl.

By JULIAN HAWTHORNE.

Garth.	Sebastian Strome.
Ellice Quentin.	Dust.
Fortune's Fool.	Beatrix Randolph.
Miss Cadogna.	Love—or a Name.
David Poindexter's Disappearance.	
The Spectre of the Camera.	

By Sir ARTHUR HELPS.
Ivan de Biron.

By Mrs. CASHEL HOEY.
The Lover's Creed.

By Mrs. GEORGE HOOPER.
The House of Raby.

By TIGHE HOPKINS.
'Twixt Love and Duty.

By Mrs. ALFRED HUNT.
Thornicroft's Model. | Self Condemned.
That Other Person. | Leaden Casket.

By JEAN INGELOW.
Fated to be Free.

By HARRIETT JAY.
The Dark Colleen.
The Queen of Connaught.

By MARK KERSHAW.
Colonial Facts and Fictions.

By R. ASHE KING.
A Drawn Game. | Passion's Slave.
"The Wearing of the Green."

TWO-SHILLING NOVELS—*continued.*

By HENRY KINGSLEY.
Oakshott Castle.

By JOHN LEYS.
The Lindsays.

By MARY LINSKILL.
In Exchange for a Soul.

By E. LYNN LINTON.
Patricia Kemball. | Paston Carew.
World Well Lost. | "My Love!"
Under which Lord? | Ione.
The Atonement of Leam Dundas.
With a Silken Thread.
The Rebel of the Family.
Sowing the Wind.

By HENRY W. LUCY.
Gideon Fleyce.

By JUSTIN McCARTHY.
A Fair Saxon. | Donna Quixote.
Linley Rochford. | Maid of Athens.
Miss Misanthrope. | Camiola.
Dear Lady Disdain.
The Waterdale Neighbours.
My Enemy's Daughter.
The Comet of a Season.

By AGNES MACDONELL.
Quaker Cousins.

KATHARINE S. MACQUOID.
The Evil Eye. | Lost Rose.

By W. H. MALLOCK.
The New Republic.

By FLORENCE MARRYAT.
Open! Sesame! | Fighting the Air
A Harvest of Wild Oats.
Written in Fire.

By J. MASTERMAN.
Half a-dozen Daughters.

By BRANDER MATTHEWS.
A Secret of the Sea.

By JEAN MIDDLEMASS.
Touch and Go. | Mr. Dorillion.

By Mrs. MOLESWORTH.
Hathercourt Rectory.

By J. E. MUDDOCK.
Stories Weird and Wonderful.
The Dead Man's Secret.

By D. CHRISTIE MURRAY.
A Model Father. | Old Blazer's Hero.
Joseph's Coat. | Hearts.
Coals of Fire. | Way of the World.
Val Strange. | Cynic Fortune.
A Life's Atonement.
By the Gate of the Sea.
A Bit of Human Nature.
First Person Singular.

By MURRAY and HERMAN.
One Traveller Returns.
Paul Jones's Alias.

By HENRY MURRAY.
A Game of Bluff.

By ALICE O'HANLON.
The Unforeseen. | Chance? or Fate?

TWO-SHILLING NOVELS—*continued.*

By GEORGES OHNET.
Doctor Rameau. | A Last Love.

By Mrs. OLIPHANT.
Whiteladies. | The Primrose Path.
The Greatest Heiress in England.

By Mrs. ROBERT O'REILLY.
Phœbe's Fortunes.

By OUIDA.
Held in Bondage. | Two Little Wooden
Strathmore. | Shoes.
Chandos. | Ariadne.
Under Two Flags. | Friendship.
Idalia. | Moths.
CecilCastlemaine's | Pipistrello.
Gage. | A Village Com-
Tricotrin. | mune.
Puck. | Bimbi.
Folle Farine. | Wanda.
A Dog of Flanders. | Frescoes.
Pascarel. | In Maremma.
Signa. | Othmar.
Princess Naprax- | Guilderoy.
ine. | Ouida's Wisdom,
In a Winter City. | Wit, and Pathos.

MARGARET AGNES PAUL.
Gentle and Simple.

By JAMES PAYN.
Bentinck's Tutor. | £200 Reward.
Murphy's Master. | Marine Residence.
A County Family. | Mirk Abbey.
At Her Mercy. | By Proxy.
Cecil's Tryst. | Under One Roof.
Clyffards of Clyffe. | High Spirits.
Foster Brothers. | Carlyon's Year.
Found Dead. | From Exile.
Best of Husbands. | For Cash Only.
Walter's Word. | Kit.
Halves. | The Canon's Ward
Fallen Fortunes. | Talk of the Town.
Humorous Stories. | Holiday Tasks.
Lost Sir Massingberd.
A Perfect Treasure.
A Woman's Vengeance.
The Family Scapegrace.
What He Cost Her.
Gwendoline's Harvest.
Like Father, Like Son.
Married Beneath Him.
Not Wooed, but Won.
Less Black than We're Painted.
A Confidential Agent.
Some Private Views.
A Grape from a Thorn.
Glow-worm Tales.
The Mystery of Mirbridge.

By C. L. PIRKIS.
Lady Lovelace.

By EDGAR A. POE.
The Mystery of Marie Roget.

By E. C. PRICE.
Valentina. | The Foreigners.
Mrs. Lancaster's Rival.
Gerald.

Two-Shilling Novels—*continued.*

By CHARLES READE.
It is Never Too Late to Mend.
Christie Johnstone.
Put Yourself in His Place.
The Double Marriage.
Love Me Little, Love Me Long.
The Cloister and the Hearth.
The Course of True Love.
Autobiography of a Thief.
A Terrible Temptation.
The Wandering Heir.
Singleheart and Doubleface.
Good Stories of Men and other Animals.

Hard Cash.	A Simpleton.
Peg Woffington.	Readiana.
Griffith Gaunt.	A Woman-Hater.
Foul Play.	The Jilt.

By Mrs. J. H. RIDDELL.
Weird Stories. | Fairy Water.
Her Mother's Darling.
Prince of Wales's Garden Party.
The Uninhabited House.
The Mystery in Palace Gardens.

By F. W. ROBINSON.
Women are Strange.
The Hands of Justice.

By JAMES RUNCIMAN.
Skippers and Shellbacks.
Grace Balmaign's Sweetheart.
Schools and Scholars.

By W. CLARK RUSSELL.
Round the Galley Fire.
On the Fo'k'sle Head.
In the Middle Watch.
A Voyage to the Cape.
A Book for the Hammock.
The Mystery of the "Ocean Star."
The Romance of Jenny Harlowe.
An Ocean Tragedy.

GEORGE AUGUSTUS SALA.
Gaslight and Daylight.

By JOHN SAUNDERS.
Guy Waterman. | Two Dreamers.
The Lion in the Path.

By KATHARINE SAUNDERS.
Joan Merryweather. | Heart Salvage.
The High Mills. | Sebastian.
Margaret and Elizabeth.

By GEORGE R. SIMS.
Rogues and Vagabonds.
The Ring o' Bells.
Mary Jane's Memoirs.
Mary Jane Married.
Tales of To-day. | Dramas of Life.
Tinkletop's Crime.

By ARTHUR SKETCHLEY.
A Match in the Dark.

By T. W. SPEIGHT.
The Mysteries of Heron Dyke.
The Golden Hoop. | By Devious Ways.
Hoodwinked, &c.

Two-Shilling Novels—*continued.*

By R. A. STERNDALE.
The Afghan Knife.

By R. LOUIS STEVENSON.
New Arabian Nights. | Prince Otto.

BY BERTHA THOMAS.
Cressida. | Proud Maisie.
The Violin-player.

By WALTER THORNBURY.
Tales for the Marines.
Old Stories Re-told.

T. ADOLPHUS TROLLOPE.
Diamond Cut Diamond.

By F. ELEANOR TROLLOPE.
Like Ships upon the Sea.
Anne Furness. | Mabel's Progress.

By ANTHONY TROLLOPE.
Frau Frohmann. | Kept in the Dark.
Marion Fay. | John Caldigate.
The Way We Live Now.
The American Senator.
Mr. Scarborough's Family.
The Land-Leaguers.
The Golden Lion of Granpere.

By J. T. TROWBRIDGE.
Farnell's Folly.

By IVAN TURGENIEFF, &c.
Stories from Foreign Novelists.

By MARK TWAIN.
Tom Sawyer. | A Tramp Abroad.
The Stolen White Elephant.
A Pleasure Trip on the Continent.
Huckleberry Finn.
Life on the Mississippi.
The Prince and the Pauper.

By C. C. FRASER-TYTLER.
Mistress Judith.

By SARAH TYTLER.
The Bride's Pass.	Noblesse Oblige.
Buried Diamonds.	Disappeared.
Saint Mungo's City.	Huguenot Family.
Lady Bell.	Blackhall Ghosts.

What She Came Through.
Beauty and the Beast.
Citoyenne Jaqueline.

By J. S. WINTER.
Cavalry Life. | Regimental Legends.

By H. F. WOOD.
The Passenger from Scotland Yard.
The Englishman of the Rue Cain.

By Lady WOOD.
Sabina.

CELIA PARKER WOOLLEY.
Rachel Armstrong; or, Love & Theology

By EDMUND YATES.
The Forlorn Hope. | Land at Last.
Castaway.

OGDEN, SMALE AND CO. LIMITED, PRINTERS, GREAT SAFFRON HILL, E.C.

www.ingramcontent.com/pod-product-compliance
Lightning Source LLC
Chambersburg PA
CBHW021717110726
47902CB00005B/1231